NONFICTION
The Gift of Love

Starstruck

AMY CLIPSTON

THOMAS NELSON
Since 1798

Starstruck

Copyright © 2023 Amy Clipston

All rights reserved. No portion of this book may be reproduced, stored in a retrieval system, or transmitted in any form or by any means—electronic, mechanical, photocopy, recording, scanning, or other—except for brief quotations in critical reviews or articles, without the prior written permission of the publisher.

Published in Nashville, Tennessee, by Thomas Nelson. Thomas Nelson is a registered trademark of HarperCollins Christian Publishing, Inc.

Thomas Nelson titles may be purchased in bulk for educational, business, fundraising, or sales promotional use. For information, please email SpecialMarkets@ThomasNelson.com.

Publisher's Note: This novel is a work of fiction. Names, characters, places, and incidents are either products of the author's imagination or used fictitiously. All characters are fictional, and any similarity to people living or dead is purely coincidental.

Any internet addresses (websites, blogs, etc.) in this book are offered as a resource. They are not intended in any way to be or imply an endorsement by Thomas Nelson, nor does Thomas Nelson vouch for the content of these sites for the life of this book.

Library of Congress Cataloging-in-Publication Data

Names: Clipston, Amy, author.
Title: Starstruck : a novel / Amy Clipston.
Description: Nashville, Tennessee : Thomas Nelson, [2023] | Summary: "Bestselling author Amy Clipston returns with another romance full of charm, music, and a happily ever after for a small-town waitress and a touring rockstar"-- Provided by publisher.
Identifiers: LCCN 2023016806 (print) | LCCN 2023016807 (ebook) | ISBN 9780840708915 (paperback) | ISBN 9780840708922 (epub) | ISBN 9780840708939
Subjects: LCGFT: Novels. | Romance fiction.
Classification: LCC PS3603.L58 S73 2023 (print) | LCC PS3603.L58 (ebook) | DDC 813/.6--dc23/eng/20220623
LC record available at https://lccn.loc.gov/2023016806
LC ebook record available at https://lccn.loc.gov/2023016807

Printed in the United States of America

23 24 25 26 27 LBC 5 4 3 2 1

For Pam—I can't believe it's been almost thirty years since we met as pen pals. Thank you for being a wonderful friend to me and a loving godmother and aunt to my boys. We love you!

1

The delicious aroma of the Barbecue Pit's pulled pork wafted over Heather as she zipped around the restaurant delivering sandwiches, hush puppies, and coleslaw. It was a typical busy Thursday evening, and the happy buzz of conversations filled her ears. She nodded greetings to familiar faces, grateful for the regular customers who visited her family's restaurant in her hometown of Flowering Grove, North Carolina.

Heather dashed back to the kitchen, slipping her notepad in the pocket of her black waist apron as she pushed through the double doors. She placed four pulled-pork specials on a tray and hefted them up high in the air before peeking over at the counter, where her parents worked hard putting together more orders. She smiled. The restaurant would be her parents' legacy, and she was so thankful to be a part of it.

Weaving through the sea of tables, Heather approached number ten. "Here you go—four hot specials."

She placed the plates in front of the members of the Baucom family—Lenny, Jean, Brinley, and Connor. They were regulars who had been coming for as long as she could remember. In fact, she was certain Connor had grown at least six inches since the first time she recalled seeing the family sitting at one of their tables.

1

Heather rested the tray under her arm. "Is there anything else I can get for you?"

Lenny lifted his plastic cup, which was mostly melted ice. "How about some more sweet tea?"

"Absolutely." Heather took the cup and scanned the table. "Anyone else need a refill?" When the rest of the family members shook their heads, she smiled. "I'll be right back."

Heather heard a commotion behind her, but she continued toward the drink station. While filling the cup, she glanced toward the front of the restaurant, where Allie, working as hostess tonight, led a group of nearly a dozen young men to the largest booths, located in the far corner. Customers at nearby tables appeared mesmerized as the men sauntered past. Some of the younger patrons pulled out their phones and pointed them toward the young men as conversations seemed to crescendo.

Curiosity nipped at Heather as she placed the full drink on the counter. It seemed as if the men in the large party were important or famous, but they didn't look familiar to her.

"Heather! Heather! Heather!" Wendy, Heather's younger sister, appeared at her side. Wendy's light brown ponytail, which sported blond highlights, bobbed excitedly. "You are not going to believe who just walked into our restaurant!" Her honey-brown eyes sparkled in the fluorescent lights buzzing above them. "I can't believe it! I mean, what are the chances that they'd choose *our* restaurant?" She gasped, then her breaths came in short bursts.

"Calm down." Heather touched Wendy's slight shoulder. Her excitable younger sister seemed to constantly overreact, often reminding Heather of a teenager instead of the twenty-two-year-old she truly was. "Take a deep breath, count to ten, and then tell me what on earth you're going on about."

Wendy giggled and then cleared her throat. "Sorry." She

pulled in a breath through her nose and then pivoted toward the dining room. "Tables number sixty and sixty-two."

Heather peered toward the far corner, where the large group of young men sat. "I see two tables of guys who look like they're in their twenties. So?"

"Don't you know who they are, Heather?" Wendy's words were clipped and measured, as if she were speaking to a four-year-old.

Heather lifted the refilled cup of sweet tea as annoyance filtered through her. "No, I don't, and I really don't have time for this. Just tell me so I can deliver this drink to Mr. Baucom and then check on my other tables."

"They're Kirwan." Wendy gave a little squeal. "Kirwan!"

"I have no idea what that means."

Wendy huffed. "The band, Heather! Haven't you ever heard of Kirwan? They've had like five number-one hits in the past year!"

Unimpressed, Heather shrugged. "Okay . . ."

"Ugh!" Wendy gave Heather's shoulder a light smack. "Maybe if you listened to something other than Dad's music, you'd know how amazing they are. I can't believe they are in our restaurant. They're super famous!"

Then she looked toward the table once again and gave a dreamy sigh. "I'm so thrilled Allie sat them in my section. I've always dreamt of meeting Kayden Kirwan. He's so hot." She grinned. "Maybe we can get an autographed photo of them for our Wall of Fame. We've only ever had local celebrities eat here, but Kirwan's a big-time rock band!"

Before Heather could respond, Wendy flitted off. Although she was only four years older than Wendy, at times she felt as if they were ten years apart in age. Shaking her head, she hurried over to deliver Mr. Baucom's drink before checking in on the surrounding tables.

"Excuse me, Heather."

She spun as Mrs. Price motioned for Heather to join her at her table. "Yes, ma'am?"

"Marvin and I were just discussing your scrumptious treats." The older woman slipped on her reading glasses and then pointed to the dessert menu. "What do you recommend we order?"

Heather stood a little taller, pushed her dark brown ponytail off her shoulder, and lifted her chin, ready to discuss her favorite subject: the desserts she prepared for her family's restaurant. She relished arriving early in the morning to prepare them for the day. Baking had been her favorite hobby for as long as she could remember, and she was thrilled when her parents encouraged her to add her desserts to the restaurant's menu ten years ago when she was only sixteen. They also let her name the baked goods, all inspired by her love of reading.

"Well, I'm not one to brag, but I've been told my Bookish Brownies are quite good. I also have some fresh Chocolate Chunk Novel Cookies." She pulled her notepad from her apron pocket.

Mr. Price brushed his hands together. "How about we order both and share them, Shirley?"

"Absolutely. You know, you really should think about opening a bakery," Mrs. Price said.

Heather beamed. "That actually is a dream of mine."

"Well, darlin', you should make that happen."

"Thank you, ma'am. I'll bring your desserts right out."

Mr. Price held up a finger. "And add two cups of coffee as well."

Heather scribbled on her notepad. "Perfect. I'll be right back." She scooted around the Prices' table, and a loud fuss drew her attention back to the far corner of the restaurant. There, a group of young women had gathered around one of the booths.

She paused for a moment and took in the sight. The women

took turns posing for selfies and asking for autographs from two of the young men, whom Heather assumed were members of the rock band. Each of the guys had blond hair that was longer on top and styled with hair gel. They wore tight jeans and plain black t-shirts that showed off their fit physiques. The young men looked to be related—perhaps brothers—with similar cheekbones, angular jaws, and bright blue eyes. They seemed to eat up the attention as they grinned broadly at the young women. Clearly, they were professionals.

Her eyes flicked to the second booth, where a young woman lingered by another man who nodded and smiled, apparently listening to what she had to say. He shared the same bone structure as the other two men, as well as the same blond hair and blue eyes. He, however, looked older—closer to thirty—and his expression held a warmer and more genuine quality. Still, he turned on a megawatt smile when the woman held up her phone for a selfie.

Heather shook her head and continued toward the kitchen, where she hurried over to the dessert section to fill the Prices' order.

"I heard we have a rock band out there." Mom looked up from the grill, where a few buns were warming for another pulled-pork barbecue plate.

Heather had always believed Wendy favored their mother. Not only did both women stand at five feet, six inches—two inches shorter than Heather—but they also shared the same thick, light brown hair. And while Mom's bobbed style had started showing flecks of gray, her beautiful face was youthful with only a few lines around her eyes.

Heather snorted. "Yeah. They're having an all-out autograph session, which I find confusing since I've never even heard of them."

"It's good for business when celebrities visit and then post about it on social media," Dad called from the freezer. Most people who noticed the wrinkles around Russell Gordon's eyes and mouth, as well as the gray threading through his dark brown hair, would correctly guess he was in his midfifties. But Dad always insisted he was young at heart.

"We need to add them to our Wall of Fame," Mom announced.

Dad held up a frozen bag of hush puppies in agreement. "You're right, Nora!" His deep-brown eyes sparkled—the same dark eyes he'd passed on to Heather.

"You both sound like Wendy," Heather grumbled.

"Hey, all publicity is good publicity, Heather!" Dad sang, loading the hush puppies into the oil.

Heather placed the desserts on a tray before beelining toward the drink station to pour two mugs of coffee. She placed the desserts and coffees in front of the Prices, then returned to check on her other customers and take orders from the customers who had just been seated.

When she found Mr. and Mrs. Funderburk sitting at table sixteen, she grinned. "Good evening," she greeted them. "Let me guess. You each want a barbecue plate with extra hush puppies and coleslaw, along with two large sweet teas." She scribbled the order on her notepad.

"How did you know that?" Mr. Funderburk asked with a twinkle in his eyes.

Heather chuckled. "I believe you've ordered the same meal every Thursday for as long as I can remember."

"That's right, sweetheart. It's the best meal we have all week long." Mrs. Funderburk handed Heather the menus. "We won't need these."

An hour and a half passed in a flash as Heather took

care of her guests and cleared their tables. She was wiping down a recently vacated four-top when a cacophony of voices sounded from the back of the dining room. She whipped around toward the large booths in the corner and found the celebrities and their entourage at one of the tables pelting each other with hush puppies.

Heather felt her posture go rigid, and she sucked in a breath as frustration poured through her. Cleaning up after little kids was one thing, but having to sweep up a food fight caused by grown men was something Heather could not tolerate.

She absently fiddled with the rag as the food war continued, but relief filled her when the men—more like overgrown babies—finally stood to leave. They dropped a stack of bills on the table before meandering toward the exit and filing out onto the sidewalk. As she watched them go, Heather bit back the urge to follow them out onto Main Street and reprimand them for wasting food and making such a mess.

Instead she swallowed her anger, picked up the dustpan and broom, and pushed the cart she used for bussing through the sea of tables to the back corner.

"You've got to be kidding me," she grumbled as she took in the booth, peppered in hush puppies as if an explosion had occurred.

Wendy appeared at her side and took the dustpan and broom from her hands. "Let me help you. I'll start on the floor, and you can wipe down the table and the booth."

Annoyance flashing through her, Heather turned toward the wall of windows lining the front of the restaurant and glared out toward the rockstars and their entourage. The two good-looking blond guys still lingered out front, posing for more photos with adoring, squealing fans.

Heather faced her sister, who was already sweeping. "So

those jerks use our restaurant for an autograph session, behave like children, make a mess, and then just start another party for groupies out on the sidewalk?" She made a sweeping gesture toward the front of the restaurant. "How can you possibly still be their fan?"

"Well, they left us an awfully nice tip." Wendy held up a stack of bills and waved it in the air. "I've never seen anyone leave 200 percent. Have you?"

Heather narrowed her eyes. "I'll give them a nice *tip*. How about next time, they can eat somewhere else?"

"What on earth happened here?"

Wendy's gaze snapped to something behind Heather, and her honey-brown eyes widened. She stood up straight and touched her hair as if making sure each strand was in its proper place.

Heather swiveled and faced the man behind her. She recognized him as the older one from the second table. She surmised that he stood at least six feet one, similar to her father's height, if not a little taller. His shoulders were broad, and his muscular biceps seemed to strain against the sleeves of his gray t-shirt. Well-worn jeans hugged a trim waist, and his blue eyes reminded her of the Caribbean Sea, which she'd seen only in photos. She hated to admit that those eyes were mesmerizing.

For a moment she couldn't speak as she took in this gorgeous man up close, but then she shook herself back to the present. His bandmates had desecrated her family's restaurant, after all.

"I'll tell you what happened." Heather leveled her gaze with his. "These so-called rockstars with big heads left us a mess. *That's* what happened. And they think leaving us a big tip makes up for their immaturity."

Wendy gave an awkward laugh. "We don't mind cleaning this up, and we appreciate the tip. My sister didn't mean that the way it came out."

"Yes, I did." Heather faced her sister. "Do we deserve to be treated as second-class citizens who were put on this earth to clean up after some 'celebrities'?" She made quotation marks with her fingers. Then she aimed her glare at the man again. "Do they treat everyone like this or just restaurant workers?"

Wendy poked Heather's arm. "Heather, hush."

"Why should I hush?"

Her younger sister gave her a pointed look. "Because he's one of the lead singers of the band." Her eyes seemed to say, *"Please—for once—listen to me, Heather!"*

Heather didn't allow that information to stop her. "Did you forget something in the booth, sir?"

He touched the nape of his neck and had the gall to look nervous or possibly embarrassed. "I'm sorry. I didn't realize my brothers did this. I just went to use the restroom and make a phone call, and when I came back, I saw they had left without me." He held out his hand to Heather. "I'm Alex Kirwan."

She hesitated but gave his hand a quick shake. Then she started to load the dirty dishes into a plastic dishpan on the cart.

"How can I help?" he offered.

"Don't be silly, Alex." Wendy waved him off. "I'm sure you have somewhere to be, right? You don't want to miss your ride."

"They know that if they *actually* leave me, they'll never hear the end of it." He turned those sky-blue eyes toward the front door, and for a moment Heather was almost certain they had narrowed. "Besides, they're busy. I have time to help." He bent and started picking up hush puppies and dropping them into one of the plastic tubs on the cart.

Wendy shook her head. "You don't need to help us. We're used to cleaning up messes."

"Never one this bad," Heather groused.

"Heather!" Windy hissed.

Alex pulled a leather wallet out of the back pocket of his tight jeans. "Let me give you some more money to pay you for your time."

"No, thank you." Heather stood up to her full height, scowling. "We don't want any more of your money."

Alex exhaled, his expression somber. "I understand that you're upset. I am too. I'm embarrassed by my brothers, and I plan to let them know." He divided a glance between the sisters. "What can I do to make this better? Are you coming to the show in Charlotte tomorrow night?"

Wendy frowned. "I couldn't get tickets. They sold out too fast."

Heather swallowed a snort. *Sold out? Who are these guys?*

Alex's smile was wide, and Heather hated to admit how nicely it lit up that handsome face of his. "Now that's something I can fix. How would you like VIP tickets and backstage passes to the show?"

"Are you serious?" Wendy's voice resembled a squeak, and Heather was careful not to roll her eyes. No wonder these guys had such high opinions of themselves, with young women like her sister swooning in their presence.

He slipped his wallet back into his pocket, then retrieved a cell phone from the other back pocket. "Yes, I'm serious. How many tickets would you like?"

"Um, two, I guess." Wendy looked at her sister expectantly. "You'll go with me, right?"

Heather shook her head. "I don't think so. You should definitely take Deanna."

"She's in Maine visiting her grandmother."

"Well, there has to be someone else you can take." Heather gathered up the utensils and sorted them into the slots on the cart.

"Heather . . ."

"I'm sorry, Wendy, but I'll be washing my hair tomorrow night," Heather quipped.

"My big sister is a bit of a kidder," Wendy said with another nervous laugh. "She and I *will* be there."

Heather crossed her arms. "I don't think—"

"Yes, we will," Wendy interrupted, spearing Heather with another stern expression.

Alex swiped on his phone and began typing. "What are your names?"

"Wendy and Heather Gordon," Wendy said.

He typed some more and then met Wendy's gaze. "Got it. Your backstage passes and tickets will be at the will-call window." Then he looked at Heather. "Again, I'm really sorry about this. Their behavior is inexcusable, and I'll make sure they understand that."

Heather swallowed as she took in his earnest expression and felt her anger fade—slightly.

Then he pointed to his table, which wasn't nearly as messy, and his face turned sheepish. "Also, could I possibly get a to-go box for my cookies? I think they were called something like Chocolate Chunk? I didn't get a chance to eat them."

"My sister makes all of the desserts," Wendy announced, smiling at Heather.

Alex's blond eyebrows lifted. "Is that right?"

"Yup," Wendy said. "She's going to open her own bakery someday." She pointed toward the kitchen. "I'll get you a full box to take." Then she hastened toward the back, leaving Heather to stand there and stare awkwardly at the tall, handsome singer.

Heather blinked. "Excuse me," she muttered, then continued placing plastic cups in the top dishpan and dumping napkins in the bottom one.

Alex picked up the dustpan and broom and began cleaning up the floor under the table. Heather sneaked a peek at him, and when their gazes met briefly, she once again found herself mesmerized by those blue eyes.

"Here you go." Wendy came hurrying back, holding up the box like a trophy. "A fresh batch for the road."

Alex set down the broom, took the box, and nodded at Wendy. "Thank you." He opened the top and added the cookie stack from the table. Then his eyes bounced between the sisters. "I'll see you tomorrow night then."

"We can't wait," Wendy said.

Alex's eyes lingered on Heather for a moment longer, then he traipsed toward the exit, nodding at admiring faces on his way to the door.

"Isn't Alex a hunk?" Wendy cooed as she watched him go. "He's almost as handsome as his younger brother Kayden."

Heather looked at her sister and rolled her eyes before turning back to the booths.

2

Alex balanced the box of cookies in one hand, then pushed open the door with the other before walking out into the cool, early-April evening. The sky was clear and dotted with stars, and the scent of moist earth mingled with the delicious smells from the restaurant.

He sucked in a breath as he took in the crowd gathered around his brothers, who were still signing autographs and posing with fans for selfies and group photos. Alex was so tired of the circus that his life had become since he and his brothers had won that music group contest nearly three years ago. Since then, his schedule had turned into nonstop performances, interviews, photo sessions, tours, and social media posts.

If only he could get a moment to catch his breath. To rest. To write songs. To find some meaning in all the chaos.

Kayden stood in the center of the group of fans with a wide smile on his face. He posed with his arms around the young women, who nearly swooned in his presence. With his baby face, bright smile, and magnetic personality, Kayden had been born to perform.

Although Alex and Kayden shared the role of lead singer, Kayden was the most popular member of their trio. He was the band's heartthrob, the brother for whom the girls would tearfully scream during shows. And Alex and Jordan were happy to give their youngest brother that role, since being the main object of affection was more pressure than they wanted. But Kayden loved being the center of attention.

Kayden turned, and when his eyes met Alex's, his face lit up. "Alex, get over here for a group photo with these nice folks." He motioned for Alex to stand between him and Jordan, their middle brother, who always seemed happy to just follow along with Kayden, even though he was twenty-four and two years older.

Pasting a bright smile on his face, Alex set the box of cookies on a nearby bench before posing for photos, shaking hands, and signing autographs. He breathed a sigh of relief when the crowd finally dissipated.

Alex retrieved the box of cookies, then followed his brothers toward the two Escalades waiting in the restaurant's parking lot. The roadies who had joined them for a rare evening out piled into one of the vehicles, while Alex climbed into the third row of the second one, just behind his brothers.

The two black SUVs roared to life and rolled out toward Main Street, heading back toward Charlotte. As if on cue, both Kayden and Jordan extracted their phones from the pockets of their jeans and began absently scrolling through social media.

Alex leaned forward and tapped each brother on the shoulder, startling them. "So who started the food fight while I was on the phone with Mom?"

Jordan cut his eyes to Kayden, who lifted his chin.

"Well, I *could* say it was Jor, but it was really me." Kayden chuckled. "I tossed a hush puppy to him, and after that, all heck broke loose."

Alex pressed his lips together. "Did you see the mess you left for the two servers to clean up?"

"In Kayden's defense," Jordan began, "we left a nice tip. I mean, *really* nice."

A memory of the fire in the brunette's dark eyes flashed through Alex's mind, along with her furious words: *We don't want any more of your money.*

"When are you two going to grow up? You're not sixteen anymore." Alex drew in a breath through his nose. "Have you thought about how that behavior looks to our fans? How many people were taking photos and videos of us tonight? What if one of them posted a video of you two acting like kids on social media? Do you want that all over the internet?"

Kayden's lips flattened. "We didn't make *that* big of a mess."

"Yes, you did, and two young women had to clean it up." Alex rubbed his hand over his chin as he recalled his awkward conversation with the brunette—Heather, he remembered. He would never forget the adorable freckles marching across her perfect nose, even though he'd probably never see her again. "It was horrendous."

Jordan grimaced. "You're right, Alex. We didn't think it through. We just got caught up in the moment."

Kayden rolled his eyes. "You need to learn to relax, Alex. We can't work all the time. Sometimes we need to let loose."

"I let loose in the gym or by reading a book. I don't let loose by acting like a spoiled kid in a public place."

Kayden frowned. "You're right. I'm sorry for making us look bad and for not considering how our behavior would affect other people." He shook his head. "I'm sorry they had to clean that up."

"I helped them a little bit, but it was obvious that the older of the two sisters just wanted me to leave. She'd clearly had enough of us. I doubt we'd be welcomed back to that restaurant." Alex brushed his hand through his hair.

Jordan nodded. "We really should have thought about that."

Their youngest brother stared out the window at the passing traffic, and Alex could almost hear his thoughts. Then Kayden angled his body to face Alex in the back seat.

"Is there anything we could do to make it right, Alex?" Kayden asked.

"I offered them VIP tickets and backstage passes to the show tomorrow night. The younger waitress was excited by the idea, but the other one wasn't impressed."

Kayden scoffed. "She wasn't impressed?"

"Not at all." Alex almost laughed as he recalled Heather's indifference to the idea of attending their concert. It had been a long time since a woman had turned him down that way, and for some reason, he found it hilarious as well as intriguing. "But either way, if they come, you should apologize to them."

"We will," Jordan said. "And we'll have Brooks give them the royal treatment," he added, referring to their tour manager.

Kayden nodded. "We'll make sure they get all the swag."

Road noise filled the SUV as Alex's brothers turned their attention back to their phones. He blew out a relieved sigh. The past couple of weeks had passed by in a blur as their tour had kicked into gear. It had been a fog of flights, long drives in SUVs or buses, hotel rooms, interviews, meet and greets, and performances.

Although Alex was grateful for his band's success, he still felt unfulfilled. It wasn't that he didn't appreciate the adoring fans who spent their hard-earned money to purchase Kirwan's music and concert tickets. Instead, he felt indebted to those people. Yet he carried around a gaping pit in his soul when he considered his life. He felt called upon to do more than just perform—to do something worthwhile and make a difference in the world. He was almost thirty and wanted more than this lonely life on the road.

But he couldn't abandon his brothers. Even though they were grown men, Alex had felt responsible for them both ever since their father passed away fourteen years before, killed in a car crash on his way home from the grocery store. Alex had been only fifteen when a drunk driver crossed the centerline and hit their father's car head-on. He could still recall the details of that day as if no time at all had passed.

Alex closed his eyes and tried to evict those thoughts from his head. Dad was gone, and it was now Alex's job to make sure his mother and his brothers had what they needed. He would always put their needs before his.

When they arrived at the hotel, Alex was relieved to avoid interacting with anyone in the lobby. He rushed back to his suite, then changed into shorts and a tank top before loping to the gym, which was empty.

He went through the motions of his usual workout, running on the treadmill and then lifting weights, grateful for a chance to release his frustrations. When a young couple entered the facility, Alex wiped down his equipment and gave the couple a friendly nod before hurrying toward the exit, hoping they wouldn't recognize him.

He returned to his room and took a long shower before pulling on a fresh pair of shorts and a faded concert t-shirt. He retrieved the acoustic guitar he carried with him everywhere he traveled, then started plucking out a tune that had been lingering in the back of his mind for a few days.

As his thoughts meandered, he once again recalled what Heather had said in the restaurant when her sister had asked her to attend the concert with her.

"I'm sorry, Wendy, but I'll be washing my hair tomorrow night."

Alex laughed as the comment rolled through his mind. How refreshing it would be to have more conversations with a woman like Heather. She didn't seem like the kind of woman who'd tell him only what he wanted to hear and hang on his every word. Instead, she'd be blunt and honest, and Alex would relish it.

But he was certain he'd never encounter Heather again.

When a yawn overtook him, he set his guitar back in its case, turned off the lights, and climbed into the king-sized bed. He needed his rest so he could tackle another day filled with interviews, rehearsals, and a sold-out show—another chance for him and his brothers to give the fans what they deserved.

⌣

The following evening, Heather leaned against the concrete wall outside the amphitheater. The evening air was cool, and faint aromas of popcorn and french fries wafted over her. Excited conversations buzzed as people hurried by, many of them clad in t-shirts sporting the Kirwan band members' faces or the band's logo.

She snickered to herself, still stunned by this group's popularity. She wondered how many people would still like these guys if they had witnessed the display of immaturity and rudeness last night in her family's restaurant.

Yet as much as Heather had wanted to stay home tonight, she couldn't say no to her sister. Wendy had begged and begged, going so far as to arrange for the other servers to take their shifts at the restaurant. Wendy had even offered to drive, even though Heather insisted she would pick her up on the way to the concert.

As she waited for Wendy to fetch their passes, Heather just hoped the concert would end quickly so she could go home and spend the evening paging through her cookbooks and reading the latest suspense novel she'd picked up at the library.

"Here we go!" Wendy nearly skipped over to Heather as she held up a lanyard attached to a large laminated card that said "VIP" in neon orange. Wendy slipped the bright green branded lanyard over Heather's neck, then handed her a ticket. "I'm so excited I could scream."

"Me too," Heather muttered. Wendy grabbed her arm and led her through the crowd to the gates, where their purses were checked and their tickets scanned before they could enter the amphitheater.

Once inside, Wendy headed straight toward the merchandise stand. She seemed to study the wall of t-shirts, hoodies, posters, signed postcards, stickers, hats, and jackets, all of which featured the Kirwan logo and photos of the three band members. Heather silently marveled at the knot of people standing in line to purchase the overpriced swag.

"Should I get a t-shirt and maybe a hoodie?" Wendy tapped her lip.

"I think they owe you one of everything after the mess they made last night."

Wendy frowned. "You need to let that go."

"I don't think I ever will." Heather studied the back of the laminated VIP ticket and took in the brooding faces of the three Kirwan brothers, wondering which one was Kayden, the man who had apparently stolen her sweet sister's heart.

"Let's go find our seats."

"Huh?" Heather looked up as her sister made a beeline toward the seating area. "Wait for me!"

The sisters journeyed down steps and past many rows of seats, drawing closer and closer to the front.

"Are we ever going to get there?" Heather snapped.

Finally, they came to the third row and found their seats in the center section—right in front of the stage.

"This is a dream come true!" Wendy exclaimed. "I can't believe we're this close."

Heather glanced around and frowned, imagining just how long it would take to get out of here when the concert was over. They would most likely be stuck in traffic until next Tuesday. She sat down, folded her arms over her chest, and slumped back in the chair.

Wendy bumped Heather's elbow with her own. "Why don't you try smiling, big sis? If nothing else, this is a fun night out for us. When was the last time we had a girls' night?"

Heather sighed and felt a spark of guilt. "You're right. It has been a long time."

Wendy pulled her phone from the pocket of her purple hoodie and held it up, then snuggled in beside Heather. "Say cheese!"

Heather grinned for a selfie, and Wendy opened her Instagram app. "Are you really going to post that?"

"Of course I am." Her fingers flew over the phone, and she posted: Waiting for #Kirwan to perform. Can't wait! #bestconcertever

Please. Heather pulled her phone from the back pocket of her jeans and found a text message from her best friend waiting for her.

MCKENNA: How's the concert going?

HEATHER: Waiting for it to start. Hope it won't be too long.

MCKENNA: When has a concert ever been short? News
    flash: You might actually have a good time.

HEATHER: Doubt it.

MCKENNA: All you ever do is work, so relax and enjoy it.

HEATHER: You're the one who runs her own hair salon and
    rarely gets a break. Take your own advice! Have a good
    night and see you tomorrow.

Heather surveyed the crowd as the seats around hers and Wendy's slowly filled. Most of the audience members around them were young women, but she was surprised to see some young men and a few middle-aged and older couples. It seemed that Kirwan's music appealed to people in all walks of life, which Heather found fascinating.

Thirty minutes later, the opening act, which included a band of three young men and a young woman, took the stage. They sang a few techno songs that reminded Heather of the music from a club she attended in high school. Some members of the audience danced along, but Heather couldn't wait for it to end.

During one of the songs, she leaned over to her sister and tapped her on the shoulder. "Tell me Kirwan doesn't play techno music."

"No, they don't." Wendy chuckled. "You honestly don't know any of their songs?"

Heather shrugged. "No."

"I should have played some of their music in the car on the way over."

Heather nodded.

Wendy gave a knowing smile. "I bet you'll recognize a few of their songs once you hear them."

Heather clapped out of relief when the opening act finally exited the stage and roadies dressed in black jeans and shirts disassembled their equipment and set up for the next performance.

Soon the stage was empty. The lights went out, and the air seemed to crackle with anticipation as the audience began to clap and cheer.

Wendy folded her hands and squealed. "I can't wait to see Kayden again!"

Then a chord from an electric guitar filled the air, and the concertgoers jumped to their feet as the members of Kirwan came out one at a time.

The people in front of her leapt to their feet, so Heather had to stand too. Wendy grabbed Heather's arm again and shook it.

"Ow!" Heather hissed, but her sister was too busy screaming to hear.

While one of the brothers took his place behind the drum set, Alex and the brother who had a youthful face walked up to the microphones.

Alex slipped the strap of a bright red electric guitar over his shoulder and waved to the crowd. He looked even more gorgeous than she recalled from last night. He was clad in a tight-fitting blue t-shirt that somehow made those beautiful eyes bluer. His chiseled jaw was clean-shaven, and his tight jeans hugged his trim waist.

The other brother picked up a purple bass guitar and approached a microphone. "Hey, Charlotte! How's it going?" A chorus of shrieks responded to his question, and he laughed. "Are you ready to rock tonight?"

"All right!" Alex chimed in. "How about we start it off with a song you might have heard?" The crowd cheered as Alex turned to his brother and said, "One, two, three, four."

They played the opening bars to an upbeat song that sounded vaguely familiar to Heather. And when Alex started singing, Heather was mesmerized. His voice was smooth and comforting, and it somehow warmed her like a soft, comfortable blanket.

The man was superhot, *and* he could sing!

"Hey, Heather! Put your tongue back in your mouth."

"What?" Heather faced her sister, who was laughing at her. "What do you mean?"

Wendy bumped her shoulder. "I told you they were hot, but Kayden is mine."

"Which one is Kayden?"

Wendy looked offended. "Are you kidding? He's that beautiful man playing bass."

"You can have him," Heather said before turning her attention back to Alex.

Next thing she knew, she was singing along and having the time of her life.

3

More than two hours later, Heather stared at her reflection in the ladies' room mirror. She and Wendy had strolled backstage after the concert, and while a security guard led Wendy to meet the band, Heather had excused herself to the restroom to freshen up.

She frowned as she took in her appearance. After dancing, clapping, yelling, and even singing during the concert and two encores, the perfect thick french braid Mckenna had crafted for Heather had loosened, leaving tendrils of dark hair to frame her face. If only she had a brush, she would try to fix the braid. But she hadn't been able to fit a comb or a brush in her tiny blue crossbody.

To make the situation worse, her makeup had faded, but she was grateful she had dropped a tube of lip gloss into her purse before rushing out the door tonight. Heather swiped the gloss across her lips and then groaned. Why was she fussing with her appearance before going to meet a rockstar? She was acting like a groupie.

Well, if not a groupie, then she was just as bad as her younger sister, turning into gelatin at the sight of Kayden Kirwan. Would Heather react the same way when she came face-to-face with

Alex? After tonight she would never see him again. In fact, he probably had already forgotten her name. She expected he'd just shake her hand, sign an autograph, and tell her to have a nice night before traveling to the next city for more young women to ogle him.

I've lost my mind!

Huffing out a breath, Heather squared her shoulders and brushed her hands down her baby-blue hoodie. Then she marched toward the restroom door and pushed it open. Her eyes moved up and down the hallway as she debated where she might find her sister.

Heather retrieved her cell phone from her back pocket and unlocked it. Her thumbs were typing out a text to her sister when a warm, melodious voice, accompanied by an acoustic guitar, floated over her. She closed her eyes and stilled. The voice sang about an endless love, a match made in heaven, and an unbreakable bond that would last throughout the ages.

As if pulled by an invisible magnet, Heather followed the voice to a room at the end of the hall. She stood outside, allowing the song to serenade her as if it had been written just for her.

When the song ended, she couldn't stop herself from clapping and pushing the door open. Inside she found Alex Kirwan sitting on a stool and holding an acoustic guitar on his lap. He had changed into a faded black t-shirt emblazoned with the Beatles' logo, and his hair looked as if it had just been brushed. The small space resembled dressing rooms Heather had seen in movies, with a large mirror surrounded by lights, a few chairs, a sofa, and a rack containing hangers.

When Alex blessed her with an affable smile, she froze like a deer in headlights. Her feet seemed to be cemented to the floor.

"Heather Gordon," he said. "What a surprise."

He remembers my name! She opened her mouth to respond, but her words were trapped in her throat.

He set the guitar on a nearby stand, and she finally found her voice and the ability to walk. She took a step toward the doorway and pointed her phone in the direction of the hallway. "I—I'm so sorry, Alex. I was looking for my sister. Please excuse the intrusion." She started out the door.

"Hang on a minute."

Heather spun to face him. "Yes?"

"I'm glad you decided to skip washing your hair tonight and come to our concert instead."

Was that a spark of amusement glimmering in those sky-blue eyes?

When she laughed, a grin lit up his attractive face. "Yeah, well," she began, mirroring his teasing tone, "I figured my hair could wait until tomorrow."

"I'm happy to hear it." He pointed to a nearby chair. "Have a seat and tell me what you thought of our show. I have a sneaking suspicion you'll give me an honest review."

Heather sank onto the chair. "It was good. I actually recognized some of your songs." When she realized what she'd said, a hot flush of embarrassment infused her cheeks, and she wished she could take back her words. "I'm sorry. Wendy keeps telling me I need to listen to more pop music instead of 'oldies,' as she calls them."

"Oldies?" Alex looked intrigued. "Do you mean like the Beatles?" He pointed to his shirt. "Or maybe the Monkees? Or the Beach Boys?"

"Not exactly. My dad sort of raised us on nineties alternative and grunge."

Alex's smile widened. "Oh. You mean Nirvana, Soundgarden, Stone Temple Pilots, and Pearl Jam?" He picked up the guitar again and started crooning the lyrics of Audioslave's "I Am the Highway."

Heather grinned and joined in as he played the chorus.

"That was outstanding!" he exclaimed after they finished their song. "Maybe we should sing a duet at my next concert. We're heading to Greensboro tomorrow. If you're not too busy washing your hair, maybe you can join us."

Chuckling, she shook her head. "I don't recommend calling me onstage for a duet. Unless, of course, you want the audience to leave early."

He laughed, and she enjoyed the deep, joyous sound, trying to commit it to memory.

"What was the song you were singing when I came in?" she asked, recalling the beautiful ballad detailing forever love. She wondered if he had written it for his girlfriend or wife, but his hands were naked of any jewelry. Was a beautiful woman waiting for him at home, wherever his home might be?

"It doesn't have a title, but I like to play it every once in a while."

"It's beautiful." She paused, hoping he would share more. When he remained silent, she added, "Did you write it for someone special?"

She cringed at herself. *Don't be awkward, Heather!*

He shook his head as he set the guitar back on its stand. "My dad wrote it for my mom a long time ago."

"Oh. Do you ever perform it?"

He laughed again, and to her he seemed so . . . *humble.* "No, and I probably never will, but thanks for the compliment."

When she realized she was staring at him, she averted her eyes. On a counter in front of the mirror, she spotted a familiar book. She set her phone on a table beside her, popped up from the seat, and crossed the room to pick it up. "Is this yours?"

"Yes. Do you find it impressive that I can read and write?" His eyes sparkled with more delight. Was he this friendly to every fan he met?

She decided to join in the teasing. "Why, yes. Especially since I once read that rockstars are all high school dropouts, and not one of them has ever finished an entire book."

He guffawed. "Well, I beg to differ. I'm always reading something. I like hardcovers and e-books too." He lifted a gray backpack from the floor, pulled out a tablet, and held it up.

"I'm impressed that you're an exception."

He grinned. "Thank you. I'll take that as a compliment."

"I loved this book so much that I read it four times." She held the book up, examining the cover. "In fact, Emil Zimmerman is my favorite author. I can't wait for his next book to come out. Waiting until August is like torture for me." She flipped the book over and ran her hand over the dust jacket, recalling how she'd been pulled right into the suspenseful story, living it alongside the main character.

"Is that right?"

She looked up and found Alex watching her intently, and she felt itchy under his stare. "Yes. It's actually my dream to open a bookstore."

"I thought it was a bakery."

She opened her mouth and then closed it, feeling like a fish out of water. How did he know that about her?

"You look surprised, but your sister mentioned it last night. By the way, I've been enjoying your amazing cookies. I shared them with our crew, and they disappeared quickly. They're the best I've ever had, and I bet your bakery will be a great success."

His compliment sent a wave of heat through her. "Thank you. Actually, I would love to open a combined bakery and bookstore." Then she hedged. "That's a dumb idea, right?"

"I think it's unique and brilliant."

Her shoulders sagged with the reality of the situation. "More like *unattainable*. I've been saving money and working on a business plan for a while. I want to open a place in my hometown, but the real estate is either not available or too expensive."

"Don't give up on your dream, Heather." He pointed to his chest. "My brothers and I are proof that dreams come true."

She set the book back on the counter and returned to her chair. "Where is everyone else?"

"They're doing their usual meet and greet after the concert. Our PR rep always sets up a special session for the VIPs." He pointed to her lanyard. "Like you and Wendy."

"Why aren't you there too?"

He lifted a shoulder in a half shrug, and his expression became sheepish. "I actually prefer a little quiet after the concerts. Kayden and Jordan are always excited to meet fans, but I need a little time to wind down and recharge my batteries first."

"Oh, I'm sorry." Heather jumped up. "It was so rude of me to just barge in here. I'll go find my sister."

Alex held his hand up. "No, please, don't go." Reaching into a nearby refrigerator, Alex pulled out two bottles of water and held them up. "How about a drink?"

Heather smiled and took the bottle from him as surprise filtered through her. "Thank you."

"Cheers." He held his up as if to toast her.

Heather opened the bottle and took a long drink, enjoying how the cool liquid felt on her parched throat after cheering and singing all night.

"So your family owns that restaurant, right?"

She nodded. "Yes, my parents opened it after they were married. It's been a fixture in Flowering Grove ever since."

"Well, it's legendary. My tour manager likes to research areas

29

we visit, and it came up on a list of recommended restaurants. We all agreed that it lived up to its hype. The food was outstanding."

"Thank you."

He ran his fingers over the condensation on his bottle. "I assume Flowering Grove is your home?"

"Yes, I was born and raised there. My sister still lives with my parents, but I live with my best friend. We rent a house that her parents own. Actually, her parents own most of Flowering Grove. They own several retail spaces as well as some rental homes. In fact, her parents own the salon she runs on Main Street. Mckenna has been doing hair for as long as I can remember. She used to style our Barbie dolls' hair when we were kids. We share a little brick ranch on Ridge Road a few blocks away from the restaurant. You can't miss it."

She chuckled. "Mckenna is obsessed with flamingos, so we have a flamingo welcome sign and a flamingo garden flag that says something silly like 'Do the Flamingo.'" She made air quotation marks with one hand. "And then we have a whole flock of these solar-powered, glass-blown flamingos that light up in the dark. Our neighbors must think we're nuts, but that's Mack for you!"

She realized she had gone off on a tangent, and her cheeks flamed again. *Stop talking, Heather!* She cleared her throat before taking another drink in an attempt to cool her humiliation.

Alex lifted a blond eyebrow and tilted his head. "How interesting."

"I'm sorry." She motioned toward the door. "I really should get out of your hair. I'm sure you want to rest before you get back on the road."

Alex nodded. "Unfortunately, I do need to make an appearance tonight. I'm sure they're wondering if I ran off to the hotel." He set his bottle of water on the nearby counter and then made a sweeping gesture toward the door. "But we can go together. After you."

Heather entered the hallway, then fell into step with Alex as they made their way to a large open area. There she spotted Wendy and a half dozen people surrounding the younger two Kirwan brothers.

Wendy beamed as she gazed up at Kayden, who seemed to be in the middle of a story about another performance. As he spoke, the group around him laughed.

Alex joined his brothers and greeted the other VIP guests. His smile was pleasant as he signed autographs and posed for photos. Heather noted that he was the tallest of the brothers—a few inches taller than Kayden and several inches taller than Jordan, the drummer.

When Wendy spotted Heather, she sidled up to her. "I was just about to go to the restroom and check on you. Where have you been?"

"I was talking to Alex."

Wendy gasped. "You were?"

Heather couldn't stop her grin.

"Tell me everything!"

"I accidentally wound up in his dressing room when I was looking for you, and we just talked about music and books." She shrugged as if it wasn't a big deal. "He was really nice."

"Cool!"

The other VIPs said goodbye to the brothers before a security guard led them toward the exit. Once they were gone, Alex said something to Kayden and Jordan and then motioned them toward the sisters.

"Heather and Wendy," Alex began as they approached, "these are my two younger brothers, Kayden and Jordan, the two idiots who trashed your family's restaurant last night."

31

Jordan, the shortest, held his hand out to Heather first. "I'm sorry. We were out of line."

Heather shook his hand. "I appreciate the apology."

Kayden shook her hand next. "I would blame it all on Jordan, but it was my fault. I was the doofus who started it all."

Heather laughed. "No harm done."

Kayden and Jordan took turns shaking hands with Wendy, who began quizzing them on their songs and favorite concerts.

Alex beckoned a man dressed in jeans and a blue polo shirt with the Kirwan logo on it. "Brooks, would you please get these ladies two of our special swag packs?" Then he turned to Heather. "Brooks is our tour manager."

"Oh." Heather nodded and tried to think of something to say to keep the conversation going, but nothing came to her. After a moment of nervous silence, she finally blurted, "So if you're reading Emil Zimmerman, does that mean you like suspense books the most?"

Alex smiled. "It's my favorite genre."

"Mine too. Have you ever read Elise Harvey's books?"

He shook his head. "No, I don't think so, but I enjoy Sean Monroe's."

"Oh yes!" Heather snapped her fingers. "*The Shadow in the Woods* was excellent."

"One of my favorites."

Heather and Alex both grinned, and for a moment, she felt as if they shared a special bond. Then she shoved that ridiculous thought away. Who was she kidding? He was a rockstar, and she was a server in her parents' restaurant.

Brooks reappeared and handed string bags with the Kirwan logo on them to Wendy and to Heather. "Here you go. Thank you for coming to the show tonight."

Wendy thanked him, then turned her attention back to

Kayden. Heather shouldered the bag and found herself wishing for more time with Alex.

"I'll look up Elise Harvey's books on my tablet as soon as I get back to the hotel tonight," Alex said, holding out his hand to Heather. "I really enjoyed talking to you tonight, Heather."

She clasped his hand and was almost certain he held on for a moment longer than necessary. "I did too."

Wendy took hold of Heather's arm. "We had a blast tonight. Thank you so much," she sang, pulling Heather toward the security guard standing by the door.

Before they exited the building, Heather looked back to where Alex stood. He was still watching her, and her skin prickled.

⁓

"Kayden Kirwan is the most gorgeous man on the planet!" Wendy exclaimed as she climbed into the passenger seat of Heather's gray 2010 Honda Civic. "This was the best night of my life. Thank you so much for coming with me." She pulled her phone from her pocket. "I need to text Deanna and tell her everything. She's going to be so jealous that we met the Kirwan brothers, but it's not my fault she went to see her grandmother."

Heather nodded as she pulled out of the parking lot and headed toward Tryon Street. Her sister's words were only background noise to her own thoughts, which rehashed her all-too-short conversation with Alex Kirwan.

On one hand she mentally chastised herself for the crush she had developed on him, but on the other hand, she couldn't stop recalling the interest she thought she'd found in his expressions while they talked. But why would a rockstar be interested in someone as boring and ordinary as she was? Heather also knew that having a crush on someone unattainable was safer than getting her heart broken by a real boyfriend, which was exactly what her ex-boyfriend, Jeff, had done to her.

"Oh wow!" Wendy announced, opening the swag bag. "Wait until you see what's in here. We got a water bottle, a Sharpie, a thumb drive, a hand towel . . . Oh! And here's an autographed photo of them. We can hang this on our Wall of Fame at the restaurant."

Heather nodded, keeping her eyes on the road as she merged onto Interstate 485. "That's great."

"I took a bunch of pictures too." Wendy turned her attention back to her phone and pulled up her photos. "I can't wait to show Deanna. I got a selfie with Kayden and Jordan. Deanna prefers Jordan because she says he seems so quiet and down-to-earth, but Kayden is just so hot!"

While Wendy continued to gush over Kayden's swoony qualities, Heather lost herself in thoughts of Alex, wondering if he had enjoyed their conversation as much as she had. Surely she had imagined their connection, but he seemed so genuine. *He must meet thousands of women per year. Why would he even remember me after tonight?*

"Now admit it, Heather. You had fun," Wendy insisted, breaking through Heather's ridiculous thoughts.

"I had a great time."

Wendy clapped her hands. "I totally knew you would!" She leaned toward Heather. "Are you going to stream their music now?"

"Yes, I will. They were really good. Thank you for making me go with you."

"You're welcome." Wendy laughed as she began texting on

her phone. "I'm sending Deanna all of these photos. I can't wait to share the details."

Heather swallowed a sigh. She was certain she'd never see Alex Kirwan in person again, but she indulged the foolish hope that he might remember her name.

4

Alex and his brothers signed autographs and talked to the employees at the amphitheater for another hour before he returned to his dressing room to gather up his stuff and head to the hotel. He slipped his guitar into its case, threw his clothes in a duffel, then picked up his book and smiled as he recalled his conversation with Heather. He hadn't met a woman who wanted to discuss books with him since . . . well, ever. The women who crossed his path never wanted to talk about anything other than his music.

Alex grinned as he considered Heather. Their conversation had been fun and interesting. He had enjoyed how she'd teased him and how she hadn't treated him like a celebrity. Instead, she spoke to him like a peer, like someone she wanted to get to know as a person. He relished how she admitted she hadn't really known his music. She seemed to him like an honest person.

And it was a bonus that she was so attractive, with dark hair framing her pretty face, her chocolate-colored eyes, and those adorable freckles across her petite nose. She was trim and also taller than most women he knew.

Alex was still contemplating her when he spotted a cell phone on the table beside the chair where she had sat earlier.

He examined the light blue case, then flipped it over and touched the screen. A photo of two black-and-white cats sitting on a sofa stared back at him. The corner of his mouth quirked upward.

"So Heather is a cat person," he mumbled.

"Alex, you ready?"

He turned to face Brooks, who was standing in the doorway. "Yeah," he said, pocketing Heather's phone and following his tour manager toward the exit. "I'm going to need to run a quick errand tomorrow on our way to Greensboro."

"What kind of errand?" Brooks asked as they jogged down the steps and out to the parking lot. An Escalade waited for them, its engine running.

"One of the women who came from that restaurant left her phone in my dressing room."

"We'll have a courier deliver it."

Alex opened one of the back doors of the SUV and shook his head. "No, I want to deliver it to her."

Brooks studied him for a moment and then nodded. "All right, but I heard Robyn say you have a tight schedule tomorrow."

"Thanks." Alex climbed into the back seat behind his brothers, who were engrossed in a conversation about the encore set list for Greensboro.

While the SUV motored toward the hotel, Alex pulled his tablet out of his backpack and searched for the Barbecue Pit's webpage. He clicked on a heading that read "Our Story," and a Gordon family photo filled the screen. He took in the image, noting how Wendy seemed to have her mother's coloring while Heather took after her father with darker hair and eyes.

He studied Heather's beautiful face, taking in those intriguing freckles. He longed to spend the evening discussing books with her and learning more about her life. His thoughts moved to her dream of owning a bookstore with a bakery, and he clicked on the link to the restaurant's menu and found his way to Heather's desserts.

As he read the list of delectable treats, each one of them featuring a bookish name, a strange excitement filled him at the thought of seeing her again tomorrow.

⌒

"Oh no. No, no, no." Heather groaned as she pointed a flashlight around the floor of her car later that evening. "It's got to be here somewhere!"

When she had arrived home after dropping her sister off at their parents' house, Heather realized her phone wasn't in her crossbody or her jeans pocket. After checking her hoodie pocket, she hurried into the house to ask Mack to call it—but her best friend was already snoring in her bedroom.

Heather had located Mack's phone on her bedside table and unplugged it. Then she found a flashlight in the junk drawer in the kitchen and trotted back out to the car. Using Mack's phone—for which she knew the passcode—Heather called her own number. She hoped to hear her ringtone, a clip of Pearl Jam's "Even Flow," singing out to her, but panic gripped her when she didn't hear the song or the sound of her phone vibrating. Instead, her voicemail picked up.

Heather slipped Mack's phone into her pocket and began searching the car anyway. Maybe the phone was hiding under her seat with a drained battery—or not. After patting down the entire car, Heather knew for sure the phone had to be elsewhere.

With another groan, she sank down onto the driver's seat and mentally retraced her steps. When had she used her phone last?

She had texted Mack during the concert, but then she couldn't remember it after that. She'd definitely lost it at the amphitheater. Heather closed and rubbed her eyes. What were the odds that someone had found it?

Heather would have to call the amphitheater tomorrow and hope someone turned it over to the lost and found. If not, she'd have to buy a new one. She let out a frustrated sigh. The last thing she needed was the cost of a new phone added to her monthly bill when she was doing her best to save every penny for her bookstore and bakery.

She locked her car before heading back into the house, where her two tuxedo cats met her at the door with a chorus of meows.

"Shh," she told Jet as she stroked his head. "You're going to wake Mack, and you know how grouchy she is if she doesn't get her eight hours of sleep."

Molly peeped and then nudged Heather's shin.

With black-and-white faces, black backs and legs, and white chests that gave them the appearance of wearing tuxedos, Jet and his sister, Molly, were nearly identical from afar. But Heather often thought the black around Jet's eyes looked like a mask, which made him distinguishable from his sister, along with his larger size.

Heather shooed the cats into her room, then tiptoed into Mckenna's room across the hall and returned her phone. Her friend continued to snore softly while Heather padded out and quietly closed the door.

Heather gave the cats some food and water in the kitchen before she showered, climbed into her queen-sized bed, and switched on her laptop. Molly curled up on the pillow beside her while Jet took his usual spot, flopping down on her left foot.

The memory of Alex's handsome face and brilliant smile filled her mind as she searched for Kirwan's website. She browsed the page, taking in their tour schedule, information about their fan club, photos of the band on tour, and a list of songs.

She clicked on a link to a video and sat mesmerized as Alex and Kayden crooned into microphones. Then she shook her head. How ridiculous she was! Why was she obsessing over this guy? She was just as immature as her sister!

Heather closed her laptop, flipped off her lamp, and snuggled down under the covers. After whispering good night to her cats, she waited for sleep to find her.

⌒

"Why are we delivering her phone?" Kayden asked from the third-row seat of the Escalade the following morning.

Alex pointed at the upcoming sign. "There's Ridge Road. Turn here, please," he told Easton Powell, their driver. Then he craned his neck toward his brother. "Because she left it in my dressing room. Wouldn't you want your phone back?"

"Yeah, but why didn't you just leave it with security?" Kayden's expression seemed suspicious.

"Because I want to deliver it myself." Alex faced the windshield. "Look for a house with a lot of flamingos out front."

"Flamingos?" Jordan snickered from his seat beside Kayden. "Like, plastic ones?"

Alex shook his head. "Heather said her roommate has a flamingo welcome sign, a garden flag, and a bunch of solar flamingos that light up at night."

"Is it that house?" Jordan pointed toward a brick ranch

with an older, gray Honda Civic and a late-model green Subaru Outback out front.

And just as Heather had described, a flock of ceramic flamingos lined the path leading to the front door. The welcome sign and garden flag were there as well, seeming to smile in the early morning sun.

Kayden smirked. "Well, that's . . . different."

"I find it rather quaint and cheerful," Easton quipped as he nosed the large SUV into the driveway and slipped it into Park behind the Honda.

Robyn Morris, their publicity manager, turned around from the passenger seat and speared Alex with a look. "Please make it snappy. We have a schedule to keep."

Although she was barely five feet tall—even when clad in the high heels she always wore—Robyn was a force to be reckoned with when on a mission. With her curly dark hair, dark eyes, bright red lipstick, and red-framed glasses, she knew her way around a publicity plan and was ever determined to keep her band on schedule.

Alex pulled Heather's phone from his jeans pocket, then wrenched the door open. "I'll be right back."

He climbed out of the Escalade, pushed the door shut, and started up the path, smiling as he moved past the happy flamingos on his way to the small front porch. Then he opened the storm door, knocked on the wooden door's red frame, and waited. He hoped Heather would answer, and that the two vehicles in the driveway indicated she and her roommate were home.

Alex glanced out toward the small front yard as two squirrels raced up a nearby tree. A few birds sang their morning songs to the clear blue sky and bright, early-April sun.

Turning back toward the house, he lifted his hand to knock

again just as the red door creaked open. A petite young woman with dark hair, red highlights, and a cute, pixielike face looked up at him. She blinked, and he was almost certain recognition flashed in her blue eyes. "May I help you?" she said.

"Mckenna, right?" he asked.

A quizzical expression filled her features as she opened the door wider. Two tuxedo cats sat behind her, watching him with their ears back. "That's right."

"I'm Alex." He held up Heather's phone. "Heather left this at the amphitheater last night, and I wanted to return it."

Mckenna tilted her head. "You're Alex Kirwan."

"That's right."

"Come on in." She motioned for him to enter the house. "You aren't allergic to cats, are you?"

"No."

"Good. Jet and Molly won't bite. They'll just sniff you. Do you normally return phones for fans who leave them at your concert?"

He laughed as he stepped into a small family room, complete with a beige sofa, a love seat, a coffee table, end tables, and a flat-screen television. "No, not usually. This is a special circumstance."

"Well, she'll be delighted to have it back. She's been on hold with the amphitheater for about thirty minutes now asking about it, and I need my phone back from her so I can head to work. Make yourself comfortable, and I'll go get her." Mckenna drifted to a hallway and called, "Heather!"

Alex moved to a nearby bookshelf and took in an impressive book collection. He ran his fingers along the bindings, recognizing some of the titles and authors. Then he examined framed photos of Heather and Mckenna at the beach, smiling while waves crashed behind them. He couldn't help but smile at all the family photos featuring Heather and a few of Mckenna.

When he felt something rub against his leg, he looked down. A black-and-white cat blinked up at him.

"Hello there. What's your name?" he asked the cat.

The feline responded with a purr before rubbing against his shin once again.

Alex turned toward the hallway when he heard voices sound behind him.

"Heather," Mckenna called again. "Come out here."

"Just a minute. I'm still on hold with customer service," Heather responded from somewhere in the house.

"Your phone is here."

A beat of silence passed, and then Heather said, "What?"

"I said your phone is here," Mckenna called. "It's been delivered personally by a very handsome man."

Alex barely held back a laugh. More silence filled the air, then Heather appeared at the end of the hallway dressed in an oversized shirt and blue lounge pants decorated with different-colored cats. Her dark hair sat in a messy knot on top of her head, with wisps falling around her makeup-free face.

Alex sucked in a breath. She was gorgeous. Those freckles! He couldn't stop staring at her.

Her hand, which had been holding a cell phone to her ear, dropped to her side. "Alex?" Her voice was a shocked whisper, and her eyes widened as she walked toward him. "Wh-what are you doing here?"

"You left something in my dressing room last night." He held up her phone.

She blinked and then ran her hand down her clothes. "Oh goodness. I never expected to see you again. I'm a wreck."

"No, you're not. You look great." He met her at the edge of the hallway and handed her the phone. "I saw a missed call from Mckenna's phone when I got up this morning. I was wiped out when I got to the hotel room, but if I'd heard it ringing, I would have answered and told her I had your phone."

Heather shook her head. "I had actually used Mack's phone to call *my* phone." She paused and narrowed her eyes as if trying to figure something out. "How did you find my house?"

"You told me you lived on Ridge Road and your yard was decorated with flamingos." He pointed toward the front door.

Mckenna took her phone from Heather's hand and grinned. "I told you those flamingos were awesome." She snickered as she walked through the doorway leading to the kitchen.

"They definitely helped me find you. We're on our way to Greensboro, but I wanted to stop by to return your phone and ask you a question."

She blinked those long, dark lashes. "Uh, okay."

"So," he began, mustering all the courage he could find inside himself. "I was wondering if I could have your number." Then he held his breath, hoping she was single and would say yes.

Heather opened and closed her mouth, looking completely flummoxed. "Why would you want my number?"

"So I can text you."

She pointed to her chest. "Why on earth would you want to text *me*?"

"To talk about books, of course." He jammed his thumb toward the impressive bookshelf, but she continued to watch him with a mixture of curiosity and bewilderment. "So what do you think?"

She unlocked her phone and handed it to him. "Of course."

Excitement coursed through Alex as he added his number to her contacts and then sent himself a message. His phone dinged in his back pocket as he gave her phone back to her. "Now you've got my number too."

"Great." She smiled, and happiness filled him. What was it

about this young woman that seemed to bring his heart back to life after so long?

A horn tooted outside, lowering him back down to earth. "I have to run, but it was great seeing you again. We have a crazy schedule today before tonight's show, but I'll text you."

"Thank you for delivering my phone."

"You're welcome. I hope you have a nice day, Heather." He waved at Mckenna standing in the doorway to the kitchen, watching him curiously. Then he crossed the room to the front door.

"Alex, wait!" Heather suddenly called.

He whipped around.

"Would you like some cookies for the road?"

He clasped his hands together. "That would be fantastic."

"Just give me a minute."

Mckenna stepped aside as Heather bolted into the kitchen.

Moments later, she returned with a to-go box and held it out to him. "Here are some of my Oatmeal Raisin Romance and Butterscotch Thriller cookies."

"Thank you," he said as he took the box.

"It's the least I can do." She blessed him with another smile. "Be safe on the road."

"I will." He told each of them goodbye, then hurried out to the waiting SUV and climbed into the back seat.

When he glanced at the house, he spotted Heather standing in the doorway holding a large black-and-white cat. He opened the window and waved, and she returned the gesture as Easton backed the vehicle out of the driveway.

Jordan reached over the seat as the truck motored down the road. "Please tell me you have more cookies in that box."

"Take a few." Alex handed him the box, then pulled his phone from his pocket. He quickly created a contact for Heather, adding her home address along with her phone number.

When Alex looked up, Kayden was watching him. He prepared himself for an interrogation.

"Why are you chasing after that woman, Alex?" his youngest brother asked. "Are you afraid she's going to post a negative story about us on her social media after what happened at her family's restaurant?"

Robyn's head snapped around from the front seat. "What happened in the restaurant?"

"This has nothing to do with Thursday night. She's past that already," Alex said.

Jordan held the box open, and Kayden chose a cookie.

Robyn frowned. "Tell me what happened. Do I have a publicity fire to put out?"

"It's fine. I handled it." Alex held his hand up to calm their PR manager before filling her in on the food fight. "Heather accepted our apology, and everything is fine."

Kayden swallowed a bite of butterscotch cookie. "Then why are you chasing after her?"

"I'm not chasing after her. I just want to be friends."

Kayden snorted. "Friends. Right."

"Let's hope the traffic isn't bad," Robyn said. "We're cutting it close with your first appointment. We have two radio interviews, two television interviews, and a meet and greet before the soundcheck. We can't waste any more time."

While Robyn went on about their schedule, Alex glanced out the window and smiled. With Heather's number now in his phone, he looked forward to the chance to get to know her better.

5

Heather tried to catch her breath as the sleek black SUV drove down Ridge Road and out of sight. She set Jet down on the floor. She was grateful she had grabbed him before he followed Alex out the front door. When she turned, she met Mckenna's surprised expression.

"Girl, we just had a rockstar in our den. You need to explain yourself."

"I'm actually not sure what's happening." Heather entered the kitchen and slipped a vanilla latte pod into the Keurig, placed her favorite cat mug under it, and hit the Start button. Then she leaned back on the counter and cupped her hand to her forehead, trying to calm her racing heart. Soon the delicious aroma of coffee overtook the kitchen.

Never in a million years would she have imagined she'd see Alex Kirwan again—yet he was just in her house. Had she dreamt it?

Mckenna stood in the doorway with her hands on her small hips. "You said you had a meaningless conversation with Alex Kirwan in his dressing room last night. But he just delivered your phone to you and asked for your number."

"We did have a meaningless conversation, which is why I'm just as confused as you are."

"Heather, I have five minutes before I'm officially late for my first appointment at the salon, so I need you to tell me what *really* happened in that dressing room—pronto."

"I *did* tell you what happened," Heather insisted, holding her hands up. "I wandered into his dressing room looking for my sister, and I babbled on about books and your flamingos. We didn't talk about anything important. So I have no idea why he came here. He probably collects women's numbers!"

"Uh, I don't think so. He said he wants to talk about books."

"Sure." Heather snorted and then looked down at her pants. "I can't believe I'm wearing my cat pajamas." She covered her face with her hands. "I feel like the biggest idiot on the planet."

"But I heard him say you looked great."

Heather moaned again, then picked up her mug and took a sip.

"Why would he deliver your phone and ask for your number if he didn't want to get to know you?"

"Yeah, sure. He wants to get to know a woman who works as a server in her parents' restaurant and hopes to open a bookstore with a bakery someday." Heather pulled out a loaf of bread and dropped two pieces in the toaster.

"Heather, he likes you! It was written all over his face."

"I doubt it." Heather reached down and filled the cat bowls with dry food, and Jet and Molly trotted in to inhale their breakfast. "He's probably just after one thing."

"But he's on the road all the time. Why would he ask for your number if he just wanted something physical?"

Heather considered the thought, then shook her head. "I'm

a nobody compared to him. I'm a working-class citizen, and he's a megastar. Why would he want to get to know me?"

"Because he *likes* you, silly. That's why." Mckenna pulled her in for a hug. "Just wait until you get that first text message. He'll be falling in love with you in no time, and you'll be a rockstar's girlfriend."

"I doubt that."

"Whatever!" Mckenna waved her off on her way to the front door. "Have a great day and let me know if you hear from him. Meanwhile, I'm meeting Kirk Jenkins for lunch."

Heather grinned. "He's been asking you out for a month. You finally told him yes?"

"I did." Mckenna spun when she reached the front door. "Maybe Kirk and I can double date with you and Alex someday."

Heather laughed. "Yeah, right. Get out of here."

"Love you! Bye!"

"Love you too," Heather called after her. Once Mckenna was gone, Heather unlocked her phone and scrolled through her contacts until she found Alex's number. He had identified himself as "Alex K." Her heart skipped a beat as she wondered when she'd hear from him again.

The *pop* of the toaster startled her back to reality. Reluctantly, she turned her attention to getting ready for a day at work.

⌒

"Let me get this straight," Wendy said later that morning, standing next to her sister in the restaurant's kitchen. "Alex Kirwan was *at your house?*"

Heather nodded as she iced a carrot cake. "That's what I said." She tried not to grin as she recalled how gorgeous Alex had looked in those tight jeans and his worn gray hoodie. Who was she kidding? That man would look hot wearing a burlap sack. When she remembered she had been wearing her pajamas when he stopped by, though, her smile dissolved.

A timer dinged, and Heather turned to her mother. "Would you please pull the cookies out of the oven and slide the next tray in?"

"Of course." Mom opened the oven, and the delicious aroma of strawberry shortcake cookies wafted through the kitchen.

Deanna Burris, Wendy's best friend, pinched the bridge of her nose as if trying to comprehend the situation. "So you talked to him briefly last night, and then he came to your house today?" She shook her head, and her natural red curls bounced back and forth. "I can't believe it!" She faced Wendy. "If only I had visited my grandma last week and you had gotten three tickets, then maybe I could have gone, too, and met Jordan."

"Could you imagine if Kayden and Jordan had come to see *us*?" Wendy asked.

The two young women held hands and screeched.

Heather frowned at her mother, who rolled her eyes.

"Can you two calm down?" Dad called from the far end of the kitchen. "I have a headache."

Wendy bit her lip. "Sorry, Dad." Then she and Deanna shared a smile before turning back to Heather. "Would you please put in a good word for me with Kayden?"

"And for me with Jordan!" Deanna held her hand up as if asking a question at school.

Heather stared at them and wondered if they were sixteen instead of twenty-two years old. "I'll probably never hear from him again. It was just a crazy thing that happened."

Mom chuckled. "I disagree. He'll be back for more cookies."

Heather laughed, and Wendy and Deanna joined in.

Later that morning, Heather finished icing a chocolate cake and turned to her mother, who was preparing a large batch of coleslaw. "I think we're ready for the Saturday lunch and dinner rush."

Mom wiped her hands on a towel and sidled up to Heather. "So tell me every detail about Alex Kirwan that you didn't tell your sister and Deanna."

"There really isn't anything else, Mom. We talked about books and music. And I rambled like an idiot about my dream of having a bookstore and bakery. I even told him about the flamingos in front of our house, which is how he found it." She glanced left and right and then leaned in close. "I had this strange moment where I felt like we had a connection, but how can that be true? We're from different worlds, Mom. Why would he be interested in me?"

Her mother's pretty face lit up with a knowing smile, and she touched Heather's cheek. "Because you're a beautiful, intelligent, sweet, amazing young woman who has a lot to offer."

"But I'm sure he meets hundreds of women every week who are much more successful, attractive, and interesting than I am. So, again, why would he want to get to know *me*?"

Mom rested her hand on Heather's shoulder. "I believe he saw something in you that he hasn't seen before." She touched Heather's cheek. "I know Jeff broke your heart, but not every man is like Jeff. You're a strong, beautiful, intelligent woman, and you shouldn't be afraid to put yourself out there again."

Heather cringed at the sound of her ex-boyfriend's name.

"Besides," Mom began as she gestured around the large kitchen. "You never know. People find love in the most unexpected places."

"Love?" Heather couldn't stop her sarcastic laugh. "I hadn't even heard of his band until they came to the restaurant."

"An unexpected meeting is the best kind!"

Heather shook her head as she pulled off her apron, which was splattered with cake batter and icing. "I'm going to get ready for lunch service."

"Have faith, Heather. You never know where a friendship with Alex might lead," Mom sang.

As much as she wanted to believe her mother, Heather doubted she would ever be more than an acquaintance to Alex Kirwan.

After changing her apron and fixing her hair, Heather pushed through the double doors leading out to the dining room. There she found Wendy and Deanna standing in front of the sea of photos on the restaurant's Wall of Fame.

"Heather! Come here!" Wendy waved her over. "We added the autographed Kirwan photo we got in the swag pack."

As she approached the wall, Heather's eyes focused on Alex's face. He and his brothers all posed with serious expressions, and though he looked handsome, he didn't look at all like the man she'd met. In fact, he hardly resembled the man who laughed with her and teased her. She wondered if she'd met someone else—the *real* Alex Kirwan, the man behind the rockstar image.

She chided herself. How could she possibly know the real him yet?

Wendy rested her hands on her hips. "Well, Heather? What do you think?"

"It looks great." She sighed, certain she'd find herself staring at his photo during the day and wondering where he was and what he was doing. Perhaps her heart was already doomed.

Later that afternoon, the band stood onstage for their sound-check at the arena in Greensboro. "This next question is for Alex," Brooks announced into a mic. "What is your favorite song you've ever performed?"

Alex looked out over the crowd of fan club members. Their VIP tickets admitted them to the soundcheck before the concert, during which the band tested the equipment by singing songs selected by fans. The VIPs also had the chance to email questions, meet the band, and receive special fan merch.

"Hmm." Alex brushed the stubble on his chin with his fingers as he contemplated the question.

Although he'd been asked the same question hundreds of times, he tried to vary his answer as often as possible. He considered naming the song he'd sung when Heather had appeared in his dressing room, but it wasn't a song he'd ever performed in public. He racked his brain for an answer, but Heather had preoccupied his thoughts all day long. Even while he was powering through the interviews earlier in the day, he found himself wondering how Heather's day was going.

"I guess I'd have to say 'One More Time.' We won the Battle of the Bands contest with that song," Alex finally said.

The fans cheered, and Alex nodded a thank-you before tossing the question to Kayden. "What about you, Kay? Which one is your favorite?"

"Oh, that's easy." His youngest brother grinned. "It's 'Let's Dance' for sure. That was our first number-one hit."

The crowd cheered again.

"Why don't we play it, huh, Jor?" Kayden faced Jordan, who sat behind his drum kit.

Jordan shrugged. "Sure."

As Alex played the opening chords of the song, he tried to focus on the performance and not his thoughts of Heather.

After the soundcheck was over, Alex and his brothers walked down the steps to talk to the fans until the security guards escorted them out of the hall. The fans could then reenter the venue in a couple of hours before the concert started.

When Alex finally made it back to his dressing room, he retrieved a butterscotch cookie from the box Heather had given him and shook his head. He had eaten so many of her cookies today that he would have to hit the gym extra hard.

He pulled his phone from his pocket and unlocked it.

"Alex?"

He turned toward the doorway, where Robyn now stood. "Yeah?"

"There's a special fan who would like to meet you."

Alex slipped his phone back into his pocket. "Who is it?"

"His name is C. J., and he's eight. He's been in and out of hospitals since he was eighteen months old. His mother reached out to me and asked if you could possibly meet with him since you're his hero."

"Wow." Her words tweaked his heart. He didn't feel worthy enough to be anyone's hero, especially a child's. "I'd love to meet him." His favorite part of being in the music business was meeting kids. He considered it his privilege to have the chance to talk with them—especially those brave kids who dealt with pain and illness.

Memories of Alex's own childhood suddenly flooded his mind. He recalled the boy named Carson who had lived beside him when Alex was ten years old. Carson was only eight when he had been diagnosed with leukemia.

Alex's parents sent him over to Carson's house with small

gifts, and the boys would play games and watch cartoons together. He visited Carson at least once a week before Carson's parents had moved to be closer to a specialized cancer center. To this day, Alex often wondered where Carson lived and how he was doing.

"Great. I'll go get C. J. and his mom." Robyn turned to go.

"Wait," Alex said, and she swiveled toward him once again. "Is there any chance we could find a children's hospital to visit in the next couple of days?"

"I could work on that. I'll see if I can get a photographer to go with you and shoot something for our social media accounts."

Alex shook his head. "No, I don't want to do it for the publicity. I don't want anyone to know I'm there. I just want to spend some time with the kids and try to brighten their day." He hoped he could touch another child's life the way he hoped he had helped Carson all those years ago.

Robyn's expression became solemn. "Oh, I see. I'll make some calls and see if we can fit it into the schedule."

A few minutes later, a small, skinny boy with a pale complexion, light green eyes, and light blond hair stood tentatively in the doorway to Alex's dressing room. For a moment Alex's heart was caught in his throat, but he took a deep breath and smiled.

"You must be C. J.!" Alex held his hand out. "I'm Alex Kirwan. It's an honor to meet you." He sneaked a look behind the boy and spotted a young woman with the same green eyes beaming at him. "And you must be his mom. Please come in."

C. J. grinned and followed Alex into the dressing room. "Wow! Is that your guitar?" He pointed to the acoustic guitar in the corner.

"It is."

"Would you please play something for me?"

"It would be my honor. What would you like to hear?"

C. J. looked up at the ceiling as if it held all the answers. "How about 'Maybe Tonight'?"

"Is that your favorite song?"

The boy nodded with enthusiasm. "Yeah."

"Good choice." Alex hopped up on a stool while C. J. and his mother each sank onto a chair. As he began to tune the strings, he felt his heart lift. He felt led to help children and their families—families like C. J.'s. He just had to figure out how to go about it.

6

Heather's back, legs, and feet ached when she dragged herself into her house later that night. She kicked off her shoes at the front door and then looked up, surprised to find Mckenna and Kirk watching a movie on television. Jet and Molly were both sprawled out on the back of the sofa, snoring softly.

"Hi," Heather managed to say through a yawn.

Mckenna paused the movie and leaned forward. "Why are you home so late?"

"Jane called out, so I offered to work a double since Wendy had plans with Deanna tonight." She blew out a sigh. "It was a typical crazy Saturday. Allie, Joyce, and I were hopping all night long."

Kirk smiled. "I hope you made some big tips though."

"Not bad!" Heather nodded toward the hallway. "I'll let you two enjoy your movie."

Mckenna held her hand up. "Wait. Did you hear from Alex?"

"Who's Alex?" Kirk's dark eyebrows lifted.

Heather waved him off. "He's no one, and no, I didn't hear from him."

Her jaw clenched as she walked toward the kitchen, regretting telling her friends and family members about Alex. It seemed that all day long someone was asking her if she'd heard from "her rockstar," and every time she had to say no. Of course, Mckenna had witnessed the entire scene this morning, but Heather was tired of talking about it. It was humiliating that Alex had asked for her number and then didn't reach out.

But the questions weren't the only issue Heather had dealt with today. She had also become obsessed with checking her phone. It had gotten so bad that she finally set her phone in her parents' office in order to stop herself from looking at the screen, constantly hoping to find a text message from Alex K.

Heather had tried to evict thoughts of him from her mind, but he remained there, taunting her. The photo of him and his brothers staring back at her from the Wall of Fame all day long didn't help the situation either. She poured herself a glass of iced tea, then took a long drink.

"Why don't you text him?"

Heather swiveled to where Mckenna grinned at her from the doorway. "No, I'm not going to chase after him like some lovesick groupie."

"I highly doubt Alex gives his phone number to groupies."

"You should be out with your boyfriend and not worrying about me and my nonexistent relationship." Heather finished her drink and set her glass in the dishwasher.

Mckenna grinned. "He's not my boyfriend . . . yet."

"You like him though." Heather smiled. "I'm happy for you."

Mckenna hugged her. "Alex is going to text you. I can feel it in my bones."

"You're silly." Heather laughed. "Go enjoy your night." She padded down the hallway to her room, took a long shower, and then climbed into bed. After checking Kirwan's social media pages, she began adding the band's music to playlists on her phone.

Then Heather pulled the latest novel she'd been reading from the pile by her bed. She tried to concentrate on the words, but her thoughts kept meandering to Alex. She dropped the book onto the bed beside her. Unbidden, memories of her ex-boyfriend, Jeff, also invaded her thoughts. Heather had been convinced that she and Jeff had a future, but that all changed when his ex-girlfriend came to visit family in Flowering Grove. Then he met his ex for lunch—and left Heather for good.

She frowned. She was just bad at relationships, and she was better off alone. After all, she had her bookstore to plan. That would be her future. She needed to put all distractions out of her head and stop driving herself crazy.

Heather heard a rustling near her cracked door, and Jet pushed himself through. He meowed at her before flouncing into her room and jumping on the bed.

"You're the only boyfriend I need," Heather told the cat before kissing his head. She took another book from her bedside pile, this time her favorite dessert cookbook, and flipped through it until her eyes longed to close.

⌒

Late Tuesday afternoon, Alex followed his brothers out of a television station and waited at the curb for their SUV to arrive.

Jordan jammed his hands into his jacket pockets. "Since we have a few hours off, why don't we go find a place to eat and hang out? Maybe play some pool?" He glanced around downtown Raleigh, North Carolina. "There has to be a good place nearby, right?"

"That sounds like the perfect way to relax tonight. It's been too long since I've beat you at a round of pool." Kayden gave Jordan's shoulder a playful punch.

Jordan snorted and looked at Alex. "What do you say, Alex? Are you in?"

Alex shook his head. "No, thanks. Robyn arranged for me to spend a couple of hours at a children's hospital visiting some patients."

Jordan's expression lit up. "Oh, I didn't see that on our schedule. Did she add that today?"

"We can come with you and mug for a few photos," Kayden said. "Robyn is always telling us we need new material for Facebook."

"I'm actually not going for the publicity. In fact, only their community relations person knows I'm coming."

Kayden's brow furrowed. "What do you mean?"

"I just want to say hi to the kids without the cameras around."

"Oh." Kayden shared a look with Jordan. "Do you want us to go with you?"

Alex shook his head. "No, you guys go have fun. I'll see you at the hotel later."

The SUV pulled up to the curb, and Alex climbed into the passenger seat while his brothers took their places in the back.

"Where to?" Easton asked as he steered the vehicle away from the curb.

"I'm heading to the children's hospital, and these two want to go play pool." Alex swiveled to face his brothers. "And don't cause a commotion or start a food fight. If you do, you'll have to deal with Robyn and me."

Kayden looked up from his phone and pinned Alex with a furious look. "We're adults, and you're not our dad."

Alex winced. Problem was, he'd felt like their dad since he was fifteen years old—and he probably always would feel responsible for them since their father was gone.

"You can trust us, Alex. We won't have another incident like we did in Flowering Grove." Jordan held a hand up as if to stop an argument from erupting. "You two just calm down."

Alex settled back in his seat and faced forward, hoping Jordan was right.

Alex pushed open his hotel room door and set his guitar case on the sofa. He yawned and checked the clock by the television, then was surprised to find it was after eight o'clock. He had lost track of time at the children's hospital, and afterward he'd stopped for something to eat.

He smiled as he considered the afternoon. He had brought his guitar and spent more than two hours talking to the kids, singing, and laughing with them. His heart felt full when he saw their faces light up. He only wished he'd brought something to give the kids as keepsakes. He'd have to discuss that with Robyn.

After choosing a bottle of water from the minifridge, he flopped onto the sofa and turned on the television. He flipped through the channels, but his mind raced with thoughts about the next time he'd get to pay a visit to a hospital. Today's visit reminded him of the time he'd spent with Carson as a kid. While Carson had always seemed sad when Alex first arrived, he always wore a smile by the time Alex left to go home. Alex loved bringing his friend some happiness, and he felt a similar satisfaction after spending time with the resilient kids at the hospital.

Once again, he found himself longing for something more than his current life. While he enjoyed writing songs and performing, he wanted something more meaningful. He craved someone to spend his life with—someone with whom to share a family. Someone with whom to grow old.

His mind filled with memories of his father, and his chest squeezed. If he closed his eyes, he could still hear his father's voice as he sang to his mother when he thought Alex and his brothers weren't around. He could still see his parents dancing in the kitchen or holding hands as they walked through a store together. Alex wanted a relationship like that, a love like that.

But Alex hadn't dated in more than two years—not since Celeste had broken up with him, insisting he was wasting his time trying to turn the band into anything more than a hobby. She had been the last woman he'd trusted with his heart.

After Celeste broke up with him, Alex had given up on love, despite his best friend Tristan's insistence that Alex would meet someone who would believe in him and stand by him through thick and thin. Still, Alex had poured all of his effort into the band, as well as making sure his mother and his brothers were taken care of. That was his duty as the eldest son, after all. His job was to put the family first until they no longer needed him.

Yet now, as he sat in the hotel room and stared at a television, he felt loneliness creeping into his heart. He needed a distraction—like going to the gym or even opening the latest book he had downloaded.

He glanced around for his tablet, and his eyes focused on the box of cookies sitting on the coffee table. He thought of Heather again and smiled. He could still see how that gorgeous grin had lit up her face when she'd handed him the box of cookies.

Inside the box, only two oatmeal raisin and one butterscotch cookie remained. No, what had she called them? He snapped his fingers as the names echoed in his mind—Oatmeal Raisin Romance and Butterscotch Thriller cookies. He laughed to himself, adoring the bookish names for her tasty treats.

He chose an Oatmeal Raisin Romance cookie and then picked up his phone. He had planned to text Heather sooner, but every time he opened his phone, he either was interrupted or realized it was too late at night to message her.

But shortly after eight wasn't too late, was it? After finishing the cookie, he began to type a message to her.

When Alex's thumb hit Send, his mouth dried.

He laughed at himself and ate the last oatmeal raisin cookie. He was acting like a teenager who was terrified of being rejected by the prettiest girl at school.

What was it about Heather that made him so nervous?

He didn't know yet, but he wanted to find out.

⌒

"Busy for a Tuesday night," Heather told Dad as she navigated the vacuum cleaner from the dining room into the supply closet beside the kitchen.

Dad nodded as he started the dishwasher. "Yes, it was! I was surprised that large party came in right before eight."

Heather closed the closet and spun to face him. "If I'm being totally honest, I considered telling them we were closing. But I knew you and Mom would disown me if I turned them away."

"Did they leave a nice tip?" Dad asked with a grin.

She frowned. "Yes, they did."

"And that's why we don't turn anyone away, no matter how close to closing time it is."

"So I've been thinking . . ." She retrieved a cookbook from a nearby counter, then hopped up on a stool beside him.

Dad lifted his dark eyebrows. "About . . . ?"

"My dessert menu. What if I added more flavors of cheesecake?" She flipped to the section of the book she'd marked with a sticky note. "We only have New York–style now, but what if I added pumpkin, chocolate, white-chocolate raspberry, chocolate peanut butter, and key lime? Of course, I'll give them funny names that are related to books. Do you think customers would like that?"

Dad studied her, and she shifted on the stool. Could he tell she'd been up late reading cookbooks, trying—in vain—to banish thoughts of Alex from her mind?

For the past couple of nights, she had convinced herself that Alex hadn't texted or called because he'd forgotten about her, lost her number (impossible!), or met a woman who was much more interesting than she was. She'd considered deleting his name and number from her phone, but she couldn't convince her fingers to push the button. For some silly reason, she was still holding on to hope.

"Heather, are you still considering opening a bakery?"

She shrugged. "I want to, but it doesn't seem possible."

"Of course it is. Don't you think your mom and I had doubts when we opened this place?" He gestured around the kitchen.

"I'm sure you did."

"You should follow that dream. You're so talented, and you're persistent. I still remember how you tackled those math classes when you were in high school. You were determined to pass, and you worked until you not only passed but earned a B plus."

Heather frowned. "This is different."

"Dreams come true, Heather. I'm sure of it."

His words transported her back to her conversation with Alex in his dressing room. She could still hear his encouraging voice:

"Don't give up on your dream, Heather. My brothers and I are proof that dreams come true."

Heather swallowed a groan and once again tried to kick Alex out of her mind. It was ridiculous to miss a man she'd just met—let alone to hope he'd be thinking of her.

She sat up straighter on the stool and met her father's kind gaze. "I had this crazy idea of combining the two things I love, books and baking, and opening up a bookstore with a bakery."

"That's brilliant!" he declared. "I know you've been reading books about opening your own business, and you've taken online courses too. Plus, you've been working on your business plan for more than a year now. You've been saving money, and your mom and I can help you. You can do this, Heather. It's time you made that dream a reality." When his cell phone started ringing, he picked it up from a nearby counter and looked at the screen. "It's your mom. I'd better get it."

"Hi, Nora," Dad said into the phone. "Heather and I are just finishing up here. We had a party of ten come in just before eight."

While Dad took his phone call, Heather stood and considered his encouragement. Her dream was to have her own place on Main Street in Flowering Grove, but she knew opening such a business could be risky. While she'd worked for her parents since she was a teenager, she had never managed anything without their help. The idea of striking out on her own scared her.

She set the cookbook on a shelf beside the counter, then went to gather up her things from her parents' office.

When she turned over her phone, she found a text message on her screen. She blinked when she read the name of the sender—Alex K—and her stomach did a flip. With a gasp, she dropped into her mother's desk chair and read the message.

ALEX: How does one go about ordering more of your scrumptious cookies?

Heather's hands trembled as she stared at his words. The text had been sent more than an hour ago. Had she missed the opportunity to chat with him?

"There's only one way to find out," she whispered, then typed a response.

> **HEATHER:** Normally one must have a permanent mailing address at which to receive said scrumptious cookies.

She held her breath. Would he respond? Or was he busy doing important rockstar things after nine at night?

When conversation bubbles appeared almost immediately, the air escaped her lungs in a loud *whoosh*.

> **ALEX:** Hmm. That could be a problem if one is always on the road. But alas, the cookies were superb and worth the extra workouts at the gym.

Heather's cheeks heated at the mental picture of Alex working out in the gym—of his large, sinewy biceps flexing as he lifted weights. She smacked her forehead to dislodge the image.

Stop it! Stop it!

She cleared her throat and responded.

> **HEATHER:** I'm thrilled you enjoyed them, despite the extra workouts. If one has an address of where one might be, I might be able to persuade the baker to send another box to you.

She bit her lip and tried to think of something to keep the banter going while she awaited those precious conversation bubbles.

> **ALEX:** Have you always loved to bake?

"Heather?" Dad stuck his head into the office. "Is everything all right?"

She jumped with a start at her father waiting in the doorway. "Oh yes. I received an unexpected message."

"It's almost ten. Are you heading home?"

"Yes, I am. Sorry." She slipped her purse and tote bag over her shoulder, then followed her father to the back of the parking lot.

The early-April air was cool, and the stars sparkled in the night sky. She couldn't stop her smile as she pulled her keys from her purse. Her heart seemed to beat in double time.

"Be safe driving home," Dad said as he unlocked his Tahoe.

She opened her car door. "I will. Tell Mom and Wendy good night for me."

Once seated in her car, she shot off another quick text to Alex.

HEATHER: I'm just leaving the restaurant. I'll text when I
    get home.
ALEX: Sorry. I didn't mean to bother you. Drive safely.

Heather laughed as she typed: You're not a bother. And to answer your question, have you ever heard of an Easy-Bake Oven? If not, then Google it while I drive. That's where I got my start.

7

Heather burst into the house and found Mckenna typing on her laptop in front of the television, with Heather's cats lounging on either side of her, each giving themself a bath.

Mckenna picked up the remote and turned the volume down. "Your rockstar boyfriend and his brothers were on TV tonight. They have a concert in Raleigh tomorrow, and they were on the news."

"He finally texted me!" Heather held up her phone and danced around.

Mckenna squealed, and both cats ran to hide behind the entertainment center. "Let me see!"

"We're just talking. I'll be in my room." She hurried to her room, kicked off her shoes, and flopped on the bed.

Mckenna appeared beside her and leaned over to read the messages. "Ooh! He likes you!"

"Hey!" Heather swatted her away. "He just wants more cookies."

Mckenna snorted as she stood. "Yeah, right. I want a full report when you're done talking to him."

"I'll keep you posted," Heather called after her.

As Mckenna walked out of the room, Jet scampered in, hopped up on the bed, and snuggled up to Heather, purring.

Heather's heart raced as she looked down at her phone and found that Alex had texted ten minutes ago.

> ALEX: You must be tired after working late. I'll let you go. Have a good night.

"No, no, no," she whispered as she leaned back on a pillow and typed: It's not too late to text unless you're tired.

His response was immediate.

> ALEX: I'm wide awake. Now about that oven. Is this what you still use for your cookies?

She grinned, relieved he was willing to keep the conversation going.

> HEATHER: The oven is too small for my desserts. But would you believe the original Easy-Bake Oven is somewhere in my mom's attic? It was hers when she was little!

She tried to think of a similar question to ask him.

> HEATHER: How about you? How did you discover your love of music?
>
> ALEX: My dad. He was in a band.
>
> HEATHER: Really? Would I have heard of any of their songs? Was it a nineties grunge band?
>
> ALEX: Unfortunately, I ruined their chance at fame. Mom made him get a real job when she found out I was coming along, but he never stopped writing songs.

HEATHER: He must be proud of you and your brothers though.

When Alex's response didn't come right away, worry threaded through Heather. Had she said something wrong? Or had he fallen asleep? Her shoulders tightened but relaxed when the conversation bubbles reappeared.

ALEX: My dad passed away fourteen years ago, when I was fifteen.

Heather clutched her chest, and her eyes stung. She couldn't fathom life without her father. Alex, his brothers, and his mother must have missed him every day.

HEATHER: I'm so sorry.
ALEX: Thanks. I think he would have enjoyed seeing us perform. So—tell me about your day.

Heather shrugged as if Alex sat beside her. She typed: Nothing too exciting. Just baking and then serving food. I want to hear about your day too. Mack said she saw you and your brothers on the news. You're in Raleigh, right?

ALEX: Yeah, we did some interviews. The concert is tomorrow night.
HEATHER: That's exciting! I can't imagine being interviewed on the news, but I'm sure you're used to it.
ALEX: It's usually the same interview questions over and over again.

Heather scoffed as she typed: Is it tedious having people fawn over you and your brothers?

After a moment's pause, the conversation bubbles returned.

ALEX: It's not that people fawn over us exactly. Sometimes
I feel suffocated by the fame. I want to do more with
my life than answer interview questions.

Heather tilted her head as she typed: Like what?

ALEX: Help people. Make a difference.

Heather smiled. Was he opening up to her? She typed: How
was the Greensboro concert?

ALEX: It was good. They're all a blur after a while.
HEATHER: Did you sing that song your dad wrote?
ALEX: No. We don't normally do acoustic sets during the
concerts.
HEATHER: You should sometime. Then everyone will turn
on their camera flashlights like the audiences used to
do with their lighters. Very retro.
ALEX: Retro? ☺

Heather laughed at his smiley face.

HEATHER: I'm serious. An acoustic set would be awesome.
ALEX: I'll mention that to the guys.

Heather looked down at her cat curled up beside her and
tried to think of something else to ask Alex. But before she
could, he pinged her first.

ALEX: Have you read The Lost Castle by Ronald Siebert?

71

Heather huffed out a relieved breath and typed: No. I haven't read anything by him.

ALEX: What are you reading right now?

Heather picked up a cookbook from her bedside table—*Delectable Desserts* by Karen Thomas—took a photo of it, and sent it to him with a note: I highly recommend it.

ALEX: I'll have to add that to my TBR pile. ☺

She chuckled. You have a to-be-read pile?

ALEX: I do. I keep it on my tablet.
HEATHER: You'll have to send it to me.
ALEX: Can't do that. It's top-secret information.
HEATHER: Ooh. Now I really want to see it.
ALEX: But you might post it on social media to embarrass me.

Heather snorted. So my hundred TikTok followers will see it?

ALEX: I'm sure you have more than a hundred friends.
HEATHER: Hardly. So what is your schedule like on concert days?
ALEX: Breakfast on the run. Media interviews. Soundcheck with the fan club members. Concert. Meet and greets.
HEATHER: What's a soundcheck?

Alex's bubbles appeared right away, and he seemed to be typing for a while before sending: It's when the band tests the equipment, about two hours before the show starts. The fan club members can buy VIP tickets to attend. Our tour manager runs the soundcheck, and the fan club members vote on which songs we play to check the sound quality. When it's over, we hang around and talk to the VIPs for a bit. They have to put their cell phones in these little locked cases so they can't take photos or record the session. That way if we sound terrible, the fans can't post it anywhere. It's like an intimate experience—just us and the fans.

> HEATHER: That sounds fun. So if I joined your fan club, I
>   could get a VIP ticket to the soundcheck too?
> ALEX: I suppose so. ☺
> HEATHER: How does one join the Kirwan fan club?
> ALEX: That information is on our website, of course.

Heather chuckled, loving their playful banter: Well, I'll have to check into this fan club of yours.

> ALEX: What's your schedule tomorrow?
> HEATHER: I'm meeting my sister at the little coffee shop on
>   Main Street before work. Then more baking and serving
>   meals.
> ALEX: You have a full day too.

Heather tried to imagine his voice saying the words to her. She wrote: But your day will be more exciting than mine.

> ALEX: I should let you get your sleep.

Heather glanced at the clock and found it was almost eleven. Where had the time gone?

> HEATHER: Who needs sleep? Oh, right. You, probably.
> ALEX: Would it be all right if I text you again?

Heather took a deep breath and decided to full-on flirt with him: You'd better, Alex K.

ALEX: Yes, ma'am. Good night.

She sent one last "good night" text and then waited, hoping to see those delightful conversation bubbles dancing on her screen again.

"From that look on your face, I'm guessing the conversation has been very good," Mckenna asked from the doorway.

Heather ran her fingers over her phone. Although she and Alex hadn't discussed anything too private, the conversation felt confidential, and she couldn't betray his trust. "We just talked about our day." She summarized the high points, leaving out what Alex had shared about his father.

"You got yourself a rockstar," Mckenna sang.

"No, I don't think so. He's just lonely." Heather imagined him sitting in a hotel room and texting her, and her heart tripped over itself. "I think we're just . . . friends."

Mckenna shook her head. "I imagine he really trusts you if he gave you his phone number and texted you."

Heather wanted to believe she was a special friend to Alex. After all, he had already become important to her.

⌒

Adrenaline pumped through Alex's veins as he set his cell phone on the arm of the sofa. If only he could spend all night texting Heather. In fact, FaceTime would be even better. That way, he could see her beautiful face and watch her react to the things he said.

Suddenly full of energy, Alex jumped up from the sofa and

jogged into the bedroom. He quickly changed into shorts and a tank top and then headed to the gym.

While he ran on the treadmill, he stared at a late-night talk show on a flat-screen television on the wall—but his thoughts remained on Heather. Alex had worried she wouldn't respond at first, fearing she wasn't interested in getting to know him. Or maybe she already had a boyfriend and just hadn't made that clear.

Alex was relieved to have a normal conversation with someone—especially a woman. They chatted like two friends, not like a celebrity and a fan. No one else in his life wanted to talk about books, and he'd laughed out loud when she recommended a cookbook to him. It occurred to him that it would be a blessing not to have to play the role of rockstar with someone like Heather. He'd felt himself opening up to her, even though sharing his private feelings rarely came easy. He could only hope she felt the same way about him.

The steady cadence of Alex's feet pounding on the treadmill echoed in the gym as an idea overtook his mind. He was grateful to have a confidante, and he wanted to show Heather just how much their new friendship meant to him. What was something nice he could do for her?

⌢

"Whoa! Hold on there." Wendy held her hand up as she sat across the table from Heather in Bloom's Coffeehouse the following morning. "Did you just say you spent more than an hour texting with Alex Kirwan last night?"

The delicious fragrance of coffee filtered through the shop as Heather wrapped her hands around the warm mug in front of her. She had shared a summary of her discussion with Alex, leaving out what Heather considered the personal pieces. Those details seemed too private to repeat, and she felt protective of her new friend.

Heather sipped her decaf Americano. "Yes, I think it was about an hour."

Wendy gasped. "Just imagine being married to him. You'll be Heather Kirwan." She tapped her chin. "Does it go against proper etiquette to flirt with your brother-in-law?" Her eyes widened. "Oh, I don't mean I'd flirt with Alex. I mean Kayden, of course."

Heather shook her head. "You're making too much of this, Wendy. I hate to burst your bubble and your dreams of dating Kayden, but I truly think Alex just wanted someone to talk to."

Despite her words, she had to admit to herself how much she enjoyed their easy banter and Alex's fun sense of humor. Chatting with him again couldn't happen a moment too soon.

"Did he tell you anything about his schedule this week?" Wendy lifted her cappuccino and took a sip.

"Not really. He just shared that concert day was very busy, and he explained what a soundcheck was."

Wendy's pretty face lit with a dreamy smile. "We should try to go to a soundcheck sometime. That would be so fun. Do you think he'll invite you to another concert? Maybe he can fly us out for a weekend so we can hang out with the band." Her golden-brown eyes widened. "Oh! And maybe Kayden will ask for *my* phone number! Could you imagine if we both married Kirwan brothers? We could have a double wedding and save Mom and Dad money. Not that the Kirwan brothers couldn't afford to pay for it all."

Heather drank more coffee while her sister went on about becoming rockstar wives, touring with the band, attending award shows, and having handsome husbands by their sides for forever.

What Wendy imagined was a childish daydream, but deep

down, Heather *did* hope for something more. Even a few more fun text conversations would do.

⌒

Alex folded his six-foot-three frame into the third row of the large SUV later that afternoon. The morning had flown by quickly while he and his brothers attended fan events at a guitar store and a record store before having lunch with a couple of entertainment reporters for local magazines.

Although he had enjoyed talking with the folks he'd met, Alex's mind wandered back to Heather. He longed to call or FaceTime with her instead of texting. The thought of hearing her voice and, even better, seeing her face sent a zip of excitement through him.

Alex glanced out the window, and when he spotted a bookstore down the road, an idea hit him. "Hey, Easton," he called to the driver. "How much time do we have before soundcheck?"

"Why?" Robyn asked, turning to face him from the front seat.

"I want to run into that bookstore."

She checked her watch. "I don't know. We're cutting it close."

"It will only take a minute. I promise."

Kayden eyed him from the seat in front of him. "Are you crazy? You'll be swarmed as soon as you walk in there. We made that mistake at the pool hall last night. Right, Jor?"

"Well, after we signed autographs and posed for photos for about forty-five minutes, we had a good game of pool." Jordan snickered.

"I'll be fine." Alex leaned over the seat and plucked Jordan's University of Oregon ball cap from the spot beside him. Then he raked his hair back with his fingers, pushed the hat onto his head, and slipped on his sunglasses.

Jordan grinned. "It's obvious it's still you, Alex. That pathetic disguise won't work."

"Yes, it will." Alex sat up taller and faced the front of the SUV. "Easton, would you please stop at that bookstore?"

Robyn eyed him from the passenger seat. "Tell me what you want, and I'll run in for it."

"I just want to pick out a book and take it to the post office."

"The *post office*?" Kayden's brows pinched together. "Why?"

Alex held up a hand toward Robyn, ignoring Kayden's questions. "I promise it won't take long."

Robyn pursed her lips and gave a resigned sigh. "Fine. I'll come with you to keep the crowd at bay, but you'd better make it quick."

"Thank you."

After Easton found a parking spot, Alex and Robyn hurried into the store. Alex blinked as his eyes adjusted to the fluorescent indoor lighting. There was no way he could read the authors' names and book titles while wearing his dark glasses. He pocketed the shades, pulled down the bill of the ball cap, and hunched his shoulders as he weaved through the stacks.

Robyn seemed to struggle to keep up with his long strides, her high heels clacking behind him. When he finally spotted the suspense section, he picked up speed and muttered an apology as he moved past other customers on his way to the shelves. Then he perused the authors' names, holding his breath and hoping to find the one he sought.

Alex felt someone's eyes burning into his back as he pulled a book from the shelf.

"Is that Alex Kirwan?" a woman whispered.

His shoulders stiffened, and he slammed his eyes shut. Another woman sucked in a breath in response, and he bit back a groan. *Oh no. Robyn was right.*

"Kirwan is in town this week!" a second woman announced. "Alex?" a third woman asked.

He held the book against his chest and nodded at the three curious women. Then he glanced over at Robyn, who pushed her red glasses up the bridge of her petite nose. She shot him a look that seemed to say *I told you* before pointing toward the cash registers.

He headed straight for the cashier, careful to keep his head bent. He was grateful he only had to wait a few moments before a young woman with braces and bright blue eye makeup called him to the counter.

"You look familiar," she said as she rang up the book.

Alex retrieved his wallet from the back pocket of his jeans and tapped his card against the screen before returning the card and wallet to his pocket. "I get that a lot. I have one of those faces."

She studied him. "Huh." Then she dropped the book and receipt into a bag and handed it to him. "Have a nice day."

"You too." He took a few steps toward the door but was stopped by a group of young women blocking the exit. They stared straight at him, their faces bright with wide smiles and their phones poised in the air.

So much for making a quick exit.

Robyn shot him another look. "Now do you see why I offered to pick up the book for you?" she snapped.

"You were right," he muttered, plastering a smile on his face.

Robyn lifted her dark eyes. "Could I please get that in writing?"

"Don't push it." Alex approached the crowd. "Hi, everyone."

"Could I have your autograph?" A woman pushed her receipt and a pen toward him.

Another gave a loud sigh. "Would you please sing for us?"

"Where's Kayden?" someone called.

Alex signed several receipts and the sleeve of a woman's shirt before posing for nearly a dozen selfies. "I'm sorry, but I have to get to an event. I hope you'll come and see our performance tonight."

He waved and allowed Robyn to steer him through the sea of people toward the door.

"Now we're behind schedule, and you know I can't stand to be late," Robyn snapped.

Alex exhaled in frustration. While he appreciated the band's success, he wished he could run into a store without being ambushed by fans.

Then one of Heather's comments rolled through his mind: *"Is it tedious having people fawn over you and your brothers?"*

He frowned as he and Robyn rushed to the SUV and climbed in. He didn't mean to sound like a spoiled celebrity, but he missed being an ordinary person who could shop without attracting a crowd.

"How'd it go?" Kayden asked after Alex was settled in his seat.

Alex handed Jordan his hat, then shoved his hand through his hair.

Robyn gave Kayden a pointed look. "Let's just say he should have let me get the book for him."

Alex's brothers laughed.

"I told you the hat wouldn't work," Jordan said.

Alex pulled the book from the bag. "Robyn, any chance you have a notepad and pen in your giant purse?"

Robyn pulled a pen and a square yellow pad of stickies from her enormous red bag and passed them over her shoulder.

"Is the book for Mom?" Kayden asked as Alex jotted down a note.

Alex stuck the note in the front of the book and closed it. "A friend."

"Which friend?" Jordan asked.

"Could we stop by FedEx or UPS?" Alex called to Easton.

"No." Robyn's response was terse. "I'll ship it while you're at the soundcheck." She pointed to the notepad. "Write down the address."

Alex did as instructed, and Kayden leaned over the seat. "Heather Gordon in Flowering Grove . . . Is that the brunette with the freckles?"

Alex nodded.

"Why are you sending her a book?" Kayden looked confused.

Jordan's eyebrows lifted. "You really like her?"

Alex huffed. He wasn't in the mood to be ribbed by his brothers. He handed the book, pen, and notepad over to Jordan. "Please give these to Robyn, Jor."

"Seriously, Alex?" Kayden demanded. "You're interested in that woman?"

"Have you been talking to her?" Jordan asked.

"A bit." Alex shrugged, refusing to say more.

Kayden leaned over the seat toward Alex. "Why would you limit your options when we have so much opportunity?"

Alex stared at his youngest brother and felt a muscle flex in his jaw.

"Dude, are you trying to find another Celeste?" Kayden's expression suddenly warmed. "Look, I know she hurt you. Do you really want to go down that road again?"

Alex folded his arms over his chest. "How about you worry about your own personal life while I worry about mine?"

Kayden scoffed.

Alex ignored his brother's sarcastic expression. True, he didn't know Heather very well yet, but for some reason, she seemed to fill an empty space in his heart. His brothers could have their own opinions, but he knew deep down there was something special about this woman.

8

Later that evening Heather delivered two pulled-pork barbecue plates to Mr. and Mrs. Simpson. "Here you go," she said, setting the platters in front of them. "Would you like some more sweet tea?"

Mrs. Simpson shook her head. "I'm fine, sweetheart."

Her husband nodded in agreement.

"Enjoy your supper. I'll be back soon to check on you." Heather headed toward the kitchen, waving to familiar faces on her way.

She pushed through the double doors and pulled her phone from her pocket, checking for what seemed like the hundredth time that day to see whether Alex had texted. Her shoulders sagged when she found her screen was blank.

"Have you heard from your rockstar again?" Wendy called.

"Again?" Mom asked. She pulled a large container of salad out of the refrigerator. "He called you?"

Dad scooped macaroni and cheese out of a large dish and into smaller bowls. "Since when does Heather know a rockstar?"

Mom slammed her hands on her hips. "Seriously, Russ? Don't you *ever* pay attention? You were here the day Wendy

82

and Deanna were squealing over the singer who stopped by Heather's house to return her phone. It was Saturday!"

Dad blinked and nodded.

"Never mind." Heather held up her hands. Then she picked up two orders that were ready.

Mom squeezed Heather's shoulder. "Oh no. I want to hear this."

"Fine," Heather said. "He texted me last night, and we chatted for a while. That's it. No big deal."

"Oh, it *is* a big deal," Wendy sang.

"Which singer?" Dad asked. Then he snapped his fingers. "Wait. Is he one of the guys who came here for supper Thursday night?"

Heather set the meals on a round tray and lifted it to her shoulder. "It's nothing."

"Alex Kirwan likes you, Heather," Wendy insisted as she collected more plates. "That *is* something!"

"Alex Kirwan likes Heather?" Misty Helms, one of the servers, said as she joined them in the kitchen. She was a pretty, blond twenty-one-year-old who loved nothing more than town gossip. "How did she meet him?"

Heather huffed and hurried out into the dining room, hoping to leave the questions behind. She worried the rumors would be rampant soon, and if she never heard from Alex again, she'd have to deal with the humiliation of the whole town knowing her business.

⌒

Later, Heather retreated to the ladies' room and was grateful to find it empty. The restaurant had welcomed a steady stream of customers that Wednesday evening, and although the crowd hadn't been overwhelming, Heather still yearned for a quiet moment to take a breath in private. She fished her phone from her pocket and was disappointed once again to find no new messages.

She scrolled to Kirwan's website and perused the fan club page. An idea for a funny text she could send to Alex came to her, but then she shook it off. Since she didn't want to appear needy or clingy, she should wait for him to text her first.

When she clicked on the band's Instagram page, her eyes found a photo of the band onstage along with the caption: "It's a great night in Raleigh!"

She imagined Alex singing, and her pulse picked up speed. Then she cupped her hand to her forehead and closed her eyes. Why was she wasting her time thinking about a *celebrity*? She was kidding herself if she believed his interest in her might be real.

The door to the bathroom opened, and Heather pasted a smile on her face. A middle-aged woman stepped inside, and Heather nodded a greeting her way before pushing through the door and reentering the dining room.

Heather shoved her phone into her pocket and tried in vain to stop her train of thought. As she approached one of her tables, she took a deep breath. If she were never to hear from Alex again, she needed to be satisfied with that. She would recover from this ridiculous crush and carry on with her normal, peaceful life.

Alex dragged himself into his hotel room and dropped onto the sofa. Every bone in his body ached, and his throat was sore. He was completely wiped out from the concert and the meet and greet afterward.

He checked his phone but found no messages from Heather. He opened his last text from her and poised his thumbs over the keyboard, but then he glanced at the clock on the wall. It was after one in the morning.

Groaning, he dropped his phone onto the sofa beside him. Though he had promised to text her, he couldn't risk waking her up after such a long and exhausting shift at her parents' restaurant.

Alex pushed himself up from the couch and ambled to the bathroom for a hot, relaxing shower. If Heather's book arrived at her house tomorrow, then maybe she would text him. He wondered if she'd had a busy night and sold every last one of her baked goods. Then he wondered if Heather thought of him as often as he thought of her.

⌒

Heather yawned as she pushed a grocery cart down the aisle the following morning. In front of her, Mckenna searched the shelf for her favorite cereal. Her first appointment at the salon wasn't until eleven, so the roommates had decided to go grocery shopping together. Heather was excited for time to catch up with Mckenna, even if it involved a mundane task like buying eggs and milk.

Heather stopped the cart and leaned forward on the handle while her best friend compared a name-brand cereal with the store brand. "How are things going with Kirk?"

Mckenna's pretty face lit up with a smile. "He has a wonderful sense of humor, and we never seem to run out of things to talk about."

"That's a good sign."

Settling on the store brand, she set the box in the cart. "It is, but I want to hear about Alex."

"There's nothing to tell." Heather dodged her best friend's curious gaze by feigning interest in a display of granola bars.

"In other words, he hasn't texted you, and you haven't texted him."

"Correct." Heather picked up a box of peanut butter–flavored bars and began examining the ingredients.

Mckenna snatched the box out of her hands.

"Hey! I was reading that."

"No, you weren't." Mckenna set the box back on the shelf. "Now stop avoiding the topic and tell me why you haven't texted him."

Heather stepped to the side when a young mother pushed a cart past them. A toddler with bright red hair sat in the seat, running a toy car over the handle while making car noises with his mouth.

Heather met Mckenna's impatient expression. "I just . . . don't want to bug him."

"Bug him?"

"Yes, bug him. Nag him." Heather rested her forearm on the cool metal grocery cart handle. "He's a busy celebrity, and I'm a server in my family's restaurant. I'm just trying to play it cool."

Mckenna clucked her tongue. "Heather, none of that matters, because he likes *you*. Why are you worried you're not good enough? Is it because of Jeff?" She snorted. "If so, then *please*! Jeff was a moron because he couldn't see how amazing you are."

"You have to say that because you've been my best friend since kindergarten." Heather rolled her eyes.

"No, it's because I know you."

Heather pushed the cart forward. "What else is on our list?"

"The list can wait because we're going to talk about this." Mckenna put her hand on Heather's arm. "You need to text

86

Alex. Keep that line of communication open with him so he knows you're thinking of him."

"I don't want to be a needy female. I can be patient, and he can reach out to me."

"Either you text him or I'll do it for you." Mckenna grabbed Heather's phone from the pocket in her blue hoodie.

"Give me that!" Heather reached for it, but somehow her short best friend wiggled away from her. "Come on."

An elderly couple walked past and gave each of them confused expressions.

Heather's cheeks burned with embarrassment. "We're attracting attention, Mack. Stop acting like a teenager and give me my phone."

"Text him." Mckenna handed it to her.

Heather nodded. "All right." With her heart hammering in her chest, she opened her last text from him and stared at the screen, trying to think of something to say.

"Come on, Heather. Just do it."

"Fine." Heather took a deep breath and recalled her idea for the text she'd almost sent him last night. "Here goes nothing," she whispered.

HEATHER: When one joins the Kirwan fan club, is one guaranteed authentic swag? How can one be certain the autographed merchandise is genuine?

Mckenna stood up on her tiptoes and peeked over Heather's shoulder. "What on earth does that mean?"

"It's a joke."

Her best friend grinned. "You have inside jokes after only one conversation? Man, he's *totally* into you!"

Two young women moved past her and shot her a look.

"Keep it down," Heather admonished. "Let's finish our shopping."

They traipsed through the aisles, moving down their shopping list. Heather perused her phone every couple of minutes and felt her spirit sinking each time she found the screen empty of any responses from Alex.

When their cart was finally full, Heather steered it to the end of a line. She leaned forward on the handle and studied her phone. She went through a mental list of reasons Alex hadn't responded—he was in the middle of an interview, he was meeting a group of fans, he was sleeping, or he was just busy doing something important celebrities did.

"Ooh, Heather," Mckenna gushed as she held up a gossip magazine. "Look at how superhot your boyfriend is." She pointed to a photo of the Kirwan brothers posing on what looked like a red carpet, with a wall behind them emblazoned with logos for the latest Marvel movie. The caption read: "Alex, Jordan, and Kayden Kirwan pose at the premiere for the newest Marvel movie featuring their hit song, 'Driving Fast.'"

Heather studied the photo, taking in the three brothers' serious expressions and their expensive-looking dark suits. Alex looked so good he took Heather's breath away for a moment.

Mckenna tapped the photo of Alex. "He cleans up well, huh?"

Heather's eyes widened as she took in every detail of the gorgeous man. "You could say that."

"Yes, and just think, Heather: he could be *the one*."

"I doubt it."

Mckenna lifted her chin. "You need to believe in love again. Don't let your ex-boyfriend ruin your future relationships. He was the one who had the problem, not you."

Heather smiled. "Thanks, Mack."

When it was their turn to pay, they loaded up the conveyor belt and split the cost of the groceries before loading their bags into the trunk of Heather's car.

"I need to go get set up before Mrs. Hasty arrives for her appointment, but don't forget to text me when you hear from Alex. And you *will* hear from him." Mckenna gave Heather a hug. "Love you."

Heather chuckled. "You drive me crazy, but I love you too."

"I drive you crazy because you know I'm right. See you later." Then she jumped into her car and headed to the salon.

Heather climbed into the driver's seat and checked her phone once more. Finding the screen still free of any texts, she started her car, connected her phone to the stereo with the help of a Bluetooth adapter, and turned up the volume as Kirwan music poured through the speakers.

Happiness rippled through her as Alex's voice serenaded her with her favorite Kirwan song, "Always."

She concentrated on the sound of his voice as she drove, imagining him singing the beautiful love song for only her, declaring his undying, forever devotion. The song had touched her heart when she'd first heard their music, and it had immediately become her favorite. She had listened to it over and over until she had memorized most of the words.

As Heather sang along, her mind raced with questions. Had Alex written the song, and if so, did he have a special woman in mind when he penned those precious lyrics? She despised the jealousy that slithered through her as she envisioned Alex singing for another woman.

She had to laugh at herself. Alex was only her friend at best. She had no claim over him!

When she reached her house, Heather unloaded and put away the groceries, fed her noisy cats, and then dropped onto the sofa. She thumbed through the gossip magazine, which Mckenna had insisted on buying for her. She flipped past the articles and found the photo of Alex and his brothers, then studied the photo once more before checking the clock on her phone. The morning had flown by—and now it was time to head to the restaurant to start her baking for the day.

That same morning, Alex settled in the seat on the band's bus and yawned. When he heard his phone buzz with a text, he instantly hoped the message was from Heather. Instead, he found a text from Tristan Douglas, his best friend since middle school.

> TRISTAN: What state are you in today? Or I guess I should
> ask: Do you even know which state you're in?

Alex dialed Tristan's number instead of texting a reply.

Tristan answered on the second ring. "Are you calling because you need me to track your phone and tell you where you are?" Alex could hear the smile in his old friend's voice.

Alex shook his head as if Tristan could see him. "No, we're somewhere in North Carolina or Virginia . . . I think."

Tristan laughed.

"How's life in the publishing world?"

While Alex had skipped college to pursue his music goals, Tristan had studied literature in college and found his dream job at a publisher. These days he was working his way up to acquisitions editor.

Tristan sighed. "Oh, the usual. Dealing with an author who never seems to meet his deadline."

"And how's your lovely wife?" Tristan had met Justine in college and married her three years ago before settling down in Alex and Tristan's hometown of Cascade, Oregon.

Alex had always thought Tristan and Justine's relationship was as close to perfect as his parents' had been. From what he could tell, they rarely argued, and the love he saw in their eyes when they were together was clear. They always held hands, even when they seemed to think no one was watching.

Alex craved that kind of love, and he prayed he could find it someday.

"She started working at a new accounting firm a few weeks ago, and she really likes it."

"That's fantastic." Alex grinned. "She's much smarter than we are, isn't she?"

Tristan chuckled. "Totally. How's the rock-and-roll life?"

"It's all a blur of handshakes, photos, screaming fans, and loud music." Alex kneaded his temples.

Tristan clucked his tongue. "You poor thing."

Alex snorted.

"When are you coming home for a visit or to stay awhile?"

"I actually don't know. I need to take a look at the schedule. I think we have a break in—" When Alex's phone buzzed, he stopped speaking. "Hang on one sec. I just got a text message." When he read a message from Heather, he couldn't hold back his laugh. Then he held his phone up to his ear once again. "Sorry about that."

"What's so funny?" Tristan asked.

"I got a text from a new friend."

"A new friend, huh? Tell me more . . ."

Alex shared an abbreviated story of how he met Heather at the restaurant, including the detail about how unimpressed she'd first seemed.

"She actually said she'd rather wash her hair than go to your concert?" Alex could hear the amusement in Tristan's voice.

"She sure did. She'd never even heard of the band."

"I like her already."

Me too. "She never fawned over me or my brothers, and I appreciated that about her. It was so refreshing to have a real conversation with someone who seemed interested in me as a person—not the guy I am onstage. We actually talked about books, Tristan. She blew me away after she saw a book in my dressing room. I think we talked more about books than anything else."

"She sounds like your type."

"That's what I thought, but Kayden disagrees."

"What does he have to say about it?"

Alex rested his right ankle on his left knee and balanced his phone on his shoulder. "He thinks we have too many options to limit ourselves right now."

"Kayden is young, so his priorities are different from yours. I'm glad to hear you're interested in dating after what happened with Celeste. It's been more than three years, Alex."

He frowned at the mention of his ex's name, but deep down, he knew his best friend was right. It was well past time to move on.

"I bet life on the road can be lonely, and you've been alone too long," Tristan added.

Alex turned toward the window and took in a blur of trees. "Well, the problem is that she's in North Carolina and I'm always on the move. I'm not sure if she's up for traveling, but it's nice to have a friend."

"Friendship is a great start. Justine and I started as friends."

They talked for a few more minutes, catching up on recent news and Alex's concert schedule for the next week.

A voice sounded in the background, and Tristan said, "I need to go, but it was great talking to you. I love living vicariously through your celebrity life for a few moments."

Alex chuckled. "I actually enjoyed living vicariously through *your* life for a few moments."

"Talk to you later, buddy. Call me when you're headed back to Cascade."

"Who knows when that will be."

"Oh, to live such a charmed life."

"Charmed life?" Alex asked. "Now I know for sure I'm talking to a book editor. Take care, man."

After disconnecting the call, Alex opened Heather's text and read it once again:

HEATHER: When one joins the Kirwan fan club, is one guaranteed authentic swag? How can one be certain the autographed merchandise is genuine?

Then his thumbs moved over the digital keyboard, his mind whirring with ideas for responding to this funny, beautiful woman.

9

ALEX: I can guarantee that if one were to join the Kirwan fan club, one would receive only authentic Kirwan swag.

After sending the text, he contemplated Tristan's encouragement to start dating again. Celeste's rejection three years ago had plunged Alex headfirst into focusing on his family and his career instead of his love life. On one hand, Alex agreed and could almost see himself in a relationship with Heather. She had seemed genuinely shocked when he'd asked for her number, and when he considered all of the eager fans he'd met, he knew he'd never met anyone like her—ever.

But on the other hand, he tried to imagine someone like Heather—a woman who hoped to own her own bookstore and bakery—trying to adapt to his atypical lifestyle. Would she even consider building a future with someone who was constantly on the road? It was common knowledge that most celebrity relationships were doomed to fail.

The conversation bubbles appeared, and Alex's chest thumped with excitement.

HEATHER: And you're stating this fact as a person of swag authority?

A burst of laugher escaped his lips as he typed a reply: Why, yes, of course. Part of my job is to approve the fan club merchandise.

HEATHER: Is that so? Well, you seem to have a ridiculous number of duties for one person—singer, songwriter, performer, AND fan club merchandise manager? I sincerely hope you're well compensated for the many hats you wear, Mr. Alex Kirwan.

He let out a hearty chuckle. He adored her quick wit and how she kept him on his toes.

Kayden moaned from somewhere in the bus. "Dude, some of us are trying to get some sleep."

"Sorry!" Alex responded to Kayden before typing: I can assure you, Ms. Heather Gordon, that I am sufficiently compensated.

HEATHER: 😊

ALEX: Ms. Gordon, may I ask what size t-shirt you would require?

HEATHER: Oh no, no. I wasn't asking for free swag. I'm just teasing you. How was Raleigh?

ALEX: Good. Lots of loud music. What shirt size do you want?

HEATHER: Don't send me a t-shirt. I can pay for one! Did you do an acoustic set?

ALEX: No, but I really am going to mention that to the guys though. If you don't tell me your t-shirt size, I'll have to guess. Do you really want me to embarrass myself and send you the wrong size? That could be detrimental to our friendship, and I feel like we have a good thing going here.

Closing his eyes, he sucked in a breath, hoping he hadn't said too much or gotten too sentimental.

But Heather replied right away: I'm offended you believe our friendship hangs in the balance over my t-shirt size. And I normally wear a medium. Seriously, though, I can pay for it. In fact, I'll see if Wendy wants to join your fan club too. Although, she might already be a member. On to other topics. Are you in Virginia? (Not that I'm stalking you!)

Relief filtered through him. He wrote: You are quite stubborn, and feel free to stalk. Actually, I believe I stalked you first when I followed the flamingos to your house.

HEATHER: 😵

ALEX: I'm honestly not sure where we are at the present time. I just see cars and trees flying past me out the window of our bus. What size shirt does your sister wear?

HEATHER: You're not going to drop this, are you?

ALEX: Nope!

HEATHER: Remind me: Who's the stubborn one?

Alex bit back another laugh as he wrote: The size, please, ma'am.

HEATHER: *dramatic sigh* Medium also.

Alex nodded. He would text his fan club manager later.

ALEX: Thank you. What are you up to today?

HEATHER: Waiting for cookies to bake.

ALEX: What kind of cookies?

HEATHER: Novel Chocolate Chunk!

ALEX: Yum. I can almost smell them. Have I mentioned that
I love the names of your delectable treats?

HEATHER: Wish I could send you some. (And thank you.)

ALEX: Me too.

He glanced out the window and pondered what to say next.

ALEX: I have a burning question for you.

HEATHER: Ask away.

ALEX: Why flamingos?

HEATHER: What do you mean?

ALEX: Why all the flamingos at your house?

HEATHER: Oh! Well, that's all Mack. Pink has been her
favorite color since she was born, so I think that's why
she's obsessed.

Alex smiled and then typed: Interesting. What's your favorite
color?

HEATHER: Hmm . . . I guess baby blue.

ALEX: Noted. And favorite animal?

HEATHER: That's easy. Cats.

ALEX: So Molly and Jet are yours.

HEATHER: Yes. I'm impressed you remember their names.

ALEX: I pay attention.

HEATHER: My turn with the burning question.

ALEX: Shoot.

HEATHER: Do you write your own songs?

ALEX: Yes, we collaborate on most of them, but some of
them we write solo. Our producer always helps.

HEATHER: Did you write "Always"?
ALEX: Yes, I did.

Alex nodded as memories of the time when he'd written that song hit him hard and fast. More than four years ago, he was working at a coffee shop during the day and performing there at night, hoping to make it big.

"Always" was the first love song Alex had been proud of, which is why his brothers insisted they record it when they received their first contract.

HEATHER: Would you think less of me if I told you I've
listened to "Always" enough to memorize it?

Alex's pulse leapt at her confession. He wrote: Not at all. I'm flattered since you don't normally like our type of music.

HEATHER: Ugh. I'm so embarrassed! Could we please just
forget our first conversation completely?

He grinned as he imagined her blushing.

ALEX: Absolutely not. Your honesty is both refreshing and
intriguing. Keep being straightforward with me.
HEATHER: May I ask another burning question?
ALEX: Of course.
HEATHER: Did you write it for someone specific?

Alex hesitated and bit his lip. Of course "Always" had been about Celeste. Memories of her hit him like waves pounding the sand. Although the breakup had happened more than three years ago, he still hated to talk about her. As his thumbs hovered over the digital keyboard, he considered completely opening his heart to Heather and sharing his painful memories. While he yearned to get closer, he wasn't certain he was ready for that kind of intimacy. It felt too soon.

HEATHER: I'm sorry. I made it weird. Let's forget I asked. Do you have any pets? What's your favorite color?

Guilt pummeled Alex. He didn't mean to embarrass Heather for asking him a question. He wrote: You don't need to apologize. I wrote that song for someone who is a part of my past. I don't have any pets of my own since I spend so much time on the road, but my mom has a dog. Oh! And my favorite color is blue.

HEATHER: Tell me about the dog! Breed? Name? Can you send me a photo?

He located a photo of his mother and her chocolate Labrador and sent it to Heather.

ALEX: Meet Elvis and my mom.

HEATHER: Aww! What a great name! They are both beautiful. What is your mom's name?

ALEX: Mom is Shannon. And Elvis is a big teddy bear. He would knock you over trying to kiss you if you met him. He has no manners.

HEATHER: Elvis sounds like the perfect dog. You have your mom's eyes and her smile. What does she do?

ALEX: She teaches high school English in my hometown.

HEATHER: Did you inherit your love of reading from your mom?

ALEX: Yes. You?

HEATHER: I just always loved books. I remember my
parents reading to me at night.

Alex cherished every detail she shared about her life. Each one made her even more fascinating to him. Favorite childhood book?

HEATHER: Goodnight Moon, of course. Yours?
ALEX: Are You My Mother?
HEATHER: Classic!

He relaxed in the seat and swallowed a laugh, then asked: Are your cookies done yet?

HEATHER: Are you spying on me? The timer just went off.
Hang on one sec.

"Alex, your grin is a mile wide. Who are you texting?"

Turning, Alex found his middle brother watching him. For a few moments, he'd forgotten his brothers and Robyn were on the bus with him. "No one."

Jordan lifted a blond eyebrow. "Is it that woman from Flowering Grove?"

Alex pressed his lips together.

"Dude, Kayden's right. It's not smart to get involved with a fan."

"She's not a fan," he insisted, looking back down at his phone as conversation bubbles danced on the screen.

HEATHER: Okay. First batch out of the oven and second
batch in.
ALEX: Photos, please.

Images of golden-brown cookies filled his screen, making his stomach growl. He typed: Yum, I can smell them through my phone.

HEATHER: 😊
ALEX: Am I keeping you from working?
HEATHER: I'd rather text you than work, but sadly, the
    lunch rush will start soon.
ALEX: I should let you go.
HEATHER: Wait! I need to tell you something else.
ALEX: Yes?
HEATHER: I was in the grocery store this morning, and
    Mack bought me a magazine that has a photo of you
    and your brothers in it.

A few moments later, Heather sent a photo of the band at the latest Marvel movie premiere. Alex groaned and typed: Ugh!

HEATHER: Why "ugh"? That's a great photo!
ALEX: I look like I have a stomachache.
HEATHER: No, you have a handsome, brooding look on your
    face.

Excitement filled him at the compliment. He wrote: Handsome, huh?

HEATHER: Droves of female fans chase after you. I'm sure
    you've heard you're handsome before.

He shook his head as he recalled the fan in the bookstore yesterday who had asked him where his youngest brother was.

ALEX: I think you have me confused with my brother Kayden.

HEATHER: My sister would agree with that. She has a major
    crush on him.
ALEX: Your sister and every other woman in the country!
HEATHER: Not every woman . . .

His eyebrows lifted. Was that a confession?

HEATHER: Well, duty calls! I need to go take orders. Have a
    safe trip. Text me soon?
ALEX: I will. Have a good day. And check your mail for some
    fan club swag.
HEATHER: Remind me again: Which one of us is stubborn?
    Goodbye, Mr. Alex Kirwan.
ALEX: Goodbye, Ms. Heather Gordon.

Alex snickered as he shot off another message to his fan
club manager about gift packages for Heather and Wendy. Then
he checked the shipping status of the book he'd sent her overnight, finding it would be delivered to Heather's house later that
afternoon.

"You really like her, don't you?" Jordan asked.

Alex heaved out a deep breath. "Yes, I do."

"Why?"

When Alex's eyes met his middle brother's confused expression, he frowned. "Because I do, Jor. She's sweet and funny, and
we have a lot in common."

"In common? Like what?" Jordan gave him a palms-up,
looking unconvinced.

"I'm still getting to know her," said Alex. "We're just friends.
What's the harm in that?"

"It's not a good idea to get attached in our business. She
could be using you."

Alex shook his head. "She had no idea who I was when we met."

"I know, but now that's she's figured out we're successful, she might have changed her tune."

Alex pointed to his chest. "I was the one who initiated exchanging numbers."

"Just be careful. We don't have time for relationships. Kayden has the right idea—that we should just be having fun right now."

Alex disagreed, but he kept his opinion to himself. His friendship with Heather seemed to be the bright light his lonely life needed, and he wasn't ready to give that up just yet.

⌒

"Tell me the latest news!" Wendy asked as she met Heather by the drink station later that afternoon. Wendy's service shift had just begun at the restaurant.

When Heather grinned, Wendy grabbed her arm.

"You heard from him?" she asked, and Heather nodded. "Tell me everything!"

Heather summarized their conversation by text, and Wendy hugged her. "I'm so happy for you."

Heather tilted her head. "Are you a member of their fan club?"

Wendy chuckled. "No. Why?"

"Never mind!" Heather pulled off her apron, grateful it was time to go home and rest her tired feet. "Have a good shift."

Heather called goodbye to the kitchen and waitstaff, then gathered her purse and tote bag before strolling out to her car.

On the short ride home, she sang along to Kirwan's music and imagined Alex singing the songs to her. Questions about the woman from his past pinballed through her mind, and she wondered if he was dating anyone now. If so, he wouldn't be texting

Heather, would he? Alex didn't seem like a cheater, but how well did Heather truly know him? Her pulse zinged at the thought of being something more than his friend.

Heather steered her car into the empty driveway as another notion smacked her in the face. What if Alex thought of her only as a heartsick fan?

Glowering at the idea, she gathered up her purse and tote bag and climbed out of her car. When she reached the front steps, she found a package addressed to her lying on the porch. The sight stopped her in her tracks.

She picked up the package and read the return address: a PO Box in Portland, Oregon.

"What on earth?" Heather whispered to herself before hurrying into the house.

10

Heather tossed her tote bag and purse onto the sofa and shooed away her cats, who were walking in circles around her and singing their usual chorus of meows. "Calm down, you two. I'll feed you in a minute."

She dug a pair of scissors out of the junk drawer in the kitchen and cut open the large shipping envelope. When she pulled out a copy of *The Lost Castle* by Ronald Siebert, she gasped. Was this the book Alex had asked her if she'd read?

She opened the hardcover and found a yellow sticky note with the following message:

> Heather,
> Do you want to read this so we can talk about it together?
> It could be the start of our own private book club.
> Fondly,
> Alex K.

She studied his neat, slanted script and imagined him writing this note to her. Then she hugged the book to her chest and danced around the kitchen, nearly tripping over her cats, who continued yammering for food.

She could barely contain her happiness. Alex Kirwan had sent her a gift! A thoughtful, wonderful, amazing gift! Perhaps they were becoming friends—but with a splash of something more?

After she finished her silly dance, she filled the cats' bowls, gave them fresh water, and hurried to the sofa. She flopped down along the cushions, set her book beside her, and pulled out her phone.

She opened her last text from Alex and began typing: You can send me gifts, but I can't send you any. No fair!

Then: By the way, thank you for the book.

She whispered to herself, "I'll treasure this forever."

Conversation bubbles appeared but then stopped, and she sucked in a breath. Then her phone began to ring with Pearl Jam's "Even Flow," and Alex's name floated on the screen.

Her stomach dipped and her hands trembled as she held the phone up to her ear. "Hello?"

"I have to admit that is the most interesting thank-you I have ever received for a gift," he said. His voice reminded her of silk, and she could hear the smile on his lips.

She grimaced and touched her forehead as embarrassment threaded through her. "I'm so sorry. What I meant to say was that I really, really appreciate the book. I would like to send you cookies as a thank-you, but you're on the road and—"

Alex's laughter filled the speaker, and she enjoyed the wonderful sound. "I understand what you meant, Heather. And you're welcome."

She relaxed on the sofa. "You didn't need to call me."

"Oh." His voice took on a serious tone. "You'd rather text?"

"Yes—I mean, no." She slammed her eyes shut and took a deep breath. *Get it together, Heather!* "Okay. Let's try this again. I'm falling over my words." She paused to gather her thoughts. "I meant to say that you're so busy, and you shouldn't feel the need to call me when you have more important things to do."

"Actually, we just got back from an event, and talking to you is the perfect break. It's what I'd rather do."

Happiness warmed her cheeks. "I'm glad." She moved her fingers over the smooth book cover. "I love the book, Alex. I can't wait to read it." Her gaze moved to the package. "What's this PO Box address from Oregon?"

"It's the one we use for the fan club."

"Oh?"

"The same fan club you and Wendy are now members of."

"Thank you for getting us into that exclusive club," she said. "So Portland, Oregon. Is that where you live?"

"I grew up in a town outside Portland named Cascade."

"What's it like there?" She kicked off her shoes and rested her feet on the coffee table. Molly jumped onto the sofa beside her and began giving herself a bath.

"Small town, suburban. It has a little shopping area like Flowering Grove, but the weather is cooler and the Cascade Mountains can be seen in the distance."

She tried to imagine it. "It sounds nice. Do you live near there now? You don't have to tell me if you don't want me to know."

"I thought we were past that secrecy thing since you have my personal cell number."

"Well, I'm planning to post that on social media, along with your address, Social Security number, your mother's maiden name, and your bank account number as soon as I gather it all."

"I knew I was getting a whole scam-artist vibe from you," he teased. "Yes, I live in Cascade, and my mom does too. I have a modest house there, but my brothers live in the ritzier part of town across the river."

She held her hand up even though he couldn't see it. "Whoa. Wait. Did you say you have a 'modest' house?"

"Yes, I do. You find that surprising?"

"No, actually, I find it shocking. You and your brothers have been on top of the pop charts for, like, over a year, right?"

"Two, actually."

"That means you've been, um, financially stable for a while now."

"That's true."

Heather was silent, questions rolling through her mind, but they seemed too rude to ask aloud.

Alex laughed lightly on the other end of the line. "Let me guess: You're wondering why I'm not living in a mansion and keeping my Ferrari collection in my huge garage."

"I mean, well, yeah." She brushed her thumb along the binding of the book.

"That's more my brothers' style than mine. I'm more of a saving-for-a-rainy-day kind of guy. I'm like my mom, I suppose."

"Fascinating."

He chuckled. "My brothers and I have been trying to get my mom to move to a bigger house, which we would all chip in on, but she's happy staying in the house where the three of us grew up." He was silent for a beat, and she imagined him wading through something in his mind. "She says that's where she and Dad decided to settle, so she wants to live with those memories around her."

Heather's heart clenched for him as she thought of her own parents. "That's beautiful."

"Yeah. Sorry to be a downer. I want to hear about your day."

"Not much to tell! It was ordinary. I'm just shocked you're able to talk to me at this time of day."

He seemed to hedge for a moment. "Would you think less of

me if you knew I've been waiting for your text since your package was delivered?"

"Did you sneak out here one night and install cameras?"

"No, but I was watching the tracking number online."

Now it was her turn to laugh.

"I love your laugh," he said.

Embarrassment filled her, but she suddenly felt bold and said, "I love yours too."

"Thank you. Now tell me about your day. For real this time."

She summarized her trip to the grocery store and her time at the restaurant, naming off some of her regular customers and highlights from the dessert menu. "Now your turn."

"We're in Charlottesville, Virginia, now. We're becoming brand ambassadors for this new energy drink, so we met with some of the bigwigs from the company and filmed a promo for the drink. Then we checked into the hotel, and I took a chance on the gym being empty. Since it was, I worked out for a while. I got back to my room, took a shower, and ordered room service. Then I started playing around with some ideas for new songs."

"Wow," she said as she leaned over, petting Molly with her free hand. "That's a very busy day. Tell me about the songs you're writing."

"There's not much to tell. I have a few stray lines, but I can't seem to make them work together."

She bit her lip, and a yearning overtook her. She wanted him to sing to her so badly she could feel it in her bones. But asking him to sing over the phone felt like such a silly request.

"What's on your mind, Heather?" His question was soft in her ear.

"It's kind of stupid."

"I'm sure it's not."

She groaned and covered her face with her free hand.

"Now you *have* to tell me."

"Okay." She hesitated. "Would you sing for me?" She winced, awaiting his laughter or rejection.

"Sure. Which song?"

Surprised, she relaxed. "Um . . . Well, would you mind singing 'Always' for me?" Then she felt ridiculous once again. "I feel so dumb, but you know I'm obsessed with that song."

"At least you're obsessed with a song in which I sing lead instead of Kayden."

"I told you that not all fans are obsessed with Kayden . . ."

His laughter felt light. "I'll have to put my phone down so I can play. Hang on." After a moment, Heather heard an acoustic guitar being strummed, and Alex's voice crooning through the phone.

Heather closed her eyes and soaked in the velvety sound of his voice, trying to imagine him singing to her in person. If only he had called her over FaceTime so she could actually watch him sing.

The song ended all too soon, and she wished she had recorded it. Once again, she wondered about his ex and if he had a current girlfriend.

"How was that?" he asked.

"Perfect."

"Any other requests?"

"I don't want to ask too much during our first call, but I'll keep a request list for future conversations."

He laughed, and she heard him take a drink.

Heather turned her attention back to the book. "Now about this book club. Will we have weekly meetings? Do we take turns picking books for us to read?"

"Hmm. Those are valid questions. I've honestly never been in a book club, so what do you recommend?"

"Well, it depends on your availability. I would prefer to meet at least once a week, but only if your schedule permits."

"I think it would be best if we kept the schedule a little fluid." She could hear the smile in his voice, and it sent a chill racing up her spine.

"Oh, we can definitely do that if it would keep our attendance rate consistent."

"And yeah, we should take turns recommending books. Did you already have our next book in mind?"

Heather hopped up from the sofa and sprinted into the kitchen, where she picked up a cookbook from the shelf in the corner. "I think you would enjoy one of my favorites. It's called *Easy Desserts for the Busy Baker* by Rose Canup."

His laughter was boisterous. "That sounds like a riveting choice."

"It will keep you up late at night for sure," she quipped as she returned the book to its spot on the shelf.

A noise sounded in the background, and Alex said, "Hang on one sec."

Heather heard rustling and then a woman's voice, and she hated the jealousy rolling through her. She closed her eyes and reminded herself that she wasn't Alex's girlfriend—not even close.

"Sorry about that. That was Robyn."

"Who's Robyn?" she asked, working to keep her voice even.

"She's our PR guru. She keeps us in the news, sometimes to our detriment. She also keeps us in line and on schedule. She's sort of like our surrogate mom when we're on the road. Anyway, she stopped by to tell me that she arranged a meeting for some special fans, and my appointment with them is coming up. I made time to see them today since our concert's tomorrow night."

"Special fans?" she asked, intrigued.

Alex seemed to hesitate for a moment. "They're some kids who have special circumstances. Lately I've started trying to squeeze in a visit to a children's hospital or even a Boys and Girls Club."

She smiled. "Aww. That's—that's amazing."

"Thanks. My brothers don't get it, but it matters to me."

"Why don't they get it?"

"They think that if we make any public appearances there should always be a photographer or a TV crew. They want content for our social media pages, but I think that sometimes you need to do good things for people without expecting recognition."

"So you want to give back."

"Exactly. Our career is turning out well, and we're blessed. We need to turn that blessing into something other than money and fame."

Her heart swelled with affection for this man she barely knew, and at that moment, her crush seemed to turn into something more.

"Heather? Are you there? Did you fall asleep?"

"Yes, I'm still here." Her voice sounded thick. "I'm just processing what you said."

"And . . . ? What do you think?"

She took a deep, trembling breath and decided to tell him the truth, no matter how risky it could be. "I . . . I think you're incredible."

"Back at you," he said before more noise sounded on his end of the call. "I'm sorry, but I have to run. Talk soon?"

"Yes. I'll start reading right way so we can talk about this book when you have time."

"Sounds good. Thank you for chatting with me."

She sat up straight. "Thank you, again, for the gift—which brings up another issue. How do I send *you* a gift?"

"Hmm," he said. "I'll have to get back to you on that."

"Okay. Goodbye, Mr. Alex Kirwan."

"Goodbye, Ms. Heather Gordon."

"You hang up first."

He laughed. "No, you!" A loud knock sounded on his end of the line. "I really do have to go," he said. "Talk to you later, Heather."

Heather hung up, grabbed a sofa pillow, and squealed into it. When she looked up, Molly studied her with wide green eyes. Heather laughed and stared at the note Alex had written her before hugging the book to her chest and collapsing onto the sofa.

⌣⁓

Alex couldn't stop grinning when he ended the call. He had enjoyed every moment of talking to Heather. When the knock on the door became louder and more insistent, he jogged over to it and opened it. There Robyn stood, glaring up at him.

"I'm sorry. I was on a call. Just give me a minute." He held up a finger, promising he wouldn't delay.

Robyn gave a loud, dramatic sigh and pointed to her watch. "If you want to do this, then we need to leave *now*."

"I know, I know," Alex muttered on his way to the bedroom, where he changed into a fresh pair of jeans and a t-shirt.

He could already admit that he was smitten with Heather. He enjoyed talking to her and the way she made him laugh. If only he had a photo of her to look at when the loneliness crept in.

He brushed and styled his hair as he contemplated how he could see her again in person. He couldn't plan a trip right away, so maybe she would consider a video call next. He'd especially found it sweet when she asked him to sing to her.

At the same time, his brothers' words bothered him. Could

someone like Heather ever truly love him for him, and not for the celebrity? Would she be willing to put up with his life on the road?

Alex pushed his wallet into his back pocket and imagined their first book club meeting. Then an idea for another surprise book for Heather hit him, and a smile overtook his lips. He quickly shot off a text to Tristan: Hey, buddy! Could I possibly ask you a favor?

Then he strode toward the door.

Later that evening, Heather folded her legs under her and sipped a cup of tea while her two cats snuggled nearby on the sofa. She had spent the last couple of hours reading *The Lost Castle*, stopping periodically to stare at the note Alex had written to her.

She had even caught herself tracing the letters of his name with her finger. She breathed out a sigh and wondered if she'd receive more handwritten notes from him.

Her mind kept replaying his response when she'd told him that she thought he was incredible.

"Back at you."

Heather felt as if she was floating on a cloud, but at the back of her mind she worried that she was making more out of their conversation than he had intended. What if he only wanted to be friends? She knew in her heart that she wanted more, *so* much more, out of this relationship. But how was something like that even possible? He was constantly on the road and lived a totally different lifestyle—the kind of lifestyle Heather could hardly imagine.

She felt a gentle nudge and turned to see Jet beside her. He rested his paw on her leg and blinked up at her.

"Hey there, handsome. Did you want some love?" She kneaded his head and his chin, and his loud purr reminded her of a car engine. When he snuggled back down on the sofa, she turned her attention back to reading.

Soon she was lost in the story, and her eyes began to feel heavy. She yawned and felt her eyes close.

A door closed and Heather jumped up, suddenly awake.

Mckenna dropped her tote bag and purse on the floor and then landed on the recliner across from Heather. "Hey, sleepyhead. How was your day?"

"Fabulous. Yours?"

"Ooh." Mckenna leaned forward, eyes twinkling. "It sounds like you have a story. Tell me everything."

"Okay." Heather sat up straight. She explained how she and Alex had texted earlier and then handed Mckenna the surprise she found on the porch when she got home. Then she shared the highlights of their conversation on the phone.

Mckenna's eyes widened. "He *sang* to you?"

Heather nodded.

"Oh!" She covered her mouth with her hand. "That's so romantic! When do you think you'll talk again?"

Heather shrugged. "I don't know. But it won't be soon enough. I'll text him in a couple of days if I don't hear from him." She shook her head. "Who am I kidding? I'll probably text him tonight." She handed her best friend the sticky note. "Look at his handwriting."

"He signed it 'fondly.' He's fond of you!"

Heather's heart skipped a beat. She was fond of him too.

11

Thank you, Charlottesville!" Alex called into the microphone to the cheering audience. "You've been a great crowd."

Kayden held up his arm. "We love you! Good night!"

Alex and Kayden bowed while the crowd continued to clap, whistle, and scream. Jordan came out from behind the drum set and waved before tossing his drumsticks into the crowd. Then the three of them bowed once more and exited the stage.

It had been another sold-out show with another lively audience. Alex had gotten chills when he and Kayden stopped singing the words to "After a While" and let the audience continue singing at the top of their lungs. They had shared a grin before Kayden told the crowd how amazing they sounded. Since the fans had been so energetic, they decided to add two more songs to their encore before ending the show for the night.

Adrenaline roared through Alex's veins as he stepped off the stage. He gladly took an ice-cold bottle of water and a towel from one of their assistants.

"Thank you, Jenny," he told her before drinking almost the entire bottle in one gulp. Then he dabbed the towel over his sweaty face, hair, and neck.

Brooks hurried over to them. "I need you guys to come with me. We have some VIPs here."

Alex frowned. So much for relaxing after a long concert.

Kayden clapped his hands together. "Any hot women?"

Jordan snickered.

Brooks nodded. "You might say that. A couple actors, athletes, and models are anxious to meet you."

Kayden pushed his hands through his sweaty blond hair. "Make sure to get some photos."

Alex rolled his eyes. He wanted to unwind and check his messages, not plaster a smile on his face and hobnob for another hour. His throat and his feet were sore, and he really needed to get out of these sweaty clothes. He took a step away from Brooks and his brothers.

"Give me a minute, all right?" Alex rushed off to his dressing room, took a deep breath, and found his phone.

Tapping the screen, he found a handful of messages—one from Tristan, one from Mom, and one from Heather. His stomach dipped at the sight of her name.

He opened Heather's message first and read:

> So I'm about a third of the way through this book, and I'm anxious for our first book club meeting. I don't care what you try to tell me because I know the butler totally did it. 😊 And, by the way, I'm sure your concert is going fabulously. Wish I was there. That reminds me— have you added your acoustic set yet? Text me soon. Fondly, Ms. Heather Gordon

Alex grinned down at his phone. He started to reply but stopped when he heard Brooks call his name. He turned to face the doorway, where his tour manager watched him with an impatient expression.

"Alex, I know you're exhausted, but we'd like the entire band here for this photo op, please." Brooks held his hands up. "You can relax soon, I promise, but we need to get on the road soon too. We have early interviews tomorrow in Virginia Beach."

Alex blew out a resigned sigh. "Yeah, I know. I'm sorry."

He locked and pocketed his phone, then strode behind Brooks to where the VIPs were gathered with his brothers. He forced his lips up into a smile and nodded a greeting to everyone as he approached.

While he was grateful that people wanted to meet them, he was emotionally and physically depleted after being onstage. Posing as "rockstar Alex" wore him out, and he was ready to go back into his shell as "introvert Alex" for a few hours.

"We're so excited to meet you, ladies," Kayden announced, opening his arms for the models, who giggled and took turns hugging him.

Alex shook his head in awe. These meetings were easy for Kayden. No, they were second nature for him. He was the true showman out of the three of them.

Jordan stood nearby talking to a couple of young men who were built like basketball players. Two pretty women, whom Alex assumed were their wives or girlfriends, stood beside them.

Alex forced himself to turn to two preteen girls beside him. Since their parents looked familiar, he assumed they were the actors. "Hi, I'm Alex."

"We know who you are," one of the girls said.

"I'm Morgan, and this is DeeDee." The other girl held up a notebook and a permanent marker. "Could we have your autograph?"

Alex smiled as he took the marker from her hand. "I'd be honored."

⁓

The hum of the engine filled the large bus, and although it was nearly two in the morning, Alex was wide awake. After more than an hour of talking to the VIPs, Alex and his brothers had loaded up on the bus, which was now headed to their next destination.

He had stared at Heather's message, eager to respond, but he didn't want to risk waking her. He should have been sleeping, but his mind buzzed. He pulled his iPad from his backpack and tried to work on lyrics for a song, but nothing came to him. All he could think about was Heather and how much he missed her.

Then an idea sparked in his mind. If he couldn't text her, then he would do the next best thing and write her a letter. He opened the Notes app on his iPad and started to type.

Dear Ms. Heather Gordon,

I'm sitting on a bus that's somewhere in Virginia and headed to somewhere else in Virginia. I received your text message, but since it's nearly 2:00 a.m., it's too late to text you. I'd feel terrible if I woke you. I hope you're sleeping well. Hopefully you'll be willing to share your email address with me so I can email this to you tomorrow.

Tonight we had a good concert. It was typical, really. The crowd was great—loud and excited. The best part is always when they sing along to the songs. Sometimes Kayden and I stop singing and let the crowd keep going. There's no feeling like that—hearing someone else sing our songs to us gives me chills every time. It never gets old!

We are blessed beyond measure with this job. People actually pay money to come to our concerts. Sometimes I think about that fact, and it blows my mind. When I was seventeen years old, writing songs was a way to deal with my grief over losing my dad. I never imagined that someone would pay their hard-earned money to buy my music or spend even more money to hear my brothers and me sing in person.

If only those moments of inspiration and wonder could sustain the loneliness I feel when we're back on the road, and I'm staring out the window of a bus or airplane or car, thinking about what "normal" people are doing in their "normal" lives—interacting with people in their offices or grocery stores or churches or even the post office. My life used to be normal too. It's funny to think that my brothers and I play sold-out concerts in pavilions and arenas, but I feel like the loneliest person in the world when I'm traveling to the next venue.

After the concert tonight, I went backstage hoping to just retreat to my dressing room. I constantly feel like I'm two people—Rockstar Alex and Regular Guy Alex. It's exhausting to be Rockstar Alex, the one who has to perform and put himself out there for shows, meet and greets, interviews, and appearances. When I'm done with Rockstar Alex events, I feel so drained that I just want to unwind. Regular Guy Alex is the one who likes to hide in the gym or behind a book.

Well, my hopes of hiding in my dressing room with my phone and your message were dashed when I learned I had to entertain some VIPs. There were a few models, two athletes and their wives, and a couple of actors waiting for us.

Kayden was right on task—joking, flirting, and posing for photos with the women. Jordan quickly fell into a conversation with the athletes. It took me a few minutes to find my extroverted personality again, and then I chatted with the actors and their kids. It was over pretty quickly, thank goodness. We took group photos, some of which you'll maybe find in a magazine next time you're at the supermarket. We'll all look happy, but inside, just know I'm dying for some time to recharge my emotional batteries!

I just realized that I'm pouring my heart out to you. Is that strange? You're probably wondering if I'm crazy, but I just felt a connection with you the moment you walked into my dressing room and talked to me like I was a normal person. You didn't start crying or ask me to autograph your arm. You didn't say things you thought I'd want to hear or pay me ridiculous compliments about my musical talent. I felt the foundation of a friendship form instantly, and I hope you feel that way too. But I just realized I haven't asked how you feel about it. Am I making a correct assumption that you want to be friends— really good friends—with me?

I also realized that you haven't mentioned your bookstore/bakery dream the last couple of times we've spoken. How are your plans coming? Are you looking for a location?

And while we're at it, let's keep asking each other our burning questions. Here's mine for you.

Burning question: What was your best day ever and why?

Well, my eyes are finally starting to feel heavy. I look forward to sending this to you and also speaking to you again.

Oh, and the butler didn't do it. ☺

Fondly,

Alex K.

With a yawn, Alex powered down his tablet, pushed it into his backpack, and finally closed his eyes.

Heather awoke later that morning to find Jet purring loudly while curled up on her chest. She smiled as she scratched his head, and he leaned into her hand, his purr growing even louder.

"It's a shame you're not spoiled," she quipped.

Reaching over with her free hand, she retrieved her phone on her nightstand and tapped the screen. Disappointment wriggled through her when she found it free of any text messages. She figured Alex had endured a long night after the concert and would eventually reach out. She just hoped it would be sooner rather than later.

Heather maneuvered out from underneath her large tuxedo cat, then padded to the kitchen with her cats meowing loudly at her heels. After feeding them, she prepared scrambled eggs, toast, and hot tea for herself. She took a seat at the kitchen table and scrolled through social media while she ate.

"Good morning!" Mckenna sang as she fluttered into the kitchen wearing a purple dress and matching purple heels. Heather would never understand how Mckenna tolerated standing all day in those shoes, but Mckenna insisted they were comfortable.

Heather nodded as she swallowed a piece of toast. "Good morning. What's on your agenda for the day?"

"I have a date with Kirk tonight. I'm so excited. I really like him and think he might be the one." She slipped a mocha latte K-Cup into the Keurig and pushed Start before dropping an English muffin in the toaster. The scrumptious aroma of the latte quickly overtook the kitchen. "Have you heard from Alex?"

Heather shook her head. "He had a concert last night."

"I'm sure he'll message you as soon as he wakes up."

"I hope so." Heather sipped the rest of her tea, then stood to load her dishes, utensils, and mug in the dishwasher. "Anyway, I need to get ready for work."

Mckenna smothered her English muffin in butter, then poured her latte into a green travel mug with her name on it. "Me too. I have a client coming in twenty minutes."

"Have a fantastic day, Mack." Heather leaned in for a quick hug and returned to her room to get dressed.

The engine of Mckenna's Subaru motoring out of the driveway sounded while Heather styled her hair in a tight french braid. Then she located her keys, purse, and tote bag and started for the front door.

She grabbed the knob just as her phone dinged with a message, and her heart nearly skipped a beat. She pulled the phone from her pocket and smiled when she saw "Alex K" on the screen.

ALEX: Good morning. Do you have an email address?

HEATHER: Doesn't everyone?

ALEX: ☺ Would you feel comfortable sharing your email address with me?

HEATHER: That sounds like a loaded question. Are you going to subscribe me to a bunch of spam websites that will fill my inbox with ads for items I will never need?

ALEX: Of course.

HEATHER: Good. Here's my address: bakergirl97@email.com

ALEX: Baker Girl, huh? I may need to call you that.

She grinned as she typed: I dare you.

ALEX: You dare me, huh? Well, now I have no choice but to call you that, Baker Girl.

Heather laughed.

ALEX: I need to apologize in advance for what I am about to
     email to you.
HEATHER: You have my attention now.
ALEX: It's just a rambling email I wrote to you at two this
     morning.

Heather tittered as excitement overtook her. He had been
thinking of her at 2:00 a.m.? She typed: I can't wait to read it.

Alex seemed to pause for a moment, then the conversation
bubbles returned. The email is on its way to you. And I'm sorry, but
I have to go. We have another interview that we're running to now.
And then probably a thousand more before the concert tonight. I'll
text when I can.

HEATHER: Okay. Have a good day, Alex.
ALEX: You too, Baker Girl.

Heather opened her email on her phone and then sank down
onto the recliner, letting her purse and tote bag fall to the floor.
Her mouth dropped as she read his words. She couldn't believe
how much of himself he had shared in that one email. It was as
if their friendship had suddenly deepened, morphing into something even more special.

When she finished reading the letter, she glanced at the
clock. If she didn't get to the restaurant soon, she wouldn't
have time to finish her baking before the lunchtime rush—and
Saturday was their busiest day of the week.

Her two cats sat in the kitchen doorway, watching her gather
up her things. "Have a good day. Molly is in charge," she joked
before stepping out into the clear April morning.

She breathed in the warm, clean air and admired the cloud-less blue sky. Birds sang in the nearby trees, and two rabbits hopped toward Mckenna's bright yellow daffodils.

As soon as Heather started her car, Alex's voice began serenading her through the speakers. Her mind buzzed with excitement as she drove to the restaurant. Alex Kirwan had bared his soul to her! He had shared secrets, and she couldn't stop herself from falling for him.

What would she say in response to his letter? She wanted to know how serious he was about her—but first, she needed to know if he had a girlfriend. Perhaps that should be her burning question for him.

12

The day had been a flash of appearances, soundcheck with the fan club, followed by another concert. Now it was the middle of the night, and Alex was back on the bus heading to Maryland. He had hoped to catch a few minutes to check email, but every time he pulled his tablet from his backpack, Brooks seemed to need him for something else. But now he was finally alone, and he could do what he wanted—which was to check in with Heather.

When he opened his email and found a message from her, his heart stuttered. Taking a deep breath, he began to read her response.

Dear Mr. Alex Kirwan,

I'm sitting in my parents' office at the restaurant while taking my break. It's about 4:00 p.m. I offered to work a double tonight because Allie, one of the servers, asked for the night off to spend time with her boyfriend. I work doubles often since I honestly don't have a whole lot else going on in my life right now, and I'm also saving money for my bookstore and bakery. I'll tell you more about that project in a minute!

But first, I have to admit I'm thrilled to have been on

your mind at 2:00 a.m. It sounds like you had a very busy day, but I'm sure most of your days are like that.

That must be an intense feeling to hear other people sing your songs to you. I sing your songs in the car, but I would never sing to you in person. That would be far too embarrassing. I'd rather bake you a cake or cookies, which is my special skill. Wendy has a much better voice than I do.

You deserve every ounce of your success, and I truly mean that. You are so very talented, and your fans adore you. You are blessed, but you have also earned it, Alex.

And your loneliness touches my heart. I had never thought about how isolating it would feel to travel so much and not be able to live a "normal" life. It also never occurred to me that you might be an introvert since you appeared so comfortable onstage. I noticed that Kayden seems to be more . . . larger than life, I guess. But you look like you're in your element when you perform. It seems to come naturally to you. If you're nervous, then you hide it well. Are you an extroverted introvert?

How could you tell me you met with models, actors, and athletes and not share who they are? That's cruel! Would I know their names? Were they nice?

Alex, I'm honored and humbled that you feel a connection with me, and it's definitely mutual. Although I must admit I still don't know why you picked me when you certainly have more exciting women who cross your path. I'm enjoying getting to know you, though, and look forward to learning more about you. Feel free to text, call, or email me anytime you want to talk.

As for my bookstore and bakery idea, well, it's just that—an idea. Maybe it's more of a goal—a rather lofty goal since I have no idea when I'll be able to make it a reality.

I've read multiple books about opening a small business, and I even took a couple of online business classes through the local community college. I have been working on a business plan with my dad, and I've been saving money for years. I want to open it here in Flowering Grove, but I haven't found a storefront that I can afford. But I really haven't pursued finding a spot either. So there's the truth—I dream about it, but I haven't actually found the courage to make it happen yet.

Now to answer your burning question. My best day ever, huh? There was this one time when I was about fourteen and Wendy was ten, and my parents closed the restaurant so we could spend the day at Carolina Adventureland, which is an amusement park that sits just over the North Carolina state line. We spent the day enjoying the rides, eating fun food, and laughing. It was so amazing! Just seeing my parents relax and have fun without working was a gift.

What was your best day ever?

Now it's my turn to ask burning questions. I like including them over email because it gives me a chance to ask what I'd never have the nerve to ask in person. However, I'm going to change the rules and ask two:

1. Do you have a girlfriend?
2. What's your middle name?

How's Virginia Beach? And how did your visit with your "special guests" go the other day? Did you sing for them?

Don't worry—I haven't forgotten the book. I read for a while last night while I waited for your message, and I'm not saying that to make you feel guilty. I'm clearly aware of how busy you are. But the book is so good, and now I'm not sure who the murderer is. Could it be Ray? And why is it called *The Lost Castle*? The title doesn't make any sense. How can you lose a castle? It's not like it can get up and walk away. Plus, there's no castle in the book. They live in condos! Still, I'm invested. We need to plan that book club meeting.

Oh no. My break is over. It went too fast! By the way, I think you need a better email address: RockstarDude or BestSongwriterEver would be more interesting than your current email handle. What does AKKFordF250 mean anyway? Is that your truck or something?

Hugs (is it okay to say that?)—

Heather (aka Baker Girl—but you're the only person who's allowed to call me that!)

Alex chuckled as he read and reread her response. This woman was incredible. She was so funny and easy to talk to, and the connection he felt to her seemed to grow with each text message, phone call, and email.

But once again he wondered: How could they make a relationship work?

The question settled over him as he hit Reply and began his response.

To my Baker Girl,

It's delightful to climb onto the bus at nearly 2:00 a.m. and find an email from you waiting for me. In fact, reading your message was the highlight of my day. And without further ado, I will jump right in to respond.

It sounds like you have a very busy schedule, especially working so many double shifts. Are you off the same days each week, or does it vary? My days on the road are overwhelming, but I'm looking forward to a few days off. I hope you get a few days off sometimes too!

You're sweet to say I deserve my success, but in all honesty, there are plenty of bands out there who are more talented than Kirwan and deserve success too. We managed to win a contest and catch the eye of a producer, which was lucky for us.

I'm sure you think I'm a weirdo for admitting to the loneliness of the road, but it's true. Fame can be a prison at times, and it's heartwarming to have a friend like you who is willing to listen.

Ha! I never meant to be cruel. The models were Mae Park and Lily Bradshaw. I think they're known for makeup ads. The actors were Charlie Rosenberg; his wife, Connie Whitehall; and their two daughters, Morgan and DeeDee. The athletes were Garrett Washington and Antonio Fernandez and their girlfriends. They all were very friendly. The models were captivated by Kayden, which is fine. It takes the pressure off me, and I hate trying to be cool when I'm exhausted.

Kayden has always been larger than life. My dad once said he came out of the womb performing. He was singing in the children's choir at church when he was barely four. He and Jordan have always been inseparable since they are closer in age to each other than to me. Kayden is twenty-two, Jordan is twenty-four, and I'm twenty-nine. When they were kids, they would make up songs and plays. Dad used to play piano for them while they sang.

Anyway, women have always loved Kayden. Girls were always calling him, and he was double-dating with Jordan by the time he was fourteen. Kayden craves the limelight and loves being famous. Jordan doesn't mind the attention, but he doesn't seek it out like Kayden does.

Tell me more about your sister. Are you close to Wendy?

I suppose I am an extroverted introvert, but I've never taken a personality test. How about you?

Also—I'm relieved to know the connection between us is mutual!

I think you need to start looking for a storefront for your bookstore and bakery. May I help in any way?

Your best day ever sounds wonderful! I can almost see a teenage version of you on a roller coaster, screaming your heart out. Do you like roller coasters? I do. I'd love to go to Carolina Adventureland, but I'd have to find a disguise first, I bet.

My best day ever is similar to yours. I was thirteen, and I had Dad all to myself. I can't remember why, but my brothers were off somewhere with my mom. He and I went to lunch and to the music store, where he bought me my first guitar. Then he took me home and started teaching me how to play it. We sang together and we talked about everything we loved about music. Now it's a magical memory.

I miss him. Sometimes I find myself talking to him, as crazy as it sounds. He's been gone fourteen years, but sometimes it feels like I lost him yesterday.

Now to your burning questions. I must admit I laughed out loud at the first one. If I had a girlfriend, do you honestly think I would be calling, texting, and emailing you? I can assure you that when I'm in a relationship, I'm completely loyal. I'm an all-in kind of guy, though I've been single for almost four years now. The women I've met who have been interested always seemed to want something from me, such as money or fame. I'm looking for someone who will want me for who I am, not for what I can give them.

How about you? Do you have a boyfriend?

My middle name is Kenneth, after my father—Alexander Kenneth Kirwan. What's your middle name?

Virginia was good. We did a media event and took questions from various members of the media—radio, websites, television, etc. Then we were guests on a local talk show. Later, we stopped by the beach for a festival and performed two songs. Then we had a couple of hours off, so I napped and showered before soundcheck and the show. A lot of my days look the same!

Now we're on our way to Maryland. I have no idea where we are, but Jordan and Kayden are snoring loudly.

We do need to discuss the book. I have never lost a castle or a condo, but the title will make sense toward the end of the story. And no, I'm not going to tell you whether it's Ray or not. I don't want to spoil any surprises. I'll have to call you about it when I'm able to speak during normal waking hours. In fact, Jordan just sat up and told me to be quiet because he's trying to sleep.

You're right: My email is in honor of my truck. I still have my father's burgundy 2005 Ford F-250. It was his pride and joy, and my mom gave it to me when I got my license. I also have a couple of Mustangs too. Even so, you're probably right that I should change my email address to something else. Maybe DorkyRockstarGuy. Does that fit me better?

Now it's your turn to tell me about your day. You must be exhausted after working a double. I hope you're off tomorrow. Oh, wait—that would be today, wouldn't it?

My burning question for you is: If you are single, what was your last relationship like? How did it end?

And yes, hugs from you would be something I would enjoy. Email me soon.

Hugs,

Alex

Later that afternoon Heather sat across from Mckenna at an outside table at Bloom's Coffeehouse. The sun was bright as people ambled down the sidewalk on Main Street in Flowering Grove. Heather took a sip from her vanilla latte before summarizing Alex's latest letter for her roommate. She left out the personal information he shared about his loneliness but kept the high points for Mckenna's sake.

When she finished, Mckenna blinked. "Heather! You're dating a famous singer!"

A young couple passing on the street stared at them.

Leaning forward, Heather shushed her best friend. "We're *not* dating."

"You may not be dating yet, but you're in a relationship." Mckenna held up her Americano as if to toast her. "I'm so happy for you and for me. We both found amazing guys."

Heather frowned.

Mckenna took a sip of her coffee and shook her head. "A super-successful, sweet, wonderful, handsome man is crazy about you, and you're sitting here frowning. What gives?"

"I'm just afraid of risking my heart. I really care about him, but what if he's not looking for a relationship? What if he just wants someone to email and text when he's lonely on the road?"

"Didn't he tell you that he's all in when he's dating? Didn't he say he's loyal?"

133

"Yes, but he hasn't defined what I mean to him."

"Not yet!" Mckenna exclaimed. "When the time is right, he will make it official, and you'll be as happy as I am with Kirk. And like I said, then we can all go out on a double date."

Heather took a drink of her coffee.

"I also think it's sweet that he's encouraging you to go after your dream. You want a man who will support you. That's what counts in a relationship. Kirk is understanding when I have to work late, and he respects what I do. In fact, he's impressed that I run my own business."

Heather shrugged. "I always knew you were awesome. It's about time he figured it out."

"Thank you." Mckenna chuckled. "Now it's your time to make this bakery and bookstore happen. I'm going to talk to my parents and find out if any of the retail spaces around here are available."

"I appreciate that, but I think all of the real estate around here is too expensive."

"Nonsense." Then Mckenna snapped her fingers. "Wait. Alex offered to help you. Why don't you and Alex go into business together? He can help with the start-up costs, and you can run the store."

"No, no, no, no." Heather shook her head.

"Why not?"

"Because I'd never ask him for money like that. He said he's met women who have seemed interested in him, but they only wanted something from him in the end. I'll never, ever use him."

"But he offered!"

"Doesn't matter. I want to do this on my own."

"It's okay to ask for help."

"I refuse to use him, Mack, and that's it."

"You're stubborn."

Heather touched her finger to her cheek. "Funny. I've heard that before."

They both laughed.

"Hey," Heather said. "It's been a long time since we've had a girls' day. Why don't we go get mani-pedis and then watch movies at home?"

Mckenna nodded. "Let's do it."

Later that evening, Heather placed the large bowl she and Mckenna used for popcorn during their movie night in the dishwasher before retreating to her room to email Alex.

She had enjoyed a fun afternoon shopping with Mckenna, and then they had stopped at a nail salon for their mani-pedis. When they returned home, they popped popcorn and watched two romantic comedies before Mckenna disappeared into her room to call Kirk.

Heather sat on her bed, where Jet and Molly were already sound asleep at the foot. She opened her laptop, clicked on her email, and started typing.

To my Not-So-Dorky Rockstar,

How is Maryland? I spent the day having fun with Mack. We started out at the coffee shop, then we went shopping, got mani-pedis, and watched a couple of romantic comedies. Do you like movies? What's your favorite thing to watch?

Mack and I both seem to be working all the time, so it's special when I can see her. She runs a hair salon, and when I say "runs" it, I mean she owns the business. She rents the place from her parents for a great price. I'm grateful she keeps me on as a roommate even though I bet she could pay the rent on her own.

I've been thinking on it, and I still stand firm that you deserve your success. Also, you're not weird for admitting your loneliness to me. It makes sense. I'm sorry that fame can be like a prison, but I'm glad to know I make you smile! And I'm honored to be considered among your friends.

Sounds like you met some interesting people the other night. I don't share your emails with anyone, but I did ask Mack if she had heard of the models since she's more fashion savvy than I am. She had heard of them! The actors too. We Googled the athletes and found them. I'm not surprised about women being interested in Kayden since my sister is one of them. Personally, I'd rather talk to you, but that's my opinion. And I'm sure you were cool without even trying.

So Kayden was born a performer, huh? I get that feeling from him. Since you asked, I'll tell you I'm close to Wendy, but sometimes we bicker. She's twenty-two, and I'm twenty-six. We argued more often when we were kids, but we're closer now. We do tend to push each other's buttons sometimes though. Do you argue with your brothers?

You're very sweet to offer to help with the bookstore and bakery. You did inspire me to mention it to Mack today, and she's going to talk to her parents, who own quite a bit of the retail spaces around here. She said she'd ask about any affordable storefronts becoming available soon.

I haven't been to Carolina Adventureland this season, but I do try to go at least a couple of times every year. And yes, I do like roller coasters. Do you? I'd love to find you a disguise and take you there. It must be difficult to be recognized when you go places. I'm sure that gets old.

Thank you for sharing that wonderful memory of your

father. Imagining him helping you pick out your first guitar and teaching you how to play it brought tears to my eyes. You must miss him so much. May I ask what happened to him? Was he ill? It's not crazy to think that you still talk to him. I'm sure he's listening, and that he's so proud of you and your brothers.

I'm glad to hear that you don't have a girlfriend. No, I don't have a boyfriend.

I love your full name, Alexander Kenneth Kirwan. That has a nice ring to it. My middle name is pretty ordinary. It's Rose. I'm not sure why my parents decided to name me after two flowers since they aren't very good gardeners. I don't remember a time when my mom could even keep a houseplant alive, and her garden is mostly weeds thanks to the long hours she spends at the restaurant. Does your mom garden?

I'm excited to finally discuss this book with you. I'm planning to read more of it tonight, and I have a feeling that the murderer isn't Ray since you said you won't tell me.

You definitely should change your email address to DorkyRockstarGuy, but tell me before you change it so we don't miss any messages.

I love that you kept your dad's truck. I drive the old Honda Civic you might've seen in our driveway. It's not flashy, but it's reliable. And your music sounds good in it too. I hope to get a ride in your Mustangs someday!

Now to answer your burning question. But first: If I tell you about my disaster of a last relationship, then you have to share about yours. I'm imagining you nodding in agreement, and I'm trusting you to hold up your end of the bargain. So here goes.

I dated Jeff for nearly two years, and I thought he was "the one," if that person even exists. Then his high school sweetheart came back to Flowering Grove to visit her family, and he went to lunch with her. And guess what happened after that? He broke up with me and moved to South Carolina with her. I recently heard that they're engaged, which hurts my heart.

So that was Jeff. He destroyed my heart and my trust. It's your turn. What happened with your ex?

And now you have me thinking about hugs, Alex.

Lots and lots of hugs,

Heather

She hit Send, and her pulse zoomed as she imagined Alex reading her message. Then she closed her eyes and tried to slow her racing heart.

13

Alex sat down at the desk in his Baltimore hotel suite, and his tired body relaxed as he read Heather's latest email. Thoughts of her had been his constant companion during the day, and finding such a touching, genuine message waiting for him in his email this evening had been a balm to his lonely soul.

He clicked Reply, and his fingers hovered over the digital keyboard on his tablet. Then he stilled. What he craved more than anything was to hear her sweet voice. No, he wanted to see her pretty face as well as hear her voice. It was still early enough in the evening that she would be awake. But would she want to answer a video call?

Alex held his breath and then hit the button to FaceTime her. He rubbed at a spot on the back of his neck while the phone line rang and rang and rang. His shoulders drooped, and his hope sank as the call continued to go unanswered. He considered giving up, but then Heather appeared on the screen.

She looked stunningly beautiful, her mysterious chocolate-colored eyes wide as she studied him. Her hair was wet and hanging past her slight shoulders, and her ivory skin was makeup-free, highlighting her glorious freckles. She looked as if she was wearing the same pajamas he'd seen the day he delivered her phone.

"Alex?" she asked, her voice sounding unsure.

The air was trapped in his lungs, and his words stuck in his throat. He had forgotten how beautiful she was, and he was overwhelmed with the yearning to kiss every single freckle on her face.

He cleared his throat and managed to say, "Heather. Hi." His voice sounded gruff to his own ears.

Heather looked down at her blue pajama top and then touched her wet, dark hair before giving him a sheepish look. "You, uh, caught me off guard. I just got out of the shower."

He swallowed and tried not to think too much about that confession.

"Maybe we should hang up, and I'll call you back on a voice call," she suggested. "We could save a video call for a time when I'm more prepared."

"Are you sure? I've missed seeing your face and hearing your voice. And you look perfect to me!"

Her cheeks reddened, making her look even more adorable. "Okay. I've missed your face too." Then she grimaced. "But could I have a couple of seconds to fix my hair, please?"

"Of course." He all but held his breath while she disappeared from the screen for a few moments.

When she returned, her gorgeous dark hair had been fixed in a messy bun. She sank down onto her bed and leaned back against the headboard. When a loud meow sounded, she seemed to look past the screen. "Are you saying hello to Alex?"

"Who's there with you?"

She angled the phone toward a chubby tuxedo cat curled up beside her. "Can you say hello again, Jet?"

The cat opened one eye and then closed it.

Heather laughed as she held the phone up to her face. "I guess he doesn't have anything else to say." She wound a loose lock of her dark hair around her finger. "So did you read my email?"

"I did."

"Okay." Her eyes seemed to sparkle. "Tell me about your last relationship."

He pressed his lips together. "It's not a very interesting story."

"Is she the one you wrote 'Always' for?"

He frowned with feigned annoyance. "You won't let that go, will you?"

"Nope." She shook her head. "I told you it's my favorite song."

He propped the tablet up on the desk, hunched his shoulders, and folded his arms over his chest. There was no getting around talking about Celeste. "Yes, she was."

She gave a dramatic sigh. "What was her name? How did you meet? What went wrong?"

He held up his hand. "Okay, okay. I'll tell you." Then he ran a hand through his hair, gathering his thoughts. "Her name is Celeste. We met when I was working in a coffee shop in Portland. She used to come at the same time every day and order the same drink. It took me about a month to work up the nerve to ask her out, and after I did, she said she'd thought I'd never ask. We dated for about three years. I thought we would be together for the long haul."

He ran his thumb over the edge of the desk. "We always seemed to have our issues though. We bickered a lot. I thought that was normal, so I made a lot of excuses. My best friend, Tristan, would even comment here and there about how he thought Celeste talked down to me and didn't respect me."

"Really?" She looked surprised.

"Yeah. My brothers and I would perform at the coffeehouse

some nights and weekends in addition to my long hours there as a barista. Celeste would make comments about how I should get a real job. She never really respected my dream. It should have been my first clue that something was wrong when she refused to come to my gigs. She was always too busy."

"You're kidding," Heather said.

Alex smiled, appreciating her emotional support. "Anyway, she broke up with me because she said I would never amount to much. She wanted a man who had goals and could achieve them."

"She actually said that?" Heather gasped.

"Yes, she did. And then after the band became popular, she tried to call me a few times. At first I let it go to voicemail, but then one day I decided to see what she wanted. I answered, and she said she was sorry for underestimating me and disrespecting me. She begged me to give her another chance." He rolled his eyes.

Heather seemed riveted. "What did you say to her?"

"I told her our ship had sailed. I was done. I never heard from her again after that."

"Wow," Heather said. "When did you write the song?"

"While we were dating. Our producer suggested we include a ballad on our first album. My brothers convinced me to sing it for the producer, and he liked it." Alex held his hands up. "That song is not a love song for Celeste anymore. It's just a song that happened to become a hit."

She nodded slowly, and he wished he could read her thoughts.

When she remained quiet, he said, "What are you thinking? You don't have to be afraid to say anything to me. We're past that by now, right?"

"I'm just stunned," she finally said. "You're such a wonderful man. You're so open and honest and kind. Why would she give up on you so easily?"

Her words touched him deeply, but he tried to shrug off the emotion. "I guess I wasn't enough for her."

"Her loss." Then she paused. "Have you dated anyone since her?"

"Not really. I've gone out on dates here and there, but I never met anyone I really wanted to get into a long-term relationship with." *Until I met you.* He pulled his phone from his pocket and opened her email. "How about I answer your other questions?"

"Okay."

"Let's see." He scrolled through the letter. "I like action movies."

"That's a guy thing," she muttered, and he laughed.

"My brothers and I do argue sometimes. We butt heads over things related to the band, such as publicity. We don't always see eye to eye on events. We don't always agree about our finances, but we try to figure it out. It's hard to work with family." He grinned. "I have a feeling you already know that though."

She chuckled. "Oh yes. You don't get a break from them, and sometimes your personalities clash."

"Exactly." He pointed a finger at her. Then he looked down at the letter, and when he came to the paragraph about his father, he hesitated. A lump swelled in his throat.

"Alex?" Her voice sounded full of concern. "Are you okay?"

He kept his eyes focused on the phone.

"What's wrong?"

"You asked about my dad, and I'm looking for the words." His voice was thin and reedy.

"I'm sorry." Her eyes widened, and she held a hand to her forehead. "I crossed a line. You don't have to answer."

He rubbed the stubble on his chin and looked down at his lap. "But I want to." He took a deep breath. "It was a Saturday. I was fifteen, so Jordan was ten and Kayden was eight. My mom asked my dad to go to the store. He asked me to go with him, but I was too busy playing video games." He stopped when his eyes began to sting, and he rubbed them. "I'm sorry."

"Alex, you don't have to—"

"It's okay." He sniffed. "He went to the grocery store, and an hour passed. Then two, then three. I really hadn't noticed how long he'd been gone, but suddenly I heard my mom shriek. I remember running down the stairs. Two police officers were standing in the doorway, and my mom was on her knees sobbing." When Alex's voice hitched, he stopped, took a breath, and ran his tongue over his dry lips.

Heather sniffed and dabbed her eyes with a tissue. "What happened to him?"

"He was on his way home, and a drunk driver had come into his lane and hit him head-on. He was driving my mom's little SUV, and he didn't stand a chance. The guy was speeding and out of control. I bet Dad never saw him coming." Alex sniffed again and shook his head. "I'm sorry. Sometimes it feels like no time has passed."

"I'm sorry too," she whispered, her beautiful face full of empathy.

They were silent for a moment, and Alex found a box of tissues on the desk and wiped his eyes and nose. When he looked at her again, he felt his heart crack open. "Do you want to hear something crazy?"

She nodded.

"To this day, I wonder if things would have played out differently if I had gone with him. For example, if I had gone, would we have spent ten minutes in the junk food aisle picking out some cookies that Mom would never buy for us? Then would that guy have been ten minutes farther down the road and never crossed my dad's path?" He looked down at his lap again. "Or would I have been in the front seat when it happened?" He shivered and then wiped his eyes again.

"Alex. Look at me."

He looked up and met her fierce gaze.

"You shouldn't drive yourself crazy playing *what-if*, okay? Don't torture yourself like that. The accident wasn't your fault."

"I know." He heaved a heavy sigh. "My brothers and I went through years of therapy, but sometimes I still think about what could have been."

"You look like you could use one of those hugs we keep discussing."

He grinned. "Now you're talking, Heather Rose."

Her eyes widened, and he was almost certain she was blushing again. "You remembered my middle name!"

"Your joke about your names and how your parents don't garden made me laugh. But I think your middle name is beautiful and fitting."

She looked surprised.

"And your ex is a moron for leaving you for someone else."

She blinked, almost bashfully. "Thank you. Do you want to tell me about your schedule for the upcoming week?"

He shared what was on the band's agenda with their appearances and performances, and she talked about working at the restaurant.

"And what are your plans and hopes for the future? You know, aside from more concerts and interviews and all that."

He tilted his head. "That's an unexpected question."

"You know about my dreams, so I think it's only fair I know yours!" she teased.

"You're right." He leaned back in the chair. "I guess mine are to settle down, have a family, and also do something meaningful besides play music."

"Your music is meaningful to a lot of people."

"Thank you, but I want to do something that really changes lives. I just haven't figured out what."

She nodded. "It's really wonderful that you have that goal, and I believe you'll make it happen someday."

"I hope so. What about you? Do you want a family?"

"Yes, I do. I also obviously want to run my own business. I want something that's mine."

"I see success in your future." He covered his mouth with his hand to shield a yawn. "Excuse me, Heather. I'm getting tired. I promise it's not the company."

Her smile was sweet. "I should let you go."

"But I don't want to."

She laughed. "You're like an exhausted kid who doesn't want to go to bed."

"I want to talk to you all night."

"But we have school tomorrow." She shook her finger at him.

He laughed at her playfulness.

"I love your laugh."

"Thank you, but before we call it a night, I want to hear *you* sing." He held up his guitar. "You name the song. I can play some Soundgarden or maybe Stone Temple Pilots for you to sing along to."

She shook her head with vigor. "Nope. I need to go to bed."

"All right, but can we talk soon? I can't wait for you to finish that book so we can discuss it."

"I promise I will, but you need to make me a promise too."

"What is it?"

She held a finger up. "You need to warn me before you video call me, so I can get prepared. I'd like to be properly dressed and have my makeup and hair done."

"You look absolutely perfect the way you are now."

"You're just saying that."

"No, I'm not," he told her. "I'm just telling you the truth."

Her cheeks seemed to flush a little. "Well, I want a warning next time. I need at least twenty minutes to get myself together."

He smiled. "We'll see. You have a nice night."

"You too, Alex. I can't wait to talk to you again."

"I feel the same way. Good night, Heather."

"Good night," she told him before disconnecting the call.

Alex felt like he was walking on air as he stood up and stretched. He had never trusted a woman so quickly, so easily. He felt as if he could tell her anything. He lifted his guitar and started strumming, then heard his phone ding with a text.

MOM: Are you awake?
ALEX: Yes!

His phone began to ring with a call from his mother.

"Hey, Mom," he said. "What's new in Oregon?"

"Hi, honey. I did something tonight that I haven't done in years."

"What was that?" He set down his guitar and settled on the sofa.

"I went on a date."

Alex was speechless for a moment. "With whom?"

"His name is Charlie, and I met him in the grocery store. We wound up in a conversation about produce, and the next thing I knew, he was asking me for my phone number."

Alex blinked. Was he dreaming? "He picked you up in the produce section?"

Mom laughed. "You sound shocked."

"I am." Alex sat up straighter. "What does he do for a living?"

"He's a software engineer. He's a few years older than I am

and has two grown daughters." She paused for a moment. "He lost his wife to cancer a few years ago."

"I'm sorry to hear that." Alex leaned back against the sofa. "I want to meet him when I get home."

She chuckled again. "We went on one date, Alex. I'm not engaged."

"Well, that's good news." Alex smiled. "He sounds nice. Just take it slow."

"Yes, son," she teased. "I talked to Jordan earlier, and he said you've met someone too."

Alex frowned. "What else did he tell you?"

"He told me you met a woman in North Carolina, and you've been corresponding."

"That's true," he said. "And he disapproves, right?"

"He's concerned she might be using you."

"She's not," he said with a resigned sigh.

"Whoa, now, Alex. I'm on your side."

He tilted his head. "You are?"

"Yes, I am. You're tenderhearted, and I know you're lonely on the road. I think it's great that you've met someone you like. You shouldn't be alone."

"Who told you I'm lonely?"

"You have."

"I have?"

"I'm your mother. You've made comments here and there, and I can put the pieces together," she said. "Now, tell me about her, Alex."

"Her name is Heather," he began. He filled his mother in on the last few days, describing how they met and what he'd learned about her so far. "She works a lot and loves to bake. She hopes to open her own bookstore with a bakery someday."

"She sounds wonderful. Send me a photo of her?"

Alex blew out a puff of air. "I don't have one, but I can text you the website for her family's restaurant."

"Oh yes, send me the website."

"I will. I'm hoping to go see her when I get a few days off."

"She sounds perfect for you."

"Maybe, but I don't know if she wants a life like mine."

"Love conquers all, honey. If you love each other, you'll figure out how to make it work together."

He nodded. "Yeah, well, we're just friends right now."

"You're handsome and quite a catch," she said. "I think she'll want to date you."

He chuckled. "You're my mom, so you have to say that."

"But I mean it too."

"Thank you," he said through a yawn.

"It's almost midnight there. I should let you go."

Alex could feel his eyes getting heavy. "Okay, but I'll want a full report on this new boyfriend of yours next time we talk."

She laughed. "He's not my boyfriend, but I will keep you posted."

"All right. Good night, Mom."

"Love you."

"Love you too." He ended the call, then smiled as a thought hit him. If his mom was brave enough to look for love again, perhaps he should be too.

14

Two weeks later, Mckenna and Heather stood in their kitchen. "You look beautiful," Mckenna told Heather, taking in her roommate's carefully planned look. It was Thursday night— finally, the evening for Heather's planned book club call with Alex. And for some crazy reason, it felt like a date—an actual, bona fide date—even though it was going to be virtual.

Alex had suggested they talk tonight since it was his only night off for a while. He had another concert coming up, then he'd be traveling with the band from Pennsylvania to Florida. He had only a few events that day, so he could relax in his hotel room afterward and discuss the book.

Since she had been off from work, Heather spent the entire afternoon fussing over what to wear before settling on a red sweater. She had washed her hair, and Mckenna had styled it in long waves that cascaded past her shoulders. Mckenna had even helped Heather apply her makeup.

Heather could feel her heart rate spiking as she set a bowl of popcorn on the kitchen table. "Are you sure I look okay?" She checked her reflection in the door of the microwave. "Is this red lipstick too bright? Did I put on too much eyeliner?"

"You look perfect. I promise you that if Alex isn't already in love with you, then he will be when he sees you on the screen tonight."

"Thank you." Heather hugged her best friend. "Wish me luck."

Mckenna grinned. "You don't need any luck." A horn honked outside, and she picked up her giant black purse. "Kirk's here. You have fun. I can't wait to hear all about it later." Then she waved on her way to the door.

"Bye, Mack!" Heather called. Then she turned her attention back to preparing for book club.

Alex and Heather agreed to each have popcorn and hot chocolate while they discussed *The Lost Castle*. After setting her mug of hot chocolate on the table, she looked over at the clock on the microwave, and her stomach tightened. Five minutes until her scheduled Zoom meeting with Alex.

A mixture of anxiety and excitement swarmed her chest. Could he possibly be as nervous as she was? No, of course not! Alex sang for sold-out concert halls and pavilions. Why would he be anxious about discussing a book with Heather?

Taking a deep breath, Heather sat down in front of her laptop and logged on. She fought the urge to bite her red manicured nails while she waited for Alex to enter the virtual meeting room.

She wrung her hands to shake off her nerves, and after a few moments, Alex's handsome face filled the screen. His angular jaw was clean-shaven, and his blond hair looked as if it had just been washed. He wore a pale blue Henley and looked to be sitting at a desk in his hotel room.

"Heather. Hi." When he smiled, her heart thudded, and she stared into his striking eyes, losing herself in his gorgeous pools of blue for a moment. "You look beautiful," he said.

A hot flush overtook her cheeks. "Thank you. You look amazing too." She cleared her throat. "And before I forget, I wanted to thank you for the fan club goodies. Wendy and I are thrilled with the t-shirts, hats, and pins. And it's obvious the autographed postcards are authentic."

"You're more than welcome, Heather." He grinned. "Are you ready for our first book club?"

She pointed to her copy of the book he had purchased for her. "You bet I am."

"Do you have your hot chocolate?" He held up a Starbucks cup with a lid.

She showed him her favorite cat mug. "I do."

"Should we toast?"

Warmth surged in her chest. "I love that idea."

"Great." He held his cup up higher. "Here's to many more book clubs."

"Hear, hear," she said before they each took a drink. Then she set her mug down on the table and flipped to the last pages of the book. "Should we just go through the discussion questions?"

"That sounds like fun. Do you want to go first?"

Heather smiled and felt herself relax as she began to read the first discussion question aloud.

⌒

Two weeks passed, and Heather was humming a Kirwan song as she walked from the back of the parking lot toward her parents' restaurant. The early morning air was warm and smelled of May flowers. The sky was bright blue and dotted with fluffy white clouds, and birds sang in the nearby trees. She opened the restaurant's back door and stowed her purse and tote bag in her parents' office before heading into the kitchen.

"Good morning!" she sang to her parents, who were already preparing food for the day.

Mom grinned at her. "Aren't you in a good mood?"

"The sun is up, the birds are singing, and it's a beautiful day." Heather shrugged as she retrieved her favorite cookbook from the shelf. "Who wouldn't be happy?"

She noticed a look pass between her parents, but she ignored it. Instead, she found her favorite recipe for chocolate chip cookies and began pulling together the ingredients. While she worked, she pondered how she and Alex had fallen into an easy routine of text messages, late-night emails, and voice and video calls.

She had completely fallen for him, and she desperately needed to know where she stood. She felt so close to him, but did he consider her his girlfriend? Or was she only a good friend? Maybe his special friend—like a pen pal? Or someone to help keep the loneliness at bay until he found someone better? She needed to ask but couldn't find the courage for fear of seeming needy or immature.

She frowned at the thought. She wanted to be so much more, but how could that ever work when he was constantly on the road and his permanent residence was on the West Coast? She couldn't imagine leaving her family or Flowering Grove, the only home she'd ever known. Yet Heather felt this deep, overwhelming connection to him—something she'd never felt for anyone else.

Could it be love?

She grumbled as she began mixing the dry ingredients into the wet.

"You okay over there?" Dad called from the door leading into the freezer.

Heather gave him a thumbs-up. "I'm just peachy."

He raised a dark eyebrow. "Your mood sure turned around quick."

"I'm fine. Really." She turned back to the counter and began dropping the dough onto the baking pan.

At times she felt her emotions resembled a good old-fashioned crush. Could she ever be more than just his friend and a starstruck fan? After all, she hadn't seen him in person since they'd met two months ago. Would she ever see him in real life again, or would their relationship always be through a phone?

Heather worked to concentrate on her baking for the next few hours—preparing cookies, two lemon cakes, and two chocolate cakes.

Lunchtime approached, and she greeted Wendy and Allie when they walked through the kitchen. They tied on their aprons and chattered in the dining room ahead of the lunch-time rush.

Heather washed her hands and pulled her phone from the back pocket of her jeans. She frowned when she found the screen free of any alerts. She hadn't heard from Alex since he texted yesterday morning. He also hadn't emailed last night, but he said he would be traveling and promised to be in touch soon.

She pushed her phone back into her pocket and tried to recall where Alex had said the band was headed. They had flown to Florida for a few concerts and a music festival last week. He had mentioned they had to be in the New York City area for more shows and a few television appearances soon, but she couldn't remember when. Had he even told her the dates? They had discussed so much last week, she wasn't certain.

Heather changed into a clean apron and then stilled when the voices in the dining room suddenly rose.

"No!" Wendy exclaimed. "That can't be true!"

"It's all over the news," Allie insisted. "You need to tell Heather before she finds out herself."

Heather pushed through the double doors and marched toward Wendy and Allie, who lingered near the coffee machines. "Tell me what?"

Wendy and Allie shared a horrified look, and Heather's stomach dropped.

"Tell me what, Wendy?" When her sister's lip began to quiver, anger and worry battered Heather. She folded her arms over her chest. "Tell me *now*."

Wendy gulped. "Didn't you say Alex was traveling today?"

"Yeah." Heather divided a look between them. "Why?"

Wendy gave Allie another worried look.

"What is going on?" Heather demanded.

Allie held up her phone, and the screen displayed a photo of a smashed luxury bus. The headline read: "Rock Band Involved in Deadly Crash Overnight."

Heather teetered and grabbed the corner of the counter. A wave of nausea swept over her. "No, no, no," she whispered. "No, no, tell me it's not—it's not . . ."

"Whoa." Wendy grabbed her arm. "Calm down."

Heather's mind began to spin. She covered her hot cheeks with her hands and tried to swallow back the bile rising to her throat. *Is that why he hasn't emailed or called?* She sniffed as her eyes filled with tears.

"Hey," Wendy whispered in her ear. "The article doesn't say it's Kirwan. Odds are it's some other band."

"She's right. The article doesn't say who was involved in the crash, but I thought you should know," Allie said.

No. No. No. Heather tried to swallow air to steady her breath, but the room spun out of control, along with her thoughts.

Wendy took Heather's arm and steered her toward the kitchen. "You need to sit down." She looked at Allie. "Please tell my parents what's going on."

Allie scurried ahead of them to the kitchen while Wendy guided Heather to her parents' office and toward the desk chair.

"Just call him now and confirm he's okay," Wendy instructed.

Heather located her phone and fumbled with the passcode but couldn't unlock it. "I-I can't."

"Let me." Wendy unlocked it and handed it to her. "Call him, and I'll look for more news on Mom's computer."

Heather's hands shook as she dialed his number and put the phone to her ear. "Answer. Answer. Answer!" she whispered as it rang. When it went to voicemail, she growled. "Come on—please pick up!" Then she dialed him again.

Wendy pointed to the computer screen. "Look, Heather. It says the bus was traveling northbound on Interstate 95 in Georgia when it crashed early this morning. It doesn't name the band." Her brown eyes searched Heather's. "Do you know where Kirwan was last week?"

"Florida."

"And where were they headed?"

Heather shrugged. "He said something about New York." Her lip began to tremble as her tears broke free.

"Shh." Wendy hugged her. "No need to cry. Surely it wasn't him."

"But it could be." Heather voice was soft and quaky.

"It's going to be okay."

"He's not answering his phone," she managed to say. "What if he's . . . What if he's . . ." She shivered at the horrible thought. "What if he's hurt, Wendy?"

Her sister stood up, handed her a box of tissues, and pointed to the phone. "Try him again."

Heather wiped her eyes and nose, then dialed his number a third time.

Wendy retrieved a bottle of water from the small refrigerator in the corner of the office and handed it to Heather. "Here. Take a drink."

"Thank you," Heather whispered before opening it and sipping. The cool liquid did nothing to calm her frayed nerves.

"This is why I didn't want to tell you about the accident. We don't know that it was Kirwan's bus, okay?"

Heather nodded despite the dread pooling in her stomach.

"Just keep calling him. He'll answer."

Heather sniffed. "You'd better help Allie. The restaurant opens soon, and the prep work's still not done."

"No, I'm not leaving you." Her sister looked determined.

Heather patted her sister's hand. She appreciated her emotional support but wanted a minute alone to gather her thoughts. She didn't know how she'd cope if she lost Alex, but she needed to calm down and get herself together in case . . .

Heather pushed the dark thought away. "I'll keep calling him. You go help Allie."

"I'll tell Mom to come in and sit with you."

Heather shook her head. "You know how busy she and Dad are at lunchtime. I promise I'm okay."

Wendy's brown eyes seemed to scrutinize her. "Are you sure?"

"I'm positive. Thank you for being with me, but I just need a few minutes alone. Tell everyone I'm okay and will be out there soon."

Wendy's expression finally relaxed.

"All right, but I'll be back to check on you."

"Thank you."

Wendy gave her a quick hug. "Love you."

"Love you too."

Wendy padded out of the office, softly closing the door behind her.

Heather faced the computer and skimmed the news article.

Her eyes stung anew when she read, "The names of the band members have been withheld pending notification of next of kin."

Tears pooled in her eyes as she stared at her phone. She wished she had his mother's number, but would his mother even know who she was?

She tried once more to call him but received his automated voicemail message. Out of desperation she texted him: Alex, please tell me you're okay. I saw some news about a band in a horrible accident.

She held her breath awaiting those wonderful conversation bubbles, but none appeared.

Resting her head in her hands, she tried to recall his schedule. Where did he say he was going? He *was* in Florida, and the accident happened on Interstate 95 in Georgia overnight.

It can't be him, can it?

A commotion sounded in the kitchen, but Heather kept her focus on her phone as she dialed Alex once again and pressed the phone to her ear. She heard the door to the office creak open.

"Heather?" Wendy's voice was at the door.

Heather squeezed the bridge of her nose and closed her eyes. "Not now, Wendy."

"Heather." Wendy's words were measured. "There's someone here for you."

Heather ignored her.

"Heather," Wendy snapped. "Look up."

She did as Wendy commanded and found Alex standing in the doorway with a hesitant expression on his face. Heather gasped, dropping her phone onto the desk with a clatter. She clapped her hands to her mouth as her eyes filled with fresh tears.

"Alex!" She breathed his name, not believing her eyes. But he looked real, standing there clad in tight jeans, a gray t-shirt that hugged his sculpted biceps, and a black baseball cap boasting a green *O* outlined in yellow.

Wendy ducked out of the office, closing the door behind her.

His smile made her cheeks tingle with warmth. She took in his chiseled cheekbones, angular jaw, and bright cornflower-blue eyes, and she was certain she was dreaming.

Alex stepped into the office and raised his hand. "Surprise."

"You're—you're okay." She tried to swallow, but a lump expanded in her throat.

"I'm okay." He nodded, and his smile faded. "But are you?"

She took a tremulous breath, swallowed, and then sniffed, trying to keep her emotions intact. Then all of the worry and fear she'd been holding at bay poured from her eyes. She covered her face with her hands as her tears fell.

"Come here." His voice was next to her ear, sending shivers shimmying down her back. Then his muscular arms encircled her and held her against his hard chest. "I'm here, Heather. I promise it's all okay."

She wrapped her arms around his neck as she sobbed into his shoulder. She felt herself relax as he caressed her lower back.

"I'm here, Heather," he murmured. "Shh. It's okay."

She worked to calm her tears as she held on to him. She ran her fingers through his soft hair and breathed in his scent—teakwood, soap, and something that was uniquely him. She tried to convince herself she wasn't stuck in a fantasy—but that Alex Kirwan was here, holding her in his arms.

Finally!

After what felt like several moments, she finally stilled herself and pulled away from him. He smiled down at her and wiped a few errant tears away with the tip of his finger.

"I'm sorry." She jutted her chin toward the computer screen behind the desk. "Allie told me about a bus accident, and I couldn't reach you, and . . ." She shook her head, feeling silly. "I'm a blubbering idiot."

"No, I'm sorry for not telling you I was okay. I didn't hear about that accident until I was on my way here this morning. The story was on the news on the radio. It never occurred to me that you would be worried."

He touched her cheek again, and a chill cascaded down her back. "I've been planning this surprise for a couple of weeks. That's why I didn't text or email last night. I knew that if I messaged you, I'd slip and tell you since I was so excited. But I never meant to worry or upset you. I'm so sorry."

Heather chuckled. "Don't be sorry. I'm just emotional. When did you get here?"

"I flew the red-eye this morning and got to Charlotte a few hours ago. I rented a car and drove the rest of the way. I'm staying over at the Flowering Grove Inn." He threaded his fingers with hers, and her skin warmed at his touch.

"You're staying at the inn?" she asked, and he nodded. "Do you use your real name when you travel?"

"No, I usually stay under the name Kenneth Kirkland."

"Ooh. Now I have another of your secrets to post on the web." He laughed. "That's true."

"How long are you staying?"

"I have to be in New York City early Friday morning. We're performing as part the *Good Day USA* Concert in the Park series, and then we have two concerts in New Jersey before we head out to the Midwest." He pulled her closer to him. "I wanted to see you first. My brothers flew home last night, but I chose to come here instead. I needed to see you in person." He cupped her cheek with his free hand. "I've missed you, Heather."

Without thinking, she threw her arms around his neck, and he embraced her again.

"These hugs are better than I imagined, and trust me when I tell you I imagined some really great hugs," he murmured against her hair, and she laughed. "There's that laugh I love so much."

She closed her eyes and enjoyed the feeling of his muscular arms wrapped around her once again. "I was so afraid I'd lost you," she whispered.

"I'm sorry I scared you, but I'm here now."

15

~

Alex released Heather from the embrace, and she took a step back. Then he touched the scruff lining his angular jaw, looking almost embarrassed. "Is there any chance you can take some time off and spend it with me? I know it's last minute, but I didn't want to spoil the surprise."

"Of course! I'll see if Wendy or Allie will cover for me. Let's go ask them." She pocketed her phone and turned off the computer before threading her fingers with his and leading him out to the kitchen. The restaurant smelled like coleslaw, pulled pork, and macaroni and cheese mixed with the lingering scents of the cakes and cookies she had baked earlier.

"Mom and Dad, this is Alex," Heather announced.

Dad nodded while filling a plate with hush puppies. "We met earlier. Welcome."

The door swung open, and Wendy and Allie bustled in. Allie's eyes found Alex, and she cupped her hand to her mouth as if to cover a squeal.

"Wendy and Allie?" Heather motioned them over. "I wanted to ask you a favor. Is there any way you can take my shifts at the restaurant so I can spend the week with Alex?" Then she glanced over at her mom, who was cutting Heather's cakes into slices. "Mom, would you handle my baking?"

Mom smiled. "Of course I will, and I'll call Misty and Joyce to see if they can cover a few of your shifts as well." She turned to Dad. "I'll be right back."

"Thank you." Then Heather looked at her sister again. "Would you please help out if they aren't available?"

"On one condition." Wendy's expression became clandestine as she turned her attention to Alex. "Have Kayden send me an autograph." She clasped her hands in front of her. "Thank you for the fan club swag. I really appreciate it, but I want a personalized photo that's from Kayden to me." She pointed to her chest.

Alex smirked. "I can do better than that." Then he looked at his watch. "It's after eleven here, so it's around eight on the West Coast." He pulled his phone from his pocket and unlocked it.

"What are you doing?" Heather asked.

"You'll see." He hit a button, and a video call began to ring.

Heather's mouth dropped open. "Are you calling him now?"

"Yup," Alex confirmed.

Heather turned toward Wendy and Allie, who looked as if they might burst with excitement.

Alex's screen filled with the image of Kayden rubbing his eyes. His blond hair stuck up in all directions as he yawned and then groaned. "Do you know what time it is?" His voice was gravelly.

"I do." Alex's grin was bright. "It's almost eleven here."

"Well, it's not here." Kayden yawned again. "This had better be important, Alex."

Wendy and Allie shared a shocked look, and Heather couldn't stop her laughter.

Alex's smile didn't dim. "Good morning to you too, baby

brother. I need you to talk to a couple of important people for me."

"What?" Kayden suddenly seemed wide awake. "Who?"

"I'm going to introduce you to my friends Wendy and Allie. They already know who you are, of course." Then Alex handed the phone to Wendy, who looked ready to faint.

"Um, hi, Kayden. I'm Wendy. We met when you were in Charlotte. This is my friend Allie," she began.

Heather touched Alex's hand. "Is he going to get you back for this?"

Alex shrugged. "I'm not worried about it." He rested his arm around Heather's shoulders, and she leaned against his side. "What are our plans for the day?"

"Are you hungry, Alex?" Dad asked.

Alex nodded. "I am." He looked at Heather. "I was in such a hurry to get here that I haven't eaten anything."

Her cheeks went hot as she stared into his sky-blue eyes. She needed to pinch herself to make sure she was awake.

"Then have a seat." Dad pointed to a stool in the corner of the kitchen. "I'll make you a plate."

Giggles erupted behind her, and Heather took in Wendy and Allie listening while Kayden told a story about forgetting the words to a song he'd written while performing.

"Thank you, Mr. Gordon," Alex said.

Dad smiled. "Call me Russ. What would you like to eat?"

"I would love one of your barbecue plates. My brothers and I have talked about how delicious the food is here." Alex gave Heather a smirk. "The service is pretty great too."

Dad snorted.

"He has to say that because his brothers left a huge mess for Wendy and me to clean." Heather laughed, leaning on the counter beside her father.

"But without that mess, we wouldn't have met," Alex said.

"That's true."

Dad pulled together a barbecue plate and handed it to Alex while Heather retrieved utensils and a drink for him. Alex popped a hush puppy into his mouth.

"How's the tour going?" Dad asked.

Alex wiped his mouth with a napkin. "It's going well, but I'm grateful for the break."

Mom reappeared in the kitchen. "Misty said she'll come in later this afternoon, and Joyce said she can take your shift tomorrow." She pointed to Wendy and Allie, who were using Wendy's phone to take selfies with Kayden. "Ladies, you need to wrap this up. It's time to open."

Wendy frowned at Alex's phone screen. "It was nice talking to you, Kayden."

"Have a good day," Allie chirped.

Wendy handed the phone to Alex. "Thank you." She gave Kayden one last wave before she and Allie disappeared through the swinging doors to the dining room.

Alex grinned at his brother's image on the screen. "Thanks, man."

"What are you eating?" Kayden asked.

Alex angled the phone toward his plate. "The pork special at the Barbecue Pit."

"Yum. I'm jealous." Then Kayden's eyes narrowed. "You know I'll get you back for this."

Alex laughed. "Promises, promises. Tell Mom I said hi."

"I will." Kayden yawned. "I'm going back to sleep."

"Sweet dreams, buddy." Alex disconnected the call, winking at Heather. "You know he loved the attention." Then he turned to Dad. "Where did you learn to make this delicious barbecue? Is it an old family recipe?"

Dad stirred a dish of macaroni and cheese. "Would you believe it was my grandfather's?"

"No kidding!" Alex exclaimed. "And he passed it down to you?"

Happiness fizzed in Heather's chest as she took in the comradery between Alex and her father. For a moment she wondered if Alex would fit into her family, but she halted her train of thought. How could she even imagine a future with Alex when her life was here in Flowering Grove? She could never expect him to settle here, and she would never dream of leaving her home.

An arm encircled Heather's shoulder, and Mom steered her toward the line of ovens. "I am so impressed, Heather," she whispered. "Alex is not only handsome, but he's also sweet and friendly. I can see why you like him so much. I'm excited for you."

"Shh, not so loud," Heather hissed. Then she glanced behind her and was relieved to find Alex and Dad engrossed in conversation. "We're just friends."

Mom snorted. "Sure. Just friends." Then she opened the oven and pulled out a tray of cornbread. "Would you please stir the baked beans for me?"

"Of course." Heather minded the beans while her mother sliced the cornbread. Then she helped Mom butter and grill rolls for barbecue sandwiches while Alex finished eating and talking to her father.

After Alex cleaned his plate, he and Heather said goodbye to her parents. She collected her purse and tote bag from the office.

Alex pushed his baseball cap down low on his blond hair, then threaded his fingers with hers. "Let's enjoy our day together."

Happiness bubbled up inside Heather as Alex opened the back door of the restaurant and held it for her. As she stepped out into the bright afternoon, the warm sun kissed her cheeks.

Alex pointed to a black Infiniti sedan parked beside her Honda. "There's my rental."

"Fancy. Did Kenneth Kirkland rent the car too?" She tented her hand over her eyes as she looked up at him.

He grinned, and her steps faltered. "He did, actually." He guided her over to the driver's side of the car. "I have a surprise for you."

"Another one?" she asked. "Just your being here is the best surprise."

He hit a button on the key fob and the car unlocked. "Close your eyes."

She did as she was instructed, and she heard the car door open and close before she felt him place something in her hands.

"You can open them."

Heather opened her eyes and looked down. In her grasp she found a copy of her favorite author's next book. She studied the breathtaking cover, featuring a dark house with a shadow of a man in the window and an eerie, dark sky in the background.

She blinked, trying to figure out if her eyes were deceiving her. A gold foil "Autographed Copy" sticker graced the top corner of the cover, and when she opened to the title page, she found a note written in slanted black script:

To my number-one fan, Heather: I hope you enjoy this story.
Sincerely,
Emil Zimmerman

Her mouth dried as a thrill raced through her. She was holding a book signed by her favorite author—signed *for* her!

Alex's gaze was fastened on hers, and she felt light-headed. For a moment she was left speechless as she stared at him, wondering how she had managed to snag this incredible man's attention.

His blond eyebrows lifted as a slow smile spread across his lips. "I thought this could be our next book club pick. If you agree, of course. I realize it's your turn to choose, but I just had a hunch you'd like this one."

"*The Man in the Window* isn't supposed to release until August. I'm . . . I'm so confused." She stumbled over her words. "How did you get a copy of Emil Zimmerman's next book?"

He lifted a shoulder in a half shrug. "I know people."

Her eyes lingered on his lips for a moment, and she considered kissing him. But when her courage dissolved, she set the book on the hood of his rental car and wrapped her arms around his neck, pulling him close.

"I'm overwhelmed. Thank you, Alex." She rested her head on his shoulder and longed to stay in his arms forever.

"You're welcome." The low rumble of his laugh echoed in his chest. "I've been so excited to give you the book. That's another secret I've been keeping for a couple of weeks now."

She stepped out of his embrace and picked up the book again, examining the back. "Please tell me your secret. How did you manage to get copies of a book that hasn't even been released yet?"

"The truth is, my best friend, Tristan, is an editor at Zimmerman's publisher. He hooked me up with the advance copies. I had him send them to the inn here in Flowering Grove so I could give you your copy in person." He pointed to the cover. "Did you know that 'advance reader copies' of books are called ARCs?" He lifted his chin. "I know the lingo now."

They both laughed, and Heather noticed an adorable shimmer in his eyes.

Then she pointed to her car behind her. "How about we drop one of our cars off at my house and then go somewhere and talk?"

"That would be perfect."

"Great. I can get changed too." She frowned down at her black jeans and Barbecue Pit t-shirt.

"You don't need to change. You look perfect just the way you are," he told her.

"You're too sweet, Alex." Heat radiated through her as she took in his earnest expression. She pulled her keys from her pocket. "Let's go."

Heather nosed her Honda into the driveway, and Alex parked his rented Infiniti Q50 behind her. She had spent the short ride home trying to calm her racing pulse. It was a dream come true for Alex to visit her.

Alex met her at the back of her car and held his hand out to her. "Would you like me to carry anything for you?"

"No, thank you." She shouldered her bags and hugged her book to her chest. "I have my ARC."

He laughed as they started up the path together.

The front door opened, and Mckenna appeared on the porch as Heather and Alex were walking up to the stairs. "Hey, Alex!" she called. "What a surprise."

"Alex, you remember Mack," Heather said.

Mckenna stuck her hand out to him. "Of course he remembers me."

He grinned and shook her hand. "You're the flamingo fan." He pointed at the flamingo-printed tote bag on her arm.

"That's right." Mckenna laughed, then divided a look

between Alex and Heather. "Did you know he was coming to visit, Heather?"

"No. I was stunned when he walked into my parents' office at the restaurant."

Alex reached over and massaged her shoulder. "I've been planning it for weeks and am just grateful it all worked out."

"How long will you be here?" Mckenna asked.

"I'm flying to New York Thursday night."

Mckenna clapped her hands. "Oh, we can finally have that double date we've been talking about."

Heather frowned and tried to ignore the hot embarrassment overtaking her face. And despite the look she tried to give Mckenna, her oblivious best friend kept talking.

"There's this really nice restaurant in Uptown Charlotte that Kirk and I have been dying to try. Why don't we pick a night?"

Heather sneaked a glance at Alex. A strange look crossed his face, and he cupped his hand to the back of his neck. "What's wrong?" she asked him.

He gave Heather a sheepish expression. "It's not that I don't want to take you out for a really nice meal. I do. But I was hoping to enjoy a quiet week with you without any interference from paparazzi or large crowds. Fans hoping for autographs can be so disruptive—and I don't want to share my time with you."

Heather thought her heart might beat out of her chest with admiration for this thoughtful man. "I understand."

"What if we cook here?" Mckenna said.

"That would work." Alex smiled and took Heather's hand in his again. "I owe you a fancy dinner, okay?"

Heather nodded. "Of course."

"What's your schedule?" Mckenna asked.

"Wide open, though we have plans Wednesday night," Alex said.

Heather stared at him. "We do?"

"Yup." He smirked. "And I'm not going to tell you any details. It's a surprise."

"Another one?" Heather asked.

Mckenna gave Heather an approving look. "How about tomorrow night?"

"Perfect," Heather said, and Alex nodded.

"All right." Mckenna grinned at Heather and winked. "Have fun." Then she traipsed off to her waiting Subaru.

Alex stepped ahead of Heather and opened the front door. Then she slipped past him and into the house, where her cats sat blinking up at them.

"You remember Molly and Jet, right?" Heather flung her purse and tote bag on the sofa.

Alex reached down and gave each cat a head rub. "I do."

She jammed her thumb toward the hallway. "I'm going to go get changed. Help yourself to anything in the kitchen. I'll be back."

Then she hurried down the hallway, excited to spend the day with Alex.

16

Alex glanced around Heather's small family room. It seemed like only yesterday he had walked into this house to return Heather's phone, but over a month had passed. Back then they had been strangers, but now they were close friends. No, she was more than that to him. She had become his best friend—the one he trusted with all his secrets, as well as the one he wanted to trust with his heart.

He crossed the living room to the bookshelf and leaned down, taking in the titles on the bindings. He spotted *The Lost Castle* and picked it up. The conversation they had the day she had received the book seemed to have been a turning point in their relationship—the day text messages became phone calls.

A shock of energy shot through Alex. He wanted so badly to ask Heather to be his girlfriend. He had planned to pose the question to her this week, but he had to find the right moment. He also had to find the courage. Dating him would be complicated, and he just hoped she would consider taking a chance. Would she trust him with her precious heart?

When he felt something rub against his shin, he peered down at the smaller tuxedo cat. She looked up at him and blinked before rubbing her head against his leg once again.

"Hi, Molly." He reached down to pet her soft head.

The cat responded with a loud purr.

"What do you think?"

He turned toward the hallway where Heather stood. Alex's throat dried, and his pulse picked up speed at the sight of her. She wore a cream-colored sundress and white sandals. Her shiny dark hair fell in waves past her shoulders, and her beautiful milk-chocolate eyes were accentuated with just enough makeup. And those freckles were one of his favorite features.

"Do I look okay?" She wound a lock of her gorgeous hair around her finger.

Alex cleared his throat. "You look stunning."

"Thanks." She blushed and dipped her chin.

He pulled his phone from his pocket. "I don't have any photos of you, so we'll have to take some selfies this week."

"That's a great idea." She retrieved her purse from the sofa. "Where should we go?"

"I'd like to see your hometown."

"How about we get coffees and sit in the park?"

"Perfect," he said.

⌣⁊

Alex sat on a bench beside Heather at Flowering Grove Park, sipping his coffee. The delicious smells of their Americanos from Bloom's Coffeehouse mixed with the scents of the moist grass and flowers. He looked out toward the swing sets and slides, where four toddlers played and two young women stood and talked. Two chipmunks scuttled by and disappeared into a cluster of bushes.

It was the perfect spring day, and he blew out a happy sigh. Coming to Flowering Grove had been a very, very good idea.

Heather peered over at him, and her smile seemed coy. "What was that sigh for?"

"I was just thinking that I feel completely relaxed for the first time in weeks, possibly even months." He stretched his arm along the back of the bench, and when she angled herself closer to him, he moved his thumb across her shoulder blade.

"Is that because you have a few days off?"

"That's part of it, yes."

She seemed to study him. "Why did you decide to come here instead of going home to Oregon with your brothers?"

"Do you really not know the answer to that question?" When she remained silent, he decided to be completely honest. "I missed you, and the emails, texts, and calls weren't enough. When I realized we had a few days off, I decided to put a plan together." He tilted his head. "Are you glad I'm here?"

"Yes." She laughed and rested her head on his shoulder. "I just can't believe it. I feel like I'm dreaming."

He longed to kiss her, tell her how much he cared for her, and ask if she felt the same way—but he didn't want to push too hard. He'd see how the week played out first, then surely he'd find the courage to share the depth of his feelings.

"Now you've seen our coffee shop and our park."

Alex looked around. "I see why you love it here. It must be a beautiful place to live."

Heather sat up and took a sip of her coffee. "So you said we have plans Wednesday night."

"That's right, and I'm not going to tell you what those plans are. You'll just have to wait."

"Darn!" She snapped her fingers and grinned. Then her eyes sparkled as if an idea hit her. "Would you like to visit a children's hospital while you're here?"

He angled his body toward hers and pushed a tendril of her dark hair behind her ear. A whiff of her floral-scented shampoo drifted over him, and his pulse pounded. "I really want to spend time with you, but if you want to visit a children's hospital, then we'll do it."

"I'd love to see you interact with the children. Did you bring a guitar?"

He nodded. "It's at the inn."

"What if we went to the children's hospital in Charlotte tomorrow?"

"I can call Robyn and ask her to arrange it."

"Yay." She clapped.

Alex lifted his cup. "How about we finish our coffee and then you give me a tour of Flowering Grove? I want to see where you went to school."

She smiled. "That sounds fun to me too."

⌒

Heather leaned against Alex later that evening while they sat on her sofa and watched a movie. She couldn't stop smiling as she recounted the wonderful day they'd spent together. After finishing their coffees in the park, they drove around Flowering Grove and the neighboring towns while Heather shared memories of her childhood. Alex opened up to her and talked about his favorite childhood memories of his parents and his brothers.

Later they brought home takeout from Heather's favorite Chinese restaurant, and they ate and talked about everything from his tour to their favorite books. After cleaning up the dishes they rented a movie, and now Heather sat snuggled up against

Alex's side. She tried to concentrate on the action on the screen, but her mind twirled with happy thoughts about his visit. She wished the evening could last forever.

The movie ended just as Mckenna came through the door. The cats dropped down from where they had been sitting on the back of the sofa and scurried over to greet her.

"Hey, you two." Mckenna set her tote bag by the door and gave each of the cats a head scratch. "Did you enjoy your day in Flowering Grove, Alex?"

He stood and stretched. "I sure did. Heather showed me around. I love how homey it is here." He turned to Heather. "I should probably head to the inn though. Would you please walk me out?"

"Of course."

"Great." Alex nodded at Mckenna. "Good night."

Mckenna grinned. "I'll see you tomorrow night for supper."

Alex took Heather's hand in his and guided her to the door. When she passed Mckenna, her best friend gave her a thumbs-up, and Heather shot her a warning look.

Once outside in the driveway, Alex released her hand and leaned back against his car. "Tomorrow morning, can I pick you up for breakfast? We can eat at a restaurant, or we can pick something up and eat in the park."

"There's a diner over in Wadesboro that's sort of out of the way. We might be able to get a booth in the back."

"Sounds great. We should eat before we head to the hospital. I'm grateful Robyn was able to arrange for us to go. We can stop by a store on the way to buy some toys for the kids."

After they agreed on a time, Alex reached for her free hand. As he steered her toward him, her heart began to beat erratically.

This is it! He's going to kiss me!

When he leaned forward, she closed her eyes, but instead of

kissing her, he pulled her in for a hug. She tried to dismiss the disappointment that overtook her.

"I'll see you tomorrow." His voice was low as he whispered against her ear.

"I can't wait."

Then he released her and unlocked the car. "Good night, Heather," he said before climbing into the driver's seat.

Heather stood in the driveway and waved as he drove off. Then she returned to the house, where Mckenna sat on the sofa with an excited expression.

"Tell me everything." She patted the couch cushion beside her.

Heather sank down onto it, and Molly hopped onto her lap while Jet snored on the back of the sofa behind Mckenna. She filled Mckenna in on the entire day, including the plans they had made for the morning trip to Charlotte.

"But . . . ?"

"What makes you think I have a complaint?"

Mckenna harrumphed and pointed to Heather's face. "Your expression tells me you're disappointed. Just spill it, sister."

Heather groaned and covered her face with her hands.

"You know you want to tell me . . . ," Mckenna sang.

"Fine!" Heather splayed her fingers and peeked at her best friend. "He hasn't kissed me yet, and it's killing me."

Mckenna blinked. "He hasn't?"

"Nope." Heather fell back against the sofa and tickled Molly's head. "We've hugged and held hands. He even rubbed my back in the park, and I snuggled against him during the movie."

"Maybe he's nervous or afraid you'll reject him."

Heather snorted. "He's a rockstar! Who would reject him?"

"Do I need to remind you of the first time you met him?" Mckenna pointed at her. "*You* rejected him."

"That's because I didn't know him." Heather scratched Molly's chin, and she lifted her head as her purrs became louder. "He has to know I'm crazy about him. I mean, I'm sure it's written all over my face."

Mckenna gave a knowing smile. "And it's written all over his face that he's crazy about you. Give him time."

"I just wish he would ask me to be his girlfriend."

"I have a feeling that conversation will happen before he leaves for New York."

Heather sighed, hoping her best friend was right.

Eva Rios, the Charlotte Children's Hospital community relations coordinator, met Alex and Heather in the hospital lobby the following afternoon. "We're so excited to have you, Mr. Kirwan," she said. "When your PR manager called yesterday, I almost fell out of my chair." Eva's silver high heels clacked while Alex and Heather followed her down the corridor. Heather carried a shopping bag full of puzzles, coloring books, and crayons for the younger children, as well as a bag of assorted LEGO and craft sets for the older children.

"Please call me Alex, and I'm glad it worked out with your schedule," he said.

Heather sneaked a glance at him walking beside her, and a thrill shot through her. She'd had a difficult time taking her eyes off him since he'd arrived at her house this morning, somehow even handsomer than usual. His eyes seemed bright and well rested, and his face was clean-shaven, accentuating his sharp jawline and high cheekbones. His tight blue jeans hugged his trim waist, while his gray short-sleeved Henley emphasized his muscular chest, shoulders, and biceps.

After he picked her up, they'd enjoyed breakfast at the small diner in the nearby town of Wadesboro, and they were both grateful no one recognized him. After breakfast, they headed to a local store to pick up some goodies for the children. Alex had donned a baseball cap and kept his head down as they quickly visited the toy department.

Heather noticed several customers do double takes when Alex passed by them, but she was relieved no one stopped him or made a scene. Heather was both impressed and touched by what he purchased for the children. The cashier seemed to study Alex when he paid for the toys, but the young woman kept her questions to herself. Toys in hand, they drove to the children's hospital in Uptown Charlotte.

Alex adjusted his acoustic guitar case in his right hand and reached for one of Heather's bags. "Let me take that from you." His hand brushed hers, and electricity skittered up her arm at the contact.

"It's okay." She shook her head. "I've got it."

Eva faced them as they moved down another hallway, where she stopped in front of a bank of elevators and pushed the up arrow. "We're always grateful when celebrities have time to spend with the children. We normally have athletes who visit. You're our first rockstar. What brings you to Charlotte?"

"I had a few days off, and I wanted to see Heather." He gifted Heather with a sweet smile, and her heart hammered in her chest.

A *ding* sounded, and the elevator door opened with a *whoosh*. Alex placed his hand on the open door and motioned for Heather and Eva to enter first.

Eva hit the button for the fourth floor and faced Alex and Heather. "Our kids are going to be thrilled to see you. Thank you again for taking the time to visit them. It means more than you know."

"You're welcome, but it honestly means a lot to me too," Alex said.

The elevator stopped on the fourth floor, and Heather followed Eva out into the hallway before Alex sidled up to them. They walked past a nurses' station where a group of folks worked on computers and talked on phones.

A young nurse dressed in pink scrubs decorated in Disney princesses looked up as Alex walked by. Her eyes widened before she tapped a male nurse standing beside her and whispered something in his ear.

"You're being recognized," Heather sang to Alex. "Check out the nurses' station."

He craned his neck over his shoulder and flashed a smile. When he waved, he set off a flurry of whispers and gasps. "It's just part of the job," he told Heather.

Eva stopped by a row of rooms and faced Heather and Alex. "I'll go into the patient's room first and ask if she's feeling up to visitors. If the answer is yes, then I'll call you."

"Perfect." Alex set his guitar case on the floor.

Eva knocked on the first patient's room. "Hello. May I come in?"

A soft voice sounded from inside the room, and Eva disappeared inside.

Heather peered down the hallway to where the nurses gathered to watch Alex. "I think you're going to cause a riot."

"Hopefully not a riot, but possibly a selfie session," he quipped through another one of his megawatt smiles. "I don't mind. I'm in awe of the work they do."

She looked up at him, and admiration swelled inside her.

Alex's eyes met hers and then narrowed. "Why are you looking at me like that?"

"Because I think you're the coolest guy on the planet."

He scoffed, shaking his head. "I'm definitely not the coolest guy." He ran a hand gently up and down her bare arm. "But you look beautiful in that yellow sundress."

"Thank you," she whispered, overwhelmed by the compliment.

"Alex," Eva called. "Come meet my friend Aubra."

He picked up his guitar case. "You ready, Heather?"

"Yes," she said. When he motioned for her to go in the door first, she shook her head. "You're the one everyone wants to see. You go ahead."

Alex pushed open the door, and Heather followed him into a hospital room where a skinny girl, who looked to be about twelve, lay on a bed. She had pale skin, dark hair, and large gray eyes and wore a pink hospital gown.

The girl gasped and sat up as Alex walked over to the side of her bed. "Y-you're—you're Alex Kirwan!" Then she turned to the woman sitting in a chair across the room. "Mom! That's Alex Kirwan!"

The mother, who had the same gray eyes and features, nodded as excitement overtook her face. "I see that."

"And you must be Aubra." Alex held his hand out to the girl. "I'm honored to meet you."

Aubra gaped and shook his hand.

Alex pointed to a nearby chair. "Would it be okay if I sat down and visited with you?"

"Yes, of course," Aubra exclaimed.

The girl's mother turned to Heather and grinned.

Alex sat on the chair and set his guitar down on the floor beside him. "How are you doing, Aubra?"

"Better now," the girl said with a laugh. "Kirwan is my favorite band."

Alex beamed. "Is that right? That makes me so happy."

"You brought a guitar?"

Alex opened the case and showed her his guitar. "I did."

Her eyes sparkled. "Would you sing for me?"

"I would love to. What would you like to hear?"

"How about 'Dance All Night'? It's my favorite."

"That's one of my favorites too." Alex lifted the guitar and a pick.

"Did you write it?"

Alex nodded. "Yes, I did, but Kayden and Jordan helped."

"Cool." Aubra grinned.

He set the guitar on his lap and strummed it a few times before clearing his throat. Then he closed his eyes as he sang, and the sweet, melodious sound of his voice embraced Heather.

She sank into a nearby chair as she took in the scene. Both Aubra and her mother watched with rapt attention while Alex performed. Eva stood by the door, where a few of the nurses from the station had gathered. All of them looked entranced with Alex and his song.

When he finished singing, the whole room clapped, and Alex bowed his head. His expression was humble and almost sheepish.

He turned his attention back to Aubra. "I'm so honored that I got to meet you today." He nodded toward Heather. "This is Heather. We brought a gift for you. Is that okay?"

Aubra's expression somehow became brighter. "You brought me a present?"

"We did." Heather carried the bag over with the toys for the older kids. "Do you like to make bracelets?"

"Oh yes!"

Heather pulled out a craft set for beaded jewelry. "Here you go."

"Thank you!" Aubra held it up. "Look at this, Mom."

Her mother's gray eyes seemed to glitter with tears. "That is awfully nice of you to make time to see children."

"It's truly an honor, ma'am," Alex said.

"Can we take a picture before you leave?" Aubra asked.

Alex set his guitar in the case. "I would love that." He closed the case and moved over to the bed. He put his arm around the girl and smiled as her mother took several photos with her phone. Then he signed a notepad for Aubra.

Heather felt another wave of affection for Alex and the genuine empathy and care in his eyes as he interacted with the girl.

"It was a pleasure meeting you," Alex told Aubra and her mother before shaking their hands. "I hope you feel better soon."

"Bye, Alex!" Aubra called after him as he started out the door.

As Heather walked with him to the next patient's room, she was overcome with the knowledge that she had fallen in love with this amazing man. He cared so deeply for his fans and wanted to make a difference in their lives—and she hoped to the depth of her bones that she could build a future with him.

17

What do you think of our small town?" Kirk Jenkins asked Alex as they sat on Heather and Mckenna's small deck later that evening.

Alex took a sip from his can of Coke. "It's great. I'm having a wonderful time."

And it was the truth. After spending most of the afternoon at the children's hospital, he and Heather had taken a windshield tour of Uptown Charlotte before driving back to Flowering Grove for supper. And now Heather and Mckenna were preparing the meal while he and Kirk got acquainted on the deck.

"I'm sure you've been to much more exciting places while traveling with your band," Kirk said.

"That's true, but to be honest, I prefer a small town over a big city."

"Then you're in luck." Kirk held up his can of Coke as if to toast him. "Welcome to Small Town, America."

Alex laughed. "What do you do for a living?"

"Nothing as impressive as you. I work in insurance."

Alex set his can on the table between their chairs. "That's an admirable profession."

"I suppose so." Kirk shrugged. "It pays the bills."

"How long have you been seeing Mckenna?"

"A couple of months now. I think it took me about six months to convince her to go out with me. When she finally said yes, I thought I had heard her wrong."

Alex chuckled. "I can relate to rejection for sure. Heather didn't like me when she first met me."

"You're kidding!"

"No, I'm not." He snorted. "She told me she couldn't come to my concert because she would be busy washing her hair."

Kirk laughed. "That sounds like Heather."

"Thankfully, she came, and we struck up a conversation after the show." Alex explained how she had visited his dressing room and left her phone behind, then how he had delivered her phone the next day. "I somehow found the courage to ask for her number."

Kirk's dark eyebrows rose. "You're a rockstar but were afraid to ask for her phone number?"

"She had already rejected me once. I wasn't looking forward to giving her a second chance."

"Wow." Kirk swiped his hand over his chin. "I guess we all deal with that fear, huh?"

"We do. So how would you describe your relationship with Mack?"

Kirk turned back toward the sliding glass door, then faced Alex again. "I'm crazy about her. I'm pretty sure she feels the same way."

Alex nodded.

"And you and Heather?"

"She's really special. I'm hoping she'll agree to give our relationship a chance. Dating me isn't easy. My schedule is a lot to deal with."

"From what Mack has told me, I think Heather will be more than willing to make it work."

Alex smiled. "I hope you're right."

The sliding door whooshed open, releasing the delicious smells of lasagna and garlic bread.

Mckenna stuck her head out. "Supper is ready. I hope you're hungry."

As if on cue, Alex's stomach growled. He walked into the kitchen, where the women had already set the table. A bowl of salad, a basket of garlic bread, and a pan of lasagna waited in the center.

"Everything looks wonderful," Alex told Heather.

She smiled and tapped the back of a chair. "Please have a seat."

He sat, and Heather settled on a chair beside him. Kirk and Mckenna joined them, and soon they were filling their plates.

"Tell us all about your trip to the children's hospital today," Mckenna said before passing the basket of bread to Kirk.

Heather set a piece of lasagna on her plate and then scooped a piece for Alex. "It was amazing." Her eyes shone as she spoke. "Alex is so great with the kids. I wish you could have seen their faces, Mack. The kids were glowing when he walked into the room. Alex was calm as he sang for them, signed autographs, and took photos. It was so kind."

"You're exaggerating," Alex told her.

"No, I'm not. I'm so glad you asked me to go. I enjoyed seeing that side of you."

Alex's eyes locked on Heather's, and he felt an invisible magnet pulling his heart to hers.

"I think it's just awesome that you wanted to spend time with those kids. I'm sure you brought joy and hope to them," Mckenna said, breaking through Alex's thoughts.

Alex's eyes snapped to hers. "Honestly, it's a passion of mine. I wish I had more opportunities to do it."

"How did it become your passion?" Heather asked.

Alex placed his fork on his plate while memories of Carson filled his mind. "When I was a kid, the little boy who lived next door had leukemia, and my parents insisted I visit him every week."

"Oh no." Heather gasped while both Mckenna and Kirk frowned. "I'm so sorry to hear that."

"When I went to see him, I'd play games with him and watch cartoons. At first it was awkward, but then I began to look forward to it. Those memories of Carson always stayed with me, which is why I want to continue meeting kids like him."

"What happened to Carson?" Heather asked.

Alex shook his head. "I don't know. His parents moved out of our neighborhood to be closer to a cancer center. When I think of him, I hope and pray he's doing well."

Kirk took another piece of garlic bread. "Well, I think it's great that you make time to visit kids in hospitals. I'm sure they appreciate it."

"Not only the kids enjoyed seeing him." Heather lifted her fork in the air. "He also signed autographs for the nurses and a couple of doctors. They were just as excited as the kids."

"I bet!" Mckenna cut up a piece of lasagna. "Oh, Heather, I've been meaning to tell you that my parents are keeping an eye out for a storefront for you. They might have some options soon."

Heather's smile faded, and she gave her best friend a pointed look. Then she turned her attention to the pile of salad on her plate.

Curious, Alex hoped she'd look up and meet his stare, but she kept her eyes locked on her meal. He would have to ask her about it later.

"Alex," Kirk began, "are you done with the tour?"

With a sigh, Alex shook his head. "No, we're not. We're

heading to New York City and then New Jersey. Then we're doing the Midwest leg. We're eventually heading to Europe too."

"Europe?" Mckenna exclaimed. "You must be so excited."

"I'm actually looking forward to the end of it. I'd like to concentrate on more local gigs and start living a more normal life." Alex was grateful when Heather finally looked up at him and smiled.

Kirk peppered Alex with questions about the tour, songwriting, and how Alex got started in the music business. When they were done eating, Heather brought out a chocolate chip cheesecake for dessert, and Mckenna brewed hot coffee. After they enjoyed their dessert, Alex and Kirk filled the dishwasher while Heather wiped down the table and Mckenna stowed the leftovers.

Then they moved out to the deck and talked and laughed while they watched the sunset. Bright hues of orange, pink, and red streaked across the spring sky, and the cicadas serenaded them with their nightly song.

Once darkness had fallen, Alex took Heather's hand, and she walked him out to his car. "I had another fantastic day," he said.

"I did too. I enjoyed watching you at the hospital," she said. "It was the most inspiring thing I've ever seen."

"I'm grateful you went with me."

"I have a confession though."

"A confession?" He searched her eyes, wondering if she had any idea how beautiful she was with her smattering of freckles, shining dark hair, long neck, ivory skin, and beautiful smile.

She held up her thumb and forefinger. "I was a teensy bit jealous when those pretty nurses were fawning all over you and begging for your autograph and photo."

"Let me assure you: You have nothing to be jealous of. It's all just part of the persona; it's not who I really am." He rested his hand on her shoulder. "And they don't really know me, the real me, like you do."

She seemed to study him. "You said that helping kids is your passion, and you've mentioned more than once that you don't like touring. What if you committed more time to your passion?"

Alex leaned back against his rental car. "I've thought about that, but I feel obligated to my brothers."

"How do you feel obligated to them?"

He pressed a hand to his chest. "I guess since I'm the oldest, and my dad is gone, I've always felt it was my job to make sure they're taken care of, which means that if the band is touring, then I need to be a part of it. I have to make sure the band is thriving and they have what they need. When it's time to step away from the band, then I can do what I want to do—but right now, we're a package deal."

"Hmm." She folded her hands in front of her yellow sundress. "I guess that makes sense, but they're grown men, and you're entitled to follow your dreams too."

"Speaking of dreams . . ." He recalled her reaction to Mckenna when she brought up the storefront. "I have a question for you now."

"What?"

"You seemed upset when Mack mentioned your store during supper. Did you change your mind about opening it?"

She frowned and looked down at her white sandals. "You noticed that."

"Heather, you should know by now that you can trust me with the truth. No judgment."

"I know." She sighed. "I told you that Mack's parents own most of the retail space around here."

"I remember."

"She thinks I should ask you for help, and that we should go into business together."

He smiled. "I love the idea."

"No, no, no." She shook her head.

"Why not?"

"Because I want to do this on my own. And I don't want to be a woman who uses you for your money."

He rested his hands on her hips. "I don't feel like you're using me. If I did, then I wouldn't be here."

"I would never use you, Alex." Her expression was earnest.

"I know." He touched her hand. "I'd better go. You need to get a good night's sleep because we're going to be out late tomorrow."

"Doing what?" Heather grinned.

"It's still a surprise. Good night, Heather." He smiled as he climbed into the car, feeling certain his secret plan was going to knock her socks off.

⌒

"Now keep your eyes closed," Alex instructed from the driver's seat of his rental car the following evening.

Heather folded her arms across her chest and slumped back in the passenger seat. "For how long?"

"For as long as I tell you to." She could hear the smile in his voice.

She turned toward him but was careful to keep her eyes closed. "You're awfully bossy."

"Yes, I suppose I am." He chuckled. "But trust me, Heather, this is worth the suspense."

She blew out a dramatic sigh, but she also couldn't hold

back a smile. They had spent another wonderful day together—talking, laughing, sharing secrets, and taking selfies as they picnicked at Flowering Grove Park. He had brought his guitar and sung to her, sharing a few of his father's songs. Then they went back to her house, sat on her deck, and talked some more. She felt so close to him—but one thing was still missing.

They had held hands and shared hugs throughout the day, and Alex had looped his arm around her shoulders while they walked together—but he still hadn't kissed her.

She found the affection confusing. He seemed to regard her as more than a friend, so why hadn't he taken the final step of kissing her and asking her to be his girlfriend? She enjoyed every moment they spent together, but the anticipation was driving her crazy.

The hum of the engine and road noise filled the car.

"Could we at least turn on some music?" she asked. "Preferably Kirwan."

He groaned. "Anything but that drivel."

She laughed.

Soon nineties rock music began blasting through the speakers.

"I figured you'd appreciate the grunge satellite station," he said. "You need a break from that Kirwan music."

She reached over and patted his arm, enjoying the feel of hard muscle under her palm. "Thank you."

Heather sang along with the radio, careful to keep her eyes closed for most of the ride. She peeked a few times, though, and decided they were driving along Interstate 485.

After what felt like a long ride, the car slowed. Heather assumed they had exited the highway.

"Am I allowed to look now?"

"Soon."

"How did you find your way without using your phone's GPS?" she asked.

"I memorized the directions."

She smiled. "That's impressive!"

He chuckled, then drove in silence for a little longer. When the car came to a stop, he said, "You can open your eyes now."

Heather did as instructed, and her mouth dropped open when she found they were parked in front of the "Welcome to Carolina Adventureland" sign. She angled her body toward him. "You brought me to my favorite amusement park?"

"Is that okay?" His expression seemed hesitant.

"Of course it is, but what about the crowds?"

"I took care of that. They're staying open just for us."

She sat speechless for a moment, then held up her hand. "Wait a minute. You paid the park to stay open late for only you and me?"

"That's right."

Heather's heart expanded, and her eyes filled with happy tears. "I-I don't know what to say, Alex. This is the most romantic gesture I've ever received."

Alex held his hand out to her. "Let's make our own best night ever."

"I'd love to."

He drove and parked the car closer to the entrance, and then they walked in hand in hand. The air was warm, and the sky above them was dark and dotted with bright stars that seemed to sparkle for only them.

A tall man wearing a blue collared shirt embroidered with the Carolina Adventureland logo met them at the gate. "You must be Alex Kirwan. I'm Chet. We're excited to have you with us tonight."

Alex shook his hand. "I'm thrilled to be here. This is Heather."

"Welcome," Chet said. "As you requested, most of the rides are running, and we'll stay open for three hours. We also have drinks and snacks available for you at a few stations throughout the park." He held up his hand. "Oh, and the staff has agreed to keep your visit confidential."

"Perfect. Thank you." Alex turned to Heather. "Ready to give me a tour of your favorite amusement park?"

She pointed to the left. "The best roller coaster is this way."

She grabbed his hand and tugged him, knocking him off-balance for a moment. She pulled him through the entrance and past a pretzel stand, coffee shop, and chocolate shop, the delicious smells drifting over them as they hurried over to the dragon ride.

Heather stopped at the entrance and pointed at the green steel coaster. "Ta-da!" She laughed. "This is the Dragon."

"Wow." Alex rubbed his jaw as his gaze moved heavenward.

"I believe I read once that it reaches a speed of eighty miles per hour, and that the first drop is more than three hundred feet."

"That's . . . quite a drop."

She lifted a coy eyebrow. "Are you man enough to ride it with me?"

"Is that a challenge, Baker Girl?"

"Uh-huh."

He held his hand over his heart. "Well, I can't back down from a challenge."

"Great! Let's go!" She took him by the hand again, and like giddy teenagers, they raced up the stairs to the platform.

18

⌒

A young man with dark skin, spiked black hair, and an eyebrow ring grinned at them. He wore a Carolina Adventureland uniform, and his nametag read "Corbin." "You're Alex Kirwan," he said. "We were told a celebrity had rented out the place and doubled our pay for the night. Thanks so much. I'm a big fan."

"Thank *you*." Alex rubbed Heather's back. "We appreciate it."

"Climb on in and make sure those belts are tight."

Heather guided Alex to the first car.

Alex's blue eyes widened. "The front row?"

"You said you were man enough," she teased.

Corbin chuckled. "I think she's daring you."

"Well, I have to take the dare," Alex told him. "If I don't and my brothers find out, I'll never hear the end of it."

Heather and Corbin laughed.

Alex joined her in the front row, and they fastened their safety belts. Corbin gave the belts a tug, making sure they were properly restrained, then turned toward the control booth and gave a thumbs-up.

"Welcome to the Dragon Coaster! Who's ready to fly?" a feminine voice called over the loudspeaker.

194

Heather clapped and cheered. Then she turned toward Alex beside her, but he shook his head.

"I'm not so sure about this," he said.

Reaching over, she took his warm hand in hers. "Remember, this is our best night ever."

"Right," he said.

The roller coaster car jolted forward, and when he squeezed her hand, her stomach swooped. They shared a nervous look as the green car began climbing up, up, up at a steep angle.

"I'm starting to rethink everything," Alex quipped as he shut his eyes.

Heather grinned in anticipation. "Don't you trust me?"

"Um." He opened one eye. "Maybe?"

She laughed again, adoring their playful banter. She'd never experienced such an easy relationship with a man. Jeff, her ex-boyfriend, had never been so fun-loving with her. Alex was special.

The car reached the top of the hill and hesitated for a moment before it plunged, roaring down the steep incline.

Heather sucked in a breath and then screamed as Alex released her hand. The roller coaster twisted and turned, jerking her back and forth, and she shrieked and laughed. She peered over at Alex, and he howled.

The roller coaster came up around a turn, and a light flashed through the air like a bolt of lightning, snapping their photo. After a few more twists and turns, the car returned to the platform and came to a stop with a jolt.

Alex hooted and clapped.

"You liked it?" Heather asked as she unfastened her safety belt.

He unhitched his belt and climbed out from the seat. "Yes. What's next?"

"Let's go get our photo and head to the next roller coaster."

They thanked Corbin and jogged down the steps to the store below the platform, where a young woman stood at the counter, smiling wide as they approached.

"Oh my goodness, are you Alex Kirwan?" she asked before pushing her long, wavy blond hair over her thin shoulders. Her nametag said "Ariel."

He smiled. "Yes, and it's nice to meet you, Ariel." Then he looked up at the screen and laughed heartily at their photo. "I look terrified."

Heather couldn't stop her own laughter as she took in the photo of them both screaming as they came over the hill.

"Would you like the photo?" the young woman asked.

"Yes, please." Alex purchased the photo and downloaded it to an app on his phone. "I'll send it to you later."

Heather touched her chin. "You know, I could blackmail you with this one."

"I figured you'd say that." He grinned. "Now, take me to another fantastic ride."

They spent the next few hours riding roller coasters, the Ferris wheel, bumper cars, a runaway train, and the log flume. Alex purchased their photos on each of the rides, and as they strolled through the park, they enjoyed popcorn, sodas, and large pretzels.

By the end of the night, Heather's legs and feet ached, and her throat was sore from laughing, yelling, and hooting on the rides. As she held Alex's arm on the way to the exit, she felt like she was floating.

"How did we do with our best night ever?" He encircled her back with his arm and pulled her against his side.

Heather pretended to consider the question. "Hmm. I don't know . . ."

"What?" He stopped and faced her, amusement glittering in his gorgeous blue eyes. "This doesn't rank as one of your best nights ever?"

She shook her head as her smile faded. "No. This ranks as the best week of my life."

Alex's expression became serious, and he took her hands and tugged her to him. "I agree." He traced his finger down her cheek and pushed a thick tendril of hair behind her ear. "Thank you."

"For what?" she whispered, her pulse beginning to race. She craved the feel of his kiss more than she craved air.

Kiss me! Kiss me, Alex! Please!

"For being you." His gaze roved over her features and lingered on her lips before returning to her eyes. "I'm so glad I came to see you."

"I am too."

He steered her out to where his car waited. They climbed back in, and he began driving back to Interstate 77.

While they rode, she relaxed in the seat and looked over toward him, taking in his handsome profile. She breathed a deep sigh and tried to commit it to memory.

"What's on your mind?" he asked.

"I can't believe tomorrow is your last day here."

He frowned. "I know."

"When will I see you again?"

He rested his elbow on the door and pushed his hand through his thick hair. "My schedule picks up again this coming weekend, so I need to figure that out."

She hugged her arms to her waist and tried to imagine how she would adjust to sharing only emails, texts, and phone calls with him after getting used to seeing him each day this week.

He cut his eyes to her. "I'm having a wonderful time."

"Me too." *And I'm falling in love with you, Alex.* She trembled at the thought of Alex going back on the road. When he left Flowering Grove, he would be taking a piece of her heart with him.

⌒

Alex held Heather's hand as they walked down Main Street the following afternoon. They had gone out to breakfast and then decided to spend the day walking around town and talking. He longed for the hours to slow down since he would board a flight to New York later that evening. The week had flown by too quickly, and he planned to cherish every moment he had left with Heather.

After dropping her off at her house last night, he had returned to the inn and then tossed and turned in bed, frustrated with himself. He knew he was running out of time on this trip to ask her whether they could make their relationship official.

He was certain she cared for him, but he worried about the mechanics. His erratic schedule and his fame might get in the way of having a meaningful and sustainable relationship with her. Still, he wanted Heather in his life. His heart craved her company, her presence.

Alex hoped and prayed she would give him a chance. If she did, he would prove to her that he would do everything in his power to make her happy.

He adjusted his University of Oregon ball cap on his head and stepped out of the way as a young couple walking their tan-and-black German shepherd down the sidewalk passed him and Heather. He swiveled toward the opposite side of the street, then stopped walking when he spotted a bakery he hadn't noticed before.

"The Sugary Sweet Bakery," he said, reading the sign. "Sounds good."

Heather pushed her sunglasses up on her petite nose. "It's been there for as long as I can remember."

Alex looked up and down the street, taking in Miller's Dry Cleaners, the Fairy Tale Bridal Shop, and Swanson's Hardware. "This is such a neat little town. It reminds me of my hometown of Cascade." He met her curious gaze. "You'll have to come and visit sometime."

Something unreadable flickered across her pretty face. "I'd love that."

"And this street is where you'd like to open your bookstore and bakery, right?"

"Yes." She frowned. "But as you can see, none of the shops are available. Plus I don't even know if I could afford the rent." When he opened his mouth to respond, she cut him off. "Alex, we talked about this. I truly appreciate your offer to help, but I really want to do this on my own."

He smiled. "You're stubborn, which is one of the many things I find so intriguing about you."

"Thank you." She took his hand in hers once again, then tipped her head toward a store behind him. "We should check out the Treasure Hunting Antique Mall. I went to school with the owner, Christine Nicholson. Well, she was Christine Sawyer back then. I always find something fun and unusual there."

He pushed open the door. "Lead the way."

They entered the store, and Heather waved to a pretty blond at the counter who looked to be in her late twenties.

"Hi, Christine!" she called to the woman. Next to Christine stood a tall man with curly dark hair. "Hi, Brent."

They both smiled and waved before turning to address another customer.

Heather leaned in closer as they started down an aisle, and Alex breathed in the wonderful vanilla scent of her shampoo or possibly lotion. "Christine wound up marrying her twin sister's ex-boyfriend. When he came back to town, they connected. They seem really happy. She runs her store, and they also flip houses together."

"That's cool." Alex peered into a booth with a vintage turntable and a shelf of vinyl records. "Let's stop here." He began flipping through the records, taking in albums from the fifties, sixties, seventies, and eighties.

"Do you collect old vinyls?" She stood beside him.

He nodded. "Yes, but I never seem to make time to listen to them."

"I guess that means old records would be a good gift for you."

He looked down at her beautiful smile. "You don't need to buy me anything."

Heather scoffed. "You gave me an ARC from my favorite author. See? I know the lingo now too. Then you rented out an entire amusement park for me last night, but you say I don't need to give you any gifts. I told you I'm not going to use you, Alex."

Her eyes widened for a moment, and she looked around the store. Then she cringed as she faced him again. "I'm sorry. I shouldn't say your name when we're in public."

"It's okay. I'm not the only Alex on the planet."

"No, but you're a famous one." She lifted her chin. "Now back to our previous conversation. I do owe you a gift."

He pretended to consider this. "I can think of something you can give me."

"What?" She clasped her hands together.

"How about a Barbecue Pit t-shirt?"

She blinked. "All you want is a t-shirt from my parents' restaurant?"

The corner of his mouth lifted. "Yes."

"We can stop by the restaurant to get one after we finish here."

They browsed the store, taking in booths full of vintage clothes, jewelry, kitchenware, tools, artwork, and furniture. Alex got a kick out of watching Heather show him interesting items and share stories about her grandparents, who used to live nearby.

Later they entered through the back of the restaurant, where her parents worked filling orders during the lunch rush.

"Well, look at what the cat dragged in," Russell joked from the grill. "How are you enjoying Flowering Grove, Alex?"

"I'm having a great time."

Heather gave his hand a squeeze. "What size do you wear?"

"Usually a large," Alex told her.

"I'll be right back." Heather scooted through the doors leading to the dining room.

Russell placed a pile of pulled pork onto a plate and then added baked beans, grilled corn on the cob, and a piece of cornbread before setting it on the counter. "What have you two been up to this week?"

"We've spent some time in the park and visited the stores on Main Street. And last night we went to Carolina Adventureland." Alex hopped up on a stool.

Russell began filling another order. "How did you like our amusement park?"

"It was great." Alex explained how he had arranged for the park to stay open for them for a few hours last night. "I didn't want to deal with any crowds."

Russell studied him. "You rented out the entire amusement park for my daughter?"

"Yes." Alex rubbed his elbow, suddenly feeling self-conscious.

"Wow."

Nora swept in from the office. "Alex! Russ and I were just talking about you and Heather."

As if on cue, Heather returned to the large kitchen holding a light blue t-shirt. "I thought this one would match your eyes." She seemed nervous or embarrassed as she handed it to him.

"Thank you." Alex held up the shirt and examined the restaurant's logo. Then he hung the shirt over his shoulder. "It's perfect."

Nora washed her hands at a sink across the kitchen. "Today is your last day in Flowering Grove, right, Alex?"

"Unfortunately, yes." He nodded and noticed Heather's lips turn down in a frown.

Nora dried her hands with a towel. "Today is our early day at the restaurant. Our relief cooks will be here at four thirty. We'd love to have you both over for supper." She held her hands up toward Heather. "No pressure."

"That's a great idea," Russell said. "I'll pull out the grill, and we can have burgers."

"What do you think?" Heather asked Alex.

"I'd love to spend time with your folks if it's okay with you."

"That sounds like fun." Heather turned to her parents. "How about I bring dessert?"

Her father shook a finger at her. "You'd better!"

Back at Heather's house, Alex sat beside her on the deck while they drank sweet tea and ate sub sandwiches from the Flowering Grove Deli. He looked out over her small backyard and breathed in the scent of honeysuckle.

When his phone chimed with a text, he pulled it from his pocket and found a message from his mother.

MOM: How's your visit going? If you have time for a call, I'd
love to meet Heather.

"Is one of your brothers checking on you?"

He locked the phone with a *click* and took a sip of sweet tea.
"It was actually my mom. She'd like to meet you."

"I'd love to meet her when I visit you in Cascade sometime."

"I think she wants to meet you on a video call."

"Oh." Heather reached up and touched her hair. "Now?"

He nodded.

"I don't know." She cringed. "I'd need to go fix my makeup
and run a brush through my hair." She stood, and he placed his
hand on her arm.

"You're perfect. Really."

She sank down onto the deck chair and picked at a piece of
lint on her denim shorts.

"Heather?" He leaned closer. "What's up?"

Her shoulders slumped. "I just . . ."

"You just what?" When she remained silent, he said, "Do I
need to remind you that you can be honest with me? After all, I
poured my lonely heart out to you in the very first email I sent you,
and nothing you tell me can be more embarrassing than that."

Heather sat up and faced him. "What if your mom doesn't
like me?"

"Seriously?" He scoffed. "She'll love you."

"Are you sure?"

"You make me happy, and that's all moms care about, right?"

She nodded.

"Does that mean we can talk to her?"

Her beautiful smile finally returned. "Yes."

"Thank you." Alex unlocked his phone and hit the button
to FaceTime his mom, and she answered almost immediately.

"Alex! How are things in North Carolina?"

"They're great." He angled the phone toward Heather. "Mom, this is Heather Gordon. Heather, this is my mom, Shannon Kirwan."

Heather waved. "Hi!"

"Heather! I'm so excited to finally meet the woman who has captured my son's attention. It's been so long since he's dated someone."

Alex groaned. "Mom . . ."

Heather grinned. "It's nice to meet you too, Mrs. Kirwan."

"Oh, sweetie. Call me Shannon. I hear you like to bake."

"That's true. I bake all of the desserts at my family's restaurant," Heather said before sharing details of the menu.

"Oh, that sounds delicious," Mom said when Heather was done. "When Alex brings you out here, we can bake together."

Heather seemed to glow at the idea. "I would like that very much."

"How's Elvis?" Alex asked.

"He's doing fantastic." Mom looked away from the camera. "Come here, boy. Say hi to Alex and Heather." A tinkling sound came through the phone, and she angled the screen toward the dog and his wagging tail.

"Aww," Heather crooned. "What a cutie. Hi, Elvis."

Alex leaned over toward Heather. "Hey, boy," he said, and the dog barked.

"He misses you, Alex." Mom turned the phone back toward herself again. "Did you have fun at the amusement park last night?"

Heather looked surprised. "You knew about that?"

"Oh yes. Alex worked hard on that surprise."

Embarrassment heated the tips of Alex's ears, but Heather didn't seem to notice as she described what a wonderful time they'd had.

"What are your plans today?" Mom asked.

"We're having supper with my parents. I'm going to make Alex help me bake some of my Bookish Brownies."

"Not only do I love the name, but they sound scrumptious. Have one for me."

Alex squeezed into the frame again. "How are Kayden and Jordan?"

"They were here last night. We had supper with Charlie." Mom smiled.

Heather looked confused. "Who's Charlie?"

"My mom's boyfriend."

Mom shook her head. "We're just friends, and your brothers seem to approve of him."

"I need to meet him and tell you if I approve," Alex said, and his mother had the nerve to laugh.

"You'll meet him when you're back home," Mom said. "Well, I won't keep you. Enjoy your supper tonight. And I'm sure I'll see you in person soon, Heather."

"I hope so. Goodbye, Shannon." Heather waved.

"Take care, Mom. Let me know if you need anything," Alex said before disconnecting the call. He slipped the phone into his pocket, and when he looked up, Heather was watching him with interest. "What?"

"Are you upset that your mom is dating?"

"No." He chuckled. "Why would you think that?"

"You just seem concerned about her."

"I'll always be concerned about her. She's my mom."

Heather's eyebrows came together. "Hmm."

"All right." He sat up straight. "Please tell me what you're thinking."

"Your reaction was just a little strange. Are you worried she'll get married again?"

"No, it's not that." He looked down at his empty plate and tried to make sense of his emotions.

She touched his shoulder. "Alex, you can trust me."

"I know." He sighed. "I just feel like it's my job to take care of her, and sometimes I worry about her rushing into a relationship."

"Has she dated much?"

Alex shook his head. "Not in years."

"Are you afraid she'll try to replace your dad?"

"No, no. I'm twenty-nine years old. I'm not afraid of a man replacing my father." He moved his hands down his thighs and considered what was bugging him. "I'm just worried that she'll get hurt. I don't want some guy to promise her a happy life and then break her heart. I just want to protect her."

Heather rested her hand on his bicep. "That's really sweet, Alex."

"But?"

"But she deserves to find her own happiness. We all take a chance when we risk our hearts."

He nodded. "That's very true."

They stared at each other for a moment, and awareness crackled between them. He started to reach for her arm but then stopped, his courage waning. Just as Heather had said, he was afraid of risking his own heart.

Heather stood and stacked their empty plates before pulling open the sliding glass door. "How about we make those brownies?"

"Sure." Alex gathered up their empty cups and then followed her into the house, all the while trying to come up with a plan to kiss her tonight before he completely ran out of time.

19

Those burgers were outstanding, Russ," Alex told Heather's father later that evening while he sat at the kitchen table with Heather, her parents, and Wendy. "And so was the potato salad."

He had enjoyed a lively conversation with Heather's family while they ate the delicious burgers. Heather's parents had a great sense of humor, and they kept the family laughing while they shared hilarious stories of their early days at the restaurant, sweet family memories, and Heather's childhood.

Wendy kept up a constant flow of questions about Alex's band, his tour, and his youngest brother. Alex enjoyed every moment of it, even though he frequently caught Heather shooting her younger sister warning looks that seemed to tell her to keep quiet.

Nora began piling up their dirty dinner plates. "We're so glad you agreed to spend the evening with us."

"It's been my pleasure." Alex stood and gathered up the utensils.

Heather swatted his hand away. "You're our guest. I'll take care of that."

"I really don't mind helping."

"Alex," Russell said, "why don't you join me in the garage? I'd like to show you that old truck I told you about."

"Of course." Alex cut his gaze to Heather, who looked as confused as he felt. She gave him an encouraging expression before he followed her father out the back door, which led to a two-car garage.

Russell sauntered to the far side of the garage and stood by a midnineties Ford F-150 pickup truck. He rested his hand on the side of the truck bed and then smiled over at Alex. "You mentioned that you have your father's old Ford. This one belonged to mine."

Alex gave a low whistle as he took in the pristine two-toned truck, which was painted red and white. "This is gorgeous." He ran his hand over the hood and then leaned against it. "You must treasure it."

"Every time I drive it, I smile and remember so many of the good times my dad and I had together." He seemed lost in the past for a moment, and then his expression became somber. "I'm sorry you lost your father. I still miss mine every day."

"Thank you."

"I'm sure he's very proud of your brothers and you."

Alex nodded. "That means a lot."

Russell crossed his arms over his chest and tilted his head. "I can tell Heather is very fond of you."

"It's mutual."

The older man pursed his lips. "She's stubborn and outspoken, but when she cares about someone, she gives her all."

Alex swallowed, preparing himself for a lecture or an admonishment.

"You're a very successful man, and I can tell that if you want something, you're able to find a way to get it." Russell's kind but serious eyes bored into Alex. "I also get the feeling that you're humble and genuine. But, Alex, I need you to make me a promise."

"Yes, sir. Anything."

"Heather puts up a tough exterior, but deep down, she's still my little girl. Promise me you will be careful with her precious heart."

"Russ, I promise." Then he rubbed at a spot on his cheek. "I actually plan to ask her to be my girlfriend before I leave for the airport tonight. If she doesn't say yes, I'll be crushed."

The older man patted Alex's shoulder. "Considering the way my daughter looks at you, I don't think you have anything to worry about."

"I hope you're right."

"We've enjoyed your visit, and you're welcome here anytime."

"Thank you," Alex said, grateful for the hospitality of Heather's parents.

Sadness rushed over Heather as Alex steered his rental car toward her house later that night. In less than an hour, Alex would be on his way to the airport and flying to New York City, and out of her life for who knew how long. She felt a painful squeeze in her chest with each light pole they passed.

The sky was dark, and stars already glittered above them. She couldn't help thinking that Alex fit in seamlessly with her family as he laughed at her father's funny stories. In no way had it felt like his first dinner at their table.

But it was silly for her to dwell on the future when she still wasn't even sure how he felt about her. Despite sharing another perfect day with him, he still hadn't kissed her or told her he cared about her. What was holding him back?

He cut his eyes to her. "What's on your mind?"

"I was just thinking about supper." She frowned. "I'm so sorry Wendy wouldn't stop asking you about Kayden. I was ready to tell her to be quiet."

He grinned. "Would you believe I'm used to that?"

"Tell me that's not true."

"Oh, it is!" He shook his head.

"Doesn't that bother you?"

"Not at all. I'm fine being the boring older brother."

"You're not boring, Alex." She rested her hand on his arm and relished the feel of his taut muscles.

When he steered into her driveway and shifted the car into Park, another wave of sorrow hit her hard. Soon he would drive away again, and she would have only phone calls, emails, and texts to cherish instead of his physical presence.

"I'd like to walk you inside," he said.

She glanced at the clock on the dashboard. "You don't have much time before you have to leave for the airport."

"I know." Alex killed the engine and pushed the door open. "But I want to give you a proper goodbye."

A thrill raced through her as she met him at the front of the car, and then they walked up the sidewalk together. Since Mckenna was working late at the salon, the house was dark. She unlocked the door and stepped inside, where her two cats greeted her with a chorus of loud meows.

Heather flipped on the family room lights and pitched her purse onto the couch. "I have something for you." She dashed into the kitchen and retrieved a container of cookies from the counter. Then she double-timed it back to the family room, where Alex stood by the sofa, petting Jet as he blinked up at him.

She held the container out to Alex. "Here are some cookies for the road. I call them Storybook Snickerdoodles."

"Thank you." He took the container from her, and his expression became warm as something unreadable flickered over it.

Her throat swelled, and she tried to swallow. "Thank you for coming to see me." Her voice was ragged and hoarse.

Alex set the container of cookies down, and his expression simmered. He took her hands in his and rolled his thumbs over her palms. His touch left goose bumps rippling in its wake.

"I had a wonderful time, and I can't wait to see you again." Then he cupped his hands to her cheeks and brushed his lips over hers.

Desire roared through her veins as she lost herself in the feel of his mouth caressing hers. She wrapped her arms around his neck, and he pulled her close, resting his hands on her hips. Her knees weakened, and she held on to his shoulders for balance.

Alex deepened the kiss, and a moan escaped from deep in her chest. She lost track of everything as the world around them fell away. Her hands moved to the nape of his neck and her fingertips raked through his soft hair.

When he broke the kiss, she continued to grip his shoulders, working to slow her pulse.

"I've wanted to do that since I got here on Monday," he confessed.

"What took you so long?"

She was almost certain he was blushing. "I was trying to work up the courage, and now I have to ask you something."

The air stilled in her lungs.

"Heather, would you consider making our relationship official?" He huffed out a breath. "What I mean is, will you be my girlfriend?"

"Yes," she said quickly. "I thought you would never ask."

"You know my life is crazy, and I'm not sure what our relationship will look like." He frowned. "I don't even know when

I'll see you again, but I can always send you a ticket to come and spend a long weekend with me somewhere if you want."

"We can make it work."

"If the media finds out about you, it might become a circus. I'll do everything I can to protect you from it."

"I understand. I will too."

His expression relaxed. "Thank goodness. I was so worried you'd say no." He leaned down and kissed her again, sending her stomach into a wild swirl. Then he stepped back and frowned. "I have to go."

He gave Jet a final pat on the head and picked up the container of cookies before threading his fingers with hers. Then they walked to his car together, and he turned to face her. "Are you going to watch *Good Day USA* tomorrow?"

"Of course."

"Every time I touch my chin like this," he began, touching his chin, "that's the signal that I'm thinking of you."

Happiness bloomed in her chest. "I love that."

He hesitated as if he was going to say something, but then he kissed her again. "I don't want to leave you."

"If you miss your flight, then Robyn will make you leave this earth."

He laughed. "That is true." He climbed into the car, started the engine, and rolled the window down.

"Thank you for everything, Alex," Heather told him. "This week has been a dream come true."

"I feel the same way." He held his hand out to her, and she grasped it.

"Text me when you land and when you get to your hotel. I don't care what time it is. I'll worry until I hear from you."

"Yes, dear," he teased. "And you'd better start reading. We'll have another book club meeting soon."

"I can't wait. Please thank Tristan for the wonderful book."

"I will."

"Take care, Dorky Rockstar."

"You too, my gorgeous Baker Girl." He winked at her. "Good night."

She stood in the driveway until his taillights disappeared into the darkness, then she danced all the way into the house.

When she got inside, Heather picked up Jet and twirled around the room. "Alex kissed me! And asked me to be his girlfriend!" she sang as the cat flattened his ears on his head and watched her with eyes wide.

***

At the airport, Alex kept his baseball cap pulled down low as he made his way through priority check-in and hurried to his gate. He found a private corner away from the crowd awaiting the flight, leaned his guitar case against the wall, and set his backpack down beside it. Alex was careful to keep his back to the crowd and hoped no one would recognize him.

When his phone chimed with a text, he found a message from his mother.

MOM: Have a safe trip to NYC. Btw I love Heather. You have great taste and so does she.

Alex chuckled and texted: Thank you.

MOM: I approve. Did you finally make it official?

ALEX: I did.

MOM: Can't wait to meet her in person. Talk soon.

ALEX: Thanks, Mom. Miss you.

He slouched against the wall and peeked at the digital message board at the gate. Thankfully, he would be boarding soon.

He opened his messages and shot off a text to Tristan: Hey, buddy. Thank you so much for the ARCs. Heather is thrilled. I'm getting ready to board a flight to NYC. Hope you're doing well.

He slipped the phone back into his pocket. A moment later, it started ringing. He pulled it out and was surprised to see Tristan's name on the screen. "What's up?"

"I know you're about to hop on a flight, but I have some news. I've wanted to call, but I knew you were busy in North Carolina."

"What's the news?"

"Justine is pregnant."

"That's amazing!" Alex exclaimed. "I'm so happy for you. Congratulations."

"Thank you. We're keeping it quiet until we're further along, but I wanted you to know." Tristan hesitated. "We've been hoping for a while, so we're really thrilled."

"I'm sure you are."

"How was your visit to Flowering Grove?"

"Fantastic. And thank you again for the book. Heather was blown away." He recalled their last moments together, and an ache hummed inside him. Why had he waited so long to finally kiss her? "We had a really nice visit."

"Did you make it official?"

"Yes, I did." As he spoke, Alex felt someone looking at him. He glanced to his left and found two teenage girls staring in his direction. When he met their gaze, they both gaped at him before whispering to each other.

Oh no. Unease stirred in his gut, and he spun back toward the digital sign at the gate. Boarding would begin in four minutes—not soon enough. He angled his body toward the wall of windows facing the large airplane.

"Alex?" Tristan asked. "You still there?"

"Yeah. I think I was just recognized. I'm hoping we board soon."

Tristan clucked his tongue. "It must be so difficult being a huge superstar. Your public is always there adoring you."

"Ha," Alex deadpanned. "I was hoping to remain anonymous today."

"I'm surprised you didn't just charter a plane to avoid the rest of the world."

"That's not always an option."

"Well, I should let you go. Have a fantastic flight. Text me and let me know where you're gallivanting off to next. Meanwhile I'll be sitting in an office reading manuscripts," Tristan said.

"Tell Justine congratulations for me."

"I will. Take care."

Alex disconnected the call and pocketed his phone before shouldering his backpack.

When the flight attendant at the desk called for first-class boarding, he breathed a sigh of relief. He weaved through the crowd to the gate, ran his boarding pass over the digital reader, and hurried down the long Jetway to the plane. He found his row and stowed his guitar case in the overhead compartment before sliding into the window seat and pushing his backpack under the seat in front of him.

"Good evening, sir. Would you like something to drink?"

The flight attendant addressing him wore bright red lipstick, and her chestnut-colored hair was styled in a bun.

"A Coke, please."

"Coming right up." She hesitated and seemed to study him. "You know, you look just like Alex Kirwan from the band Kirwan."

He worked to keep a pleasant smile on his face. "Is that right?"

She winked at him and then disappeared, and he breathed a sigh of relief.

An older man with a receding gray hairline appeared at the aisle seat. He nodded before loading his suitcase in the overhead compartment. He took the seat beside Alex and slipped earbuds into his ears.

Alex relaxed, grateful that all signs pointed to a quiet flight. He pulled his iPad from his backpack and contemplated the last few days. He longed for more time with Heather, but he was thankful for the special hours they'd spent together.

The flight attendant returned with Alex's drink and turned her attention to his seatmate. Alex powered up his iPad, opened a new email message window, and started typing.

To my beautiful Baker Girl,

I'm sitting in a first-class seat on my flight to New York and already miss you. Heck, I missed you the moment I backed out of your driveway. And I must tell you that those were the best kisses I've ever experienced. If only I'd had the courage to kiss you when I first arrived on Monday, then maybe we could have enjoyed more of them during the week. I look forward to kissing you again soon.

I'm sorry I scared you when I didn't respond to your texts before I arrived. I was trying to keep the visit a secret. I heard on the way to the airport about the pop-music band involved in that wreck. I feel so bad for their families. I'm keeping them in my prayers.

I'm looking forward to seeing you again soon. This week I felt completely content and relaxed around you, and I cherished every moment of our time together. If you asked me what my new best day ever is, I'd say I had a best week ever instead.

I really enjoyed our trip to the children's hospital together too. I keep thinking about those kids who need help, and I want to do more for them aside from making anonymous donations and visiting them. I want to do something in my father's memory, but I can't quite figure out what it would look like. You're the first person I've shared that dream with, by the way.

Tomorrow morning we have to be on the *Good Day USA* show bright and early for soundcheck and practice for their Concert in the Park series. I probably won't sleep tonight. We'll perform two songs live and promote our next leg of the tour. After the live segment, we'll do another set for the crowd.

I've been thinking about your bookstore and bakery and how you said you didn't want to ask me for help. What if I want to help you? What if it brings me joy to see you smile?

Heather, in case you didn't know, you make me really happy. I'm so honored that you agreed to officially be my girlfriend. I plan to keep our relationship a secret and I'll protect you from the media—especially the gossip blogs and magazines.

I hope to talk to you again soon.

Love,

Your Dorky Rockstar

20

Alex stood backstage at the Concert in the Park event with his brothers the following morning. He lifted his hand to his mouth to stifle a yawn. He had arrived at the hotel at close to one in the morning, then was awake at four thirty to shower and prepare for soundcheck at the stage in Central Park at six.

Now it was finally time for them to go onstage. The loud buzz of voices on the other side of the curtain hinted at an enthusiastic crowd for their performance.

"Tell me about Portland," Alex said to his brothers. "How was your week?"

Kayden snorted and scratched the blond scruff on his chin. He looked up at the blue sky as if it held the answers. "Let's see. We slept, partied, slept, partied." He grinned at their middle brother. "Does that cover it, Jor?"

"Yeah, I believe it does, Kayden."

"So sorry I missed that," Alex said sarcastically. He had partied enough in his time. "What did you think of Mom's boyfriend?"

Jordan grinned. "He was fine, but she insists they're not really dating."

"They are totally dating," Kayden said. "He's friendly." He shrugged. "They get along well."

"How does he treat Mom?" Alex asked.

"He's nice to her," Jordan said. "He was bending over backward to help her in the kitchen."

"Good." Alex nodded, relieved that his brothers liked the man.

Kayden leaned toward Alex. "Tell us the lowdown on your Carolina girl."

"We had a great week." He summarized their time spent visiting with her family, at the children's hospital, at the amusement park, and in her hometown. "We're official now."

Jordan and Kayden shared a look.

"Why would you want to be tied down?" Jordan asked.

"Because I'm done with the single life," Alex said. "I want a family and a home." *I want what Tristan has.*

Kayden shook his head. "You won't be able to make that work easily with this life."

"Maybe I want more than this life."

Both of his brothers looked stunned.

"Hey, guys," the stage manager called. "You're on in five."

Alex turned his focus to the show and hoped Heather would be watching at home.

⌒

Heather nudged her car door closed and jogged toward the back entrance of the restaurant. Joy filled her as she recalled the text messages and long email from Alex she'd awoken to this morning. And the email was more than an email—it was a love letter! She couldn't recall a time when she'd been this happy. A quiver of longing moved through her when she remembered the thrill of kissing him last night. She couldn't wait to see him again.

She pushed through the back door and found her parents and sister in the kitchen, the three of them looking up at the small television set mounted to the wall outside the office. A commercial for laundry detergent played on the screen. Heather had texted them last night and asked if they could all watch Kirwan on *Good Day USA* together this morning.

"Did I miss it?" she asked as she hurried over to them.

Mom waved her over to the empty chair beside her. "They're on next."

"How did it go last night when he took you home?" Wendy asked.

"Well . . ." Heather felt her face flush. "He kissed me and asked me to be his girlfriend."

Her younger sister squealed. "That's amazing! Is he a good kisser?"

"A lady never tells."

"That good, huh?"

"Best ever," Heather said.

The commercial segment ended, and television anchor Tasha Edwards announced, "And now . . . Kirwan!"

The crowd in the park went wild as Alex, Jordan, and Kayden walked out onstage. A large banner with the Kirwan logo hung behind them as a backdrop.

Heather's stomach did a somersault as she took in her handsome boyfriend. He was clad in tight jeans and a snug black t-shirt, and his strong jaw was lined with a few days' worth of scruff.

Alex took his place at a microphone and waved at fans while Jordan sat behind the drums.

"How's everyone doing this morning?" Kayden called to the crowd.

The audience roared with whistles, screams, and claps.

Kayden beamed. "Are you ready to dance?" he asked, and the audience went wild again. He turned to Alex. "One, two, three!"

Then the opening chords for "Dance All Night" began, and Heather and Wendy clapped and sang along. Their parents nodded their heads to the beat of the music, and Heather nearly swooned every time the camera zoomed in on Alex. When the song ended, the band transitioned into "Over You," another dance tune Heather and Wendy loved.

After the song ended, Tasha Edwards walked onstage with her microphone. Jordan climbed out from behind the drums and scooted over to join his brothers.

Tasha turned toward the audience. "How did you enjoy Kirwan's songs?"

The crowd cheered and clapped, and she turned to Alex.

"I think they're enjoying your show," she said.

Alex combed his fingers through his hair and flashed his knee-weakening smile. "We're so glad to be back here in New York City, and we can't wait for our shows tonight and tomorrow."

"They all look so hot, especially Kayden," Wendy gushed, and Heather shushed her.

"You've been on the road for a while now, right?" Tasha asked, turning toward Jordan.

"That's right," Jordan said. "We've been touring since early March, but we're loving every minute of it. We're grateful for fans who come out to see us play."

The crowd cheered again.

Then Tasha looked at Kayden. "You are three of the most eligible bachelors in pop music."

"Is that right?" Kayden's smile was coy as he waved to the audience, and the women screamed.

"I think it's true if those cheers are any indication," Tasha said. "Now I'm sure it will break hearts if you say yes, but I must ask: As handsome and successful as you men are, have any of you found someone special?"

Jordan shook his head. "I haven't yet, but I'm definitely looking. How about you, Kayden?"

"I think *all* women are special," Kayden said with a smirk, and the crowd went wild again.

Alex laughed, and Jordan rolled his eyes.

Tasha pivoted toward Alex. "How about you, Alex?"

Alex laughed and touched his chin, and Heather clasped her hand to her mouth as she recalled what he'd promised last night.

Then Alex folded his arms across his wide chest, the muscles in his arms flexing in response. "I think Kayden and Jordan have a better chance than I do since they're younger." Then he looked at the crowd. "What do you all think?"

The crowd hooted and hollered again.

Wendy patted Heather's arm. "Way to avoid the question, Alex!"

Heather, Wendy, and her parents laughed.

"We're so glad you joined us for our Concert in the Park series," Tasha told Alex and his brothers before turning to face the cameras. "Now we'll head back to the studio for the weather report with Gary," she said before the screen cut to a weather map.

Dad muted the sound. "They put on a great show, and the crowd loves them."

"That's for sure," Mom agreed.

Heather sighed and hugged her arms to her waist. Though it was exciting to see her boyfriend on a TV screen, she wondered when she would get to hold him again.

Alex dragged himself into his hotel suite later that night. He yawned and stretched as he schlepped into the bedroom, then checked the time on the digital clock beside the bed. It was after one in the morning. He had hoped to get back to the room early enough to call Heather, but he didn't want to risk waking her up, especially if she had to be at work early in the morning tomorrow—or, actually, later today.

It had been a long and exhausting day. Alex and his brothers had been swamped by fans after the morning concert in the park. While he appreciated the opportunity to perform and meet the fans, he was wiped out mentally and physically by the time it ended.

When it was over, they had more media interviews and an event for their energy drink sponsorship before heading to the arena for practice and soundcheck. Before he knew it, it was time for the second concert of the day.

And throughout it all, Alex had thought of Heather. He missed her. He longed to talk to her and find out about her day. And if he was completely honest, he really wanted to kiss her.

After taking a soothing shower and changing into shorts and a clean t-shirt, Alex hopped up on the king-sized bed and pulled out his tablet. He opened his email app and was grateful to find a message from Heather.

He leaned back against the headboard and felt himself finally relax as he began reading.

To my Not-So-Dorky Rockstar,

First of all, I must address that kiss—no, those kisses. "Wow" is all I can say. I've never felt so transported or weak-kneed. They were truly the best kisses of my life, and

I look forward to enjoying more of them. Could we please arrange for that soon? Pretty please?

And yes, this was the best week ever, and I miss you so much. I miss your voice, your smile, your laugh—did I mention the kisses? Sigh. You have me sighing, Mr. Alex Kirwan!

I was very sorry to hear about the band members who passed away in that crash. My heart and prayers are with their family members as well.

And I have changed your name to "Not-So-Dorky" because, Mr. Kirwan, you were far from dorky on the television this morning. You were downright hot! I wanted to scream up and down Main Street: "My boyfriend is on *Good Day USA*, and he's a superhot singer!" But I know it's our secret right now.

My parents, Wendy, and I laughed out loud at how you dodged the question about dating. Very smooth! Ha ha! I was quite jealous of all those young women who got to see you in person, but I also noted that you touched your chin for me. And yes, I swooned! (Can you hear me sighing again?)

I've been pondering your charity idea all day, and I think a children's charity would be a beautiful way to remember your dad. My eyes fill with tears when I think about that coming true. I'd love to be a part of it.

As for my store, thank you for offering to help, but I don't expect you to fund my business. As I told you, Alex, I'm not going to use you for money, fame, or anything else. I just plan to use you for a lot of kisses. Sighing again . . .

I miss you, Alex Kirwan. Thank you for picking me.

Love and lots of hugs and kisses,

Heather

Alex smiled as he read her message again and again. He missed her, too, and he wanted a true relationship. But in this moment, even though he'd just left her behind, she felt so far away. He would do the best he could.

He just hoped it would be enough.

21

Heather pushed open the back door of the restaurant and breathed in the late-May evening two weeks later. Her feet and her back ached as she padded slowly out to her car in the parking lot of her parents' restaurant. It had been a long and awful Wednesday, and she was grateful it was finally over.

Everything she touched seemed to have gone wrong today. Not only had her cookies burned this morning, but when her ingredients order had been delivered, it was missing bags of flour, cinnamon, baking powder, and sugar. She had run out of chocolate cake and brownies before the dinner rush had started because she didn't have enough supplies to replace what she'd used. Then both Joyce and Misty had called out sick, and she wound up working well past lunch and into the dinner hours. To top it off, she had three tables of rude customers who sent their orders back multiple times.

But now it was time to go home, and she couldn't wait to take off her shoes, flop onto her sofa, and turn on a sappy movie.

She climbed into her car and started the engine. She blew out a deep breath, and when she turned on the stereo, Alex's voice crooned through the speakers. It had been two weeks since she'd kissed him, and she missed him more and more every day. Though they had texted here and there, and though he had emailed her earlier in the week, she hadn't spoken to him since Sunday night. He had sent a few selfies after his last concert, and while she enjoyed seeing his gorgeous smile and stunning blue eyes, she missed his voice. And she *really* missed his lips.

Heather had known they would spend more time apart than together until he finished the tour. He was currently on his way to California for a big music festival that would take place during the upcoming Memorial Day weekend, but as much as she respected and understood his schedule, she still couldn't stop the yearning that grew like a pit in her stomach. She longed to be with Alex—by his side, holding his hand, hugging and kissing him.

She put her car in Reverse and backed out of the parking spot. When her phone dinged with a text, she stopped her car and looked at the screen, hoping the message was from Alex.

MCKENNA: When will you be home?
HEATHER: About ten minutes. Why?
MCKENNA: I have big news, and there's a package waiting
for you.

Heather blinked. Then she typed: Be there soon.

She drove home and parked next to Mckenna's Subaru, then hurried into the house. After greeting her cats and depositing her purse and tote bag on the sofa, she turned to where Mckenna stood by the doorway to the kitchen. Her makeup was perfect, her hair was styled in a french twist, and she was clad in a little black dress.

"You look amazing," Heather told her.

"Thanks. Kirk and I are finally going to that restaurant in Charlotte I've been telling you about." She pointed to the kitchen. "Anyway, go and look at what came for you."

Heather stepped into the kitchen and stopped short when she found two dozen red roses sitting in clear vases on the table. "What's this?"

Mckenna walked up behind her. "Read the card quick. We need to put the vases on top of the china cabinet before your silly cats eat the flowers and get sick."

Heather picked up the card, and her eyes stung as she read the message:

To my beautiful Baker Girl,
    I'm sorry we haven't talked much, but know I miss you and hope to see you soon.
    Love,
    Your Dorky Rockstar

Heather sighed and sniffed before hugging the note to her chest. Even though she couldn't talk to Alex every day, it relieved her to know he thought of her as often as she thought of him. She just had to find a way to cope while they were apart. She leaned down, breathed in the fragrance of her beautiful roses, and touched a perfect bloom.

"Ugh," Mckenna said. "Here come Molly and Jet. Let me help you move the flowers to a safer place."

Heather fetched one vase, and Mckenna picked up the other to place on top of Mckenna's china cabinet.

"I love your cute names for each other," Mckenna said. "He's really smitten with you."

"It's mutual. You said you had news too?"

Mckenna's expression brightened. "Yes. I have big news

from my parents." She clapped her hands. "You know the bakery across the street from Christine's antique mall?"

"Of course I know the Sugary Sweet Bakery. What about it?"

"It's going to be available at the end of June. Apparently the owners found a new location, and they're anxious to move there. Why they would want to leave Main Street is beyond me, but this is great news for you." Mckenna pointed to Heather. "My parents said it's yours if you want it. They'll negotiate the rent since you're like family. They just need to know soon because if you don't want it, then they'll advertise it. It's a prime location, right in downtown Flowering Grove and near my salon. We'd be work neighbors!"

Heather's head started to spin, and she leaned back on the sofa behind her. The location *was* perfect, and since it was already a bakery, the space had everything she would need to bake and display her desserts. She'd simply have to set up the bookstore section of the shop.

Her confidence faltered as she tried to imagine her dream becoming a reality. Did she truly have what it took to be a small business owner?

Mckenna reached out and touched her arm. "You okay?"

"Yeah, yeah." Heather stood up straight. "This *is* great news. Maybe I should go to the bakery right now and take a look. I think it's still open."

"I'd go with you, but Kirk should be here any minute," she said just as a car motored into the driveway. "That's probably him. We'll talk later, okay?"

Heather gave Mckenna a hug. "Have fun. You really do look stunning."

"Thank you."

Heather walked out to the porch with Mckenna and waved to Kirk. She waited while Mckenna climbed into his Toyota 4Runner and they backed out of the driveway.

Then she sniffed and wondered what Alex was doing at that moment. If only she could fly out to see him perform at the festival. But she had to work, and he would be too busy to spend time with her anyway.

Instead, she decided to pull herself out of her funk. She fed the cats, retrieved her purse, and locked up the house before driving back to Main Street and the Sugary Sweet Bakery.

After finding a parking spot, Heather sat at a bistro table in front of the bakery and tried to imagine the space transformed. She envisioned a small area in the back corner with tables for customers to sit and enjoy their treats. Then she visualized shelves in the center of the store full of books.

Excitement coursed through her as her imagination sparked to life. Perhaps this could actually happen! She longed to discuss this with Alex and bounce ideas off him.

She removed her phone from her pocket and smiled at her locked screen photo—a selfie she and Alex had taken in the park. She enjoyed gazing at that photo, especially on days when her loneliness threatened to swallow her whole.

Then she unlocked her phone and shot off a text to him: Thank you for the beautiful roses, Alex. They are stunning.

Heather sucked in a breath and waited for his conversation bubbles, but none appeared. She recalled that he was traveling today, and she frowned, remembering a conversation when he complained that the Wi-Fi never worked correctly on airplanes, whether private or commercial.

Her thumbs flew over the digital keyboard as she sent him another message: I know you're traveling today. No pressure to respond. But I want you to know I miss you too—more than I can possibly express. And I have big news. Text or call anytime day or night. I mean that. But if you're exhausted by the time you receive this, don't feel obligated to respond. ☺

Then she entered the bakery and purchased a cup of coffee and a cinnamon bun. She took a seat at an indoor table and pondered how she would set up the store on her own. She pulled a notepad out of her purse and began sketching out a plan.

When her pen suddenly ran out of ink, she searched her purse for another one. But her hand came across the sticky note Alex had slipped inside *The Lost Castle* when he sent it to her. She studied his handwriting and felt a stab of sadness.

She unlocked her phone and pulled up his latest email, rereading lines that had spoken to her heart:

I wish we could spend more time together in person. I promise that as soon as this tour is over, we will be together more. Thank you for being patient. I miss you so much, Heather.

She locked her phone and placed it facedown on the table. She wished Alex could be with her right now to help her dream come to life, but doubt drenched her. Was she brave enough to run this store? Would she make enough money to support herself, to pay her rent, to save for a future?

Her phone chimed with a text message, and excitement rushed through her. Heather flipped the phone over and found a message from Dad: Is your car parked in front of the bakery?

She snickered and responded: Are you stalking me?

DAD: I'll take that as a yes. I'll join you.

She found a new pen and continued working on her sketch. A few minutes later, the bell above the door to the bakery dinged.

"Fancy meeting you here," Dad said as he sat down across from her.

Heather smiled. "How did you manage to get off work so early?"

"The restaurant slowed down tonight, so I felt Patrick could handle the cooking on his own. I was headed home when I saw your car." He pointed to her sketch. "What are you up to?"

Heather leaned in close to him and lowered her voice as she explained what Mckenna had told her about the space becoming available at the end of June. "Her parents said it's mine if I want it."

"That's fantastic, Heather!"

She covered her face with her hands as worry nearly drowned her.

"Hey." Dad touched her hand. "What's wrong?"

"I'm afraid." She sniffed as her emotions welled up inside of her. "I never thought this day would come. Now I'm facing the actual risk."

Dad's smile was warm. "I remember that feeling clearly when your mom and I opened the restaurant. I'm not going to sugarcoat it, Heather. It was rough in the beginning. We borrowed money from our parents, and we were terrified that we'd never make enough to pay them back and cover our bills. But in the long run, it all worked out." He chuckled as he looked lost in thought. "To be honest, some of the tough times were also the best times."

He ran his fingertip over the woodgrain tabletop. "I remember one Christmas when your mom and I barely had two pennies to rub together. We went to the dollar store for presents for each other. I got your mom some bubble bath, soap, and lotion, and she got me notepads and deodorant. When we opened our gifts, we laughed and laughed. We were just happy to have each other and our restaurant, which was barely breaking even. But we got through it." He reached over and touched Heather's hand.

"You think I should go for it?"

"Yes."

Heather tilted her head. "Why?"

"Because you've talked about running your own bakery since you were five years old and playing with that Easy-Bake Oven." He paused. "What I'm saying is that it will be tough in the beginning, but if you don't take the chance, you'll always wish you had."

"What if I can't pay my rent?"

"You have a safety net." Then Dad winked.

"Thank you." Heather sniffed as her eyes filled with tears.

Dad paused for a moment and seemed to study her. "How's Alex?"

"I think he's fine." She peered down at her drawing to avoid her father's kind brown eyes. "We've been exchanging emails, and today he sent me two dozen roses."

"Heather, please look at me," he said. "You don't seem happy. Did something happen?"

She met his eyes reluctantly. "I just miss him."

He gave a knowing smile. "Sweetie, his job will often keep you apart."

"I know. He's traveling to California for a big Memorial Day music festival." She rested her elbow on the table and her chin on her palm.

"Do you think your relationship with him is worth these tough times?"

"Yes," she said. "I've never felt this way about anyone before. Alex is wonderful. He's thoughtful, generous, funny, brilliant, and he cares deeply for his family. When we're together, everything feels perfect. We never run out of words."

Dad nodded. "I'm glad to hear that. You two seem to really care about each other. I spoke to Alex before he left, and he seems genuine. You just have to decide if you can handle the stress of being apart. Is the loneliness worth the good times when you're together?"

"Right," she whispered.

Then Dad pointed to her sketch. "Tell me about this."

"It's how I envision the store." She pointed out where the bookshelves would go and where she'd set up a small dining area. "What do you think?"

"I think it's fantastic, and if you want, I'll help you and even partner with you."

"I really want to do this on my own."

He grinned. "I'm not surprised, but don't be too proud to accept help when you need it."

They talked about the restaurant for a while before walking out to their cars together. Her father hugged her when they reached her Honda.

"I have your back," he told her. "Your mom and I want our daughters to follow their dreams, no matter where they lead."

"Thank you, Dad," she said, and he headed over to his truck.

As she climbed into the driver's seat of her Honda, she thought of Alex and felt a pang of grief for him. She knew he would do anything to have a conversation with his father like the one she'd just had with hers.

Alex had never been more grateful to arrive at a hotel room. Not only had their flights been delayed, but he and his brothers had also been ambushed by paparazzi outside the airport and then again at the hotel. He felt as if he could sleep for a week when he finally sat down on a sofa in his hotel suite.

The battery on his phone had died during his second flight, and he had forgotten to bring a portable battery charger. To make matters worse, the charging plugs in their seats weren't functioning, and his brothers hadn't brought anything to charge their phones either.

Alex plugged his dead phone and tablet into the wall, then took a long, relaxing shower. When he emerged from the bathroom, his phone had finally come back to life, and he found a host of unread texts. The two that caught his eye first were from Heather. He read them and smiled.

HEATHER: Thank you for the beautiful roses. They are stunning.

HEATHER: I know you're traveling today. No pressure to respond. But I want you to know I miss you too—more than I can possibly express. And I have big news. Text or call anytime day or night. I mean that. But if you're exhausted by the time you receive this, don't feel obligated to respond. 😊

Alex scrubbed his hand over his mouth and studied the clock by the TV. It was nearly midnight in California, which meant it was 3:00 a.m. in North Carolina.

He pulled in a sharp breath through his teeth as he read her message again.

She had said to text anytime, but 3:00 a.m. was much too late. Still, he longed to know what her big news was. Even more, he needed to hear her voice.

He sat on the corner of the sofa and replied to her text: Are you awake?

He held his breath, and the conversation bubbles appeared after a few moments.

HEATHER: Yes!
ALEX: Do you want to talk now?

HEATHER: Yes!
ALEX: You sure?
HEATHER: A thousand times yes!

He grinned as he dialed her number, and she answered on the first ring.

"Alex. Hi." Her voice was hoarse, and he winced, certain he'd woken her.

"I'm sorry. Did I wake you?"

"I don't care what time it is," she said. "I just want to hear your voice."

He wilted into the sofa. "I feel the same way."

"How was your trip?"

He made a frustrated noise in his throat.

"That bad?"

"Our flights were delayed, and we got surrounded by paparazzi and fans at the airport and then again at the hotel."

"I'm so sorry."

"Kayden was into the attention, but Jordan and I had a hard time even smiling." He exhaled an irritated breath. "Also, my phone and my tablet died on the second flight, and I had no way to charge them. I'm sorry I couldn't text you back."

"It's okay. I love my roses. Thank you."

"You're welcome. You deserve much more than roses, but I wanted you to know I think about you all the time even though I can't call you." He rested his feet on the far end of the couch. "I want to hear your news, but you must be exhausted. Want to tell me what's up and then go back to sleep?"

Heather shared her news about a storefront becoming available and Mckenna's family's offer for her business.

"Heather, that's amazing! This is what you've been waiting for. I'm so excited for you."

"Thanks." She seemed to hesitate. "I'm excited too, but I'm also nervous and scared."

"You can do this. My brothers and I felt the same way when we started trying to really pursue music, but we powered through it. You've got this."

"I wish you were here to see the store." Her voice faltered. "I really want to show you everything and get your opinion."

He rested his forearm on his brow, feeling a twinge of guilt. "I'm sorry I'm not there, but I'm here rooting for you. I'm always on your side."

"I didn't mean to make you feel bad," she whispered. "Your life is different from mine."

"But that doesn't mean I don't want to be with you."

"I miss your lips." She sniffed.

His heart flipped at her admission. "I miss yours too."

She yawned. "I'm sorry to yawn in your ear."

"I need to let you go."

"But when will I talk to you again?"

He exhaled. "I don't know yet." He tried to remember his schedule for the weekend. "I will call you, I promise. Sleep well, babe."

She clucked her tongue. "Is this all a dream or did Alex Kirwan just call me *babe*?"

He laughed. "You're not dreaming, but you might be delirious."

"Good night."

"Good night." He let her hang up first, then he flopped back on the sofa. Being apart from her was torture. He had to find a solution to this—but first, he needed sleep.

22

Six weeks later Heather stood in the center of her store—*her store*—and turned in a full circle. A mixture of excitement and anxiety drifted over her. The Sunday afternoon sunshine poured in through the large windows at the front of the shop, and she wiped her hands down her face.

She had finally taken possession of the store the day before, and while she was grateful that her dream of owning a bookstore and bakery had finally come true, the rumbling truck of reality had hit her at eighty miles per hour: She was now a small business owner. Any success or failure she experienced started and ended with her.

She scanned the dingy gray walls and the scuffed black-and-white checkerboard tile floor. Then she tried to imagine the storefront transformed into her bookstore and bakery, with bright yellow walls, aisles of bookshelves, a cashier counter, a bakery counter, and a small café area with the tables and chairs she had cleaned up and stored in the back room.

When she considered her budget for everything that needed to be purchased and done, her heart seemed to beat harder in her chest.

Then she stood up straight and lifted her chin. First, she had to clean and paint. Then she'd worry about the rest of the items on her list.

The bell on the door jingled as Mckenna came inside, her pretty face lit up in a smile as she flitted over and hugged Heather. "I thought I'd find you here!" her best friend exclaimed. "I've been so busy at the salon and with Kirk that I haven't seen you enough. So . . . how does it feel to finally stand in your store?"

Heather frowned. "It's a lot. Honestly, I'm overwhelmed and wondering if I've made a mistake. I've been thinking about the shelves I need to order, and the prices are insane. I'm grateful my dad is going to help me with the setup, and I'm going to talk to him about borrowing some money. It'll take me awhile to pay him back, but he insists on helping."

"Don't be afraid to accept it." Mckenna touched Heather's arm. "My parents were a tremendous help to me when I opened my salon, and that's okay." She smiled. "Have you heard from Alex?"

Heather pushed her hand through her hair. Thoughts of Alex always lingered in the back of her mind. She was grateful for the technology that allowed them to be in regular contact, but she missed him so much that she ached every time she envisioned his handsome face. She craved more time with him in person, but she wondered if it was selfish to feel that way.

"He's fine," she said, turning to the back wall. "I was thinking I could hang a blackboard there above the bakery display cases and list my daily specials for—"

"Whoa," Mckenna said, interrupting Heather. "Did you and Alex have an argument?"

Heather perched on a stool and shook her head. "No, I just miss him a lot. He mentioned that he has a few days off coming up soon, and I was hoping he might make plans to see me, but he never mentioned anything. It's been almost two months since I've seen him."

Mckenna's smile was bright despite Heather's disappointment. "I'm sure he misses you just as much as you miss him."

Heather picked up a notepad. "Help me make a list of everything I need for renovations?"

Mckenna dropped her purse on a nearby box, then they set to work brainstorming a list for the home improvement store.

After the list seemed long enough, Heather slung her purse over her shoulder. "I guess I'll get going."

"Kirk and I were just going to hang out today. Why don't I call him and have him meet me here so we can help you paint?" Mckenna asked.

Heather shook her head. "I appreciate the help, but I don't want to—" She paused midsentence when her phone began to ring, and when she found Alex's number on the screen, her heart did a little dance. "Hello?"

"Are you busy?" Alex asked.

"I'm about to go to the store with Mckenna. What's up?"

"Look toward the street."

She faced the front door and found Alex standing outside holding up a paintbrush. Her eyes stung with happy tears as a shocked squeak escaped her throat.

He pushed the door open and grinned at her. "When we talked yesterday, you said you were planning to paint today. I'm yours for the week, so put me to work."

Heather dropped her phone and purse on the nearby box and jumped into his arms.

⌒

"This is still the best barbecue I've ever had," Alex declared while sitting in the breakroom at the back of Heather's store later that evening. He picked up a piece of cornbread and took a bite, and she smiled over at him before sipping her Diet Coke. He had missed that beautiful smile!

She shook her head. "I still can't believe you're here."

"We're off until Thursday, and I was determined to spend the Fourth of July with you since it didn't work out for you to visit me while I was on the road."

She reached over and touched his hand. "Thank you. I've missed you so much."

"And I've missed you, Heather."

He'd hoped to help her prepare for her store opening, which was just what they'd done since his arrival. After she'd welcomed him with some amazing kisses, they drove to the home improvement store, where they'd filled a shopping cart with a few gallons of sunshine-yellow paint and other supplies. Despite her protests, he'd pulled out his credit card and paid for everything before loading it into the back of the SUV he'd rented.

They had applied primer to most of the store's walls before stopping to pick up supper at her parents' restaurant. Russell and Nora had been delighted to see him and asked him about his tour as they filled up two to-go containers with food.

Back at Heather's store, Heather and Alex had spread out their food on a folding table.

"Have you settled on a name for the store?" he asked.

She nodded and swallowed a bite of her pulled-pork barbecue sandwich. "I'm going with Books 'N' Treats."

"How about Heather's Books 'N' Treats?"

She moved her head back and forth. "Don't you think that's a little braggy?"

"No." He laughed. "Why is it braggy to include your name? It's *your* store."

She shrugged. "I don't know."

"I think it sounds perfect. Tell me about these bookshelves you're considering," he said before sipping his Coke.

Heather wiped her hands on a napkin, then opened her laptop and angled it toward him. "These are the ones I want, but I need to talk to my dad before I can buy them."

He took in the pine shelves and nodded as he moved the laptop closer to him. "They're nice. How many do you need?"

She shared the number, and he added the same number to the online shopping cart.

"What are you doing?" Her eyes widened.

Alex pulled his wallet from his back pocket and located his black credit card. "Do you want them shipped here?"

Heather's pretty pink lips pressed into a thin line. "I don't know when I can pay you back."

"You didn't answer my question. Where do you want them shipped?"

"Alex, you're not listening to me. I don't want this."

He smiled. "Consider it my contribution to your store. You don't have to pay me back. Just include a special display for the Kirwan Book Club Pick of the Month."

When she smiled, he released a deep breath. "So what's the address?"

She recited the address, and he completed the order.

"Looks like you'll have them in about two weeks."

"Thank you."

"You're welcome," he said. "After we finish painting tonight, can we do something fun?"

⌒

Alex laughed Tuesday evening while he sat on Heather's parents' deck and listened as her father shared stories of the camping trips he and Heather's mom had taken when they were first married.

Although the air was humid and the summer sun was bright, they were shielded by a red umbrella above their rectangular table. The delicious aromas of baked chicken, corn on the cob, baked beans, and macaroni salad filled his senses as he glanced around the table at Heather, her parents, and her sister. He was grateful to celebrate this Fourth of July with them, and he felt as if he were part of the family as they enjoyed the company and delicious food.

Yesterday he and Heather had spent the day painting the entire store, including the main area, breakroom, office, storeroom, and kitchen. They teased each other and laughed while they worked, and he couldn't remember a time when he'd felt so at ease with a woman.

When they finished, Heather went home to clean up while he showered and changed at the inn. He picked her up for a picnic at the park, then later that evening, they drove to a hill outside of town to kiss and stargaze.

Today they had returned to the store to add the second coats of paint. Then they cleaned up and joined her family for the cookout. It had been the perfect couple of days, and he longed for time to slow down.

That longing for time had haunted him since his last visit to Flowering Grove. How could he make Heather and this place a permanent part of his life?

"How is the store coming together?" Nora asked as she picked up a chip.

Heather swallowed a bite of chicken. "Great. We finished the painting today, and we also ordered the bookshelves and the sign for the window."

"Fantastic!" Wendy exclaimed. "I can't wait to see it, Heather."

Then she focused on Alex. "What are your brothers up to this week?"

Alex swallowed a spoonful of beans. "They both went home to Oregon. I'm sure they're having a barbecue with my mom today." He faced Russell. "Everything is delicious, by the way."

"Thank you." Russell seemed to sit up taller.

"Are you going to go to the fireworks with us?" Nora asked.

Heather faced Alex, and when her bare shin brushed against his, heat zipped up his leg. "The fireworks are a really big deal here in Flowering Grove. The entire town shuts down for the holiday. You got to see the parade while we were painting in the store."

"Yes, it was great." Alex grinned. "I love how the kids decorate their bikes and ride along the parade route."

"Tonight we have the fireworks at Veterans Field," said Heather. "Everyone brings lawn chairs and blankets, and food trucks park there. It's a lot of fun."

Alex swallowed and hesitated. While he didn't want to disappoint Heather, he also didn't want to risk drawing a crowd.

Before he could respond, Heather held up her hand. "You know what? I have a better idea. We could go back to that hill we went to last night to see the stars. We can see the fireworks from there, too, without the risk of your being recognized."

"Strawberry Hill?" Wendy asked, and Heather nodded. "Oh, that's a great idea. And even if there are other people there, you can find a secluded spot."

Alex smiled. "That sounds perfect."

"Tell us about your next steps for the store," Nora said.

Russell nodded. "And how can we help?"

Heather spent the remainder of the meal talking about the store. Then she brought out a lemon cake, which she called Love Triangle Lemon Cake. After dessert, Alex carried their plates and utensils to the kitchen while Heather filled the dishwasher, Nora scrubbed the platters, and Wendy dried them.

"You two run along," Russell said as he set their cups on the counter. "We'll finish this."

Heather frowned. "Are you sure?"

"Yes," Nora insisted. "Head out before the traffic gets bad."

Wendy set the dish towel on the counter. "Wait. You need some drinks and a blanket to sit on. Let me pack you a bag." She scurried toward the hallway leading to the laundry room.

Alex glanced at Heather, and she shook her head and grinned. He helped Heather load the dishwasher until Wendy returned with a large beach bag and held it out to Heather.

"There's a large blanket and four cans of soda in it." Wendy winked at Heather, and Alex held back a laugh as Heather responded with a pointed look.

Then Heather smiled at Alex. "Are you ready?"

"Yes." He nodded at Nora and then Russell. "Thank you for another wonderful meal."

"We hope to see you again before you leave," Nora said.

Russell nodded. "You're always welcome here, son."

Then Alex took Heather's hand. "Let's go watch the fireworks."

23

"ow's this?" Heather asked when they reached a quiet spot away from a few groups of people at the top of Strawberry Hill.

Alex peered out over Flowering Grove below them. "Looks wonderful to me."

Heather pulled the blanket from the bag, and Alex helped her stretch it out on the ground. Then they sat beside each other. He took in the sunset, which sent vivid steaks of color across the clear evening sky, and he breathed in the aroma of honeysuckle and fresh grass. The cicadas began their usual chorus while lightning bugs showed off their own sparkling display.

Beside him Heather crossed her legs and peered over at him. "I know I keep saying this, but I'm so glad you're here, Alex." She reached over and threaded her fingers with his. "I'm so grateful to be able to spend time with you and to have your help with my store. More than anything, I've wanted to share this important milestone with you. You have no idea how much this means to me."

Alex traced a finger along her jaw and then dipped his head before kissing her. She wrapped her arms around his neck and pulled him closer. As she deepened the kiss, every nerve ending inside him caught fire, and he knew to the depth of his bones that she was his true love, the one who held the key to his future. His body relaxed as he relished the taste of her.

When she pulled away, she smiled up at him, her lips swollen from the kisses. "Could we do that again before you leave?" she asked.

He laughed and rested his forehead against hers. "I'm available until my Wednesday night red-eye flight. You let me know what works for you."

Just then a *whoosh* sounded, followed by a *boom*. Heather jumped, then laughed as fireworks exploded in the sky. Alex shifted closer, and Heather rested her head against his chest.

They oohed and aahed as the show continued to color the night sky. He lost himself in thoughts of what his and Heather's future could look like—together.

Was it too soon to tell her he loved her? How could he be sure she felt the same way?

He didn't know the answer, but he knew for certain that he loved Heather Gordon and never wanted to let her go.

Heather swiped her hand across her forehead the following evening while she stood in the doorway leading to the back of her store.

"I can't believe it," she said. "We painted the trim, polished the floor, set up the café tables, and cleaned the displays in the bakery area." She gave Alex a high five. "You're the best partner I've ever had," she told him, and she meant it. Not only did they work well together, but they also spent the entire time laughing and teasing each other.

His smile made her legs feel like cooked noodles. "And you

know what else?" He rested his hand on her shoulder. "I also had a lot of fun."

"I did too."

Alex pointed to the storage closet. "How about we buy some shelving units for in there? I saw some in the store when we rented the floor polisher that I think would—" His words were cut off when his phone began to ring with a video call. He lifted his phone from his pocket, examined the screen, and frowned. "Huh."

"Who is it?"

"Tristan. I hope everything is okay." He answered the call. "What's up?"

"I saw your mom today at the supermarket, and she told me you're back in North Carolina. I thought I'd call and see how it's going."

Alex grinned. "It's going great. I'd like to introduce you to Heather." He angled the phone toward her.

"Hi!" She waved at the man with dark hair, dark eyes, and a kind smile.

"Is that Heather?" a woman's voice called from the background. "I want to meet her!" Then a pretty blond with bright green eyes appeared on the screen and waved. "I'm Justine, Tristan's wife. I've heard so much about you."

"It's great to meet you."

"When are you going to bring Heather out here to meet us, Alex?" Justine asked.

Alex held the phone up higher so he and Heather were both on the screen. "It's funny you should ask that. I was going to run an idea past Heather."

"What idea?" Heather asked, her pulse skipping.

Alex faced her. "I have some time off next month before we head to Europe, and I was going to see if I could fly you out to meet my family—and when I say *family*, that includes Tristan and Justine."

"I'd love to. I can see if Wendy and Deanna will run the store for me since they already told me they want to work for me."

"Great!" Justine clapped. "Let us know, and you can come for supper. We can girl-talk."

Heather clapped. "Oh, how fun. Then I can ask you all sorts of questions about Alex."

"I'll tell you all of his embarrassing secrets," Justine promised with a laugh.

Alex shook his head. "Oh, I don't know about that." Then he smiled. "How are you feeling?"

"Pregnant." Justine chuckled. "I'm doing well—just really tired."

Heather grinned. "When are you due?"

"October. We're really excited." Justine leaned her head against Tristan's shoulder.

Her husband nodded. "Yes, we are. How's the bookstore and bakery coming along?"

"Fantastic." Alex turned the phone around and panned across the store. "I'll give you a tour."

Love and appreciation swelled in her chest as she listened to Alex share all the tasks he and Heather had completed during his visit. She rested her hand on his waist and smiled into the camera.

"The store looks great," Tristan said.

Justine nodded. "I want to see it in person after it's done." Then she frowned. "Well, when I'm able to travel, that is."

"I would love that," Heather said.

Alex nodded. "We could definitely arrange that in the future. Other than waiting on the baby, what's going on out in Oregon?"

Tristan and Justine shared news about their jobs as well as people who Heather assumed were mutual acquaintances.

"We should let you go," Justine finally said. "I'm sure you have plans for the evening."

Alex laughed. "Actually, we were talking about going to the home improvement store to buy some shelving units."

"What exciting lives you lead," Tristan joked.

Alex encircled his free arm around Heather. "Honestly, I'd be happy watching paint dry with this one."

"We've actually done that," Heather quipped, and they all laughed.

Tristan waved. "You two have fun."

"See you soon!" Justine said before they ended the call.

Alex slipped his phone into his pocket. "How about we go pick up those shelving units and then grab supper?"

"Let's do it," Heather agreed.

⌣

Heather and Alex walked up the front steps at Heather's house later that evening, and Mckenna squealed when they came inside. "I'm so glad you're both here!" Then she shared a look with Kirk, who sat beside her on the sofa in the family room. "We have news."

They both stood and faced Heather and Alex.

"Oh?" Heather set her purse on the floor beside her two cats, who were yammering their usual greeting.

Mckenna held up her hand and squealed again. A small diamond flashed on her ring finger.

Heather's heart leapt before she rushed over to Mckenna and hugged her. "Congratulations!" Then she held her best friend's hand and examined the round-cut diamond in a gold setting. "It's lovely."

Starstruck

"Thank you!" Mckenna hugged her again. "I'm so excited I could burst."

Alex joined them and shook Kirk's hand. "Congratulations."

"Thanks." Kirk huffed out a breath that seemed to bubble up from his toes. "I'm just glad she said yes."

Mckenna smacked his arm. "Of course I did."

"Yeah, but it's so soon." Kirk brushed a hand over the dark stubble on his chin.

Mckenna's expression seemed dreamy. "But when you know, you know."

I know how you feel. Heather nodded, and out of the corner of her eye, she spotted Alex watching her. Did he feel the same way?

"Will you be my maid of honor?" Mckenna asked Heather.

"Of course I will!" Heather exclaimed.

Mckenna ran a hand through her thick locks. "I've always wanted a Christmas wedding, and Kirk loves the idea too. I have so much to think about. We need to start planning."

"You'll have to come back for the wedding," Kirk told Alex.

Then Mckenna's eyes widened. "Oh yes! Maybe we could get you and your brothers to perform at the reception."

"I don't know if we could afford you." Kirk grimaced.

Alex chuckled. "Maybe we could work something out."

"Let's toast!" Heather said on her way to the kitchen. "I think we still have some sparkling cider from your birthday party last month, Mckenna."

She found the bottle and returned to the family room with cider and cups. Then they sat down and toasted Mckenna and Kirk before discussing possible wedding venues.

Later, while Heather stood in the driveway with Alex, her mind spun with a mixture of excitement at Mckenna's news and sadness that Alex's time with her was ending.

Alex rested his hands on Heather's shoulders. "I can't believe it's time for me to leave already."

"How about you stay another week?" she teased.

His gaze seemed to soften. "If only I could . . ."

"I can't thank you enough for your help."

He trailed his fingers down her cheek, and she leaned into his touch. "I'm just grateful I could take part in the planning of your store. I'm really proud and thrilled for you."

"Thank you," she whispered, overwhelmed.

Then he kissed her, and she pulled the front of his shirt toward her as she soaked in his nearness. She felt as if millions of butterflies were dancing in her stomach.

When he broke the kiss, the intensity in his gorgeous blue eyes sent heat thrumming through her. "Will you come out to Oregon to see me next month?"

"I would love to."

Alex swallowed. "It won't be soon enough." He dipped his chin and kissed her once again. "I'll miss you every second of every day until I see you again."

"I'll miss you too."

Alex hugged her, then opened the driver's side door.

"Text me when you land, no matter what time it is."

"I will." He climbed into the truck and shut the door. After turning the engine over, he lowered the window. "Take care."

"You too." As Heather watched Alex drive away, it occurred to her that each goodbye was getting more and more difficult.

24

Three weeks later, Alex sat out on the balcony of his hotel room in Denver on a Friday night. He looked out over the traffic moving on the street below and huffed out a breath. Tonight had been another sold-out show, but every day had seemed like a monotonous fog since he had left Heather in Flowering Grove.

He missed her so much that he ached for her. They had shared calls, texts, and emails, and while he cherished every interaction, it wasn't the same as holding her in his arms and kissing her. He longed to see her again, but his next break wasn't for another week and a half. To make matters worse, tomorrow was Heather's big day—her store's grand opening— and he couldn't be there to celebrate with her. Guilt and disappointment pummeled him.

He glanced down at his phone and found it was almost midnight, which meant it was nearly two her time. He hated waking her, but doing so seemed inevitable these days.

Sucking in a breath, he opened his last text from her and typed: Are you still awake?

His phone rang with a video call, and he sat down on a nearby chair and accepted it. "Hi, babe."

"Hey." She tried to stifle a yawn as she sat on her bed and

leaned against the headboard. "I just got in from the store a little while ago." Her eyes looked tired, and he immediately regretted bothering her.

He frowned. "You're exhausted. I'll try you tomorrow, okay?"

"No, no, no!" She was suddenly bright eyed. "I've been thinking about you all day and have been dying to talk. But I knew you had a show tonight. How did it go?"

He shrugged. "It was fine. The usual. I want to hear about your store."

"I think we're ready. We're stocked with the supplies we need for the bakery, and I'm going to go in to finish my baking after I get a few hours of sleep. *If* I can sleep, that is. Wendy, Deanna, and I checked the books into the system this week and have them organized on the shelves by category and author. Plus we paired books with desserts, such as Plot Twist Cinnamon Rolls paired with Emil Zimmerman's *The Man in the Window* and then Elise Harvey's *Where Did She Go?* paired with Suspenseful Shortbread."

Alex grinned. "Heather, that is brilliant!"

"Thanks. We put together a display with the pairings, and I hope it works. Plus we cleaned the windows and hung the 'Grand Opening' banners. I have a sandwich board sign and balloons ready to go out on the sidewalk in the morning."

Then she snapped her fingers. "Oh! And an article about my store was published in the *Flowering Grove Times*, and the *Charlotte Observer* book reviewer wrote a piece on me this week, which is exciting." She pushed her dark hair behind her ears. "Now I just have to show up tomorrow and pray some customers do too."

"I'm sure your store will be a hit." Alex resisted a frown as more guilt assaulted him. "I just wish I could be there. I feel awful that I'm not."

She clucked her tongue, and her expression warmed. "Alex, you helped me so much when you were here, and I owe the bookshelves to you. They're amazing! You saw those photos I sent yesterday, right?"

"Yes, I did. They look great."

"And I'm creating a sign for the Kirwan Book Club Pick of the Month."

He laughed. "You don't really have to do that."

"Yes, I do." She lifted a finger. "By the way, we need to choose another book to read for *our* book club after life slows down a little bit for me. I haven't had much time to read while putting the store together."

"No pressure." He leaned back in the chair and took a deep breath of clean Colorado air. "I wish you were here. Denver is beautiful."

"I've never been there."

"Someday I'll bring you."

When she smiled, her beautiful, makeup-free face and charming freckles were out in full view. "So . . . I get to taste your lips in less than two weeks," she said.

He sat up straight again, and his pulse quickened. "Yes, that's true."

"I can't wait to see you."

Alex cleared his throat. "That is an understatement. I talked to my mom, and she said you're more than welcome to stay in her guest apartment."

"Guest apartment?" she asked. "Wow. That sounds fancy."

He laughed. "It's really not. It's a one-bedroom apartment above her detached garage."

She gave him a knowing expression. "It sounds really nice. Thank you." Then she yawned again and rubbed her eyes. "I'm sorry."

"Why are you sorry? It's after two your time. You need to sleep."

She covered another yawn. "I know, but I don't want to hang up."

"Text me tomorrow and send me photos?"

"I will." She tilted her head. "I miss you, Alex."

"I miss you too, babe."

He ended the call and rested his head against the wall. He longed to skip the next show and just fly out to North Carolina to be at Heather's grand opening with her. But he couldn't do that. He had obligations to his brothers and to their fans.

Then an idea came to him. He found his tablet in his back-pack in the hotel suite and powered it up to order a surprise for her. If he couldn't be there, at least he could let her know how much he cared.

Heather stood in the center of her store the following morning and surveyed it. The delicious aromas from the cookies, cakes, and breads she had finished baking earlier in the morning per-meated the room. The "Grand Opening" banner hung across the front window just above her Heather's Books 'N' Treats custom logo sticker that her father had helped her affix to the window last week.

"It's perfect, Heather," Deanna said from behind the cash register. She wore the lemon-yellow t-shirt featuring the store's logo above where the breast pocket would be, with a larger version of the logo on the back.

Wendy, also clad in jeans and a yellow logo shirt, appeared at Heather's side. She encircled her arm around her sister's shoulders. "You've outdone yourself. And I am super proud of you, big sis."

"Thank you." Heather leaned on her sister. "I can't thank either of you enough for helping me make my dream come true."

Heather had managed to get nearly four hours of sleep and then arrived at the store shortly before six to finish her baking. Then she'd thrown on a fresh pair of jeans, a yellow t-shirt, and a yellow apron before fixing her hair in a bun and hoping she could find the energy to make it through her first day as a small business owner.

Wendy hugged her. "This place is going to be a huge success."

"I hope so." Heather glanced at her phone. "We open in twenty minutes."

Just then a knock sounded on the front door. Heather spun and found a man standing outside the store, holding a bouquet of yellow roses.

"Looks like someone sent you flowers." Wendy rushed to the door and opened it. "Hi."

The man held out the vase. "I have a delivery for Heather Gordon."

Heather swallowed a deep breath as she hurried over. "For me?"

"Ma'am, I have five more of them in the truck. Where would you like me to put this one?" he asked.

"I'll take it." Wendy grinned as he handed it to her. "Six bouquets?"

The man nodded. "Yes, ma'am. I'll be right back."

"Oh my goodness," Heather said.

Deanna hurried over and took the bouquet from Wendy. "Let me help." Then she set the vase on the counter by the cash register before rushing outside to retrieve another one.

Soon Heather, Wendy, Deanna, and the man delivered the remaining five bouquets into the store, placing all of them on the counter by the cash register.

Heather admired the gorgeous flowers and breathed in their fragrance. "They're lovely!"

"Let's arrange them around the store," Deanna said before lifting one of the vases.

Wendy grabbed another one. "Great idea. I'll put this one back on the bakery counter."

"This is for you too." The man held out an envelope to Heather. "Have a great day." He nodded before turning to leave.

"Thank you," she called after him. Then she opened the envelope and found a small card with a typed message:

To my beautiful Baker Girl,
      Your opening is going to be great. I wish I could be there to cheer you on, but I'm rooting from afar. I'm so proud of you. Knock 'em dead!
      All my love,
      Your Dorky Rockstar

Heather's eyes filled with tears. She was overwhelmed by Alex's loving and thoughtful heart. She wiped her eyes as Wendy and Deanna fussed with the vases around the store.

"They look beautiful!" Deanna announced.

Wendy sidled up to Heather. "What does the card say?"

"Here." She handed it to her sister. "He's amazing."

Wendy clucked her tongue. "Aww. He loves you."

"Do you think so?" Heather asked, and her sister laughed. "What's so funny?"

Wendy held up the card. "Because he signed it 'All my love.' That means he loves you, silly!"

"But he hasn't said it out loud." Heather took the card back from her sister and tucked it safely into the back pocket of her jeans.

Deanna looked stunned. "He hasn't?" she asked, and Heather shook her head. "But it's so apparent on his face when you're together. He's crazy about you."

"Ten minutes until we open!" Wendy announced.

When Heather's phone chimed with a message, she pulled it from her pocket and read Alex's name on the screen.

ALEX: Are you ready for the opening?

"I bet he received a notification that the flowers were delivered," Wendy said, reading the text over Heather's shoulder.

"Hey!" Heather teased. "That's a private message."

Wendy laughed and gave her a gentle push. "No, it's not."

"FaceTime him!" Deanna exclaimed. "You can show him the flowers."

"That's a great idea." Heather hit the button to start a FaceTime call, then held up the phone.

Alex's face filled the screen, and when he smiled, her hand trembled. "Good morning, babe," he said.

"Thank you for the magnificent roses," she said, so grateful to see his handsome face.

"You're welcome. I wanted you to know I was thinking of you."

Heather's chest expanded with love for this precious man. "They are a wonderful addition to my opening day." She slowly moved the phone to scan the store.

"Wow. Everything is perfect!" he said.

When Heather pointed the phone at Wendy and Deanna, they waved and said hello.

Alex waved back. "Hi there. Are you ready for the opening day too?"

"We are," Deanna said.

Wendy grinned. "How's Kayden?"

"Still ornery," he quipped, and they all chuckled.

Heather held the phone in front of her face. "Thank you again, Alex."

"You're welcome, babe. It's time for you to open now, so I need to let you go."

She sighed. "Yes, I know."

"Good luck and text me later, okay?"

"I will," she said. "And I'll see you soon."

He blew her a kiss. "I'm proud of you."

"I'm always proud of you, Alex," she told him before they said goodbye and disconnected the call.

Heather walked to the front door. "Well, ladies, let's do this!"

Then she opened the door to her new future as her dream finally came true.

25

A week and a half later, Heather adjusted her backpack on her shoulder and hurried down the corridor. She then followed the signs toward the baggage claim at the Portland International Airport. After a long but smooth flight in first class from Charlotte to Portland, she couldn't wait to see Alex's handsome face in person. It had been almost five weeks since she'd hugged and kissed her boyfriend, and she yearned to feel his lips on hers again.

When she finally reached baggage claim, her eyes scanned the area until she found Alex leaning against the wall near the exit. He looked tall and lean wearing tight blue jeans, his blue Barbecue Pit t-shirt, and a black ball cap with the green-and-yellow *O* on it.

Her heart thumped as she took off toward him. His gaze tangled with hers, and a grin lit up his face as he opened his arms for her. She launched herself into his hug, and he chuckled and held her close.

"Hi," he whispered into her hair, his voice sending shivers of delight across her skin.

She buried her face in his chest and breathed in his familiar scent. "I've missed you." She looked up at him, and his lips met hers, electrifying her pulse and sending a ripple of feeling through her.

When he broke the kiss, he sighed. "I've been dreaming of this day for too long. Welcome to Portland." He lifted her backpack off her shoulder. "Let me carry that for you."

"Thank you." She took his hand in hers. "I like your shirt. I knew it would complement your gorgeous eyes."

"Thank you. A supercool woman gave me this shirt." He steered her toward the conveyor belts, where a crowd of people had gathered to await their luggage. He nodded at the digital sign displaying her flight number. "Let's get your suitcase and head to my mom's."

The belt began to move, and Heather peered around at the crowd. When she noticed two young women staring at Alex and whispering, her back stiffened.

"Isn't that Alex Kirwan?" one of the young women murmured.

Oh no. Heather felt a surge of apprehension.

"How was your flight?"

Heather's gaze darted to Alex's pleasant expression. "What?"

"Your flight." He lifted a blond eyebrow. "How was it?"

"Great. I finished that book you recommended, the one by Jessica Truman. It was really good. The ending surprised me!"

He nodded. "You thought the sheriff did it, right?"

"I did!" Heather laughed. "I never expected it to be the stepfather."

Alex chuckled.

She turned back to the conveyor belt. "That's my suitcase." She pointed to a large black bag trimmed in blue.

He lunged for it and set it on the floor before lifting the handle.

As they turned to go, the two young women approached them.

"Excuse me," the tall blond said. "Are you Alex Kirwan?"

Heather frowned at the way the women gawked at him. She crossed her arms over her middle and tried to ignore the uneasy feeling in her gut.

Alex rubbed the stubble on his chin and nodded. "Yeah, I am."

"Oh wow," the short brunette gushed. "Could we get a selfie with you?"

The blond folded her hands to plead with him. "Please?"

"Sure." He gave them a sheepish smile.

The brunette clapped. "Thank you! I'm so excited. I can't believe it's you."

"I told you he lived in Portland," the blond snapped as she retrieved her cell phone from her pocket. She unlocked it before she and the brunette positioned themselves in front of Alex. Then they posed and snapped at least a half dozen selfies. Then she gazed up at him and batted her long lashes. "Thank you so much, Alex."

Heather's stomach soured at the woman's overt flirtation.

"You're welcome," he said before giving Heather his attention. "Ready?"

"Yes." She felt the two women studying her.

"Hey! That's Alex Kirwan!" someone nearby called.

Heather swallowed back her anxiety as Alex waved.

Then he took Heather's hand and led her toward the door. "Let's go."

She stepped out into the comfortable evening air and peered up at the stars twinkling in the clear, dark sky above them. She inhaled a deep breath, grateful to have left the stifling humidity back on the East Coast. "It's only the first Monday in August, but it feels like early fall here."

"Like I said, welcome to Portland." He rested his hand on her shoulder and nestled her against his side.

As they ambled across the walkway, she marveled at the green ivy cascading down the side of the parking deck. "I have never seen a more beautiful parking garage."

"You're kidding."

"No, I'm not." She turned and faced the airport. "It's beautiful here. And that mountain I saw as we flew in was breathtaking! I took photos of it."

"That's Mount Hood."

"I love it here already."

His expression lightened. "That's what I hoped you'd say." He pointed toward the cars in front of them. "My truck is over here."

He led her through the rows of cars until they came to an older model, burgundy Ford F-250 extended cab pickup truck.

Warmth wafted over her. "This is your dad's truck."

"Yup." He placed her suitcase and backpack in the back seat. "Hop in."

She took her spot in the passenger seat, then Alex climbed in beside her. He tossed his baseball cap into the back seat before running a hand through his blond hair. Then he angled himself toward her, and the heat in his eyes nearly singed her skin.

"Now I can give you a proper hello," he said, placing his finger under her chin, urging her face toward his, and giving her a long, deep kiss.

Heather closed her eyes and rested her hand on his hard chest. She reveled in the feel of his lips against hers, his kiss sending tremors through her body like an earthquake.

Then he pulled away and turned the key, bringing the truck to life. "So tell me more about your grand opening day."

"It was amazing!" She clasped her hands together and smiled

as the details of the day filled her mind. "I don't think I told you that grouchy old Mr. Owens came by three times that day." She held up three fingers. "Three times! And he never bought a thing."

Alex scoffed. "Nothing?"

"No, but he kept swiping free samples of my Happily Ever After Scones."

Alex hooted. "That's unbelievable."

"I know." Then she snapped her fingers. "Oh! And Wendy held an impromptu story time for the little ones! She read *Are You My Mother?* and the kids loved it."

He placed a hand over his heart. "My favorite book."

"I know! It was a huge hit. She's going to start holding story time once a week. She said she'll only share the classics. She plans to read *Green Eggs and Ham* this week."

"What a great idea."

"The store has had such a great start. I'm so relieved."

He gave her a knowing look. "I'm not surprised. I knew it would do well, and I'm proud of you." He put the truck in gear.

"Oh, wait!" she cried. "Can you reach my backpack?"

His brow lifted as he shifted back into Park. He grabbed the backpack from the back floor and handed it to her.

Then she held out the shopping bag. "I got you a little something."

"You didn't need to get me anything."

"Right." She snorted. "I've lost count of all the gifts you've given me, not including the money you spent to fly me out here to see you. Please take it."

He opened the bag, and his eyes widened as he pulled out an original Beatles *Rubber Soul* record and an original *Waiting for the Sun* record from The Doors. His mouth dropped open, and he turned the records over in his hands. "Where did you find these?"

"I have connections. Remember that antique store on Main Street in Flowering Grove?"

He nodded.

"I went back and talked to Christine, the owner, and she helped me find them."

"Wow." He set the records on his lap and pulled her into his arms. "Thank you. I love them."

I love you, she wanted to say. "You're welcome," she said instead. She rested her head on his shoulder. "I've missed you so much."

He kissed her head. "I've missed you too." Then he released her, placed the records gently on the back seat, and buckled his seat belt.

Alex steered the truck down the ramp toward the automated exit machine. He fed a ticket into the slot and swiped a credit card to pay for parking.

"My mom is so excited to meet you," he said. Then he grimaced. "I'm afraid she might be pulling out photo albums from when I was a baby as we speak."

Heather guffawed. "Oh, I hope so." Then she settled back into the seat and smiled. It felt so right to be back with Alex once again.

After a short ride, Alex drove to a quiet neighborhood and parked in front of a two-story white house with a small front porch. A red front door displayed a flowery wreath with a sign reading "Welcome."

Alex killed the engine and removed the key from the ignition. Then he turned to face Heather. "Welcome to my childhood home."

"Wow." Her eyes widened to take in the house.

He chuckled. "It's nothing special."

"I think it's fantastic." Heather pushed open the door and climbed out of the truck while Alex retrieved her suitcase and backpack.

They walked up the front porch steps together, and when they reached the top step, the door flew open and a chocolate Lab bounded out with his tail wagging and tongue lolling out of his mouth.

A woman, whom Heather immediately recognized as Shannon Kirwan, stood at the door. She looked just as Heather remembered. She was slender and approximately an inch taller than Heather, and she had graying blond hair in a stylish, short, layered cut, along with bright blue eyes and a warm smile. Heather guessed the woman was in her early to midfifties.

"Heather!" Shannon declared, her arms opened wide. "Welcome!" Then she pulled Heather in for a tight squeeze. "I'm thrilled Alex finally brought you out here to meet me."

"Thank you for having me." Heather stepped out of her hug and then stooped to pet the dog. "Why, hello, Elvis. It's an honor to meet you too."

The dog responded by licking her face, and she laughed.

"It's always good to see you, Alex." Shannon hugged him.

"You too, Mom."

Shannon beckoned them into the house. "Come in. I picked up a coffee cake and I'll put on a pot of coffee as well."

Heather followed Shannon into the house, and the dog trotted behind them. They stepped through a small foyer into a spacious family room with a sprawling black leather sectional sofa, a couple of armchairs, and a large flat-screen television hanging on the wall above a fireplace. The furniture and the television looked new.

"This is beautiful," Heather said.

Shannon smiled. "Thank you. My sons insist on buying me new furniture fairly often, even though it's completely unnecessary." She seemed to share a look with Alex.

"That's because Mom won't let us buy her a new house, so we have to find other ways to spoil her," Alex said as he set the suitcase and backpack in the foyer.

Shannon lifted her arms. "Why would I want a new house when everything I need is right here?"

Heather peered around the room. "I think it's perfect." She turned toward a hallway and grinned when she spotted some old family photos hanging. She pointed at them. "May I?"

"Of course." Shannon motioned for Heather to follow her.

Alex groaned. "Oh no. Well, I'm going to use the restroom while you two ladies talk about me."

"Yay." Heather laughed as Alex fled the scene.

Shannon flipped on the light. "Here's Alex as a baby." She began pointing to photos. "And here's his father, Kenny."

Heather gasped as she took in how adorable Alex was. She recognized his smile and those gorgeous blue eyes. She examined a photo of Kenny and said, "Alex resembles him."

"He does." Shannon seemed lost in memories as she studied the photo. "Alex is also a lot like him. He's quiet and reserved and always puts his family first. He's caring, generous, and loyal." She turned to Heather. "And he really cares about you."

Heather smiled. "I care about him too."

"I'm so glad he met you. It really warms my soul to see him happy." Shannon touched Heather's shoulder. "Thank you for bringing my son's heart back to life."

Heather's eyes stung with joyful tears. "I don't know what to say, except that he's done the same for me."

"Alex is such a good man. He will go to the ends of the earth for you."

Heather nodded. "I've already gotten that impression, and I'm so grateful and surprised he picked me."

"I can tell you're special too." Then Shannon turned back to the gallery of photos and began sharing more stories of Alex's childhood. Heather tried to commit as many as possible to memory.

Soon Alex appeared at the end of the hallway. "Are you done embarrassing me yet, Mom?"

Shannon laughed. "I suppose so. Let's have some coffee and cake. Heather, I want to hear all about your store."

Heather followed her into the large kitchen, and Shannon brought a coffee cake to the table while Alex started the coffee maker. Soon they were sitting at the table, enjoying the evening treat while Heather talked about her store and shared photos with Shannon.

After a while, exhaustion overtook Heather. She covered her mouth in vain, hoping to hide her yawns.

Alex placed a hand over hers. "It's almost two in the morning on the East Coast. You need to get some rest. I'll show you where you're staying."

"Let me give you a key to the apartment and the house." Shannon chose a set of keys from a set of hooks on the wall and handed it to Heather. "If you need anything, just come in through this back door."

"Thank you." Heather pushed the keys into her pocket.

Alex retrieved her suitcase and backpack and then opened the back door before motioning for her to walk through first. They stepped out onto a large deck, then walked down the stairs before following the path to the three-car garage, sided in white to match the house.

"Was this garage one of the gifts you guys gave your mom?" she asked.

"My dad had built a one-car garage when I was a kid. My brothers and I added two more bays and the apartment a couple of years ago." He nodded toward the deck. "We also expanded the deck. We wanted to install a pool, but she told us it wasn't necessary."

They followed the path to a side door on the garage. Heather unlocked it and flipped on a light before ascending the steep steps. Then she stepped into the large apartment, which included a full kitchen, a table and four chairs, and a den with a sofa and television. She opened a nearby door and found a bathroom, then walked to the far end of the apartment and the large bedroom.

"What do you think?" Alex asked her.

She covered her mouth to shield another yawn. "It's perfect."

He chuckled and took her into his arms. "Looks like you need some rest. I'll pick you up for breakfast before sightseeing, okay?" He kissed her. "And have I told you how happy I am that you're here?"

"No, you haven't." She gave him a coy smile.

"I'm really, really, really glad you're here, Heather." He brushed his lips over hers again. "Good night. I'll see you in the morning."

"I'll be waiting for you." She grinned as she watched him go, so grateful to finally be in Oregon with him.

26

I love it here," Heather said as Alex steered his truck into downtown Portland. "I'm having so much fun."

Alex had picked her up around nine in the morning. They had eaten at one of his favorite places for breakfast before driving out to Crown Point to see the amazing Vista House. The scenic spot along Highway 30 had a breathtaking view overlooking the Columbia River. Heather had held Alex's hand while she took in the scene, marveling at the winding river and glorious mountains.

After stopping for lunch, they then headed to downtown Portland.

"I'm glad you're enjoying your visit." He gave her a sideways glance.

She angled her body toward him. "Where are you taking me now?"

"It's a surprise."

Heather stuck her lip out in a flirty little pout. "No fair."

"It will be worth the wait." He drove through downtown and parked in a garage. Then he grasped her hand and led her down to the street.

Heather pushed her hair behind her ears and scanned the buildings and the light-rail. "This city is just so cool!"

Alex chuckled. "You're easily impressed."

"I love the weather, and the mass transit is so progressive."

He adjusted his baseball cap on his head and put an arm around her. "I love seeing the world through your eyes."

She smiled up at him. *I love you*, she wanted to say again.

Alex steered her down another block and then pointed to the corner. "Ta-da!"

Heather's mouth dropped open as she took in the huge sign for Powell's Books. Then she looked up at Alex. "It's a bookstore."

"Not just any bookstore. It takes up an entire city block."

She squealed with delight. "Let's go!"

"Yes, ma'am." They crossed the street and entered the store.

For the next hour they browsed the stacks, and Alex encouraged Heather to pick out as many books as she wanted. After Alex had an armful of suspense novels for Heather along with two cookbooks she'd picked out for him as a joke, they strolled to the front of the store and took their place in the long line.

Alex studied the suspense title on top of the pile. "This one looks good." He flipped it over to examine the back.

While Alex read the blurb aloud, Heather cut her eyes to the crowd surrounding them, curious to see whether anyone recognized him. She spotted a few young women whispering and pointing in their direction.

Oh no. Here we go again.

"Next in line, please," called a cashier with a nose ring, an eyebrow ring, and bright purple hair.

Alex stepped up to the counter and set the books down. "How's it going?"

The young woman blinked at him as recognition flickered in her hazel eyes. "You look just like Alex Kirwan."

"I hear that a lot." He pulled his wallet from the back pocket of his jeans and found a credit card.

As the young woman began ringing up the books and a tote bag Alex had picked out, a low whispering buzz swept through the room. Alex paid and placed the receipt into the top book before slipping everything into the tote bag, thanking the cashier, and heading for the door. He turned to Heather and held his hand out to her.

Heather took his hand and blew out a deep sigh. They were in the clear. She must have imagined the attention the teenagers were giving Alex.

"That's Alex Kirwan!" a young woman announced.

The air in Heather's lungs seized as a crush of people gathered around them.

"What books did you buy, Alex?" a young man called.

"Is she your girlfriend?" another woman hollered.

"Where's Kayden?" a teenager asked.

Trepidation crept up Heather's spine, and her body began to tremble as a sea of phones were pointed at her and Alex. *Click*s sounded in the air.

"Hey, everyone." Alex released his grip on her, then held up his hand as a manufactured smile turned up the corners of his lips. "I'm just in town for a few days, so I wanted to stop in and pick up some books. I'm sorry, but we're on our way to an appointment. Thank you for understanding. Have a great afternoon."

Then he reached for Heather and guided her through the crowd and out the door.

"Are you okay?" he asked once they were across the street from the store and walking swiftly toward the parking garage.

She nodded, then released a shaky breath.

He held her closer to him. "I'm so sorry that happened."

"It's—it's not your fault."

Alex stopped at the entrance to the garage and swiveled to face her. "Are you sure you're okay?"

"Yeah," she said, still working to steady her breathing.

"I'm really sorry." He pushed a tendril of her hair behind her ear. "Unfortunately, that happens all the time. It's not easy to get used to."

She bit her lip and nodded, doing her best to stay calm. But deep down, she knew that sort of attention was something she could never, *ever* get used to.

⁓

Heather sat across from Alex in Ohana, a restaurant in Milwaukie, Oregon, later that evening. "This is wonderful. I've never had Hawaiian food before," she said. Then she took another bite of teriyaki chicken and savored the taste.

"It's one of my favorites." Alex wiped his mouth with a napkin. "So what was your favorite part of today?"

"Hmm." She set her fork beside her plate. "That's a tough question. I'd have to say just being with you is my favorite part."

He shook his head. "Nope. I need something more specific."

She laughed as she cut her eyes around the restaurant, hoping none of the other patrons recognized him. She dreaded a repeat of the fiasco in the bookstore. "Browsing the books at Powell's was fun, but I loved the breathtaking view at Crown Point too."

Alex reached across the table and touched her hand, his blue eyes filling with concern. "Are you all right?"

"Yeah. Why?" She tried to smile.

He seemed to study her. "You look . . . preoccupied."

"What happened in the bookstore kind of freaked me out."

She ran her finger along the rim of her glass. "When all of those people crowded around us and then pulled out their phones to take photos, it was a lot for me to handle."

He huffed out a breath. "I'm sorry."

"You need to stop apologizing for being famous."

"I don't like to see you upset. I'll do my best to protect you from it all, okay?"

"Okay." She felt herself relax despite the niggle of worry that lingered in the back of her mind.

After they finished their meals and Alex paid the check, they retreated to the sidewalk. Heather breathed in the comfortable air and smiled up at the sky as the sun began to set. "The weather is perfect, as is the company. Let's have more nights like this, okay?"

"Eventually, I'd like to have every night like this."

She stopped walking and faced him as her heart made a dizzying *thump-thump*. "What do you mean?"

"Well, what I mean is—"

"Alex?" a woman's voice called. "Alex Kirwan, is that you?"

Heather pressed her lips together as frustration erupted inside her. She pivoted toward a beautiful blond hurrying toward them. The woman had long sunshine-colored hair, bright blue eyes, a long neck, and slender legs—and Heather got the distinct impression that she wasn't a fan. No, this woman knew Alex personally. And Heather's frustration morphed into confusion and then worry. She swiveled toward Alex as an unreadable expression flickered over his features.

He pinched the bridge of his nose. "Celeste. Hi."

Heather stiffened. *Celeste.* So this was the ex-girlfriend—the *gorgeous* ex-girlfriend, who looked to be at least five feet ten.

Celeste divided a look between Heather and Alex.

"Uh, Heather," Alex began with a sweeping gesture, "this is Celeste Mayer."

Heather managed a quick nod.

"Hi," Celeste said before turning her focus back to Alex. Her gaze raked over him as she sized him up and grinned. "You look good, Alex—*really* good, as a matter of fact. You work out, huh?" Celeste twisted a lock of her incredible hair around her finger.

Heather set her jaw as jealousy wrapped around her lungs and squeezed.

Alex shifted his weight on his feet and then took Heather's hand in his. "It was nice bumping into you, but we really need to get going."

"That's a shame. Well, take care. It was great seeing you too," Celeste called as Alex guided Heather toward the end of the block where they'd parked his truck.

"I'm so sorry," he muttered. "I never expected to see her."

Heather remained silent as envy continued to sear through her. She never expected Celeste to look like a supermodel!

Once they had climbed into the truck, he turned to face her. "I know I keep asking you this, but are you okay?"

Heather blinked. "She was stunning."

He snorted.

"Why are you laughing?"

"Because she's invisible next to you."

"Are you teasing me?" She pointed in the direction of the restaurant. "Did you see her hair and those legs? And how about those blue eyes? I mean, she looks like a supermo—"

Alex cut off her words with a kiss.

When she finally came up for air, she worked to catch her breath. "What was that for?"

"To remind you that *you're* my girlfriend. You're the woman I want in my life, not her." Then he touched her nose. "And you know what my favorite feature of yours is, right?"

She shook her head.

"Those freckles." He moved a finger over her cheeks. "After I met you the first time in your parents' restaurant, I couldn't stop thinking about your adorable freckles and how you told me you would be too busy washing your hair to come to my show."

She laughed.

"There's that smile I love so much. Now, forget about Celeste and start thinking about a movie we can watch tonight." Alex started the truck, then steered out to the road.

And Heather finally felt herself relax.

⌒

Alex laughed as he sat in the dining room the following evening surrounded by Heather, his brothers, mother, and Charlie, his mother's "friend," who clearly was her boyfriend by the way he kept touching her shoulder. His eyes were glued to her as she shared a story about driving off with Alex's sippy cup on the roof of her station wagon.

"I heard this horrific rattling noise, so I pulled over and got out to find the cup rolling around inside the roof rack. The sound was just terrifying. I had thought to myself, *What is Kenny going to say when I tell him the car is broken?*"

Heather chuckled and shook her head. "That sounds like something I would do."

"Heather, this chocolate cake is fantastic," Charlie said.

"Thank you." Heather smiled as she lifted her cup of coffee. "Shannon and I made it together."

Mom nodded. "We had fun, didn't we?"

"And the beef stroganoff was great too, Shannon," Heather said.

"I'm glad you liked it."

"So, Heather," Kayden began from across the table, "where has Alex taken you so far this week?"

"Yesterday we went to Crown Point and then to Powell's."

Kayden grinned. "Of course, a bookstore."

"Well, it *is* the best bookstore in the nation," Alex said.

"Yes, it is," Heather agreed. "Then we ate at Ohana."

"Oh, I love that place." Jordan gave a dreamy smile.

"I did as well," Heather said. "And today we got up early and drove out to Seaside. I was so thrilled to finally see the Pacific Ocean."

Mom's eyes brightened. "Did you like all of those cute little stores?"

"Yes, I did," Heather said. "I bought fun gifts for my parents, my sister, and a couple of friends. I still can't believe you don't have any sales tax here. That is crazy."

Mom stood and began picking up their empty plates. "How about we clean up and then play a game or watch a movie?"

"A game sounds like fun," Charlie said. He lifted his mug and reached for Mom's, Kayden's, and Jordan's.

After the table was clear and the dishwasher was humming, they moved to the family room and soon were involved in a rousing game of Pictionary. Alex was delighted by the way Heather laughed along with everyone. She seemed relaxed—at ease among the rest of his family.

After the second round of the game, Jordan and Kayden said good night to everyone. After hugging Mom and Heather, they took turns shaking Charlie's hand.

Kayden slapped Alex's arm. "We'll see you at the airport bright and early Friday."

Alex nodded. "I'll be there."

"Bye, bro," Jordan called before both brothers headed outside.

Charlie kissed Mom's check. "I'll call you tomorrow, Shannon," he promised. Then he shook Alex's hand. "It was nice to finally meet you."

"You too," Alex told him.

Heather excused herself to the restroom. After she disappeared down the hallway, Mom turned to Alex. "What do you think of Charlie?"

Alex crossed his arms over his chest and rested one shoulder against the wall. "He's nice, but don't tell me you're just friends."

"Well, we're sort of dating."

Alex snorted. "Just call it what it is. We're all adults."

"I don't want to upset you."

"Mom," Alex began, "you're a grown woman, and you've been alone for a long time. We all just want you to be happy."

Mom smiled. "Thank you." Then she peeked toward the hallway before leaning in closer to Alex. "I've already told you I approve of Heather, but I think you need to snatch this one up."

"You're right, but I don't know how to find a balance. My schedule is a circus, and she has a great life back in North Carolina. How do I make it work?"

"I don't know the answer, but you need to figure it out. She's crazy about you, and you're crazy about her. You two belong together."

"I hope so." Alex nodded, grateful for his mother's blessing. He just prayed he could find a way for them.

27

Heather held Alex's hand as they walked out of the children's hospital the following afternoon. "That was fun." She leaned her head against his shoulder. "I love seeing you interact with the kids. You truly have a gift."

"I was surprised you wanted to go to a hospital since today is our last day before I head to Europe tomorrow." He pulled his keys out of his pocket, and they jingled in his hand.

They entered the parking garage and headed toward his car, which waited at the far end of the second floor.

"I really do enjoy watching you with the kids. Plus, I'm just happy to spend time with you." She grinned as they approached his powder-blue 1966 convertible Mustang with a white top. "I have a confession though."

Alex's lips twitched. "Uh-oh. Sounds serious."

"Now don't be jealous, but I kind of have a crush on your gorgeous car." She ran her finger along the quarter panel.

He snickered as he unlocked the trunk and stowed his guitar case, along with a bag of leftover toys. "Well, I can't blame you there. I have a crush on her as well, but my feelings for her are nothing compared to how I feel about you."

Heather took her spot in the passenger seat and opened the window.

Alex rested his forearms on her door. "Would you like to ride with the top down?"

"Yes, please."

He leaned in and kissed her. "Your wish is my command."

"When did you buy this beauty?" she asked as he went through the motions to lower the top.

"She was my first purchase when my brothers and I got our record deal. My dad always dreamed of owning one, so I bought it in memory of him."

"That's really sweet."

"Later I got a newer Mustang too. I'll show it to you when we go by my house tonight. My dad was always a Ford fan, so I blame him for my love of them." He finished lowering the top and then joined Heather in the car. "Now we're free until it's time for supper at Tristan's. Where to next?"

"You mentioned that you got your start at a coffee shop, right?"

He perched a pair of mirrored sunglasses on his face and then started the car. "That's true. I worked as a barista during the day and then performed there with my brothers a few nights a week."

"Wanna take me there?" she asked.

He put the car in Reverse and began slowly backing out of the parking spot. "It's actually not far from here."

"Awesome." Then she recalled the mob scene at the bookstore and felt her smile flatten. "Do you think it'll be busy?"

"Not on a Thursday afternoon."

"Perfect." She reached over and rested her hand on his as Alex drove out of the hospital parking garage and motored the car through Portland.

Soon he parked in a lot near a strip of businesses. He closed the convertible top, locked up the car, and retrieved his guitar from the trunk before they entered Java and Tunes.

The aroma of coffee overwhelmed Heather as she took in the restaurant. Two baristas worked at a counter spanning a sea of wooden tables and chairs and a stage at the far wall. She imagined Alex here serving coffee, then singing with his brothers onstage before they became international superstars.

Nearly a dozen patrons sat at the tables, while a few more stood at the counter awaiting their orders.

"Alex Kirwan! What brings you back to this little hole in the wall?" a man called out. A buzz then sounded throughout the coffee shop as patrons turned their heads toward the counter.

Heather felt her body stiffen as Alex made a beeline to the counter and shook a balding man's hand.

"Gene!" Alex set his guitar case on the floor, then leaned over the counter to give the man a one-armed hugged. "You look amazing." Then he motioned for Heather to join him. "I want you to meet Heather."

The older man shook her hand. "You got yourself a great man here," he said.

"I agree." Heather beamed at Alex, and he responded with a sheepish expression. She silently marveled at how a celebrity could be so humble. He truly was the opposite of his youngest brother, who always seemed to bask in the spotlight.

"What can I get you two?" Gene offered.

Alex nodded at Heather. "What would you like?"

"A vanilla latte, please," she said.

Alex pulled out his wallet. "I'll take an Americano."

Gene waved him off. "Your money's no good here."

"I owe you for giving my brothers and me our first break."

"Pshaw!" Gene grunted. "We're grateful you shared your talent with us. I'm not taking your money."

Alex shook his head as he pulled out a stack of bills and shoved it into the tip jar.

"Your orders will be right up, and I'll bring them out to you," Gene said. "Will you perform for us?"

Alex glanced at Heather as if asking permission, and she shrugged. "Why are you looking at *me*?"

"Are you comfortable with me singing with all these people here? They might take videos."

"I'd be grateful to hear you. You haven't sung for me since I got here on Monday," Heather said, overwhelmed by his thoughtfulness.

Alex removed his guitar and a yellow pick from the case, then pointed to the tables. "Where would you like us to sit?"

Heather chose a seat near the back of the restaurant. Alex set the case on the chair beside her and kissed her cheek before sauntering toward the stage, where a microphone stand and a stool waited for him.

Someone near the center of the crowd began to clap, and soon the entire restaurant was filled with patrons' claps, cheers, and whistles.

Alex raised his hand in response before flipping on the microphone, settling on the stool, and adjusting the microphone stand to his height. "Testing," he said, and his voice sounded throughout the coffee shop. "Hi, everyone. I'm Alex."

A few folks in the crowd clapped, and when someone yelled, "We know!" the audience members laughed.

Alex chuckled. "Some of you may or may not know that I got my start here, and I'm so grateful to Gene, who not only hired me as a barista but also let my brothers and me sing on this very stage." He propped a foot on the bottom rung of the stool while a few folks continued to clap. "My life has changed a bit since the last time I was here, and it feels great to be back."

Scanning the audience, Heather spotted a few folks holding up phones. She imagined that videos of Alex's performance would be uploaded to social media within hours or minutes.

Alex strummed the guitar, and someone whistled. Then he pulled the microphone closer. "This is one you might know." He licked his lips and then began the opening chords of the hit "The Faster We Go."

Heather rested her elbow on the table and her chin on her palm as she marveled at how completely at ease Alex seemed in front of an audience full of strangers. She would have passed out from stage fright before she even made it to the mic.

As he sang, she tried her best to freeze the moment in time. Then she pulled out her phone and snapped two photos. If only this day could last forever.

Gene came to stand beside her and set the two cups of coffee on the table. "He is one talented fella."

"Yeah, he is." She released a deep breath.

Gene kept his eyes focused on Alex. "And he's humble too."

"That's very true." Heather took a sip of her latte. "Delicious. Thank you."

"You're welcome, sweetie. Enjoy." Gene gave her shoulder a light pat and then returned to the counter.

Alex finished the song, and the crowd cheered, clapped, and whistled once again.

"Thank you so much." He strummed a chord. "Next I'd like to sing a song for a special person." His eyes focused on Heather. "This one is for you, babe." Then he began the opening chords of "When I Dream," a lyrical love song, and happiness buzzed through her.

When a few folks in the audience turned to look at her, her

face felt hot and prickly. A few of them focused their cameras on her, taking her photo and recording her. She hugged her arms to her chest and tried to tamp down her self-consciousness.

After Alex finished the song, he took a few requests. "Thank you for allowing me a chance to revisit my roots for a while," he said, standing and grinning over at Gene. "Be sure to tip your barista."

The audience clapped, and he took a bow before stepping down from the stage. Members of the crowd stood and began shooting questions at him.

"How long are you in town?"

"Could I have your autograph?"

"My sister is never going to believe that I got to see you perform today. Could I get a selfie with you?"

Alex pointed to the table where Heather sat. "I'm going to drink my coffee, but you're welcome to stop by for autographs." He strolled back to the table and tucked his guitar and pick into the case before sitting beside Heather and sampling his drink.

"As always, you were amazing," she told him.

He kissed her cheek. "Thank you, babe."

Heather did her best to hold back her shock when she caught a few folks recording the kiss on their phones. Would her photo be plastered all over the internet? And what kind of fallout would she and Alex face when the world found out he was dating someone?

While these questions swirled in her mind, Alex patiently answered questions, posed for photos, and signed autographs for what felt like the next half hour.

While she sat beside him and watched him work the crowd, Heather kept wondering where she belonged in his world. After all, he was famous, and she was no one.

After signing the last autograph, Alex covered Heather's

hand with his. "Ready to go? We should probably head out so we're not late for supper."

"Good idea. We need to stop somewhere to pick up dessert too." They gathered their things to go, and as Heather and Alex exited the small coffee shop, she breathed a sigh of relief to be leaving the prying eyes behind.

Alex stretched his arm out and rested it on the back of Heather's chair. Then he ran his thumb along her shoulder blades and inhaled the warm evening air. He detected a hint of rain as he looked out over Tristan's deck, appreciating the beautiful view from the side of the mountain where Tristan's house was perched.

The sky above them was dark and clogged with gray clouds. They had enjoyed a scrumptious meal of steaks and loaded baked potatoes. It had been a perfect evening to spend with friends, and Alex couldn't be happier.

"Your store sounds amazing, Heather. I'd love to see it someday." Justine absently moved her hand over her distended stomach.

Heather picked up her glass of Diet Coke. "I would love that."

Justine gave her husband a pointed look. "We need to take a trip to North Carolina. I told you I wanted to see the Outer Banks someday."

"Well, dear, I think we might be a little busy for the next couple of years, so your dream trip may have to wait." Tristan pointed to his wife's belly, and they all laughed.

Joy coursed through Alex as he took in the smiles Heather shared with Justine and Tristan. Once again, he marveled at how well Heather fit into his life.

Justine held on to the table and hoisted herself up from her chair. "I need to get these dishes cleaned up so we can enjoy that carrot cake you brought."

Heather stacked up their plates, and Tristan took the platter of leftover steak from Justine. "You insisted on cooking, so I will handle the dishes," he said, meeting Alex's gaze. "Alex will help me because even famous people do the dishes. Right, buddy?"

"I'm glad to help, but normally my butler handles mine," he quipped, and everyone laughed.

Heather added utensils to her stack of dishes. "I can help too."

"No, you won't," Justine said. "You're going to come with me to see the nursery."

Heather's expression lit up. "I'd love to!" She blessed Alex with a sweet smile, then followed Justine into the house.

Tristan eyed Alex from across the table. "What are you waiting for, man?"

"What do you mean?"

"Give her a ring. Marry her, Alex. She's perfect for you. She's sweet, funny, hardworking, and crazy about you."

Alex cupped his hand to the back of his neck. "I agree, but we've only been dating three months, and I haven't even told her that I love her yet."

"*Do* you love her?" Tristan asked.

"Yes, I have for a while. I was going to tell her tonight."

"Then tell her. Don't wait too long."

"I know." Alex blew out a deep breath. "My mom said something similar last night, but I'm afraid Heather won't want to deal with my schedule and the chaos of being with a celebrity."

"If you love each other, you'll find a way to make it work."

Alex nodded, and his throat dried at the idea of telling Heather exactly how he felt.

Heather entered the nursery and took in the white walls decorated with gray and blue silhouettes of dinosaurs, with a matching dinosaur mobile dangling over the white crib. The room also held a bookshelf full of colorful books, along with a white changing table and dresser. "Ryker" was spelled out in blue letters above the crib. "This room is stunning," she told Justine.

"Thank you." Justine sank down gingerly onto a white rocking chair and picked up a stuffed Tyrannosaurus rex. "I saw a few ideas on Pinterest but then gave it my own spin. I just hope little Ryker loves dinosaurs as much as his dad and I do."

Heather chuckled. "I'm sure he will with a room like this!"

After a brief pause in the conversation, Justine looked at Heather and said, "I've known Alex for about six years now. Maybe seven. And I've never seen him as happy as he is when he's with you."

Heather studied Justine but didn't find any signs of a lie on her pretty face.

Justine tilted her head. "You look like you're not quite sure if you should believe me."

"Well, we ran into Celeste Tuesday evening." Heather brushed her finger over the edge of the crib.

Justine made a face as if she were smelling something foul. "I'm sorry to hear that."

Heather couldn't stop her laugh.

"Let me guess." Justine held up her hand. "She was super phony, right?"

Heather folded her arms over her chest. "She made a point of telling Alex how good he looked and how obvious it was that he went to the gym." She narrowed her eyes to slits. "It was like she was undressing him with her eyes. It made me sick."

"I never liked her, and I never trusted her either. Celeste only cared about what Alex could do for her."

Heather nodded. "He told me something similar."

"But you're different. You're good for him."

Heather gave her a palms-up. "I'm just not sure how I can fit into his life since we're so different. I'm nothing but a small business owner from North Carolina."

"First of all, don't sell yourself short. Your store sounds very cool. And second, Alex hates the fame. I think he'd give it up for you."

Heather shook her head. "I don't want him to give up anything for me."

Justine pushed herself up from the chair, set the stuffed animal on the seat, and walked over to Heather. "Compromise is the key. Tristan and I are different, and that's what keeps it interesting. You can make it work if you want to. Trust me on that." Then she touched Heather's arm. "I could go for some of that delicious carrot cake right about now. What do you say?"

Heather smiled as she followed Justine to the stairs, grateful for a new friend.

⌒

After they left Tristan and Justine's house, Alex drove his Mustang up a steep hill and stopped in front of a gate. He pushed a controller on his sun visor, then steered past the open gate before pushing the button to close it. They motored down a long driveway that stopped in front of a one-story house with a three-car garage.

"Wow. It's gorgeous." She turned toward him. "I thought you said you had a modest home."

"I do compared to my brothers' houses."

Heather shook her head and laughed.

He hit another button on the sun visor, and the garage door

on the far right hummed and lifted. He nosed his car into the garage and turned to Heather. "Welcome to my home."

"Thank you." She climbed out of the car and turned toward a royal-blue, late-model Mustang. "This one is gorgeous too. I officially have crushes on both of your Mustangs."

He closed the driver's side door and came to stand beside her. "The next time you come, you can drive them and tell me which one you like more."

"I would be honored."

He slung his arm around her shoulders. "Come on. I'll give you the twenty-five-cent tour."

Alex closed the garage door and gestured for Heather to step inside the house first. As soon as her foot touched the tile floor, an alarm began to bleat.

He followed her and then typed a code into a keypad on the wall. "Sorry. I had this installed along with the gate when we started touring." Then he began explaining the layout of the house. "Over here is the laundry room—"

"Does the butler handle your laundry or only the dishes?" Heather teased.

"He usually takes care of both, but he's off on Thursdays," he said with a grin. Then they walked into a tremendous kitchen with an eat-in dining area and a huge island.

She blew out a low whistle. "I could give line dancing lessons in here."

"Now that I'd like to see." He stepped into a formal dining room complete with a mahogany table with eight chairs. "I never use this room."

"You should. It's lovely."

Then they walked to a large den with a tan leather sectional with built-in recliners, a coffee table, and an entertainment center with a flat-screen television. On the far wall, she spotted a credenza with a turntable, speakers, and a shelf of record albums. "Here's the family room."

She ran her fingers along the sectional. "Nice."

"Thank you." He pointed to a wall of windows. "But the deck might be my favorite."

She looked out at the gorgeous view of the city below and gasped.

"Impressive, isn't it?" He crossed his arms over his wide chest. "That's what sold me on the house."

She nodded.

"My bedroom is over there." He pointed toward a short hallway. "And a bathroom, of course." He crossed to a staircase that went down. "There are three more bedrooms and a rec room downstairs, along with two more bathrooms. One of the bedrooms is set up like a little music studio with my guitars." Then he faced her. "And there you have it."

She smiled up at him. "The house is amazing, just like you are."

"You are easily impressed, Heather Gordon." Alex shook his head and then touched her nose.

She pointed to the hallway. "May I use your restroom?"

"Sure. Just leave a quarter on the tank."

She chuckled and made her way down the hall. After using the facilities, she washed her hands and checked her image in the mirror. Sadness already lined her face, reflecting the gloom she felt about another long separation from Alex. Tomorrow she would fly back home to North Carolina while he jetted off to Europe, and she wouldn't see him again for at least a month. How would she cope with saying goodbye to him again?

Heather finger-combed her hair before exiting the bathroom. She spotted the french doors leading to the deck open, and she padded out to where Alex leaned on the railing, overlooking the lights glowing in the city below. The air was cool and held the promise of rain.

She stood behind him for a moment, and worry threaded through her. "Alex? Are you okay?"

He swiveled to face her. "I'm better than okay." Then he extended his hand to her. "Come here."

She closed the distance between them and entwined her fingers with his.

"Heather, this has been the best week of my life. I'm so glad to have you here with me."

She smiled. "I feel the same way."

Then he reached into his pocket. "Thank you for making me so happy." He placed something metal and cool in her hand. "You have carried my heart since I met you, and I hope you understand how much you mean to me."

Opening her hand, she found a gold necklace with a diamond-encrusted heart pendant, and her mouth fell open. "Alex . . ." She breathed his name. "This is too much."

"I love you, Heather," he said, his voice tremulous. "I've loved you for a while, but I was afraid to tell you. I'm not afraid anymore."

"I love you too," she whispered as happy tears stung her eyes and a mist of rain kissed her cheeks.

He dipped his chin, and her breath hitched in her lungs as his lips met hers. Happiness blossomed in her, and she melted against him as the light sprinkle continued to fall on her bare skin.

She looped her arms around his neck and pulled him closer. He deepened the kiss, and the contact made every cell in her body catch fire. She closed her eyes and savored the feel of his mouth against hers as the drizzle transformed into soft raindrops.

He broke the kiss as larger drops began soaking his gray t-shirt. "I think it's raining."

"You think so?" She reached up and ran her hand through his wet hair.

They both laughed as the rain fell harder all around them. Then she grabbed his wet shirt and tugged him toward her. "Kiss me again, Alex."

"Yes, ma'am." His grin was wicked, and she swallowed against a sudden rush of desire pulsing through her body.

When Alex's lips found hers once more, she wished she could hold the moment forever.

28

"How did you sleep last night?" Alex asked Heather the following morning while they rode in a sleek black SUV to the airport.

As if on cue, Heather covered a yawn with her hand. After kissing in the rain last night, they had trudged back into the house and dried themselves off with towels. They then spent their remaining time together snuggling on the sofa and watching a movie.

Later, Alex had dropped her off at his mother's house. Heather packed and tried to sleep, but she'd stayed awake most of the night trying to prepare herself to say goodbye to Alex in the morning.

She rubbed her tired eyes. "I slept a little."

"I'm sorry we ran out of time." He took her hand in his.

She smiled. "That's how time works, I guess."

His smile faded, and worry trickled through her. "There's something I want to say to you," he began. "My life is chaotic and sometimes complicated, but I want to do everything in my power to make you happy—if you'll let me."

She was overwhelmed with love for this incredible man. As

she shifted toward him to kiss his cheek, he turned his head and met her lips with his.

"I love you, Alex," she told him, placing a hand over her heart necklace.

He nodded toward the pendant. "Take care of my heart, okay?" When he grinned, her pulse took on wings.

"I'll do my best."

The driver stopped the car in front of the sign for departures, then met them at the car's open trunk. Alex gave the driver a handful of bills and thanked him before unloading their suitcases and backpacks and setting them on the sidewalk.

Alex adjusted his baseball cap on his head and met Heather's gaze. "Are you ready?"

"No, not really." She shouldered her backpack and purse. "I don't want to say goodbye to you." Her voice was strained, and she felt a catch in her throat.

He touched her cheek. "I know, babe, but I promise I'll see you as soon as I get back from Europe."

"I'll be waiting for you." She touched her necklace. "And I'll take good care of your heart."

They walked together into the terminal, and Heather followed him to the priority check-in. She glanced around at the crowd of passengers standing at the kiosks or waiting in line at the luggage drop. She was relieved no one had seemed to notice Alex and hoped it would stay that way.

Heather and Alex typed their information into the kiosk and printed their boarding passes and luggage tags before moving to the counter, where a young woman dressed in a blue pantsuit, her dark hair styled in a tight bun, greeted them.

Alex motioned for Heather to go first.

Heather handed the clerk her ID and boarding pass while Alex set Heather's suitcase on the scale.

"You're flying to Charlotte today?" the woman asked.

Heather nodded. "Yes."

"Have a nice flight," she said before she faced Alex. "And you, sir?"

Heather held her breath while the clerk examined Alex's license. When recognition flashed across her face, Heather sucked in a breath.

The woman's eyes flickered to Alex's face, and a sweet smile overtook her lips. "Mr. Kirwan."

Heather peeked up at Alex, but his expression remained pleasant.

The woman handed him his license and boarding pass and then moved his suitcase to the conveyor. "Have a nice flight."

"Thank you." Alex lifted his backpack onto his shoulder and then reached for Heather's. "May I take this one for you?"

She shook her head and set it on her shoulder along with her purse. "I got it."

"Stubborn," he teased before threading his fingers with hers and leading her toward the priority TSA line. "You okay?"

"I thought for sure she was going to freak out when she realized who you are," Heather whispered as they took their place in the long queue.

Alex shrugged. "I try to be prepared for anything."

"How do you stay so calm?"

"Just because I'm acting cool doesn't mean I'm not silently praying she won't cause a scene."

Her brow furrowed as questions roared through her mind.

"What's going on in that pretty head of yours?"

Heather pivoted as more people lined up behind them. She spotted two teenaged girls, so she moved closer to Alex and lowered her voice. "Doesn't it bother you when people invade your space?"

"Sure, but I've come to accept it as part of the job."

"It doesn't upset you when you're just minding your own business and people yell your name and demand your time?" she asked. "Like when we were in the bookstore, and they were so pushy? They acted as if they own you and you owe them an autograph or photo. They just pulled out their phones and started recording you. They didn't even ask for permission."

Alex nodded, then took a few steps forward as the line moved. "Heather, you have to understand that I do owe them if they buy my music or spend their hard-earned money on my shows."

"But they don't own you, Alex."

He blew out a deep breath.

"You're entitled to your privacy," she said. "For all we know, they've already posted those videos of us online."

His handsome face filled with concern. "And how would you feel about that?"

Heather's stomach dipped at the idea of her face being plastered all over the internet. "I—I don't know."

"I wish my life was less complicated than it is." He touched her face. "If I could change it, I would. And you know I would leave it all behind for you if I didn't feel obligated to my brothers. I'm sorry that I can't."

"Don't apologize for your life," she said. "I love you for the wonderful man you are."

His blue eyes softened, and he tugged her closer to him.

"Next in line, please!"

Heather followed Alex over to the TSA agent, and they made their way through the security checkpoint before walking out to the concourse.

"Your flight leaves before mine," he said.

She released a breath. "I know. We're running out of time."

"Let's walk over to your gate and find a place to talk."

Alex held her hand, and they strode down the concourse toward the gate for her flight. Heather's eyes scanned the area, on alert for anyone who might recognize him. When they reached the gate, they both checked the digital display.

"Looks like we have about ten minutes before they'll start boarding," he said. He pointed to a far corner. "We can go stand over there and wait."

Alex kept his eyes focused on the floor until they reached the deserted area. When he set his backpack down, his phone chimed with a text, but he kept his focus on Heather.

"Do you want to check your message?"

"No." He took her hands and closed the gap between them. "You have my undivided attention until you leave."

"But that might be important."

He gave her a look. "Not as important as you."

She lifted her eyebrows.

"If it makes you feel better, I'll check it." He pulled out his phone, read the screen, and then showed it to her. "It's Jordan letting me know that he and Kayden are on their way to the airport. Our equipment and instruments are also on their way, and the crew will meet us in LA."

"Are you taking a private plane from there?"

"Exactly." He studied her. "But why do you want to spend our last few minutes discussing the tour when we could be kissing?"

She grinned. "Now you're talking."

He leaned forward and ran a thumb along her jawline before meeting her with a kiss. She encircled her arms around his neck and breathed in his scent, enjoying the security of his muscular arms wrapped around her middle. She reached up and plunged her fingers into his soft hair, accidentally knocking the ball cap off his head.

She stepped back and laughed. "Whoops. I got lost in the moment." She picked up the hat and handed it to him.

"It's okay." He pushed his hair back and repositioned the hat.

"Is that Alex Kirwan?" someone called.

"I *told* you that was Alex Kirwan!" someone else yelled. "I saw him over at the security checkpoint."

Heather spun as a crowd headed toward them with their phones out. Dread hit her so hard and fast it felt like someone had punched her.

"Alex! Where are you headed?" someone called.

Heather's stomach plummeted as panic spread through her.

Alex rested his hand on her shoulder. "It's okay," he whispered in her ear. "Just take deep breaths." He held up his hand as his lips turned up in a smile that didn't quite meet his eyes. "We were just saying goodbye, and we'd appreciate it if you could stand back, please. Thank you." Then he turned back to Heather. "Breathe, Heather. You look like you're going to pass out."

Then the crowd began lobbing questions like grenades.

"Is she your girlfriend?" someone asked.

"Are you flying somewhere together?"

"Where did you meet?"

"Are you engaged?"

"We're now boarding our first-class passengers on Flight 183 to Charlotte through gate C36," a man called over the loudspeaker. "All first-class passengers can board through lane one."

Alex's expression fell. "That's you, Heather. Go."

Her words were trapped in her throat as she looked up at him.

"I love you," he said. "I'll text and call you, okay?"

She nodded as tears stung her eyes.

"Hey. It's okay." Leaning down, he kissed her once more, and she was certain she heard camera apps clicking. "I love you, Heather," he repeated.

"I love you too," she managed to say.

Alex nodded in the direction of the gate and gave her hand a gentle squeeze. "Go get on that plane."

Heather let him go, then weaved through the sea of people gathered around them. She hurtled toward the gate and ripped her boarding pass from her pocket. When she reached the counter, she looked back at where they had been standing.

Anger replaced her anxiety when she spotted Alex still surrounded by a mob of people. He waved, still watching her, and she returned the gesture before handing the flight attendant her boarding pass and hurrying down the Jetway.

Her phone chimed as she set her purse and backpack beneath the seat in front of her. She yanked her phone from her pocket and found a message from her best friend.

MCKENNA: Have you boarded the plane yet? I hate to bother you, but I feel like I should warn you about something.

Fear jolted Heather as she imagined something bad happening to a member of her family or maybe her store.

HEATHER: Just got on the plane. What's up?
MCKENNA: You're sitting down?
HEATHER: Yes. Please just tell me.

Conversation bubbles appeared, and as they continued, more worry and horrible scenarios overtook her mind.

HEATHER: Hurry up and tell me, Mack!

Finally, Mckenna's message came through.

MCKENNA: I ran into Wendy during my lunch break yesterday, and she told me Deanna was reading some gossip
blogs online. You're already trending.

HEATHER: What do you mean by "trending"?

MCKENNA: There are photos and videos of you and Alex
all over the internet. Wendy was afraid to tell you, but I
felt like you should know. Check this out.

Heather clicked on the link Mckenna sent. It took her
to a website called Celebrity Secrets, where she found photos
of her and Alex at Powell's, along with photos and a video of
Alex kissing her cheek at the coffee shop. Her eyes stung as she
perused the comments.

Who's that girl?

Alex can do so much better.

What does he see in her?

*She's so ordinary! Does that mean I can find my own famous
sugar daddy too?*

"Oh no." Heather sniffed as her eyes overflowed, sending
tears trailing down her hot cheeks.

"Are you okay, miss?"

Heather's head snapped up to meet the gaze of an older man
dressed in a flight attendant uniform. "Yes," she managed to say,
her voice thick.

"Would you like something to drink?"

"Water, please."

He nodded and then disappeared toward the front of the
plane.

Heather's phone dinged again.

MCKENNA: Are you okay? I didn't want to spring this on
you, but I would want to know if I were in your shoes.

There are other websites with photos too, but you
should ignore the comments. It's so obvious Alex
loves you. You're beautiful and amazing, Heather! You
deserve all the happiness you've found with him. Forget
about those internet trolls!

Heather's thumbs hovered over the digital keyboard on her
phone, but she couldn't form a response. Her mind was reeling
with anger and anguish. The world now knew she was dating
Alex Kirwan.

Was she strong enough to face the scrutiny? And what would
happen if the media found out her name? Would her life be
changed forever?

Her phone dinged again.

MCKENNA: Heather! Please answer me and tell me you're
okay!
HEATHER: I'm okay.
MCKENNA: Are you really? Ugh. Maybe I shouldn't have
told you.
HEATHER: I'm glad you told me. I'm just a little shocked.

She ran her fingers over her heart pendant and closed her
eyes, trying to concentrate on Alex and the last kiss they'd
shared—but her mind kept returning to the nasty comments
about her.

The flight attendant returned and handed her a cold bottle
of water.

"Thank you," she said.

A middle-aged woman with graying black hair appeared
in the aisle and sank into the seat beside Heather. She nodded,
then pulled a paperback novel from her designer bag.

Heather's phone chimed with another text. She considered not reading it, but when her curiosity overwhelmed her, she read Alex's name on the screen.

ALEX: Are you okay?

Heather considered telling him no and sending him the link to the gossip website, but she decided not to worry him. Instead, she chose to digest the news before starting a conversation they couldn't finish until they both had made it to their destinations.

HEATHER: Yes. You?
ALEX: I'm fine. I survived the crowd and hid out in a
    restroom for a while.

He paused for a moment and then added: I'm sorry.

HEATHER: Don't apologize, Alex. It's not your fault. And by
    the way, I miss you already.
ALEX: Me too. Have a good flight. I love you.
HEATHER: I love you too.
ALEX: Text me when you get to Charlotte.
HEATHER: I will.
ALEX: ♥

Heather wiped her eyes, then clicked back to the gossip website for another look. As she read comment after comment questioning who she was and why Alex would be interested in her, she realized the website had substantiated her fears. She had no business believing she was good enough for Alex or could ever belong in his world. And with that admission, Heather felt her heart begin to crack.

29

As soon as the plane landed on the tarmac in Charlotte, Heather shot off a text to her father.

HEATHER: Just landed.
DAD: Your mom and I are in the cell phone lot. Let us know
    when you have your luggage.

While the plane taxied to the gate, she rested her head against the back of the seat and looked out at the dark sky, which was clogged with gray clouds that seemed to mirror her mood.

While she'd slept in spurts during the long flight home, she had pondered the gossip website and the cruel comments from strangers. She couldn't stop the doubt that crept into the back of her mind, confirming her worries that had haunted her since Alex had first texted her five months ago. She didn't belong with him, and she never would. There was no way for an ordinary person to have a relationship with a celebrity, no matter how much they cared for each other.

Her phone dinged, and she found a message from Alex that he'd sent hours earlier.

ALEX: We're boarding. I'm thinking of you and hoping you
    have a good flight. Text me when you land. Love you,
    Baker Girl.

She sniffed and moved her fingers over the diamond heart
pendant as a horrible feeling of dread seeped through her. How
could they ever make things work amid such criticism? He
deserved someone better than she was, just as the gossip pages said.

When the plane came to a stop, she gathered up her backpack
and purse and waited for her turn to exit. She quickly moved out
to the gate and navigated hallways jammed with other travelers
on her way to the baggage claim.

She located the conveyor for her flight, then found a quiet
spot to stand. Out of the corner of her eye, she observed a tall man
dressed in jeans and a t-shirt coming toward her.

"Excuse me," he said. "Are you Heather Gordon?"

Heather's back stiffened as she tried to place the man. "Who's
asking?"

"How long have you been dating Alex Kirwan?"

Her blood went cold at the question. "How did you . . . ?"

The man smirked as he pulled out his phone and pointed it at
her. "How did you meet him?"

Heather pushed past him and began to circle the conveyor
belt. The room began to close in on her. She had to get out of
there. Where was her luggage?

Come on! Come on!

"From the photos and videos I've seen, you and Alex seem
pretty serious," the man called after her. "Are you engaged to him?"

Her eyes stung, and nausea rolled through her. She glanced
around the crowd for a security guard or a police officer. Surely
there was someone who could help her.

"Ms. Gordon! Ms. Gordon!"

She shot him the nastiest look she could muster, but then she remembered that he was recording. Surely this footage would wind up on the internet. How would she be perceived if she yelled at him?

But this man was harassing her! Didn't he deserve her ire?

The conveyor belt hummed, and she finally spotted her luggage. She grabbed the handle and whipped the suitcase off the belt.

Doing her best to keep her emotions in check, she unlocked her phone and dialed her father's cell phone number.

"Heather." Dad's voice calmed a fraction of her stress. "We're pulling around."

"Thank you!" She disconnected the call and rushed out the automatic doors, dodging other travelers and then marching along the sidewalk.

A line of traffic crawled down the road at a snail's pace.

"Come on, Dad. Come on," she grumbled.

"Ms. Gordon! Ms. Gordon!" the man called after her. "Please just answer one of my questions about you and Alex Kirwan!"

Heads turned as people standing on the sidewalk peered over at her, curiosity glimmering on their faces.

When Heather finally located her father's Tahoe in the sea of cars, she released a breath in relief. She rushed to the SUV as it came to a stop. Her father gave her a quick hug, then opened the tailgate, loaded her suitcase, and closed the trunk. Heather hopped into the back seat, and her father merged back into the line of traffic.

Mom turned around from the passenger seat and touched Heather's hand. "Honey! How was your trip?"

Heather opened her mouth to respond but dissolved into tears instead. She covered her face with her hands as all her worry, grief, and anger leaked from her eyes.

"Oh no." Mom leaned back and placed a wad of tissues in her hands. "Honey, what happened? Did you and Alex break up?"

Heather wiped her eyes and nose. "No."

"Then what's wrong?" Dad looked at her in the rearview mirror.

Taking a deep breath, Heather explained how Alex had attracted crowds wherever they went, how Mckenna had sent her the link to the gossip website, and how she'd encountered a gossip reporter in the airport.

Dad frowned. "We told Wendy not to share that with anyone. I'm sorry Mckenna texted you about it."

"You knew about it?" Heather asked.

Mom's expression turned grave. "We did, but we were hoping you wouldn't see it. You shouldn't worry about what people say about you online. Heather, you are a strong, intelligent, courageous, beautiful woman who is deserving of love. You have always been true to yourself. You've built your own business without asking for help, and your dad and I couldn't be prouder of you. All that matters is what you think of yourself, and any man would be lucky to have you in his life. You don't need to change for Alex or any man. You are perfect the way you are. And those online bullies are only jealous of you, which is why they say cruel things."

Heather stared at her lap and sniffled. "I don't know if I can do this."

"What do you mean?" her mother asked.

"I don't know if I can be in a relationship with someone this famous. It's all too much." The truth of her own words pierced her heart.

Mom touched her arm. "You're exhausted and jet-lagged after a long trip. Why don't you rest your eyes for a little while? I bet you'll feel better tomorrow, after a good night's sleep."

Heather sniffed and nodded, but deep down, she knew no amount of sleep would fix her broken heart.

⌒

The following afternoon, Heather pushed through the front door of the store and found nearly a dozen customers browsing the stacks of books. Another handful stood at the bakery counter, and others sat in the café area eating treats and drinking coffee.

Sorrow bogged her steps despite the store's activity. She had tossed and turned most of the night, debating how to handle her relationship with Alex. She wanted Alex in her life, but she didn't know how to handle the media frenzy. The idea of living with constant gossip being spread about her online and having to interact with belligerent reporters set her on edge.

Although she and Alex had traded a few text messages, she hadn't mentioned the gossip website or told him about her run-in with the paparazzo at the airport.

She had managed to close her eyes around five in the morning and sleep until noon. When she finally dragged herself out of bed, she found Mckenna had already left for work.

Feeling lonely, with only her cats to keep her company, Heather forced herself to shower and dress. Then she drove to her store to distract herself from her churning thoughts.

"Hi, Heather!" Deanna waved from the cashier counter. "How was your trip?"

Heather forced a smile. "It was good." She nodded greetings to customers and continued to the bakery counter, where Wendy rang up a customer buying a box of Blueberry Meet-Cute Muffins.

When Wendy's eyes met Heather's, they widened. "I thought you weren't coming back to work until Monday. What are you doing here?"

"I needed to get out of the house." Heather came around the counter and put on an apron. "Need some help?"

Wendy studied her with suspicion, then nodded. "Sure."

Heather busied herself with the long line of customers, grateful for the distraction.

When they were finally caught up, Wendy turned to her. "How was Portland?"

"It was wonderful and too short." Heather wiped the crumb-covered counter with a damp towel.

"Hey." Wendy moved closer. "What's going on?"

When Heather faced her, Wendy's eyes homed in on her necklace. "Did Alex give you this?" She touched the diamonds and gasped.

"Yes. On Thursday night when he told me he loved me."

"Wow!" Wendy squealed, and Heather shushed her. "That's amazing." Then she tilted her head. "Why aren't you as excited as I am?"

Heather swallowed and gave her sister a hard look. "Why weren't you going to tell me about the gossip website?"

Wendy's expression darkened. "Mack told you."

"Yes, and you should have too. At least I was warned before my run-in with a reporter at the airport."

"Oh no. What happened?"

Heather summarized the harassment.

"Have you told Alex?"

"No." Heather blew out a puff of air and hopped up on a stool. "He's traveling, and we've only traded a few texts."

"You need to tell him."

"What can he do about it?" Heather ran a hand through her hair.

An elderly man approached the counter. "Excuse me. Do you possibly have any books by Emil Zimmerman?"

Heather's heart stuttered as she recalled her first conversation with Alex about Zimmerman. "He's my favorite, so we definitely do. I'll show you where to find them."

⸺

Heather pushed a broom across the floor a few minutes before closing time. She had sent Deanna and Wendy home nearly an hour ago since the store had slowed and they had worked such long days for her while she was gone.

She swept the pile of dirt into a dustpan and dropped it into a trash can. The bell above the door chimed, and a young woman flounced into the store.

"Welcome to Heather's Books 'N' Treats. How may I help you?" Heather asked.

"I was looking for a romance novel." The young woman pushed her short auburn hair behind her ears and adjusted her thick-framed purple glasses on her dainty nose.

Heather swallowed a groan. Just what she needed: someone browsing five minutes before closing time. "Do you know the title or the name of the author?"

The young woman shook her head and grinned.

Great.

"I'm open to recommendations. I just want one with a juicy story."

Heather could handle that. She led the woman over to the Romance section and made a few recommendations before the woman chose a cover featuring a muscular man in desperate need of a shirt. Then they returned to the counter, and Heather rang up the book. She told the woman the price before dropping it into a yellow bag.

The young woman pulled out her phone and clicked a couple

of buttons before handing Heather her credit card. "Tell me, Heather," she began, "what's Alex Kirwan *really* like?"

Heather froze, holding the woman's credit card in the air.

"How did you meet?" The woman leaned forward and rested her chin on her palm as if they were close friends sharing secrets.

Heather breathed in through her nose, trying to calm her anger. With quaking hands, she ran the woman's credit card.

"Your store just opened. Did he loan you the money for it?" Her smile became vicious. "Or did you *earn* it somehow?"

Heather added the woman's credit card and the receipt to the bag, pushed it toward her, and pointed to the door. "Get out."

"I'll take that as 'No comment.' Thanks for the book. I'll be back!" The woman strutted out of the store with her head held high.

Heather locked the door behind her, leaned back against it, and felt the blood pulsing in her temples. She was at her wits' end. She didn't know how to deal with this constant harassment. How could she possibly live like this forever?

She peered around the store, and the memories of Alex helping her renovate it whirled in her mind. She had cherished those times—quiet, happy days that mirrored the kind of life she wanted with him. She touched her heart pendant and sighed.

Justine told her that she and Alex would have to compromise to make a life together. But how could they do that when he was on his way to Paris, and she was in Flowering Grove? Neither of them could be in two places at once!

A knock sounded on the door, and Heather growled. "Go away!"

"Uh, okay."

Heather spun and found Mckenna frowning at her. "I'm sorry, Mack!" She jerked the door open. "Another gossip reporter just left the store."

"Another one? When did you see the first one?"

"Come in, and I'll make us some tea."

Heather locked the door behind Mckenna before turning on the kettle. Then they sat down in the café area to drink tea and eat leftover Protagonist Profiteroles while Heather shared details about her week.

Mckenna looked pained. "I'm so sorry I told you about the website. I realized how thoughtless it was of me to dump that on you right before a five-hour flight alone. Please forgive me."

"No need to apologize." Heather rested her hand on Mckenna's. "If you hadn't, then I wouldn't have been prepared for what came later." She tried to brush off her worry and force a smile. "Anyway, tell me about the wedding plans. How are they coming along? Christmas will be here before we know it."

Mckenna frowned. "We can talk about my wedding later. Right now, I want to know what's bugging you. Tell me how you're feeling."

Heather dipped her chin, studied her half-eaten profiterole, and considered how much to share.

"Spill it, sister."

Heather met her best friend's warm gaze. "Alex finally told me he loves me."

"That's great!" Mckenna's smile faded. "Isn't it great?"

"Of course it is. I'd been hoping he would say it since I feel the same way." Heather frowned.

"But you're upset about the gossip on the internet and the paparazzi."

"Exactly." She shared how Alex drew a crowd of fans whenever they were in public. "I'm not sure if I can live like this. I know we need to compromise, but can I spend my life wondering if anything I say or do will wind up on a gossip page?"

"You love him though."

"Yes, I do, but—"

"There can't be a *but*, Heather. You're all in or you're not."

Heather swallowed as she recalled a line from one of his very first emails:

I can assure you that when I'm in a relationship, I'm completely loyal. I'm an all-in kind of guy.

She covered her face with her hands as guilt swamped her. How could she even consider giving up on Alex when he had given her so much?

"It's okay." Mckenna scooted her chair over and patted Heather's back. "See how you feel after a good night's sleep. Then have an honest conversation with him. You can work this out together, but you have to tell him the truth about your feelings."

But how could Heather tell Alex the truth without breaking both of their hearts?

Heather stared at the ceiling in her room while Jet and Molly purred at the bottom of her bed. She'd spent most of the night tossing and turning while her worries nearly ate her alive. She blinked in the darkness as Mckenna's advice echoed in her mind:

"See how you feel after a good night's sleep. Then have an honest conversation with him. You can work this out together, but you have to tell him the truth about your feelings."

Heather angled her face toward her digital clock and read the time: 1:45 a.m. That meant it was 7:45 in the morning in France, so Alex was likely awake.

She sucked in a deep breath and shot off a text to him: Is there any chance you can talk?

Her phone began to ring right away. "Alex?"

"Hey," he said as voices sounded in the background. "I have five minutes before we're going live on a French morning show."

Her throat dried. "It's so good to hear your voice."

"Yours too." The voices in the background faded, and she imagined him moving to a quiet corner of the television studio. "Isn't it almost two in the morning there?"

"Yes."

"Why are you awake at this hour?"

"I was hoping to talk to you." She could hear the quaver in her own voice.

"What's wrong?"

"Have you seen the gossip about us on the internet?"

He sighed. "I have. Robyn showed me. I'm so sorry, Heather."

"It's not your fault." Molly came to sit beside her, and Heather moved her fingers over the cat's soft fur. "But it's been tough." She shared how she'd been harassed at the airport and in her store. "I don't know how to handle all of this alone. It's overwhelming."

Alex groaned. "I wish there was something I could do to stop it, but I can't. I was hoping to protect you from all of that, but maybe this was inevitable. I'm sorry I let you down." He took a deep breath. "And I'm committed to this tour now . . ." His voice trailed off. "We'll figure it all out as soon as I get home, okay?"

A lump swelled in her throat. "When will that be?"

"I don't know exactly." His voice was warm and smooth. "But do your best to ignore the trolls. What they say doesn't matter because we love each other, right?"

"Right." She wiped her stinging eyes.

A voice sounded in the background. "I'm sorry, babe, but I have to go. I'll call you as soon as I can."

"Okay."

"Hang in there," he said. "And don't forget I love you."

"I love you too," she replied. Then the line went dead.

30

The following Friday night, Heather parked her car behind the restaurant and dragged herself from the driver's seat. It had been a long and exhausting week after returning home from Oregon. She and Alex hadn't connected beyond a few text messages here and there. He sent a few photos from Paris, and he texted *I love you* at least twice a day, but they hadn't spoken over the phone again since the weekend before.

Heather followed Alex and his brothers on social media, taking in their photos by the Eiffel Tower and other landmarks. She'd also found more gossip about her relationship with Alex, and her spirit broke with every snarky comment she found. Internet trolls called her a gold-digging hillbilly, insisting she was using Alex for fame and fortune, and others claimed she wasn't pretty enough for him. A few more reporters had stopped by her store, and two more had called earlier in the week. Though the media seemed to be losing interest in the story of her and Alex, the dread coiling in her stomach remained.

Each night she tossed and turned, trying to get past the pain of the internet gossip. But she always came to the same soul-crushing conclusion: She didn't belong in Alex's world.

Heather pushed the back door open and found her parents cleaning the kitchen.

Her mom looked up from scrubbing the grill and smiled. "Hi, Heather. What brings you out here tonight?"

"I was hoping we could talk."

Mom swiped her hand over her forehead and nodded. "Sure. Let's go in the office."

"Where's Dad?" Heather asked as she sat in the chair across from her mother's desk.

"He's closing down the register. The waitstaff finished straightening the dining room and went on home. Why do you look so glum?"

"I feel like I'm losing my mind." Heather's voice shook as she told her mother about the reporters who had reached out to her. "I don't think I'm cut out for this kind of life."

Mom reached over and patted Heather's hand. "Oh, sweetie. You and Alex obviously love each other. Don't let some bullies get the better of you. Have you told him about what you've been dealing with?"

"We spoke briefly on the phone last week." Heather snatched a tissue from the box on the desk and wiped her eyes.

"What did he say?"

"He said he was sorry he couldn't protect me from the paparazzi and internet trolls, and he said we'd figure it out when he was back here. He also said our love is all that matters." She plucked another tissue from the box and began to absently fold it in her hands. "The problem is, he doesn't know when he'll be back, and I'm not sure I can handle this on my own."

Mom gave Heather's hand another squeeze. "He's right, sweetie. It doesn't matter what anyone else thinks about you. Besides, I'm sure he's gotten bullied by critics out there who don't like their music. There are bullies everywhere, sweetie. You'll learn that not everyone grows up. Some people are stuck in middle school."

"It's more than that." Heather ran her thumbnail over the edge of the worn desk. "I don't think I'm good enough for him. I'm just an ordinary person. I'm a small-town, North Carolina woman. I don't belong on the arm of a famous musician, Mom, and I never will."

"Heather, look at me." Mom's voice was stern.

Heather met her determined gaze.

"You belong on the arm of anyone you want. You're perfect the way you are, and Alex is blessed to have you in his life."

Heather sniffed as tears leaked from her eyes. "I still don't see how it can work between us. My life is here." She pointed to the floor. "My family and my business are here. His life will always be on the road, but I belong here."

"Do you love him?"

"Yes, I do." Heather wiped her eyes as more tears escaped. "That's what's making this decision so hard. I think I need to end it."

Mom frowned. "Sweetie, think long and hard before you make any decisions. If you do break up with him, your dad and I will support you. But we don't want you to do anything you might regret."

Heather covered her face with her hands as a sob tore from her throat.

Mom clucked her tongue, then came around the desk and hugged Heather.

But as her mom held her close, Heather felt her soul begin to shatter. Her decision had already been made. She just had to break the news to Alex. And telling him she couldn't handle the pressure was going to break her apart.

On Sunday evening, Alex sat backstage at the concert hall in Hamburg, Germany. He pulled out his phone, studied the screen, and frowned. It had been eight days since he and Heather had talked over the phone. He missed her so much—longed to see her face, hear her voice, and kiss her lips. Being apart from her was torture, and he wasn't sure how much more he could take.

Alex held up the phone and gritted his teeth. Since it was six in the evening in Germany, it was noon in North Carolina. And since it was Sunday, he knew she wasn't working in her store. Taking a chance, he shot off a text to her.

ALEX: Can you talk?

He held his breath. After a moment, the conversation bubbles appeared.

HEATHER: Yes.

With a relieved grin, he dialed her number.

"Hello?" Heather sounded tired.

"It's so good to hear your voice." He hesitated, and when she remained quiet, he just kept talking. "We're in Germany now. The Paris shows were great. The crowds have been really energized, and they sing along to our songs, which is always cool. We're going onstage in less than an hour, but I missed you so much that I had to take a chance and call you."

He leaned back in his chair and rested the phone between his shoulder and his ear. "Europe is great, but I miss you so much. Did I say that already?" He chuckled. "I can't wait until this tour is over. I'm so ready to come home. I was thinking I could come see you for a few weeks, and then maybe you can come back out to Oregon. That's if you can get away from your store, of course." He stopped talking when he realized there was silence on the other end of the line. Had the call dropped?

"Heather? Are you there?" he asked.

"Yes, I'm here." Her voice sounded thready.

"Did I wake you?"

"No."

He sat up straight as worry gripped him. "Is something wrong, babe?" When she was silent for a beat, his stomach dropped. "What is it?"

More silence filled the line.

"Heather, you can say anything to me, okay? So please tell me what's wrong. I'm listening."

"I've . . . I've been thinking," she began slowly, her voice sounding unsure. "I think we need to take a break and re-evaluate things."

He blinked, and a vise gripped his chest. "You think we should take a break," he repeated.

"Yes."

"What do you mean by 'break,' Heather? Do you mean we should break up?"

"Yes."

The air came out of his lungs in a rush. For a moment he couldn't inhale or think. The room started to spin, and bile rose in his throat.

"Alex? Are you still there?"

"I'm—I'm confused. Where did this come from?" He almost choked on the words. "Are you still upset about the internet gossip? Like I said, I'm sorry I couldn't protect you from that. I really wanted to. But we'll get through it together, okay? I promise you, we'll figure it out."

"It's more than that," she said. "I've been wondering if I could really fit in your world, and I've realized I can't." Her voice became thick and shaky. "We want different things, so it's just better if we cut our losses now and move on before we get too serious."

"I thought we wanted the same thing, which is to be together. You said you loved me." He hated the tremble in his voice. He sniffed and wiped at his eyes.

"I do love you, but I don't fit in your world." Her words came out like chipped rocks.

His mind spun as he tried to make sense of it all, and his heart felt as though it had been split in two by a dull axe. "Yes, you do fit in my world. In fact, Heather, you *are* my world."

"Alex, I can't be your celebrity girlfriend. My life and my family are here in Flowering Grove."

"We can figure it out, Heather. You can keep your life in Flowering Grove and still be with me. We can find a way. I want to make this work more than anything."

"But what if there's no end in sight to your traveling?"

Her words gutted him. He leaned forward in the chair and scrubbed his free hand down his face. "That's about to change. The tour is almost over. I just need you to be patient, okay?"

"I'm sorry, Alex, but I can't do this. It's too much. I'm not used to being picked apart on the internet."

"Heather, I'm sorry about that. I promise you that it will get better. Just ignore those idiots," he pleaded with her. "They don't matter. All that matters is you and me, and I love you, Heather. I want you in my life, and I'll do anything to prove it."

"I'm sorry, Alex. I've made myself sick trying to figure out a way to make this work, but it just won't." She sniffed. "I'll pay you back what you spent on my store."

"I don't want to be paid back. I just want your heart."

"I need to go," she whispered. "Goodbye, Alex." Her voice broke, and a sob sounded through the phone.

The call disconnected, and he studied the phone. Then he wiped his eyes and stared at the blank white wall in front of him, trying to make sense of what had just happened.

A knock sounded on the door before it squeaked open.

Jordan stood in the doorway, his eyes wide. "Alex, are you okay?"

Alex tried to swallow against his dry throat, but he couldn't catch his breath. He sagged back on the chair.

His middle brother rushed over to him. "Tell me what's wrong."

"Heather just broke up with me." Saying the words cut him to the bone. "I'm . . . I'm devastated." A chasm of anguish opened in his chest, and he took in a tremulous breath.

Jordan touched his shoulder. "What happened?"

"She kept saying she didn't fit in my world, and she's upset about the internet gossip. She also said a long-distance relationship can't work." Alex sniffed and rubbed his stinging eyes. "I asked her to be patient, but she insisted." His voice was gruff, and he dipped his chin, trying in vain to swallow back his emotion.

Kayden appeared and knocked on the doorframe. "Hey. Almost time to go onstage." He stilled and divided a look between Jordan and Alex. Worry clouded his features. "What's going on? Is Mom okay?"

"Heather just broke up with Alex," Jordan said.

Kayden grimaced. "Oh no. What happened?"

Jordan repeated to Kayden everything Alex had just shared.

"Dude," Kayden said. "I am so sorry. I was sure she was the one for you."

More grief compressed Alex's chest. "I was too." He wiped his eyes. "I have no idea what I'm going to do without her."

"I know she makes you happy, bro," Jordan said. "Don't let that happiness slip through your fingers."

Kayden gave a solemn nod. "He's right, man. You can't give up on her."

Alex shook his head, and an ache swelled in his gut. He had no idea how to make her happy, and he had no idea how to move on.

Brooks entered the room. "Five minutes, guys. Let's go."

Alex swallowed hard and followed his brothers to the stage, wondering how on earth he would find his voice to sing.

⌒

"You need to eat something," Mckenna told Heather later that evening, pushing a plate of carrot and celery sticks toward her. They sat together on the sofa and stared at a romantic comedy on the television.

Heather wiped her eyes and nose, then tossed another tissue into the overflowing trash can at her feet. She'd spent the entire afternoon crying and was convinced her face would be red and puffy for the rest of her life. After all, she would never recover from the grief of losing Alex. She kept staring at his photos on her phone and recalling the good times they'd had together. But now he was just someone she used to know.

"I'm not hungry."

Heather touched the diamond heart pendant that hung around her neck, envisioning the romantic evening when Alex had given her the necklace, told her he loved her, and then kissed her in the rain. More tears leaked from her eyes as she recalled how perfect the evening had been and how certain she was she'd spend the rest of her life with him.

Now it was over, and she kept checking her phone for missed

calls or texts from him. But why would he call her when she was the one who had chosen to end it? She'd pushed him away, and now agony and shame burned her from the inside out.

"Heather, if you're this miserable, why not call him and tell him that you made a mistake?" Mckenna said. "Tell him you love him, and you'll find a way to try again."

"But it won't work. It can *never* work." She picked up her laptop and opened Facebook before scrolling to Kirwan's page. A video interview had been posted a few hours earlier. She clicked on it, and it started to play.

Mckenna moved Molly, who had been sitting between them on the sofa, and scooted closer to Heather. "What's that?"

During the interview, a reporter stood with Alex and his brothers and asked them how their European tour was going so far. Kayden and Jordan smiled, gushing about their wonderful shows and fabulous audiences and how much they loved being in Europe. Alex, however, stood behind them with a stoic expression on his face. His eyes were dull, and his jaw was set.

"Alex looks miserable," Mckenna whispered.

Heather's lungs constricted. *She* had made Alex miserable. She had broken that wonderful man's heart, and she would have to live with that guilt for the rest of her life.

Her head began to pound as her eyes stung with fresh tears. Perhaps she had made a mistake. But how could they find a compromise when there was no way to bridge the long distance keeping them apart?

31

Alex sat on the balcony of his hotel room in Madrid and frowned as he overlooked the city. It had been four days since Heather had broken up with him, and he'd just been going through the motions ever since. He still felt as if his heart had been ripped out of his chest.

More than once, he'd considered telling his brothers that he wanted to quit the band, but he didn't want to leave them in the lurch like that. He had made a commitment to them and to the fans when they'd agreed to the European tour, and he had a duty to finish it. But he couldn't stop the daily anguish of his heartbreak.

Alex studied his phone for the hundredth time since Sunday and pondered calling Heather, but she had made her feelings clear. Then he thought about calling his mother, but he didn't want to dump his problems on her. Finally, he sent a quick text to his best friend.

> ALEX: I know it's 7:00 a.m. where you are, but is there any chance you can talk? I'm in Spain, so I'll call you.
> TRISTAN: Sure. Call me.

Alex breathed a sigh of relief and dialed. Tristan answered immediately.

"What's up?" Tristan asked.

Alex rubbed his hand down his face, took a deep breath, then poured his heart out to his best friend. He explained how the paparazzi had gone after Heather, how gossip pages were attacking her online, and how she had broken up with him, saying she didn't belong in his world and couldn't see a path forward for them.

"I promised her we'd spend more time together when this tour was over, but she just gave up." Alex leaned back in the chair. "And now I feel like I can't breathe, and I don't know how to go on. I need your advice, man. I'm lost."

Tristan huffed out a breath. "I'm shocked."

"That makes two of us." Alex snorted. "I feel like I'm walking around in a fog." He rested his feet on the rungs of the balcony. "What do you think?"

"It doesn't matter what I think. The question is, what do you want?"

"That's easy. I want Heather."

"Then go get her."

Alex shook his head. "But what about the band? My brothers? I have an obligation to them."

"Forget about your brothers, Alex. What do *you* want?"

"I want what you have with Justine, and I'll do anything to make that work with Heather."

"I think you already have your answer, Alex. You can find a way to have both. You don't need to tour forever. You hate touring, don't you?"

"That's true. I want a life—a *real* life. I want a meaningful relationship, and I want to start a meaningful charity."

"Then do it, Alex. Tell Jordan and Kayden that you want to

finish up the tour and then build a life with Heather. You can make North Carolina your home base if you want. Work that out with her. She needs a concrete promise."

Alex sat up taller as he felt a seed of hope taking root in his chest. "Thank you. That's what I needed to hear." He closed his eyes as a plan started to form in his head. "Now, how's Justine?"

"We are so ready for this baby." He could hear the smile in his best friend's voice.

"You'd better keep me posted on that."

They discussed the tour for a while, then Alex stood and stretched. "Well, I'd better let you get to work. I'm going to try to get some rest before our next event."

"You take care, man, and let me know how it goes with Heather."

"I will," Alex said. "Give my love to Justine." He disconnected the call, then sprinted into the hotel room. He knew exactly what he had to do.

⌒

"Thank you for coming in today, Mrs. Price. I hope you enjoy your Chick-Lit Coffee and Romantic Comedy Chocolate Cake, as well as your Saturday afternoon." Heather handed the woman her receipt and change.

The woman dropped the receipt and the coins into her wallet and zipped it closed. "I'm so glad you opened this store. We've needed a bookstore in Flowering Grove for a long time. I'm grateful to not have to drive to one of the malls to find a new book to read."

Heather forced her lips into a smile. "I appreciate that very much. Please come back to see us soon."

"Oh, I will, dear. You can count on that."

Starstruck

As soon as Mrs. Price walked away from the counter, Heather's shoulders wilted. It had been six days since she'd broken up with Alex, and she was still heartbroken, still grieving, still missing him, and still doubting her choice to end their relationship.

But she had no idea how to fix it. She touched the diamond heart-shaped pendant that still hung around her neck and frowned. When he'd given her the necklace, he'd asked her to take care of his heart, but she hadn't kept her promise. Instead, she had crushed his heart.

There was a sudden flurry of activity at the front of the store, and Heather leaned over the counter to get a better look. A line of customers had moved to the front window, and murmured conversations drifted around the store.

Heather thought she heard someone singing. She peered around the store in search of someone watching a video on their phone. But no, what she heard sounded like live music.

"Heather! Heather!" Wendy called from the front of the store. "Heather, come quick!"

Deanna rushed over to the bakery counter. "You've got to come now, Heather. Please!"

Heather scooted around the counter, and Deanna took her arm and nearly dragged her to the front of the store.

"Go outside. Now!" Deanna ordered.

When Heather realized that the person serenading the crowd was Alex, her legs nearly gave out from under her. Was she dreaming? She peered out the window and spotted Alex sitting on a folding chair on the sidewalk, playing an acoustic guitar and singing.

She padded to the door, pushed it open, and stepped out onto the sidewalk. Then her eyes filled with tears. A crowd had gathered around Alex, and many of the folks there had their cell phones out to record the song. But this time, Heather didn't care.

Alex had returned. He had come for her, even though she had crushed him. Relief surged through her, making her feel limp and dizzy. She didn't deserve him, but she loved him more than she'd ever loved anyone in her life. And she wanted him back, no matter the cost to her life or her privacy.

Alex looked up at her, and he continued to sing a song she didn't recognize. But the words spoke to her heart, and she was certain he had written the song for her.

> *No matter where you go, I'll never be far.*
> *You will always carry my heart.*
> *For I love you more each day and night,*
> *And nothing can keep us apart.*

Heather covered her mouth with her hand as a river of tears flowed down her cheeks. The words wrapped around her chest and hugged her close as he continued to sing.

When he finished the song, the crowd around him clapped, but he didn't seem to notice anyone but Heather. His gorgeous eyes were locked on her alone. The sound of the audience faded away, and she suddenly felt as if they were the only two people on the sidewalk on Main Street in Flowering Grove.

"Heather Gordon, I love you," he said, speaking over the crowd. "You've carried my heart since I first met you back in April. You're the love of my life, and I can't live without you. Please tell me we can make this work." His cornflower-blue eyes seemed to plead with her, and for a moment she couldn't speak.

She sniffed and tried to find her voice. "I love you too, Alex, and I'm so sorry. Yes, I want to work it out. I can't live without you either."

He smiled and set his guitar down before pulling her into his arms and kissing her. The feel of his lips caressing hers sent chills down her arms.

The knot of people around them cheered and whistled as she held on to him, but she didn't care that an audience was watching their intimate scene. All that mattered was that Alex had come for her. The rest of the world could have their opinions, but she had Alex.

And then her mother's words echoed in her mind: *"Heather, you are a strong, intelligent, courageous, beautiful woman who is deserving of love."*

Heather held on to Alex as she realized her mother had been right. She did deserve to have Alex in her life, and despite the roadblocks standing in their way, they could fight for each other and their love.

More than ever, Heather knew in her bones that she wanted a life with Alex. She wouldn't allow anyone to come between them ever again.

When Alex broke the kiss, he held Heather close.

She closed her eyes and rested her cheek on his shoulder. "I'm so, so sorry, Alex. I love you."

"I love you too, but I don't have much time. I have another flight back to Europe before the next show. Can we talk in private?"

"Yes, of course," she said, taking his hand. He waved at the crowd before picking up his guitar, and she steered him into the store, past the sales counter, and into her office. She closed the door behind them, and her gaze met and clung to his. "You flew all the way out here to talk to me?"

He touched the pendant on her collarbone and smiled. "You're still carrying my heart."

"I never stopped." Her eyes stung. "I know I made a huge

mistake by breaking up with you. I let my doubts get in the way, and it was selfish of me to expect you to give up your career for me. But I wish I could see you more than once a month."

Alex set the guitar on a chair, then took her hands in his. "That's not selfish. I miss you too." He paused for a beat. "I told the guys I'll finish out the tour, but I want to step back from the appearances. I want a normal life, and I want to build it with you. Flowering Grove can be my home too. I want to look at houses here."

"You mean that?" she asked as her heart took on wings.

"Yes, I do."

Then she frowned. "But you shouldn't have to make all of the changes. I want to compromise. I'll hire more part-timers since the bookstore is off to a good start, and I'll travel with you when I can. I want to be a part of your life, which means *every* part of your life. And I'll do my best to ignore the nasty comments on the internet."

"Heather, you are perfect in every way." He traced his finger down her cheek. "And I hope you are my future." He kissed her, and she basked in his familiar scent.

When he broke the kiss, she stared up into his blue eyes. "Did you write that song for me?"

"I've been working on it for you since I left Portland."

"I want to hear the entire song," she told him. "Now, please."

He laughed. "Yes, ma'am." He picked up the guitar, and as he sang, Heather soaked up the beautiful words of the song.

When he finished, he kissed her again. "Heather, I have two more weeks, and then I'm coming home to you."

"I can't wait."

As Alex pulled her in for another kiss, Heather settled into his arms.

EPILOGUE

FOUR MONTHS LATER

Heather twirled around with Wendy and Deanna while Kirwan performed their lively hit "Dance All Night" onstage at the Flowering Grove Country Club.

It was two days before Christmas, and Mckenna and Kirk had taken their vows earlier that day at Mckenna's family's church. Now at least a dozen of the 150 guests were clapping and swaying on the dance floor in the large room that featured a balcony overlooking the golf course.

The wedding had been perfect. Mckenna, accompanied by her father, had walked down the aisle in a beaded white gown with a long train that reminded Heather of a princess's dress. Kirk had been handsome in his traditional black-and-white tuxedo. Heather had been thrilled to stand with Mckenna as her maid of honor, while Kirk's brother was his best man. And Heather was so happy for her stunning best friend, who had simply glowed with joy while she and the love of her life recited their vows.

Mckenna's parents had planned her reception at the country club, which was decorated for Christmas—complete with candles, white lights, wreaths, garland, and even a Christmas tree in the corner of the room.

Heather, however, secretly felt the best part was that Kirwan had agreed to perform at the reception. Alex had offered to play for free, but Mckenna's parents had insisted on paying them. Alex shared with Heather that they offered a special rate since he considered Mckenna and Kirk close friends of the band.

And now, as the reception came to a close, she laughed and spun in her red gown as her sister and Deanna played air guitars along with the song. Heather stopped dancing and turned her attention to her handsome boyfriend, who belted out the lyrics to the song along with Kayden. He looked gorgeous, still dressed in the suit he had worn to the wedding. But he had removed the coat and tie and unbuttoned the top few buttons of his blue shirt. She reached up and touched her diamond pendant, which she hadn't removed since the day he had given it to her.

The past few months had been some of the happiest in her life. After Alex and his brothers finished the European tour, he'd kept his promise and come to Flowering Grove for a month. Although he stayed at the inn, he and Heather looked at a few houses, and he made an offer on a large house only a few blocks away from the one she rented with Mckenna. The owners accepted the offer, and after the closing, he and Heather worked together to decorate it.

Wendy planned to take Mckenna's place in the house after the wedding, but Heather secretly hoped that someday she and Alex might live in his new house as husband and wife.

Heather's Books 'N' Treats continued to remain busy, and Heather had hired more part-time employees to help when she and Alex were together or traveling. They had traveled to Portland in October to meet Ryker, Justine and Tristan's baby boy, who had arrived on time and was adorable and perfect in every way. Heather also enjoyed visits with Alex's mom and brothers, and together they had all taken a trip out to the coast.

The song ended, and the crowd on the dance floor clapped and whistled.

"Thank you," Kayden said. "We're so glad we could entertain you tonight during this special occasion."

Alex held his hand out to where the bride and groom stood together beside the dance floor. "We'd like to wish Mckenna and Kirk a wonderful life together. Let's hear it for the happy couple!"

Everyone clapped and cheered while Mckenna and Kirk waved.

"Now we'll all gather outside to bid them farewell as they head out on their honeymoon," Kayden added.

The three brothers climbed down from the stage, and Jordan and Kayden made their way to Deanna and Wendy while Alex joined Heather. They followed the crowd outside, where everyone assembled on the sidewalk. The crisp night air caused Heather to shiver as she took in the stars twinkling in the clear winter sky above them.

The guests waved crackling sparklers in the air as Mckenna and Kirk, who had already changed into more casual clothes, exited the country club and climbed into a sleek black limousine that would take them to the airport. Happy tears flooded Heather's eyes as she watched her best friend and her new husband drive away, bound for a luxurious Caribbean getaway.

When she felt a hand on her shoulder, Heather turned to Alex, who gave her a strange expression. He cleared his throat and nodded in the direction of the country club entrance. "Could we talk for a minute?"

"Sure." She searched his blue eyes. "Are you okay?"

"Yeah, of course." He gently took her arm, and conversations buzzed around them as they started back up the path into the building.

Heather's heels clacked on the wooden floor, and Alex steered her out to the balcony. Hundreds of white fairy lights created a romantic glow overlooking the golf course. The cool night air swept over Heather, bringing with it the aroma of a fireplace somewhere in the distance.

Alex led her to the far end of the balcony and pulled in a deep breath.

She tilted her head as worry wound through her. "Alex, what's wrong?"

"I promise nothing is wrong." He took her hand in his. "Heather," he began, "I had no idea my life would change the day my brothers decided to start a food fight while I was making a phone call at the Barbecue Pit."

She burst into laughter. "But like you said, if they hadn't made a mess, then we never would have met."

"That's exactly right. I'm so grateful they did make a mess, and I'll never forget how you gave me the third degree. Somehow I knew in that moment that you would become the love of my life."

Heather shook her head and grinned.

Alex ran his thumb along the back of her hand. "Actually, maybe I didn't know at the time you would become the love of my life, but after trading some text messages with you, it became apparent that you would be the woman I'd want to annoy for the rest of my life."

When he dropped down onto one knee, Heather gasped and pressed a hand to her collarbone.

"I was going to do this at Christmas, but after the wedding today, I realized I couldn't wait another minute." Alex pulled a ring box from his pocket and opened it, revealing a large, round-cut diamond in a white-gold setting encrusted with more twinkling diamonds.

"Heather Rose Gordon, my beautiful and wonderful Baker Girl, would you do me the honor of being my wife?" His voice held a hint of a quaver as his blue eyes pleaded with her.

"Yes, yes, yes!" she exclaimed.

Alex stood, picked her up, and spun her around. When he set her back down on her feet, he slipped the ring onto her finger, and it was the perfect fit. He kissed her, and she rested her hands on his broad shoulders.

When he stepped away from her, she worked to calm her wildly thumping heart. "Heather, I can't wait to share my life with you, but I have another question."

"What is it?"

"I've been doing a lot of thinking, and I've finally figured out how I can make a difference in the world. I want to start the Kenneth Kirwan Memorial Foundation to bring music into schools that don't have music programs, teach underprivileged kids how to play instruments, and organize concerts to raise money for children's hospitals." He touched a strand of hair that had escaped her french twist and tucked it behind her ear. "Will you help me run the foundation?"

She sniffed. "It would be my honor both to be your wife and to help you run the foundation."

"Thank you. I promise to love you for the rest of my life."

"And I will do the same."

As he brushed his lips over hers once again, she enjoyed the feeling of her fiancé's nearness. In his arms, Heather felt her body relax. She couldn't wait to see what the future held for her and her rockstar. No matter what it was, they would face it together.

ACKNOWLEDGMENTS

As always, I'm thankful for my loving family, including my mother, Lola Goebelbecker; my husband, Joe; and my sons, Zac and Matt. I'm blessed to have such an awesome and amazing family that puts up with me when I'm stressed out over a book deadline.

To my husband, Joe, thank you, thank you, thank you for putting up with my random text messages asking you about music and rockstars. You're a saint for putting up with my crazy! I love you more than words can express.

Special thanks to my mom and my dear friends Pam Agustin and DeeDee Vazquetelles for proofreading the draft of this book and for encouraging me to believe in Heather and Alex. I'm so grateful to have your love and support for each of my books.

Pam—Zac, Matt, and I had a blast visiting you and your family in Oregon. Thank you for taking us to so many fun places and for helping Alex's character come alive. I can't wait to come back to Oregon to see you again. Your friendship is a blessing!

Thank you to the Jonas Brothers for the hours of inspiration their music provided (much to my husband's dismay) while writing this book.

I'm so grateful to my wonderful church family at Morning

Star Lutheran in Matthews, North Carolina, for your encouragement, prayers, love, and friendship. You all mean so much to my family and me.

Thank you to Zac Weikal and the fabulous members of my Bookworm Bunch! I'm so thankful for your friendship and excitement about my books. You all are amazing!

To my agent, Natasha Kern—I can't thank you enough for your guidance, advice, and friendship. You are a tremendous blessing in my life. I hope you enjoy your retirement with your family—especially your precious grandsons.

I would also like to thank my new literary agent, Nalini Akolekar, for her guidance and advice. Nalini, I look forward to getting to know you better and working with you on future projects.

Thank you to my wonderful editor, Laura Wheeler, for your friendship and guidance. I appreciate how you've pushed me and inspired me to dig deeper to improve both my writing and this book. I'm so excited to work with you, and I look forward to our future projects together.

I'm grateful to editor Jocelyn Bailey, who helped me polish and refine the story. Jocelyn, I'm thrilled that we're able to work together again. You always make my stories shine! Thank you for being amazing!

I'm grateful to every person at HarperCollins Christian Publishing who helped make this book a reality.

To my readers—thank you for choosing my novels. My books are a blessing in my life for many reasons, including the special friendships I've formed with my readers. Thank you for your email messages, Facebook notes, and letters.

Thank you most of all to God—for giving me the inspiration and the words to glorify You. I'm grateful and humbled You've chosen this path for me.

DISCUSSION QUESTIONS

1. At the beginning of the story, Heather dreams of opening a bookstore with a bakery on Main Street in her hometown of Flowering Grove. When a retail space becomes available, she's at first afraid to take a leap of faith and open the store. What do you think inspires her to go for her dream?

2. Alex lost his father to a car accident when he was a teenager, and he channeled his grief into writing and performing songs. Have you ever lost a beloved family member? If so, how did you cope?

3. By the end of the story, Heather finally believes she's good enough for Alex and their relationship is strong enough to withstand the pressures of fame. What do you think causes that change?

4. What has Alex learned about himself by the end of the novel? How does that influence his thoughts about a future with Heather?

5. When Alex and his brothers were working hard to make their dreams a reality, Alex's ex-girlfriend, Celeste, broke up with him and told him he'd never be more than a barista. Have you had your heart broken

by someone close to you? If so, how did you handle that
devastation, and what did you learn from it?

6. Alex enjoys visiting children's hospitals in order to
brighten the days of children who are going through
hard times. Do you have a special charity or ministry?
If so, what is it, and how does it inspire you and those
around you?

7. Heather is discouraged when internet gossip interferes
with her relationship with Alex. Have you ever had to
deal with gossip? If so, how did you handle it?

8. When Alex first meets Heather, his brothers feel he's
wasting his time trying to get to know someone who
isn't a part of their world. Do you think their concerns
about Heather's and Alex's differences are valid? Why
or why not?

9. Heather and Mckenna have been best friends since
childhood. They're each other's support, especially
during rough times. Do you have a special friendship
like that? If so, what do you cherish the most about that
relationship?

10. Have you ever visited a small town like Flowering
Grove? If you could go anywhere for vacation, where
would you choose to go?

From the Publisher

GREAT BOOKS

ARE EVEN BETTER WHEN THEY'RE SHARED!

Help other readers find this one:

- Post a review at your favorite online bookseller

- Post a picture on a social media account and share why you enjoyed it

- Send a note to a friend who would also love it—or better yet, give them a copy

Thanks for reading!

ABOUT THE AUTHOR

Dan Davis Photography

Amy Clipston is an award-winning bestselling author and has been writing for as long as she can remember. She's sold more than one million books, and her fiction writing "career" began in elementary school when she and a close friend wrote and shared silly stories. She has a degree in communications from Virginia Wesleyan University and is a member of the Authors Guild, American Christian Fiction Writers, and Romance Writers of America. Amy works full-time for the City of Charlotte, NC, and lives in North Carolina with her husband, two sons, mother, and four spoiled rotten cats.

Visit her online at AmyClipston.com
Facebook: @AmyClipstonBooks
Twitter: @AmyClipston
Instagram: @amy_clipston
BookBub: @AmyClipston